DEER DANCER

Richard J. Gonzales

SLEEPING
PANTHER
PRESS

FORT WORTH, TEXAS

Sleeping Panther Press
A Publishing Imprint of
Fort Worth Writer's Boot Camp
4221 Parrish Road
Fort Worth, Texas 76117
www.sleepingpantherpress.com

Rachel Pilcher, Publisher

Names: Gonzales, Richard J.
Title: Deer Dancer/Richard J. Gonzales
Identifiers: LCCN 2017945316 | ISBN 9780998066127
Subjects: Novel-- Fiction | Yaqui History — Fiction | Mexican
History — Fiction | Yaqui Uprising- Fiction | Indiginous Family Life-
Fiction | Coming-of-Age — Fiction |
Classification: DDC 868.9973 GON

First Edition

Printed in the United States of America

Cover Design by Kara McEuen-Powell

Richard J. Gonzales Photo by Andrew Moseley

For the Indigenous Peoples of the Americas.

PREFACE

Since the arrival of Europeans to the Americas, the indigenous people have fought to keep their cultures, languages, religions, lands, water, and property. Whether motivated by Manifest Destiny musings, the zeal to convert to Christianity, sheer greed, or racism, the Europeans and their agents have encroached on native lands, and enslaved, spread pandemics, and corralled in reservations the original inhabitants of the Americas. A recent manifestation of this struggle was the protest at Standing Rock.

The Army Corps of Engineers authorized the building of a 1,170-mile oil pipeline from North Dakota to refineries in southern Illinois. Although most of the pipeline was built over private land, they allowed Energy Transfer Partners, a Texas-based company, to build an easement under Lake Oahu, the primary water source for the Standing Rock Sioux. Native Americans and their allies protested the building of the pipeline, fearing contamination of their water and sacred cultural sites. Camping on and near the Sioux reservation, thousands of activists formed human blockades and demonstrations to stop the construction. The local sheriff and private security shot rubber bullets, spewed pepper spray, lobbed concussion grenades, wielded Tazers, and arrested over 759 people, resulting in injuries to the protestors. Although President Barack Obama halted the pipeline construction, President Donald Trump reauthorized the building. The pipeline easement under the lake was opened on June 1, 2017, and since then, the oil flowed. As of this writing, further federal legal hearings will review environmental justice concerns raised by the Sioux nation. The struggle for protection of Native American ancestral lands and water continued into the 21st century.

Deer Dancer is set in the 1800s of Sonora, Mexico. Although the events transpired south of the border in a different century, readers will find similarities with the ongoing challenges that indigenous peoples have faced when confronted by a government intent on land grab and disdainful attitudes to its inhabitants. I wish to honor the memory of the Yaquis who have gallantly fought to preserve their culture, territory, and water since the 16th century to the present day. May indigenous American voices soar.

Richard J. Gonzales,
June 2017

TABLE OF CONTENTS

CHAPTER 1

✦

DEER CHASE

"What's he doing?"

"Dancing in the grave yard."

"He wishes to become a deer." The Little People played flutes, drums and laughed at the thought.

"A deer?"

"He's a boy."

"A boy who carries much sorrow and shame."

"He's strong. Just look at him jump." The Little People clapped.

"Danger — she's coming for him."

"Shall we warn him?"

"He'll soon know."

"Will Maso save him?"

Under the bright light of a witch's moon, Cheve Falcon chased the deer into the Yaqui graveyard filled with crooked crosses. Fresh and old mounds surrounded the church, the spiritual and geographic center of Potam. The sixteen-year-old's skin sloughed off, replaced by smooth fur and long slender limbs and supple muscles. Hands and feet sprouted into hooves and a short, thin tail blossomed. He shook it and laughed. The joy vanished when the transmutation of muscular boy to strapping deer stopped at his neck.

Cheve concentrated harder, howled but still heard his high-pitched young voice and not the sweet deer's bellow. The antlers—he yearned for antlers curled in glory like twisted tree limbs around the deer's angular head. He wiggled his disfigured nose to stir the growth of a long, smooth snout. He blinked his brown eyes to stir them into the

1

long-lashed, slanted orbs shining like the souls of saints. His ears refused to grow into the long, pointy flaps that twisted at the signs of danger and joy. The prize he pursued most in the Yaqui graveyard, the grand look of the deer head, was elusive. He sought to bask in the beauty of the night with an equally wondrous face and to find *El Feo*.

If he danced well, he could speed the change with the melody of deer music. He rocked his head and stiffened his hooves toward the ground. A flute whistle and a drumbeat throbbed in his head as he hopped and swayed, careful not to step on the small mounds or kick the tilted blue, green, pink and white crosses. Deer dancing in the graveyard should conjure a vision from the *Yo Ania*.

He paused and gazed through misty clouds at the white, pregnant moon.

"Tonight, show me tonight," he said with a strong lisp in Cajita. He searched the night sky for a comet to sweep its tail over his face. *Scrape off the ugliness, leave me a handsome, brown look – like those of Ángel and Luz.*

Slipping his tongue along the edge of his mouth slit that reached up to a crooked nose and exposed his teeth, he desired the powers of the bees that sealed their honeycombs with their saliva.

"*Ave Maria, que es en caelus…*" he shouted in Latin to *Santa Maria la Virgen* to persuade her to lead him to the man who gave him this face. Perhaps, the hunted would find the desert magic leaves to seal his facial fissure. If not, he could teach him how to look away when others stared and whispered. He could explain who and why they were cursed.

"Why am I ugly? But if my father isn't *feo*. Who is?" He chanted a mystic hymn he had heard the gray-heads sing to protect them from witches through a night of dance, cigarettes, mescal and jokes. He shuffled his feet, swaying his shoulders to transform boy head to deer head. Childhood memories of songs that praised deer beauty filled his ears. He raised his right knee, stood motionless and scented the air.

2

A cool January wind that swept down from the Bacatete Mountains, over the cactus and mesquite tree-laden plains, stirred up the desert dust. Cheve invited the playful spirits to the warmth of his covers. As he swirled, the crooked crosses swam around him, home to Yaquis who once danced and sang. The hundreds of years of fighting with the Yoris hurled many men, women and children to their graves too early.

Cheve leaped closer to the stucco church, recalling his mother's strong voice echo. Petra Falcon as *temastian* exhorted Yaquis to remember God's words, their struggle and customs.

Cheve could see her preaching to the assembly, her hands and arms moving in the air as if she were holding onto God's feet.   Worshippers cheered, laughed and jumped to her words. His feet sprung higher as if she were to take flight.

"God gave us this land. It's holy land, Yaqui land," he chanted, leaping over a grave. The blanket fell from his shoulders onto a small mound entombing a baby girl killed by smallpox.

"Yoris brought this filth," Cheve shouted. "Kill all Yoris!"

A shiver raced through his body. He prayed for a vision, but the only image floated from his mother's hypnotic voice. In the glow of the moon, her intense gaze from deep, brown eyes, flowing black- and gray-flecked hair, nose and lips shaped like a rose petal, surfaced.

A vision filled with answers to riddles could free him from his distortion. As the bright light flashed, he gasped and swerved his gaze. His breathing quickened as the illumination grew brighter. Surely, a glowing deer had come to lead him to the *Yo Ania, El Feo* and the face-shaping herbs.

He heard distant screeching, faint cries. At the first whiff of smoke, he walked toward the blooming luminosity.

"A fire," he whispered. He estimated the flames a short run from the graveyard. *Who would set such a large flame at this late evening, so close to the huts?*

"Yoris!" he shouted.

A shiver raced from his neck to his back and chest. He held his breath. Fur, legs, hooves and tail instantly evaporated. Gunshot cracked, women and children ran from the fire.

"Yoris, Yoris!" they screamed.

Rumbling footsteps and shouts of men approached from behind. Old warriors leaned forward as they swung their arms to-and-fro to stir their legs to run. This night his people were weak, Cheve feared. His father and most of the young fighters had accompanied Cajeme in talks with their Mayo neighbors. Their captain-general gambled a show of strength could secure their loyalty.

Flames now cracked and hissed. Cheve bolted, passing the grey-heads who huffed and stumbled. If he didn't have good looks, at least he ran faster than most men and boys of the eight Yaqui villages.

As he drew closer, the air simmered and crackled. A woman wailed, and children cried. He broke into the brightly lit clearing to find Cajeme's hut afire. The flames exposed the captain-general's wife pinned to the ground by several Torocoyoris. Rifle-toting Yoris on horseback oversaw the attack.

Behind the trapped woman, Torocoyoris held her squirming children by their throats and arms. She screamed repeatedly as she struggled to break free. "Leave my children alone."

Her captors laughed and fondled her breasts and legs.

"She's mine." A fat man pushed aside several of her guards. He jerked her to her feet by her hair, tore her clothes off with one strong jerk and threw the naked woman to the ground.

"No!" Cheve charged forward. A mounted Torocoyori darted his horse toward him. He zigzagged past the man's bullets that struck the ground. By the leaping fire, the man howled and cursed him. His horse's eyes bulged at the jerks and twists of its long neck. It bared large teeth as if to eat Cheve.

4

He dodged more bullets, tumbled, rose, scrambled forward. More horsemen, like rushing shadows, floated into the flickering firelight to corral him.

"Kill that rat," shouted another horseman.

Cheve came within a few feet of the rape to see clearly the woman. The corpulent rapist pumped his thighs vigorously. Several Torocoyoris tackled Cheve. One hooked an arm around his neck and jerked his head back. Another jammed a rifle butt repeatedly into his torso. His breath gushed through his mouth as pain wracked his ribs and gut.

Assaulted with images of the rape, the fire and his captors' cruelty, he struggled to stay on his feet but his legs buckled.

"Can't breathe, ugly one? I'll give you air." A man standing before Cheve brandished a knife. He made a cutting motion over his own throat.

"Release him," another ordered.

"Ugly monkey needs teaching."

"Free him now or fight me."

Cheve strained to focus on his rescuer. A sharp push to the back of his head slammed him to the ground.

He sat up and spit out grit, struggling to breathe through the pain. His ribs ached to the touch. Other Yaquis sprawled on the ground; some crawled away and moaned their failure. Three elected governors, leaders of Potam, sat hand-bound on horses.

"Get going," a familiar voice ordered him. The mounted warrior's sombrero cast a shadow over his face.

Cheve rose to a stoop, stared hard at the dark-faced man. The man's horse shuffled from side to side allowing the flames to cut scissors of light on his face.

"Ángel — what are you doing?" Cheve asked.

"Go." The man pointed his rifle.

The woman's sobs and the children's cries filled his ears. The fat man still gyrated on top of Cajeme's wife in the dirt. Her legs kicked the air. She flailed her hands on his massive back but to no avail. The fat man's grunts and panting filled Cheve with disgust. He looked away.

He limped to the closest tree, sat, and leaned against the trunk, cupping his hands over his eyes.

Pain and sense of helplessness nailed his rage to the bark. Instead of trying to rescue the woman again, he threw up and wept.

"Where's your husband, Cajeme?" the rapist called out. "Where's the son of a whore? Certainly, not here to stop me from taking you."

Grabbing the woman's hair, the man jerked her head to his face as if to kiss but instead slapped her. He rose, pulled up his pants and laughed raucously. "That's the way I like my women — with some fire in them," the Yori said.

When his men released her children, they rushed to their mother, pressing their faces into hers.

Cheve heard a gasp behind him. The bouncing firelight distorted his sister's pretty face to scowls. She reached out as if to somehow magically rescue the woman.

"My dear blessed *Virgen*, what did they do to her?" Luz said in a weepy voice. She appeared to shrink as her shoulders sagged.

He strained to stand. "Get back, Luz, out of the light."

His sister took a few steps forward and put her hand to her mouth. "No! By the blood of *Jesus Cristo*, how could Ángel do this to us, to Father, Mother?" She shook her head. "What did they do to you?"

Cheve limped with her back behind the tree. When she wrapped her arms around him and squeezed, he moaned. "Not so hard." She eased her hold, caressing his bloody face and hair.

"Mother?" Cheve asked.

"In the church, with the other women. She worried you would come."

"Ángel saved me." He nodded toward the mounted Torocoyori, as Yaquis called traitors.

The fat man climbed onto his horse. "When the coward Cajeme returns, tell him Sergeant Bocagrande raped his wife. He can find me in Guaymas. When I catch the rat, I'll hang him from the closest tree and any of you who care to join him. I'm going to squeeze your governors' balls until they squawk like parrots. They'll tell me where the rat *Caca* hides." His men laughed at the deliberate mispronunciation. "That's right — that shit-eating rat."

A horseman galloped to the sergeant. He pointed toward the south.

"Thank you, sweet whore, for your hospitality. My regards to — "

Gunshots rang.

"We go, eeeeyahh!" Bocagrande kicked his horse's flanks and bolted into the night followed by the other Yoris and Torocoyoris raiders, whooping and whistling.

Yaquis rushed forward to Cajeme's family and the beaten defenders on the ground. Horsemen with drawn pistols and rifles galloped to the burning house. People of Potam pointed toward the darkness, at Cajeme's wife and children. As quickly as they came, they charged off in pursuit of the raiders.

Unwelcomed visions came to Cheve on this night of dancing and fighting. They foretold more years of the Yaqui River stained with their blood. He foresaw plots of fresh graves, tilted, colorful crosses, rising around the church. The only path to sunny plateaus of Yaqui freedom led over the treacherous sierras of death and destruction.

"Does Mother know?" he whispered.

"No. She would have told me."

"Father will never forgive him."

"We cannot tell them yet. We must persuade Ángel to come back to us."

"How?"

"We find and bring him back." She pressed her trembling hands together as if praying, "Please, Blessed Mary, give me the strength."

The fire finished consuming Cajeme's house with hissing flames, falling wood. Two women assisted Cajeme's wife to her feet and covered her with blankets. Her children slipped under the wrap, clinging to her. They jumped at each crack of distant rifle fire that echoed from the dark.

"Oh Brother Ángel, why did you desert us?" Luz asked.

Maybe the desert winds held the answer.

Above the moans and cries of the wounded and outraged, a woman's lisped voice crackled from the fire, "Cheve, my beloved son."

Flames leaped crazily to form a laughing vision of a woman with distorted lip and nose.

CHAPTER 2

WRATH OF CAJEMÉ

"They beat war drums again."
"So much fighting." The Little People shook their heads.
"We should take their guns away."
"They'll just fight with their hands, nails and teeth."
"Cheve looks for his papa."
"He doesn't know."
"Let's tell him."
"No, he must discover the truth on his own."
"Is he smart enough?"

Cheve rode in the cool February morning behind his parents, Mateo and Petra, and sister, Luz, following drum beats to the town of Vícam. Rifle and bow toting men traveled with their families from Bácum, Tórim, Cócorit, Belem, Guirivis, Rahum, and Pótam. People streamed the roads and trails, their voices muted, in their trek to the public assembly called by the governors. In the misty dawn that enveloped them, dirt paths led to a vengeful war, a well-worn Yaqui track.

The closer Cheve approached Vícam, the hum of voices swelled. Thousands of Yaquis gathered in the dusty, central plaza square bordered by a ramada on one end and a church on the other. Dour-faced Yaqui officials, their heads leaned to one another in quiet conversations, sat under or near the ramada. Young, muscular Yaquis carrying rifles had climbed to the church bell tower. Their hands shaded their gazes over the town and beyond. Farther out, around the central assembly square, small patron saint statues stood guard in the yards of vacant reed huts. Tied dogs barked their cries for release.

9

Yaquis of all ages and sizes gathered: hardy, dark-skinned men held children on their shoulders, plump women breast-fed infants, and scraggly-haired boys offered cups of water to older men and women.

Mateo Falcon pushed his way through the throng to the front, his family in tow. Cheve felt his palms moisten and his breathing quickened. He bowed his head to avert any wandering gazes, fleeting remarks and snickers. At times, his father's importance spilled unwelcomed light onto him.

Five silver-capped canes lay fixed in the ground before the ramada, symbols of the governors' authority. Their fine, colorful blankets contrasted with their black eyes, bandaged heads and broken limbs. Cheve learned Yoris had stripped and beat them, only releasing them because they slowed the raiders' flight.

Mateo Falcon, wearing a fox's skin draped over his shoulder, panache of feathers hanging from his head, sat next to Cajemé, captain-general. A tall boy standing to the side of the governors held the Yaqui flag — a white cross in a field of blue. A hundred grim-faced soldiers clutching Mausers, arrows, and bows stood guard on both sides of the officials. Cheve sat with his mother and sister in the first row reserved for relatives of Yaqui leaders.

His face inscrutable, Cajemé gazed at the ground. He drew small crosses in the dirt with the right index finger. He, too, wore the distinctive fox's skin and feathers. As soon as the governor stood and raised both hands, the drumbeats stopped. Ghost echoes reverberated. The crowds' silence lingered like a feather falling to the ground.

"Welcome to a talking. To our purpose: Yoris and Torocoyoris," the governor shook his fists, "raped Cajemé's wife, beat his children, burned his home. They kidnapped and humiliated two governors, defied Yaqui law. We know these men, their names."

Cheve shot a side-long glance at Luz's fearful face.

"What shall we do with them?" The governor asked.

The captain-general continued to stare at the ground. Cajemé drew a large cross in the dirt over smaller ones. When he looked up, he exposed a lean, taut face with blood-shot eyes. A wry smile came to his lips as he hopped up, spread out his arms.

"My governors and most human of people, the answer is simple: Kill them!" He raised his fist. "Anyone disagree?" Cajemé asked.

The feather still lolled over the gathering.

"I'm not opposed for these crazy men to die for their grave sins against you, your family and Yaquis."

Cheve looked to his side at his mother as she spoke in a loud voice.

"They've broken Yaqui law and must die," she said. "But we should execute the guilty. Are we sure we've named the right men?"

"We have witnesses," Cajemé said. "The traitors were raised among us. Read the names."

An old man with a head bandage rose, wearing a black patch over one eye. "I've lived in the Yaqui for seventy-seven years. I know everyone here." He swept his gnarled, wrinkled hand over the crowd. "This patch may trick you to think my sight is failing. But I saw and heard clearly most of these traitors that night. I admit it was dark and I couldn't identify them all. Still I spotted most. And they were not all Torocoyoris. I heard *El Español* wag from the mouths of waiting Yoris. They hurled *chingados* and *hijos de putas* at the Yaqui traitors when they heard Cajemé still lived."

"Yoris sent them to kill me," Cajemé shouted, pounding his chest with a closed fist.

Cheve leaned back at the sudden burst of fury.

"Traitors came like scorpions in the dark, hoping to sting me while I slept. They missed, but hurt my family. Read the damn names!"

The wounded governor waved for a chubby-cheeked boy to come forward. Cheve stared hard at this boy who was said to read and write in Cajita, Spanish and English. *What Seataka flows through this young one to have so many tongues? His eyes chase the lines, curls and dots as if they were his toys.* Cheve heard that when the boy's parents discovered his ease with letters, they traded food for books with Yoris to practice his reading and writing. They also offered sumptuous meals to an itinerant priest who tutored the boy after hearing confessions, celebrating Mass and baptizing young and old Yaquis.

The governor handed a brown paper sheet to the boy. A soldier placed a box on the ground. The youth stepped onto it, looked over the list and squinted. He grinned as he pronounced the names in a tinny voice.

"Louder," Cajemé ordered. The boy shouted.

Several in the assembly gasped or wept on hearing their family member or friend called out.

Cheve bowed his head, dreading the squirt's pronouncement of his brother's name. His mother and father would be shamed at the mention of their first-born. Squeezing his eyes shut, he feared the *Á* sound lash across his back. When the boy stopped reading, he glanced toward Luz whose mouth gaped open with relief as wide as his.

"I know these men. I recognized them with my good eye." The governor pointed to his cyclopic head. "They rode here to kill the captain-general. But the *Virgen de Guadalupe* protected him."

Cheve breathed easier, but didn't know whether to thank the Holy Ghost for the old man's memory lapse or poor eyesight. Perhaps, the boy couldn't read as well as all thought.

The chubby-cheeked reader handed the list back to the governor, stepped down from the box and walked to his proud parents in the gathered crowd.

Cheve wondered if the boy realized his reading talent had just sentenced many men to death. Pride and innocence blinded him to the terror his words carved into many hearts.

"Esteemed Petra Falcon," Cajemé said, "we've identified the traitors. There is no mistake."

She nodded.

"Sons, brothers, or husbands?" Cajemé rose and raised his hands to the air. "They've disgraced all Yaquis with treachery. They're no longer Yaquis. I'll personally kill them." He flexed his fingers to demonstrate his throttlehold. He dropped his arms to his sides. More sobs erupted through the gathering. "Anyone dispute this action?"

Cajemé's challenge settled over them like an ominous cloud. Except for weeping, the Torocoyoris' grieving families remained silent.

"How will we catch them?" Cajemé asked. "The governor has told us Yoris were waiting outside Pótam that night. They're demons who aim to seize our ancestral lands. Anyone resisting, they kill. Scorpions provoke a war, send soldiers and cannons to kill us all." The captain-general walked slowly back and forth before his followers. When he glanced at the sky, Cajemé looked up as well. "But I seek no war—don't want more Yaquis to die." He held up a parchment. "I've dictated a letter to the Yori prefect in Guaymas demanding he hand over the guilty Torocoyoris to us. If they comply within ten days, we avoid war."

Cheve's face flushed, seeing the boy-reader's parents patting their son on the back. *The goat-boy wrote the letter.*

"Why should they give you these men if they know you'll kill them?" a one-armed, Yaqui elder standing a few feet deep into the crowd asked.

"Well-asked. I learned to play chess, a Yori game of war. Yesterday, my men captured ten Yori cargo boats on the Yaqui. They can have their sailors and boats back once they hand over the traitors. If not... I'll burn and sink the boats with their seamen strapped to the decks. Look." Cajemé pointed to the church tower.

Cheve gazed up and saw three hand-bound Yoris standing at the edge of the church tower. The guards pointed rifles into their backs. An audible gasp swept the assembly.

"I'm tempted to hang them now. But I have patience. You, who love the Yaqui, prepare for war against our enemies. They leave our sacred grounds or die on it. No burials.

Coyotes can clean the mess." Cajemé clinched his fist into the air.

"Many Yaquis will die," the old man said in a tired voice.

"Would you prefer your children die shoveling horse shit from stables on Yori haciendas? Do you want to give them your women at night when their wives are too lazy or too ugly? I've lived with Yoris, fought in their army against the Apaches, Mexicans and French. They take what they want and respect no God or saints. They lust for drinking, fighting, and killing. You speak truthfully, old man. New crosses will rise in the church graveyard. We live and die as free men and women in the Yaqui way." Cajemé moved to the center of the ramada and looked from side to side.

"Most human of people, how many will follow me in war against Yoris and their stable-cleaning allies?" He pointed at the Yori sailors.

Like a roused flock of birds taking flight, the gathering stood, lifting their voices in their willingness to fight. The scarred-faced boy joined the peal of approval.

"Governors," Cajemé said to the elected leaders, "our people agree to our plans."

The five governors nodded like a line of woodpeckers on the same tree.

Cajemé held up a paper. "This letter contains our demands. I need a brave Yaqui to deliver it to the Yori prefect in Guaymas. Who will take it?"

"I will," Luz jumped up, her hand outreached, startling several nearby governors, Cajemé and Mateo.

"Your daughter?" Cajemé said in a low voice.

"Yes," he said grimacing.

"Sit down, Luz," Petra insisted, reaching out to her.

"I go with my sister." Cheve leaped up next to her.

"No, no, no, both of you sit down," Petra ordered, her fingers fluttering.

"And I will escort them," a new voice sounded.

Tomas Leones, a tall, muscular soldier from Cócorit, under Mateo's command walked forward with Mauser in hand. Cheve recalled his father saying Tomas was an expert horseman, good shot with rifle and bow. On a speeding horse, he had dropped many Yoris daring to come into his aim. His deft use of the knife had gutted the spirit of all foes who challenged him in hand-to-hand fighting. Crisscross scars on his chest, arms and hands etched stories of many freed souls.

"Brave children, Mateo. Shaped into loyal Yaquis. I'll never forget your son's attempt to save my wife and children."

Standing between Luz and Tomas, Cheve formed a half smile, but didn't look up at Cajemé. A quick peek to the side revealed the solider staring at his sister. When Cheve moved closer to her, he stopped. Thousands of Yaquis would see his misshaped mouth. Despite his bravery on the night of the raid, his legs grew weak and swayed.

"You can't even stand straight," Petra said. "You're not well. Sit down, Cheve. And you, too, Luz."

"I have no children or husband," Luz insisted, her head held high. "I can ride long distances without tiring. I can shoot rifle and bow. Is it not customary for Yaqui women to negotiate with the enemy?"

"Hmm," Cajemé said with a smile. "She has your strengths, Mateo," Cajemé said. "Shall I give her the letter? You're aware of the dangers."

"Luz will deliver it," Mateo said. "But not my son, Cheve. Instead, send Tomas Leones to protect her."

"I'm strong," Cheve lisped, his face flushed. "I run faster than most. I can fight."

"The beating has taken strength from your legs," his father said. "Rest. Sit down."

Cheve glared at his father.

"A good soldier obeys orders," Cajemé said. "A good Yaqui listens to his father."

Cheve sat, staring down at the ground. *A fool. I made a fool of myself, exposing my face and pride in front of Yaquis.* When his mother placed her hand on his shoulder, he pulled away.

"Don't touch me . . . because I'm ugly." Cheve placed his hand over his face. "How did I get this face when you're so pretty? I don't look like you, Father, Luz or Ángel… Whose face do I bear? I'm not Yaqui. I'm half-beast."

"Cheve, you're beautiful to me. That's enough."

"No. I'm not a Falcon. Who am I? What am I?"

Rising on unsteady legs, he pushed his way through the crowd. He fell several times, scraped his knees, bruised hands and elbows before he reached the church. *I can climb up the tower and push one of the Yori sailors over. I'll prove worthy.* Staring up at the tower, he grew dizzy.

"Ahhhh." Pushing open the doors, he tumbled forward into the solitude of the cool, dark church. He wiped the moist corners of his eyes with the back of his hands.

Dim light shimmered from the altar where two lit candles burned. Cheve rose, shuffled to the front and watched the candle flames flicker in its natural rhythm. *Must learn to move like the flame. Win awards at the next Great Pahko. Earn title of best dancer throughout all Yaqui. People would watch with admiring looks, staring at my feet — not my face.*

Dancing with strength, grace and brightness, he would reach the spirits of the *Yo Ania,* the Yaqui world of eternal beauty and creativity. From the Other Side he would find the answer to the questions of his face: How could he exchange it for a mask of Yaqui pride? Despite the dimness, his perfect features loomed in the shadows. If he could reach and lay it over his ugly visage as he did with Pascola dancers' masks, he would find solace.

His eyes adjusted to the darkness to reveal a painting of a black-robed priest giving Communion to brown-skinned lepers on a beach. Grass-thatched huts and palm trees stood in the background. His mother had said Jesuits brought them from their native country.

In this church, his mother taught lessons about wicked Spaniards. For two hundred years, their priests had controlled the Yaqui's spiritual, economic, political worlds. They taught new farming methods, house building, music and instruments. Their schools instructed them how to read, write, number, and build tools to farm and construct houses.

Against the greedy Yoris, priests championed Yaquis, preventing their enemy from encroaching on Yaqui land or enslaving them for work in their mines and haciendas. They protected their women and girls from rape. The Jesuits' protection crumbled when Yaquis decided their freedom to self-rule was more precious than to live as the priests' peasants.

Cheve walked closer to the painting where the lepers displayed gross deformities: missing limbs, ears or eyes, crooked arms or legs, twisted faces. A boy running from a thatched hut toward the priest wore no dressings. The brown-skinned youth lacked an upper lip, like him. He started at the too familiar jagged tear. Drawing back, he winced and shook his head in disbelief. *Were there really others like him in the world?*

"Leper... Cheve the leper," he said. To the side, another painting revealed a very white Madonna cradling an equally light baby Jesus. The infant Christ's right pudgy hand held the *Virgen's* small, left breast as he suckled.

"Why was I born this way?" he shouted in the near empty church, his hands over his face.

"I've asked the same question," a woman's voice answered.

The sunlight's brightness from the open door blinded him for an instant. When the silhouette spoke again, he recognized his mother's voice.

"I took you to many healers, Spanish priests. Even to a Yori doctor. They gave me medicine, herbs, holy water, but nothing worked. I've prayed to the saints, to the *Virgen* for a miracle." She walked toward Cheve with outstretched hands. "When you suffer, I hurt with you. My son, I'm tired of hurting."

"Ease our pain, Mother... my father?"

Petra bowed her head. "Again and again with this question. I've told you many times. Listen and you'll hear the same answer. Mateo Falcon is your father."

"No! You're in church, Mother. Stop lying. I'm not a child. Who is my real father?"

She placed a hand to her eyes as if to shade them and sobbed. "He's your real father. I prayed you would never doubt that," she said through her tears. "In this church, before God I swear I tell you the truth. Don't listen to gossip. The devil whispers poison in your ears."

"Some say I'm Satan's child. No one told me. Came to me as a vision in the night. Who is he?"

She shook her head and said, "Ah! Why do you need to know? Doesn't matter, now."

"Because I want to meet the man who gave me this face. Now, his name?" He ran in an awkward gait, stumbled, fell, scrambled up, and grabbed her arms. "Tell me!"

She jerked her hands from his grip and slapped him hard.

Cheve's head whipped back. Placing his hand over the stinging cheek, his eyes widened more from shock than pain. She had never slapped him before—not in the face.

"Don't touch me." She stood erect, leaning forward. He cowered at her hard gaze that pierced the darkness. "If you want to know the secret so much I'll tell you. Perhaps it'll drive the self-pity away. Then you can stop weeping like a goat seeking a tit. The man you look for is a killer. Yoris call him *El Feo*, the ugly one."

"*El Feo?*" Cheve bowed his head. Spanish words cut a deep gash in his spirit. Like a lame horse chased across the plains by wolves, he had come to the edge of the gorge of truth. The only means of escape was to jump to the other side. He asked, "Why . . . the name?"

"Because, Cheve, he looks exactly like you."

Tears welled when he asked in a quivering voice, "Is he Yori?"

"Yes, he's Yori. Now you know. Yori blood flows in you. But it makes no difference. In spirit, you are full-blooded

Yaqui. I love you as you are. And so does your real father, Mateo. He has cherished you as much as Ángel and Luz. My son, stop tormenting yourself."

Instead, his hands shook, his vision wandered around the checkered-lighted church.

"Others must know. Cajemé, the governors must know and can't trust me. That's why I wasn't allowed to go with Luz... How did it happen?"

Petra shook her head, stepping back. "Too terrible to relive it. You know too much now."

"You were raped. That's how it happened. It's the reason I'm this way. God was angry with you for this sin and punished me for this crime. I'm a bastard."

"Enough," she shouted. "I did nothing to anger God. You bear this face because *El Feo* carried this face. Accept it. I cannot change it. No one can alter the past."

"I want to kill the man who cursed me with this face. I must find him. Where is he?"

"You sin now. It's over. God will punish him. Forget vengeance."

"Out there," Cheve pointed toward the door, "Cajemé talks of war where thousands of Yaquis may die because his wife was raped. While you were hiding in this church, I was fighting to save her. I deserve more." He walked from his mother, stopped and returned to her. "Mother, now let me tell you a secret." His voice grew petulant. "Ángel, your precious first-born, rode to Pótam on the night they raped Cajemé's wife. Luz and I saw him — he rides as a traitor — a Torocoyori."

"What? You lie. Boy-reader never uttered his name. Your hatred has twisted your heart. You want to punish me for a crime I didn't commit."

"When was the last time you saw Ángel?"

"Stop it. Get on your knees and pray to Jesus, the saints, to release you from your curse of self-pity and anger." She pointed to a large wooden cross on the altar. "You own an ugly face. Accept it. No one can cut it away. I can't. You're the only one who can mend your heart." Petra ran to the church entrance.

When she opened the door, sunlight filled the room again. Cheve averted his face from the rays. The yellow candle flames flickered out at the sudden rush of air.

"I'll find *El Feo*," Cheve shouted, pounding his fist in his hand. He paced around the empty church, ran to the elevated cross, dropped to his knees. His hands in the air to the hanging Jesus, he begged, "Help me, please, to find him." He looked away and whispered, "And kill him."

Rising from knees, he walked to the door and muttered, "I'll give you back your Yori blood, Father."

CHAPTER 3

✦

GUARDIAN ANGEL

By the next afternoon, Luz Falcon rode alongside Tomas Leones, surrounded by an armed escort of twenty Yaqui soldiers, close to the Yaqui borderlands. She studied the flat, brown desert, spotted with short shrubs, cactus, and mesquites. Luz grimaced at the fields of corn, planted by trespassers, which spread all around like yellow blankets over the land. The woman scanned the horizons for hidden Yoris, waiting to ambush them. After witnessing the rape of Cajemé's wife, she resolved to kill any man who attempted the filthy act in her shooting range. Her hands trembled, breaths grew shallow at the sordid rape images. *Focus on the peace mission. Cajemé's letter.*

As the wind swept over the land, an invisible painter changed the scenery from brown to green to yellow shades. The sky appeared bluer, clouds whiter. Desiccated bones and flying hawks offered evidence the sparse vegetation attracted predators.

In the distance, roaming cattle grazed on the plain's grass. Yori *hacenderos*, hacienda owners, had defied Cajemé's order. They built their haciendas *grandes* on rich Yaqui lands, funneling precious water from their rivers. For protection, they sent vaquero patrols to guard against Yaqui raiders. Her escorts rode with Winchesters cradled in their arms, watchful for Yori traps.

Luz reached into the leather pouch that hung from her left shoulder, across her chest and rested on her right hip. The feel of Cajemé's letter addressed to the Yori prefect raised gooseflesh on her arms.

Tomas asked several times if she grew cold, tired or wished to rest or eat. She shook her head. Luz would rest when the others decided it was time. Yaqui women could work as hard, endure as much pain as any man.

Tomas' concern flattered her. Luz smiled, slipped side-long glances at his strong hands gripping the reins of his horse, the easy manner his body swayed in the saddle, the comfortable fit of his clothes, the dark brown color of his skin, the symmetrical profile of his face. *Enough, he may catch me.* She averted her gaze.

Under the vigilant eyes of her parents, Luz had never walked alone with a man. Now she rode as the only woman among twenty-one men despite her mother's wishes. She grimaced at the remembrance of her mother's sad gaze fixed on her as she rode out with the escorts. The urge to cry swelled when Luz looked back once hoping for a blessing that never came.

After the assembly, she and her father had found her mother kneeling and weeping at one of the outdoor Stations of the Cross. Her father helped her up from the ground and asked what troubled her. Through her tears and sobs, Petra told them she had slapped Cheve for disrespectful talk to her. The guilty hand rose into the air as if in voluntary admission. Her mother told of how he wailed like a spoiled boy in the church because he couldn't accompany Luz. He insisted his disfigurement forced Cajemé to refuse his place in the mission.

Mateo shook his head and grunted his disappointment. When Petra hugged Luz, begging her not to go, Mateo pulled her away. He growled Luz would go: she had volunteered before the assembly. Cajemé expected her to complete the diplomatic mission. With his arm around her shoulders, he said he was proud of his daughter for her courage. He ordered her to help Luz prepare for the journey. As for Cheve, he would deal with him later.

That night, after setting camp in Vícam, Luz and Petra talked privately in the church while her father briefed his soldiers at the corral. Under a wooden carving of Jesus on a cross and Petra's persistent questioning, Luz admitted to seeing Ángel the night of the raid. Her mother pulled on her hair, touched Jesus' nailed feet and wept at the bitter truth.

At that moment, her mother appeared like the sorrowful Mary waiting for her son to die and come down from the cross. Luz volunteered for a personal peace mission: persuade Ángel to leave the Yoris. Should Cajemé discover the truth, the captain-general would hunt and kill her older brother. Luz made the sign of the cross and vowed never to reveal this shame to her father. She knelt with her mother in a co-conspiratorial prayer.

"Ángel," Luz said wistfully.

"What's that?" Tomas asked.

She grinned and looked away. "Nothing."

"You said something about an angel. If you look for one, then you've found him. I'm you're guardian angel on this trip."

"I have many guardian angels on this mission." She averted her face. Despite the cool air, her cheeks grew warm.

"Not for long. Others will leave us soon. We enter the Devil's Land. I'll be your sole escort to Guaymas."

"They leave?"

"If the Yoris see too many of us, they may think we're a raiding party. We must avoid all contacts until you deliver the letter. Mateo's orders."

Although she trusted her father's judgment, electric fear of capture on the open plains by a Yori party quivered her legs. She and Tomas alone couldn't fend off a hostile enemy attack. God give speed to their mares.

When they came to a stream, Tomas reined his horse to a halt, motioning the others to stop. "We'll rest, eat here."

The dismounted men allowed their horses to drink at the bank. Some rubbed their animals' long necks, patting their rumps.

Luz waded into the water with her horse, rubbing its muscular legs in long hand sweeps. The horse's back rippled in an involuntary spasm. The stream's coolness shot up through her body. Her legs shivered, but she didn't move until the others did.

They hitched horses to nearby trees, unpacked bundles of food. Luz joined the circle of men as they placed tortillas, corn, pieces of beef on a cotton blanket. Someone laid a blanket wrap around her shoulders. Tomas sat close-by.

"The water's cold," he said. "You still tremble."

"It didn't bother me," she lied, glad for his kindness.

"We cannot light a fire."

"My feet are dry." She took up a meat-filled tortilla, biting into it. "My stomach growls." Chewing rapidly, she was surprised at her intense hunger. She took up another from the spread and after several bites devoured the meal. Luz blushed at Tomas' smile. "The ride gave me a strong appetite." Her chewing slowed.

He placed several of his beef portions on the blanket. "You can have some of mine."

With a mouthful of meat and armful of embarrassment, she mumbled a protest. Her escorts bantered, rubbed their backs, or stretched out on the ground. Some draped blankets around their heads to cut the bite of the wind. From beneath hoods covering most of their faces, some sneaked curious glances at their female guest. She pretended not to notice and quelled a slight trembling of her legs and hands. *I'm the daughter of Petra Falcon. I am brave.*

"My men," Tomas said.

The escorts grew silent, rose from the ground, their attention on him.

"We thank you for your protection, but we part here. When you finish resting, return to Vícam and report to Cajemé we've arrived safely to the Yori border. With protection of the *Virgen,* Luz and I should arrive in Guaymas by tomorrow evening. Return by a different trail since the enemy may track us. Avoid contact with Yoris or Torocoyoris for now."

Several grunted their disappointment. Others nodded their acceptance of the order.

"Are you sure? Yoris out there. If they catch the young woman..." An escort dropped a blanket from his head, exposing his troubled gaze. He pointed north with his rifle.

"We must negotiate—not spill blood. May the *Virgen* escort us now." Tomas leaned toward Luz while the men inspected their firearms. In a low voice, he said, "I don't mean to offend you, but I must ask why you volunteered to deliver Cajemé's letter."

Luz swallowed a handful of corn, chewing slowly in hopes of ruminating a lie.

"Yoris!" a warrior tending the horses shouted.

She scrambled to her feet and gazed at the guard who pointed in the direction of the Yaqui plains. Luz scanned the horizon at the distant mountains, scattered mesquites, cactus and shrubs. A plume of dust whirled toward them. Dark objects churned at the base of the plume. Tomas' strong tug on her arm grabbed her attention.

"We go," he ordered. "Men, divert them. Ride slowly along the stream until they see you. Then outrun them. Make your way back to Vícam in the night. Ride now." He threw an imaginary ball to the creek.

After the Yaquis picked up their rations, they scrambled toward their horses.

Luz swept up her blanket, spilling the food to the ground. She ran after Tomas to their mounts. The animals neighed at the sudden rush of men. The blanket slipped from her hand.

"Leave it," Tomas shouted.

The letter carrier jumped onto her horse's back, the pouch secured on her chest.

At Tomas's side, she stared hard with him at the approaching party. The raised dust obscured their numbers. At the distant pops of rifle fire, Luz gripped harder the horse reins.

"They chase a rider who brings them straight to us. He must have picked up our trail. Men, lead them away. God be with you," Tomas bellowed.

Luz watched her escorts grip their weapons as they flew onto their horses. Into the once peaceful rest, the intrusive gunfire shocked her to the reality of how close death tracked them. Her breathing quickened at the sound of horses neighing, men whispering comforting grunts.

Like horses, her eyes widened, nose flared at the stench of imminent danger in a cloud of swirling dust. The lone woman galloped across the stream following her guardian angel into the devil's land.

CHAPTER 4

✵

BLOODY CREEK

Slapping his horse's rump, Cheve kicked hard into the animal's flanks. He leaned forward, yelping, "Eeeeeyahhh! Run Jewel, run."

The mare whinnied, bobbed its head, mane swaying in a tangle of hair, sweat and dust. Jewel's powerful haunches kicked into rapid pounding. Muscular motion rippled in him hope he would elude the Yoris.

On reaching the edge of a large cornfield, he surged forward. Yellow stalk leaves slapped them. In the maze of corn, pounding hooves, the swishing leaves on horse flesh swelled close behind. Cheve veered his horse to the side, raced down, swerved again and again in a labyrinth of pursuit. On the last turn, Jewel's legs slipped.

The rider grabbed the reins tighter, swayed, but immediately the mount regained balance. Four spindly legs churned in synchronized gallop. He burst from the maze of stalks onto the plain. "Oh," he moaned at the sight of the Yaquis. "Big mistake, Jewel."

Cheve looked back. The lead Yori, a mustachioed vaquero with bandoliers crisscrossed over his chest, burst from the cornfield. The man swung up a gun, pointing it at him. More men erupted like exploding popcorn. Brandished rifles, guns, and machetes glinted in the sunlight.

The Yaqui rider's bow and arrows strapped to his back, knife sheathed at his hip seemed puny to mechanical death.

A man bellowed, "*Chingado* Yaqui."

"Eeeeyahh! Yoriiiis." Cheve kicked again his horse. At the first crack of gunfire, he cringed and leaned lower against Jewel's mane. The strong musky scent of the animal mingled with his own. In their flight from death, a chain of survival coiled around the boy and horse. Their swollen hearts could only burst with a bullet.

He thought at first about leading the Yoris away, but when a bullet whizzed past his cheek, he surrendered that heroic notion.

"Mother of God, save me. Come back," he shouted to the fleeing Yaquis. "Jewel, we're alone now."

As if agreeing, the mare furiously bobbed its pointy-eared head. More gunfire cracked. Bullets kicked up dirt on both sides of the fugitive as if to guide him to the killing zone. Another quick look back revealed more than a dozen Yoris intent to kill him. Cheve stared into an undulating row of black gun barrels trained on him.

"Eeeeeeeahh!" he yelled.

He scanned the retreating Yaqui guard that followed the stream. In the distant haze of men and dust, he searched for Luz. Two riders separated from the pack of men, headed in an opposite direction toward a hill.

"Luz, Luz, wait!" he pleaded. He directed his horse in the path of the fleeing couple. "Run, Jewel, catch Luz."

His horse splashed through the stream, showering Cheve. The water failed to cool his fiery fear.

The vaqueros slowed their pursuit and stopped at the brook. Shouting at one another, they pointed and yelled at the Yaqui warriors who were riding away. Tomas' men had also slowed their flight.

Cheve's panting matched Jewel's as they stopped on an easy rise overlooking the horsemen. Relieved no bullet found its mark, he inhaled, pinched the gap of his upper lip and whistled a weak trill. The boy licked his ragged lips. With a mighty puff, this time he whistled a high-pitched Yaqui tune. He waved his arms. "I'm Yaqui."

A lilting response sailed back. He chirped giddily like a bird.

Yoris whistled in mocking imitation. Two crossed the rivulet galloping toward him. Yaqui escorts stopped, pointed and raced toward their pursuers.

After the raid, Yaquis couldn't allow Yoris to leave without tasting blood. As the two warring parties closed, he uncovered the Yaqui ploy to draw the Yoris away from Luz. He shook his head, his shoulders slumped at the ruined diversion. If only they had given him permission from the start to go, he could have avoided this.

The Yori pair sent to pursue him halted and swerved around at the first crack of gunfire.

His sister and escort fled farther away. Despite his wish to follow, his desire to witness Yaquis kill vaqueros proved too strong. Familiar Yaqui war cries bellowed. Metal clanged and glistened from drawn knives, swords, and machetes. Gun fire blasted across the plain, smoke spiraled, men and horses fell.

Jewel jumped, nearly tossing Cheve.

"Easy, horse." He stroked his animal's long, sweaty neck. It's familiar, musky smell soothed him. Blessed and cursed with excellent vision, the boy recognized several Yaquis from Vícam.

Juan de Dios, a young man just a few years older than he, led the charge. Muscular and tall, he stood out in the ranks of the Yaqui formations. One of their best horseman, many women, some even married, had sought his attention. But he ignored them, attending to military duties.

Close behind rode two older men, Vivirano Lopez and Guilliermo Fuentes, both married with eleven children between them. Flying rumors whispered Vivirano had a second wife and children in Pótam whom he visited on his frequent "hunting trips."

All three catapulted head over heels to the ground with bullet wounds to the chests. Their horses tumbled as if to genuflect before their riders died.

Cheve winced and moaned when the men fell. He drew his bow, launching an arrow that landed far too short.

The Yaqui charge faltered. Several warriors retreated from the barrage of vaqueros' bullets. Goateed twins, Cuko and Ignacio Mendoza, the best marksmen of Cócorit, raced to the lead. They lifted Winchesters, retuning fire. Bullets tore into the heads of the first two riders of the Yoris' formation, slamming them to the ground.

The Mendoza Brothers rode headlong next to one another into the Yoris' ranks. Other Yaquis followed.

They wielded their rifles with deadly ease in all directions, shooting and dodging Yori fire. Despite the confusion of dust, animals, men, and gunfire, the twins fought as a unit. Protecting each other's flanks, they inspired one another to kill with grace. In their wake, they left a trail of Yori bodies for other Yaquis to follow.

When Ignacio's mare's front legs collapsed, he jumped headlong. Cuko reared around. He shouted to his brother and extended his arm to Ignacio. As he reached up, a Yori shot Cuko in the back, hurling him to the ground next to his brother. Ignacio reached for Cuko and cradled him as several more vaqueros rode up.

Yoris plugged them until both lay still in each other's bloody arms.

The remaining men of Cócorit fought in a hail of bullets, blood, and bile. After the initial hesitation, Yaquis rode in a killing rhythm their people had learned over the centuries.

In the swirl of bodies and horses, Cheve couldn't tell if Yori or Yaqui prevailed. Men fell screaming in the common language of pain. The boy cringed at the ferocity of the clash devoid of all beauty, order. He winced as the warriors squirmed on the ground touching wounds or clutching severed limbs. After the sign of the cross, Cheve prayed God accept the souls of fallen Yaquis—Satan could harvest the rest. Men and mares lay on their sides as if listening to Mother Earth on the secret of their rebirth.

Among the few still on horses, a vaquero broke away from the melee. He rode toward Cheve, listing to his right.

His first urge was to flee, but the sight of Yaquis dying for his mistake anchored him to the spot. Pulling an arrow from the quiver, he steadied the shaft on the bow string, drew back a little and aimed. Other than rabbits and rats, he had never killed with bow. His hands grew moist and trembled.

The Yori kept coming, riding at a steady gallop. When the enemy was within arrow's range, Cheve drew the string its full length. His hands ached from holding the taut string. The bow trembled. On release, the arrow flew wide. Cheve reached for another shaft, set it in place and pulled the string.

Blood dripped onto the Yori's nose and mustache. The man's eyes were half-open as he swayed, struggling to lift his head. The horseman barely rode up the small hill and stopped a few meters away. The animal's flanks and legs were soiled with blood, dirt and grit.

Cheve eased the tension on the shaft. The bow lowered.

"*Que feo,*" the Yori said in a strained voice, reaching out to the boy he called ugly.

Cheve jabbed the man's hand with the arrow.

The vaquero howled at his new wound. Pulling back, he tottered, his hand reaching for the saddle horn. "*Chingado* Yaqui," he shouted. The shifting exposed his bleeding belly wound.

"Now let's see you run, Yori. *Correle.*" Cheve slapped the rump of the Yori's horse. The mare took a few steps, stopped and shook its large neck as if saying no.

"Eeeeeeyahhh!" the young fighter howled but the horse didn't move. "Run!" he shouted.

The animal, taking no orders from Cheve, stared.

"*Chingado feo,*" the Yori grunted, tumbled from his horse and groaned on hitting the ground. He squirmed, cradling his intestines.

Cheve edged his horse over the wounded man. "Ready to die, Yori?" He pulled the arrow back against the bowstring, aimed at the man's face. The screaming from the wounded on the river as it grew crimson grew louder. The frightful din filled his ears. Few survivors still fought ignoring the pleas in Spanish and Cajita for help. He shook his head for the howls to vanish, but pandemonium persisted like trapped bees in his ears' wax.

"*Chingado feo.*" Cheve shot the arrow into the air. He steered his horse away. "Run Jewel. Catch Luz before dark."

Kicking flanks, he galloped down the easy slope. Soon the Yaqui couldn't hear the vaquero's cursing, "*Chingado, Yaqui... animal feo!*"

CHAPTER 5

DESERT HUT

Luz rode fast after Tomas until their mounts' shadows appeared to tire and drag. She scanned ahead, fearful they might encounter more vaqueros the closer they neared Guaymas, where the closest prefect of Sonora lived. With the approaching sunset, they could rest out of sight. Until then, she rode hard pushing her mare to run side-by-side with Tomas. He knitted his brows, pursed his lips, and muttered angrily, as if talking to his men about how to kill Yoris.

Shadowy brown desert, cactus and tree-covered mountains stretched far to their right. From past fishing trips, Luz knew if they rode far enough to the west, they could swim in the waters of the Gulf of Cortez. Her cousins on the coast were known for their fishing and shell diving. When they weren't fighting, the divers traded pearls for guns, lanterns, and clothes with Yori merchants.

Tomas pulled back on the reins, cooing to his steed to slow.

Luz rode past him and circled her horse back in a wide arc.

He stopped to stare into the distance. Their mounts breathed rushing air through their nostrils in equine, curly, smoke signals. Skin sticky from sweat, hands tingling from the tight grip on the reins, her body trembled in the sudden transition from syncopated motion to desert stillness. A gray aura of steam floated around her clothes.

"See it?" Tomas whispered.

Luz scanned the desert foliage profiles in the dusk.

"What?" she said

"A hut—out there."

"Where?" She strained her eyes.

He pointed. "There. By that tree. Wait here with the horses." Tomas dismounted.

Luz groaned when her stiff legs landed. Squirming to ease her aching muscles, she rubbed the soreness.

Tomas tied the horses' reins to a tree. Walking back to her, he handed her his rifle. "Use it against Yoris — not snakes."

Luz nodded as he clutched a knife and sprinted across the plain.

After a short distance, he crouched like a cougar, springing forward as if on four paws. She gasped.

Reaching into the leather pouch, she touched the letter. The coarse page brought dim images of Ángel in the distant mesquites.

Her heart ached for her brother's return, but not as a Torocoyori. How could he raid his own village, kidnap their governors and allow the rape of Cajemé's wife? What or who bewitched him to switch his loyalty from Yaquis to Yoris?

Despite her father's high status, Cajemé would hang her brother if he uncovered his treason. Falcon family shame would certainly crush her parents. Cheve, struggling with his disfigurement, would retreat further from Yaqui life. They might find themselves exiled from the Yaqui Valley — but to where?

At the horses' whinny, she glanced up and went to them. She rubbed their moist necks, whispering, "Something frightens you?"

As sunset approached, snakes, coyotes and other night predators would soon stir. Against the darkening sky, a large bird glided overhead for a last catch before night spread its protective net over the desert. She admired the grace of the feathered flyer's effortless soaring as it searched for an unsuspecting victim. The plight of the Yaqui was the same: Yoris and Torocoyoris patrolled their borders waiting to pounce when her people were most vulnerable.

Luz looked momentarily toward the mounts. When she swerved back, the woman found the soaring hunter diving. A puff of dust popped up from the ground. Flapping wings beat hard with a ball of fur dangling from talons.

Unlike the bird's prey, Yaquis had fought back and killed the ravenous Yoris when they attacked any of the most human of people for their holy land. The cost of freedom to live on their ancestral lands was never-ending vigilance, never-ending war, never-ending tears for the dead. Luz tightened her grip on the rifle, brought it to her shoulder, lifted to the sky, aimed at the aerial killer, and slid her finger on the trigger.

"Yes, you will die, Yori, the next time I find you in my sights raping a Yaqui woman. Bang," she whispered.

Following the flight of the winged raider toward the south, she brought the rifle down when it flew out of view. Her shoulders tensed when a solitary horseman, galloping hard in her direction, appeared in the twilight. A Yori scout.

She searched for Tomas, hoping he had also spotted the rider. No sign of him. Glancing back, Luz watched the mysterious horseman race closer. The woman raised the rifle to her chest.

Run. Find Tomas.

She took a few steps but stopped. *The horses.* Luz paced, stopped next to a large shrub, planted her feet a short distance from one another. Pressing the rifle butt to her right shoulder, staring down the sights, she aimed, closing her left eye. Her sweaty hands wouldn't stop shaking the barrel. The harder she gripped, the more her hand trembled. The barrel shifted from left to right. Her jittery, right index finger passed back and forth on the trigger. Perspiration slid into her eyes. Her vision blurred.

Luz held her breath in hopes of steadying her aim. It didn't. The horse's hooves pounded louder, the rider loomed. She fired. The crack and kick of the rifle startled her. The shooter peered at the small, disfigured target.

"Cheve," she shouted, exhaled and lowered the rifle. Luz averted her face as he rode up, his horse kicking dirt and grit.

By the time she faced him, he had dismounted. "Cheve, how did you...?"

Before she could finish, he wrapped one arm around her shoulders. His other hand clutched the reins of his horse. His sweaty chest heaved against her. Jewel took a few steps forward until little distance separated her face and the panting horse. She broke away from her brother.

"Here you are." He smiled his familiar crooked grin. "Jewel never failed me." He rubbed the horse's long muzzle.

"I almost shot you. How did you escape?"

He lowered his head and shrugged his shoulders.

"How did you get away?" A harsh voice interrupted from the shrubs.

Tomas approach them, crouched forward with knife in hand.

She gripped the rifle tighter as he searched the land and listened to the noise of the desert. A late-eating bird squawked, a mischievous wind whistled.

Tomas grabbed the barrel of the rifle, taking it from her.

"Get the horses, boy."

He nodded and walked his horse toward the others.

When the boy returned, Tomas said, "Broken house is almost empty. But owners won't disturb us. Better rest there tonight. Cheve, I'm eager to hear more of your escape."

Luz wondered what Tomas meant by "almost empty."

The warrior led them a little way through the desert until they came upon a thatched-roof house. The small dwelling had the clay color of the ground that blended with the ground. Large cracks splintered the plaster finish. Overgrown shrubs covered the land around the dwelling.

A well lay a few meters from the entrance. A large mesquite grew next to the house and well, giving shade. The thatched roof exposed gaping holes.

What keen, cat-eyes Tomas owns. His eyes must glow in the dark.

While man and boy tied, fed and watered the mares, Luz walked to the doorway. A broken door hung crooked from one hinge. Fresh splinters, remnants of Tomas' kicking, strewed the ground.

Luz peered in, but the descending darkness hid most of the interior. Faint sounds of a woman's sobs floated to her.

"Someone there?" She walked into the hut. "God be with you," she called out, but no one answered. Luz walked in and brought her hand to her mouth and nose to deflect a strong, musty odor.

Claws scurried over the dirt floor; pointed nails scraped over her feet. Flinching, she searched the ground and spied several lizards dart out the doorway. A flurry of flapping roused above. Five large birds flew through the hole in the roof. White droppings littered the floor.

Twilight swept a long tail of light through the roof. Dark blue glow exposed a broken table, chairs and pottery shard strewn on the floor and bar. From the looks of the shelves, chairs and tables, she guessed the place a trading post.

Luz passed through the room, entered another.

A cross of wreathes on the wall hung over a wooden bed in the middle of the room. A crack of night light exposed bleached, skeletal remains of two people who lay nestled, their spindly arms embracing one another. The skulls' teeth pressed as if the pair had died kissing.

The woman stared at one of the heads, inhaled sharply and rushed out of the room.

CHAPTER 6

HONOR THE DEAD

Outside, she leaned against the hut wall, her body trembling. She replayed what her mother had said before leaving on the peace mission. Petra's voice telling the story of her rape by an ugly Yori, Cheve's birth, and Father's bitter struggle to allow his wife and baby to stay echoed in her ears. Compelled to go back into the hut, she sought to discover what more the bones could reveal.

One skeleton wore a shredded skirt and blouse, the other a tattered shirt and pants. The disfigured skull had the wispy remains of long hair and the other's scant hair was short. The second skeleton must be a male, she guessed, by its bigger jaw, thicker brow and square chin. The smaller skull's cheek bones were smoother, more refined and the forehead flatter.

Luz slapped her hands. A possible solution to Cheve's heartache about his face and search for vengeance leaped whole before her except for one problem. Luz' mother had told her the disfigured rapist was male.

Oh, Mother, what you told me doesn't match what's here. I don't understand.

Luz had to act fast before Cheve and Tomas returned. She knelt, crossed herself and whispered to the bones, "Please forgive me, but I do this to save my brother from the flames of hell." Rising, she reached over, clutched the skull of the female skeleton and snapped it off its brittle neck and plucked the remaining hair strands. Luz placed the head on the bed and repeated the decapitation with the male remains. After the heads were switched onto the skeletons' broken necks, she set them in their kissing posture.

"Thank you for your cooperation." Luz walked out of the post into the cool, dark air. She shivered, draped her arms

38

around herself and concentrated on her mother's story of violation.

Was this encounter with the bones a lucky coincidence? Or did someone want her to know a terrible truth hidden in the desert? Weeping swept through the air. Low sobs seemed to come from nearby in the desert.

"Cheve, Tomas . . . where are you?"

The sorrowful sounds faded.

"We're coming," a low, choked voice answered.

Luz soon saw the silhouettes of two men: one shadow rushed to her. Cheve came to her side and took her hand, intertwining his fingers into hers. Tomas shuffled, sighed and wiped his hands over his eyes. He cleared his throat several times.

"Your brother told me of my men's fight with vaqueros at the stream. Lost good warriors and friends today. Must pray and mourn for their spirits. Go inside. Will get colder soon. Take these blankets and food."

She took the supplies.

Tomas walked away, stopped, swerved, and pointed at Cheve. "Boy, you owe your life to brave Yaquis." He grimaced and his words choked. "Live yours as worthy."

Luz's eyes filled with tears. She pulled her hand away from Cheve and walked toward Tomas.

When he held up an extended arm toward her, she stopped.

"Leave me alone," he pleaded.

"Let me mourn with you for a while."

He shook his head and continued his solitary walk into the brush.

Luz walked back to her brother, took his hand and led him into the hut. "What happened at the stream?" she asked.

Cheve stepped back, looked down, and pressed his palms on the sides of his head. "Men died to keep the Yoris from following me. I didn't know your plan."

"Oh, Cheve, all those young men — if you had just stayed in Pótam."

"I'll kill many Yoris to make up for their deaths." He raised his head and pounded his right fist into the palm of his left hand, making a smacking sound.

Luz put her fingers on his distorted nose. She followed the slit that channeled from his nostrils and burrowed into his heart. "A scratch compared to your disfigured ideas. No deaths can make up for the loss of their lives. Too much fighting and killing. Cajemé's letter to the prefect will stop it."

Cheve gripped her hands and drew them away from his face. "He'll spit on you, tear up the letter as soon as you deliver it. Yoris don't want peace — they want our lands. They want to rape our women and make us slaves like they did to all people they conquered. You forget the stories Mother told us of the *Españoles*."

A loud, plaintive chant interspersed with groans punched the night air. Luz stepped to the door. A few stars, scouting for the celestial army of shining lights, twinkled.

"Perhaps, it's you I must save from slavery," she said, fresh tears welling. She walked from the door to the bedroom entrance, "Come here, Cheve."

"What is it?" He walked to his sister's side.

"Look, my vengeful brother. It's the man you seek." She walked to the side of the bed, pulled back the cover and threw it to the floor. Cheve flinched. "It's *El Feo*, your father."

"Who?" He bent closer to the bones.

"Death has cheated you of the vengeance you seek. Your search is over."

"How do you know it's him?" Cheve whispered. "It's dark here — I'm not sure."

"Let your fingers do the seeing. Touch the skull's mouth and nose." She reached down and lifted the skull from the bed to her chest.

Cheve stepped farther back until he bumped the wall.

She walked out of the house with the skull close to her own. The horde of stars had now arrived, their swords shimmering. The moon shined like a crescent shield glowing in faint, phantom light. She held the skull up offering tribute to a stellar captain-general. It glowed from the reflected light. Stopping a little distance from the doorway, Luz said, "You seek a vision, my brother. I give you one. Touch what you cannot see but your heart craves: the head of your father, *El Feo.*"

Cheve stood at the doorway and shuffled toward his sister.

"Feel the familiar valley that spreads from the nose like a canal. You know this well. Touch your own and compare. You see, the same. What more proof do you need?" She placed the skull in his trembling hands. He brought it close to his misshapen face. "The man you seek is dead. Your search is over."

While his right hand searched the disfigured skull, his left probed the gap above his mouth. "How did he die?" Cheve asked.

"Who knows? Perhaps sickness, old age or the woman in there took his life. God and the saints know." Luz touched his cheek. "Let's dig a grave for them and bury your vengeance."

"In the morning. I must see this... this relic in the daylight."

Luz followed him back into the house.

He placed the skull on the broken neck and stood at the side of the bed.

She draped an arm around his shoulder. "Let's eat and rest. Come, Cheve. Leave the dead so we may live." Luz led her brother to the other room where she spread out a blanket on a dusty table and placed the food.

They ate the dry corn and meat. After their meal, they wrapped up the remains. Sitting against the far wall with the blanket draped over them, they watched night throw its black net into the room. Outside, an armada of stars clashed with the army of darkness. Twinkling signaled the faraway furious fighting.

Cheve slumped against her shoulder. Soon, he snored.

As she shifted to the side, she laid him to the ground, rose and draped the cover over him. Resting with the deformed half of his face pressed against the ground, Cheve appeared normal in the faint light. If only life's troubles were so easily solved by pressing our faces to the ground and dreaming.

Luz swept up the blanket from the table, draped it over her shoulders, and stepped into the cool night. The chant at first sounded faint. She walked a few paces to the left. The singing grew weaker. To the right, the man's voice vibrated low and strong: the *Pascola* dancers' song of mourning.

Her mother had explained the Yaquis accepted the Jesuits' Christian teaching, especially the parts about *Jesucristo* loving them so much he sacrificed his life for them. Her mother had said the Yaquis were like *Cristo*: they sacrificed to live free on their own lands, to speak Cajita, to govern themselves according to their traditions. Through prayers to the Savior, Yaquis grew stronger from his intercession.

Petra preached they found no difficulty keeping their ancient teachings and customs. Despite the Jesuits' protests, the most human of people found comfort in their ancient dances, songs and nature. Her mother taught the Yaquis were blessed with blending Christian and natural beliefs.

Luz's pity for Tomas overwhelmed his order for solitude. Or perhaps, she admitted to herself, she wished to see this strong man cry. Following the lyrics, she stopped a little distance from the shadowy figure dancing in the dirt.

He tensed and crouched as if preparing for an attack.

"Didn't mean to disturb you," she said. "Please forgive my brother's foolishness."

His silence covered his stealthy speed as she shuddered at the feel of his hand on her shoulder.

"Perhaps if we pray together, Jesus and saints will accept their souls quicker," he said.

"Yes, I'll pray." She touched his strong hand and yearned to hold him, to comfort him. Ignoring her fatigue, Luz took up the *Pascola* chant for the dead as his body shifted and weaved on the desert floor.

CHAPTER 7

✦

MASO SINGS

Darkness and sleep slithered over the tired boy. Despite the cool night and fatigue, the blanket warmed his slender bones, toes and fingers. His muscles sagged, his breathing flowed deeply while his mind's watchman dozed.

Cheve stirred awake at melodic singing from the desert that he had never heard, but still found familiar. Looking up to the ceiling, he attuned to the music and floated into the air to capture the lyrics. Pleasant lightness, buoyancy and suspension thrilled. A soft moan from below called. He smiled to see his own, curled self. Cheve played his arms and legs freely and naturally as if he could always swim in the air. His vision penetrated shadows all around—not in the clarity of sunlight, but in the night vision of owls.

Sleep flyer descended closer to study the resting boy without stepping on the ground. Cheve admired the smooth, angular half of his face that appeared normal, handsome, strong.

As if the slumbering lad heard his thoughts, he stirred, shifted to the other side, exposing jagged gaps in bald clarity. Cheve grunted. Yes, that's the half he knew too well. The skin folded where it should not have, the nose bent and nostril too wide, the lip crumpled and thin. A bushy beard and mustache like the Yoris wore would conceal his ugliness. Although few Yaqui men grew facial hair, a red beard to match his clothes would earn him the name "Running Red Man." He'd like that distinction. Horsehair could cover that sight. Perhaps, they'd mistake him for his horse's twin. A well-crafted mask contoured for that side to match the other would work. Yes, there were ways to shape his good looks to match all the other Falcons.

Singing streamed into the room again in a foreign tongue he found enjoyable. Festive, energetic lyrics intoned a celebration nearby. His ears tingled to the upbeat tempo as if inviting to come out of the house.

His legs shifted serendipitous in an instinctive urge to dance. Cheve floated to the dirt floor, his feet shuffling, arms swaying. Yet his rapid steps left no prints nor stirred dirt on the dusty ground. Swirling toward the bed, he stopped next to the two skeletons and stared at the head his sister had said belonged to his father. He drew closer, hand extended but stopped when the bones stirred.

El Feo, owner of the skull with the jagged hole, drew the covers back in a smooth sweep. He rose, yawned, and stretched his arms out. At the sound of his spine cracking, Cheve giggled. His spindly hand reached out and shook his mate's shoulder.

The smaller figure sprang from the bed, did a loop in the air, almost hitting Cheve, and landed next to her skeletal partner at front of the bed. They stood staring at one another, pointing to each other's head. In an instant, they reached over and simultaneously grabbed the other's skull and plopped them on their own necks. Bones on bones splicing clanged.

A startled Cheve drew away into the air. The heads appeared to fit better on the new frames. The larger skeleton looked around, picked up a sombrero and swept it onto his bald pate. His mate lifted a tattered, dusty *rebozo*, lying on the dirt floor. She draped it around her narrow shoulders, swaying to the side, head cocked, for her mate to admire.

On closer observation, Cheve saw a translucent glow circle the remains. The aura took a darker reddish hue, transforming to a shimmering image of the pair when they breathed. The skeletal frames grew faint as the brighter colored shell and body shapes filled out.

The sombreroed figure was a mustachioed man with bright, brown eyes, broad nose and toothy smile. Muscular, bow-legged, he had the well-weathered mien of a hacienda worker. The skeleton-vaquero held his partner's hand, a small-framed shapely woman with plump breasts and long black hair draped across half her face. From the side she displayed a beautiful profile. When skeleton-woman faced her man of bones, he lifted her hand and kissed it.

Her eye brightened, a half smile edged from beneath her draped hair.

The vaquero leaned forward, his hand raised to her tresses. She reached up to cup his hand. Drawing his hand away, he nodded and pressed his translucent lips again on the unveiled cheek.

Skeletonette drew him closer, lifted her head, drew back her hair and kissed him hungrily. Her beauty gave way to the too familiar fissures that twisted her nose and mouth like his.

Cheve reeled in circles above the pair. He twirled to view this new revelation from different angles. He tumbled in confusion.

Who was *El Feo* . . . or was there, instead, *La Fea*?

The singing filled the room in lively tempo.

With a lift of the sombrero, the male skeleton bowed, and swept it across the floor. He replaced his hat to his head, offering his hand. Palms joined, they swirled around the room in graceful, Mexican ease. Her semi-smile curled to her bright eyes, accented her fragile beauty.

When they neared the sleeping boy, the dance pair stopped. The woman knelt next to him, swept back his hair, and traced his disfigurement as she touched her own. She wiped a few of her phantom tears from the boy's cheek.

The sombreroed man tapped her shoulder.

Nodding, she leaned close to the boy, kissed him and whispered into his ear. "Better if you were never born, Cheve."

The floating boy winced at the stinging words. He clenched his fist, his eyes moistened. The sleeping twin moaned, tears seeped from his closed eyelids.

The man tugged on the woman again.

She placed her smooth cheek on the boy's craggy one for a moment. The woman rose to the arms of her skeleton lover. Shimmering bones resumed their twirls to the sweet song.

"Who are you?" Cheve shouted floating farther up, crossing himself.

The woman appeared oblivious to him, swirling and gliding in synchrony, attuned to her man and music. Their hips gyrated and pressed close to one another. He yelped and kissed her neck, cheeks and lips.

"You're not my mother. You're a *bruja*, a witch." Cheve darted down, cocked his head, pursed his lips and spat. His saliva salvo sailed through her to land nowhere.

He exposed his penis to piss on her, but the music intensified like a wave of bee notes carrying honey.

"Cheve, come and dance with me." A loud voice boomed from outside. His rod secured, he floated through the hole in the thatched roof. Stars illuminated the desert floor with hues of white, gray, blue and shadows. Silhouettes of mesquite trees, cactus, brush and distant, dark mountains staged a calm, cool, inviting desert welcome.

He sailed over Luz, asleep beneath a blanket. At her feet lay Tomas, who snored a heroic bellow to match the insect choir. He stopped to grind his teeth as if he chewed his sorrow for his dead warrior friends.

As Cheve glided over, he said, "I'm sorry, Tomas, I'll kill many Yoris to atone," and sighed.

Singing flowed like a water fall from the other side of the pond. The crescendo of words swept up the closer he neared.

Lyrics peaked as he stopped in midair to behold a large deer at the water's edge. The tallest man in Pótam, known for their heights, would reach the shoulder of this beast.

Deer's round eyes glowed green, mouth tilted up as if swallowing stars, crimson, pointy tongue flickered to taste the sky. From a long, vibrating neck quivered melodic verses. Antler tips shimmered red, reflecting in the water like bejeweled fish. Hooves sparked yellow flashes as it struck the ground.

The deer bent its head to drink from the pond. The closer it neared the surface of the water, the clearer its grand face shone from the reflection of stars, moon, glowing eyes and horns. Antlered head rose, water dripping from its mouth.

Cheve backed away unsure of where to hide, but then remembered his mother's lessons of the desert and the "Other Side."

"Maso," the boy said. In wonder, he gazed on the legendary wild deer of the *Sea Ania*: the flower world, the mystical land of the Surem, the Little People that lived underground. Even though the animal's lyrics were neither Cajita nor Spanish, the words poured into his ears a clear understanding of the *Sea Ania* song.

From his mother's teachings, he knew the Surem as the original Yaquis who remained hidden when the singing tree vibrated the prophecy of Spanish Christianity coming to their lands. The words sang of other side, in the east, underneath the dawn, of the *Huya Ania* wilderness beauty, of the trees, rivers, turtles, birds, caves, mountains, of the Surem, dancing and playing among the flowers. The words painted with music the harmonious blending of air, land and fauna of old.

"Allow me to dance with you, Maso," Cheve said. "Teach me the steps."

When Maso ran through the desert, singing of the *Sea Ania*, the boy followed. Cheve floated above the desert floor as skunks, snakes and mountain lions scurried from the deer's path. Never had he covered ground so fast, even during his speediest runs. No aches throbbed in his legs as pain normally coursed when he raced other boys and men in the village contests. Instead, he flew like a true falcon shooting through the air. His breathing flowed as evenly as if awakened from a pleasant sleep. Light, giddy and bold, he flew with arms stretched out in front in his pursuit of the bouncing red-tipped antlers with flashing hooves.

Maso reached the foothills of the mountains, climbing agilely, vaulting in leaps and springs. Its hooves crushed rocks and grit in powerful lunges and lightning strikes. When the deer's glow vanished in the thick forest, the boy circled the trunks, spiraling higher. Tree clusters blocked moon and star light to shine the way. No glimmer shone, but instead the faint melody from above echoed. Floating to a tall tree, he stood on the highest branch and peered through the gloom.

Scent of fir limbs enveloped him in a pleasant welcome. He crooned the song of the Surem in hopes the magic deer would reveal itself. As the Maso's lyrics grew fainter, the boy's grew stronger. In the *Huya Ania*, the wilderness world, he sang new words that praised the power and beauty of the little animals — the snakes, scorpions, badgers, lizards, frogs and turtles. The hymn tumbled from his lips like wind-propelled flower petals.

His mother's advice resonated: Few with *Seataka* — the gift of seeing the spirit world — would meet Maso. The deer would choose only a few to teach *Huya Ania* secrets. Grand honors bestowed to the Yaqui who learned the graceful steps to the deer melody that many struggled for years to master. As a deer dancer, his performances would impress Yaquis, his family, and Cajemé himself. He would bring much pride and honor to the Falcons. All shame would slough away as he took on the skin of the deer dancer.

Above treetops, a fleeting light, soft, distant music wafting from farther up the mountain beckoned. Higher, higher up, he shot. Flying straight toward the green glow, he trembled as the light grew stronger. At the mountain top, Maso chanted next to a cave's entrance. As Cheve glided down next to the magical beast, the deer twisted its head from side to side, and shuffled its hooves in a rhythmic accompaniment to his serenade. Despite its size and weight, the deer twirled with a lightness of a flying arrow.

Cheve bent forward, twisting his neck in imitation of the deer. His arms and legs repeated the gyrations of subtle hooves, swaying his hips to the shakes of the Maso's tail. The deer's musky smell filled his nose with gritty pleasure.

Boy and beast danced, sang in harmony, their muscles arched in synchrony, voices blended in duet, and spirits interlaced like the lattices of woman's braid. All sense of self dissolved, melding Cheve's and Maso's hearts. The boy's deer dance trapped him in the timeless allure of beauty and motion. He closed his eyes to revel in ancestral, rhythmic vibrations plumbed dancing with the Little People or their desert ally, the deer.

Unaware of day, night, life or death, only the now, he shivered at the solitude of his voice, stopped his nimble steps and opened his eyes. Shimmer of yellow light illuminating the cave entrance replaced the green glow. Close to the cave, he winced at the room's brightness. His temporary blindness gave way to thousands of candle flames dancing and swaying throughout the chamber.

The deer stood in the middle, his antlers barely scraping the roof.

"Maso, Yaqui spirits?" He entered farther into the cavern toward the motionless deer. Glad he had paid attention to his mother's lessons, he knew every Yaqui possessed a candle burning in a mountain cave. When their flame extinguished, their life ended. Candles of different sizes, many extinguished sat on cave shelves and the floor. Cheve searched for a clue as to which one flickered for him, hoping for a tall one that burned slowly. Many had melted down to their base, their wax twisted and sagging at the base like sad, old men. Others stood without flame despite a long stalk. Tempestuous wars had blown disease, famine and hateful gusts over their people for years. Why hadn't they surrendered like all the other *Indios*?

"You dance better than most, but your singing requires practice." Maso's voice sounded guttural, low and loud. "Are you brave enough to see the *Surem*, Deer Dancer?"
Although Cheve had never spoken nor heard the animal's language, he understood.

"Yes, ready to meet them," he said fluently in the talk of the forest as if he had conversed in deer-speak all his life.

"Then enter the snake's lair." Maso angled its antlers to the next chamber lying in blackness.

Cheve stepped from the candle lights of flickering life and pending death into the shadow, stopped and peered. Slithering slaps, lapping gurgles, smacking lips drew near. Red orbs loomed, growing as they advanced closer. A large snake, whose head scraped the ceiling, drooled saliva onto the ground. A scaly, open maw revealed a long, forked tongue gyrating before it. Black spots on its thick, yellow, tubular body bulged as it flexed on the cave floor.

Cheve took a few tentative steps as the serpent undulated closer, jaws opening even wider. He saw blinking eyes and wiggly fingers from inside its maw. The boy gagged at the offal stench. Clenching his fists, he had nothing to fight the serpent except for his hands and feet. The serpent's trunk filled the chamber, offering no space to run around it.

"Where are the Surem?" Cheve cried to Maso.

"There, before you," the deer answered.

The snake glided forward.

"Don't see them."

Cheve jumped back, his hands flaying the air, his back bumping against the cave wall. His feet ran in place.

"*Surem*, show yourselves," he shouted.

The snake's maw opened wider. "They're inside waiting for you, boy." The serpent lunged.

"Ahhhh!" the boy screamed, closed his eyes and covered his head with his hands.

He tumbled like a straw doll, breath swooshed out, hands reached, feet kicked into empty air. He heard Maso call, "Deeeeer Daaaancer," but he couldn't answer.

When he flopped onto the ground, he opened his eyes to find himself lying on the floor of the partially-thatched post. He gazed around into the darkness but found no one, at least alive, there.

Cheve rose. The feel of his feet on the dirt floor felt comforting. The tumbling in his head abated as he stomped his soles on the ground. He shuffled to the bed of skeletons. By the dim moonlight, he saw nothing appeared to have shifted. A sombrero lay in the corner along with a tattered *rebozo.* The arms of the bones rested over one another as they had when he first saw them.

A dream of the Yo Ania, nothing else. His mother had warned of desert enchantment from wandering witches casting nightmares onto unsuspecting travelers. But dancing with Maso wasn't a nightmare—it was a dream made real without mushrooms or leaves. He tapped his head and chests. *I'm awake now, but the beauty is gone.*

Bending over the bed, he stared at the heads. The one with the gap lay on the neck of the smaller body. Cheve shuddered. He crossed himself for protection from *brujas.* He left the hut a little way, gazing at the desert. The star light illuminated the wilderness but no longer in the clarity of his dreams. He searched futilely for the pond where the Maso drank. No songs or glows were heard or found. Returning to his blanket, he lay on the ground, opening and closing his eyes.

Sleep slipped past his weary eyelids, but before he pitched into darkness, he wiped tears and soft traces of a kiss from his cheek. A distant, gentle singing-whisper of "Other Side" whisked him to desert calm.

"Maso . . . Maso, protect me," he mumbled before he dreamed again of the *Yo Ania.*

CHAPTER 8

✵

WOMAN IN BLACK

Luz trailed Tomas and Cheve, shivering from the cold, stinging rain. Distant lightning strikes and their delayed clamorous booms kept her attention honed to the gray-charred skies. Tomas had told them the downpour provided protection in the open since most riders wouldn't venture out. As proof, several horsemen galloped passed them as if the flurry of rain drops concealed the Yaqui party. She accepted the prize of reaching Guaymas without capture outweighed the risk of God's bolts.

Their skittish horses trudged through the mud and reached the outskirts of the Sonoran city that evening. They stopped on a mountain pass overlooking the city by the bay. Wooden, thatched-roof houses, homes of half-breeds, mulattos, Yaqui servants and Yori poor, sprawled over the mountainside.

Through the watery curtain, Luz saw as they descended the houses give way to stucco homes and brick buildings that filled the city to the sea edge. Fish and merchant boats huddled in the rain-splattered waters at the dock. As the masts swayed under wind gusts, sailors scurried over their crafts to secure their cargos. One shimmied up a mast to tie down the sails. Several pulled thick ropes like umbilical cords from hulls to anchor their shifting crafts to the pier.

At sudden brilliant flashes, Luz gazed at ornate buildings, fountains and toward the center a large plaza. "Such a beautiful city," Luz said on seeing Guaymas for the first time. A fortress stood at one end of the center square. She pointed at several men with rifles who stood guard at its entrance.

Tomas nodded. "*Palacio Del Gobierno*," he shouted.

Their destination, the office of the Yori prefect, lay within sight.

She touched the leather pouch that held Cajemé's letter and smiled: it would soon reach the governor's hands. Another flash revealed a large, church bell tower standing at the opposite end of the plaza, across from the *Palacio Del Gobierno*.

When a loud bell tolled an evening Mass, the Biblical passage of rendering onto Cesar his coins and to God one's soul inspired her to say, "We must go to church to give thanks for our safe arrival and to pray for the success of our mission."

"Pray we get out of this Yori rat hole alive," her brother said.

"Cheve!" She sat higher on her horse.

He grunted, slapped his horse's rump, kicked it in the flanks and sprang forward.

"Boy hasn't learned." Tomas shook his head.

Since the discovery of the skeletons, Luz hoped his desire to find his father would end. Her ruse failed.

A dream about the bones frightened him, but he refused to give details. Cheve insisted on taking the skull to a *curandera*, a healer, who lived in the Bacatete Mountains. With a touch of her hands, she could read the skulls' history. She could divine their secrets only heard in deathwatches, lovers' embraces and confessionals.

When Tomas shouted at him to give him the skull, Cheve tossed the head to the ground. The warrior buried the bones a little distance from the house. He planted on their burial mounds two small crosses he had made from the limbs of a mesquite trees. Luz sang a Latin prayer for the dead she had heard her mother sing many times, promising everlasting joy in the company of saints and the presence of God.

They followed Cheve down the mountain road. When their horses' hooves slipped on the muddy path, Tomas shouted, "Get off the horses. Walk them in."

Instead, the boy quickened his horse's pace.

"Cheve, stop," Luz yelled.

A smirk skewed his face to an even more twisted mask.

The horse stumbled on the rain-slicked path, one hind leg slipped and the other back leg caught its full weight. The animal danced sideways until the right front leg buckled. The horse's head bent low until its muzzle slammed the road. A thunderclap boomed overhead, and a bolt exposed horse and rider tumbling forward at a steep angle.

Cheve catapulted through the air, flipping into the wet, slippery mud. He lay half-buried, his legs and buttocks sticking out.

Jewel's neck had twisted to an unnatural, sharp angle. The animal's large, dark eyes stared blankly to the cloudy sky as rain poured down its muzzle.

Luz slipped onto her back as she ran toward her brother. Her arms and legs flailed until she stopped a short distance from him, rain washing over her. She looked up at the dark sky, through the rain drops plopping her face. The cold mud swept up between her legs.

"Luz, you hurt?" Tomas asked standing over her.

"No." She sat up, took his hand and struggled to her feet. She shook her body to unload the mud. The strength of his arm comforted her. She resisted the urge to embrace for his warmth.

Her brother coughed and spewed mud on his hands and knees, his blackened face dripped wet grime. Helping him to his feet, she wiped the sludge off his face and walked back with him to Tomas, who stood over the dead horse.

The man jerked Cheve from Luz "Boy, you killed your horse."

His explosive speed forced her to gasp. Luz' first impulse was to pull him away, to spare him the sight. By Tomas' glare and grip, she knew she couldn't. Besides, his anger at Cheve's foolishness seemed right.

"Jewel, get up . . . up, my little horse, get up," Cheve pleaded. He fell to his knees and slid his hand along the twisted neck to the head and muzzle.

As he bent the neck, bones cracked and the horse's long head flop to the side.

"Breathe, Jewel. Come back alive." He bent closer to the animal to whisper into its pointy ear. Wrapping both arms around the horse's head, he placed his cheek against Jewel's mud-streaked snout and rocked. He mumbled, "Jewel, sorry... sorry, Jewel... Jewel." The rain, incessantly pattering over their bodies, hid his tears.

"Enough. Time to go," Tomas said to the boy.

"No, I can't leave him," Cheve said.

The man handed the horses' reins to Luz, and jerked the boy to his feet. He grabbed him by his hair.

"Tomas, please . . ." she said staring at her brother's gaped mouth and widened eyes.

"Don't interfere." He held up his free hand. "Caused the death of some of my best men and now your horse because you don't like your face. Don't look at your sister . . . look at me eye to eye like a true Yaqui. Your face doesn't scare me. I've seen worse, especially after a fight with Yoris."

As Tomas jerked his hair, Cheve yelped. "Shut up, boy. You think you're the only one suffering? Let me tell you a real, ugly story. I had a beautiful wife and two healthy sons. One night the Yori and Yaqui traitors raided Pótam.

"Burned my house. Killed my family. This is all they left me." Tomas released his grip on Cheve's hair, opened his shirt, and threw it to the ground. Crinkled, leathery skin covered his torso and back. The burn scars continued below his waist. Tomas clutched Cheve's hair again, jerked the boy's head down and brought it close
 to his chest. "Touch it . . . I said touch it." He forced the boy's right hand onto his stomach.

Cheve grimaced as his palm swept over Tomas's chest and belly.

"The fire reached below." The muscles on Tomas' face rippled.

"Many Yaquis in our villages have lost arms, legs, hands and eyes? Some are pock-marked for life because of the Yori' sickness. You're ugly. But no one scorns them or you for this. You shame yourself. Your self-pity is a like a snake coiled around your neck. You let it bite my men and now your horse. The serpent tightens its grip and chokes life from you. Best to cut off its head, boy." Tomas shook Cheve's hair. His head bobbed like a drunken puppet. "I don't want to hear anymore talk about your face or finding your father. Obey my orders or I'll tear open another hole in your nose and make you uglier. Understand, boy?"

Cheve nodded.

Tomas released his grip and picked up his shirt.

Luz stared at his burn scars that revealed searing heart wounds.

The boy ran to Jewel and opened his mouth as if he wanted to cry, wiping his hands over his eyes.

When Tomas took the reins from Luz, she placed her hand over his. Hard eyes grew soft. She took a step toward him to whisper, but he broke the grip and led the horses away. With a sigh, she placed an arm around Cheve and followed Tomas. They dared not look back.

Mountain dwellers stirred to quell their hunger.

* * *

By the time they reached the church, well-dressed Yoris were descending the cathedral stairs. They called out in Spanish to the drivers of waiting carriages or walked under umbrellas held by dark men dressed in peasant white.

Despite the rain, bare-footed women wearing *rebozos* wrapped around their shoulders and heads trailed after the churchgoers and held out their hands. Some drew back the colorful wraps from their chests to reveal a baby suckling. The well-dressed simply shook their heads, waved them off or ignored them.

Tomas tied the horses' reins to a tree a short distance from the church and told Luz and Cheve to go into the cathedral while he guarded the animals. With the evident hunger, he didn't want to risk losing any more horses.

When she entered the church, Luz slowed her pace to gaze at the large stained-glass windows. Angels surely created the art work. The colored paintings, finely chiseled statues of saints and the Virgin Mary brought tears to her eyes. She found the portal to heaven: glints of gold from the altar, vaulted ceiling, scintillating candles, and polished, marbled floors must lead to God's throne. Scent of incense lingering whispered to her heavenly riches lay in store for the holy. *Good Yoris surely would want to share their spiritual rewards with her people. Then why were they so hostile to Yaquis if they believed in the same God?*

A fat priest wearing an embroidered red vestment leaned on a brown cane with a gold engraved handle and silver tip. He spoke with several Yoris close to the rear of the church.

Nuns dressed in black habits and white wimples swept the aisles and cleaned the pews. Others knelt before statues, kneading rosary beads, their lips formed silent words.

After the ride in the chilly rain, Luz breathed easier in the peace of the clean, bright, holy place. Tracking mud and dripping rain, she and Cheve walked by the priest and Yoris and knelt in a pew toward the back.

A black-veiled woman, a few pews ahead, knelt before a statue of a saint, her hands pressed together. The sculpture depicted a loin-clothed man, tied to a tree. Arrow shafts pierced his arms, chest and legs. The saint's soft, blue eyes stared upward as if his body's suffering meant little to his soul's imminent communion with God.

Luz crossed herself, closed her eyes and prayed until she heard a tapping against the pew.

"*La misa* is over. The church is closed," a gruff voice in Spanish said.

She opened her eyes to see the portly priest with slicked-back hair and heavy jowls, leaning on his cane at the side of the pew.

Luz smiled. "Father, we've traveled a long way to see the prefect. I have a letter for him from Cajemé. It's about—"

"Cajemé? You're Yaqui—the two of you?" the priest asked pointing at them. He glanced toward the men at the back of the church and then at her.

"Yes, Father. We seek sanctuary until—"

"No, no, no, impossible. The church does not meddle in *la politica*. You must go." The priest's tapping cane rapidly echoed the urgency of his demand. He glanced again at the *caballeros*.

"Father, I don't understand. We have no place to go. We know no one in Guaymas."

"We know Ángel," Cheve said in a small voice.

"There, you see, you do know someone. I'm sure this Ángel will live up to his name and take you in."

"But we just arrived in Guaymas and don't know where he lives. Since we're traveling Catholics—could you help...."

The priest, his fat face and jowls shaking, as if struck with a sudden seizure, motioned up and down for them to rise. Luz's body stiffened, her throat constricted and shivered the more the priest shook.

"I cannot allow you to stay. The government forced the Jesuits out of México when they took your people's side. I cannot help you. My Order would not risk it. I could lose my church."

"And what of your soul, Father?" Luz blurted. "Should you hold onto it tighter?'

The priest's eyes narrowed, his lips pursed. He seized Luz's shoulder and pulled her up close to his face. A faint scent of wine oozed off him.

"You dare to lecture me on my soul in my own church? What do you know of theology, you insolent *india*? Get out!"

His grip hurt Luz. Shocked by the priest's anger, she darted into the aisle, tripped on the priest's cane and fell to the floor. Her hands plopped into the mud. Embarrassed, she rose with Cheve's help, wiped her soiled hands on her skirt and stood with wet head bowed before the well-girded Shepherd of Christ.

"I'm sorry, Father. Please forgive me," she said in a trembling voice. "I have a weakness for speaking too quickly. But we Yaquis are good Catholics. We know and follow the Church's teachings. We come in peace meaning no trouble."

"If Yaquis were such good Catholics," he shouted, "your people would have laid down their arms by now and accepted the rule of the government. Get out."

Stung by his words, Luz looked up and searched for the right Spanish response to earn his mercy. The words eluded her tongue. Instead, she held up her dirty hands, palms pressed together to him.

"Don't touch me, you dirty savage. Out, now!"

"Luz, let's leave," Cheve said in Cajita, "This toad hates us. Let's find Ángel, he'll take us in."

"Where do we look?" she said in their tongue.

"Speak *Cristiano*," the priest bellowed. "Quit that barking. You're not in the wilderness any longer."

"Father, aren't we brothers and sisters in Christ," Luz said. "How can you treat us this way?"

"I can because you people are the Cains of Sonora. The mark of evil is on you. Just look at him." The priest gripped the pew thrusting his cane at Cheve's face, a few inches from the disfigurement. The boy averted his head. "You'll be shunned from civilized society until your people surrender to the government, give up your wild customs, do penance." He bobbed on the balls of his feet, his free hand jerking up and down. He huffed rapidly, mouth opening and closing like a hooked fish out of water. Candlelight reflected a wild-eyed gleam from the head of the pious, pompadour *padre*.

Several nuns stopped their sweeping and polishing. They held their brooms up as if prepared to use them for a more thorough cleaning of the church. The nun who prayed to the martyred saint held a silver cross of a rosary to her lips.

The vested cleric gestured toward the open door where sheets of rain fell and lightening flashed. His body trembled like a dog with foaming sickness paroxysms. His cane tapped against the marble, sounding war tom-toms.

Her mouth agape, Luz stared at the man that supposedly spoke for God. The malevolent, raging voice sounded diabolical. A tug on her arm drew her back.

"My sister, we must leave before the soldiers come." Cheve gripped her hand and pulled her along toward the open door. His hold and the motion of her legs broke the spell of dumbness.

"I will pray for the strength to forgive you, *padre.*" Luz forced out through flowing tears and followed Cheve past the Yoris who stared at them.

"Leave this holy place, children of Satan," the priest screamed, filling Luz's ears with the painfully resonant truth. This cleric was filled with a hatred for Yaquis equal to any Yori solider.

Once outside, the cold rain and wind lashed her body again. She was a foolish, naïve woman to believe the priest would help them. Perhaps Cheve was right, Yoris couldn't be trusted.

When she reached Tomas and the horses, she fell into his arms and wept against his chest. His strong body comforted and warmed her.

She cuddled even closer until their stomachs rubbed and their legs touched.

Tomas patted her wet hair and swept a hand to her cheek. Palming her chin, he tilted her head up.

A fleeting worry she should not be this close to Tomas surfaced like a worm from its hole, but was driven back by the dove of compassion. "No place to stay. The priest wouldn't…."

"Then we dance together in the rain," Tomas said. "In the morning we'll see the prefect. We can tell him we swam from Cócorit to avoid his men." His smile filled her with warmth as he wrapped an arm around her shoulder.

The boy stood by the steaming horses rubbing their necks and muzzles.

"Come here, Cheve." Luz released her hold on Tomas and opened her arms.

"The priest called us evil," he said.

"His fears force him to lose his senses," a woman's voice said in Cajita. "This war with your people has driven many to arm with hate."

The woman, dressed in black, stood next to her brother. She recognized her as the nun who knelt a few pews ahead of them before the arrow-pierced statue.

"You're not evil. And you're correct—we're brothers and sisters in Christ. Father Julio is just *loco* right now." The woman in black tapped her forehead.

Luz walked toward the nun who looked about her age, with unusually bright green eyes, a warm smile and a strong voice. The black habit could not hide her pretty, white face or her slender build.

Tomas asked, "How is it you speak Cajita so well for a..."

"For a Yori. I know what you call us." The veiled woman laughed. "But, please call me Sister Carolina. But I'm not an official nun yet—still a novitiate, a nun-in-training. No vows taken. I learned your language from a close Yaqui friend. In exchange, I taught him proper *Castellano* and some English. But we cannot talk long. I must go back to the convent soon. You must get out of the rain or the fishermen in the morning may mistake you for shrimp. Come, follow me."

"Where do you take us, Sister Carolina?" Luz drew back.

"To school. Yori school, around this corner. I teach there. If the church will not give you sanctuary, then my school will. But we must be clever, quiet and have no lights. Yes? Cheve, I heard you say you look for someone called Ángel—Ángel Falcon?"

"Yes, my brother. You know him . . . where he lives?" Cheve stepped closer to the young nun.

"Do you?" Luz walked nearer to the woman in black.

"Yes, I know him well," she said and for an uneasy moment her brow furrowed, and then melted away replaced by a bright smile. "And where he lives." She stepped between Luz and Cheve and took their hands.

"To school. I will teach you all you need to know in school. You can bring the horses — but I don't teach horses — although I've taught burros."

"Burros?" Cheve asked.

"Burros are what we call hard-headed children who refuse to learn — stubborn as burros."

Luz's worries began to shrivel in the rain with this pleasant woman. She took a few steps until Tomas grabbed her arm.

"Wait, Luz. We don't know this . . . veiled woman. A trap. She may lead us to Yori soldiers."

Standing in the ankle-deep mud, in rain-soaked clothes with drenched hair plastered to her head, Luz said, "All Yoris are not burros. Please, Tomas, it's getting cold. Let's brave this invitation."

Lightening blistered the sky and the thunderclap startled the horses.

"May God protect us," Tomas said. He untied the animals and led them after Sister Carolina, Luz and Cheve to Yori school.

CHAPTER 9

SCHOOL LESSONS

"Yori girl is nice."
"It's safe in the school."
"Danger waits for them."
"They're too tired to notice."
"Ángel will protect them."
"He can't. He's Torocoyori."
"Tomas is strong."
"Carries too much hate."
"Priest is hateful."
"They live in the land of hate."

Cheve sat wrapped in a wool blanket in the cool darkness at the teacher's desk, his belly filled from the beans and bread the novitiate had smuggled. His weary body yearned for sleep as the sister apologized for feeding them the sparse meals. She would have brought more but feared notice by the quiet but ever vigilant Order of the Perpetual Virgins.

Faint light from street lanterns offered some relief from total blackness. Sister whispered to keep away from the windows. She encouraged them to remove their wet clothes, explaining the darkness and blanket would safeguard their modesty.

Cheve and the others, rubbing their arms and legs, declined and shivered. He gazed at the outlines of a chalkboard, desks, pictures and a bookcase. A large cross hung on the wall behind the teacher's desk.

Tomas thanked the nun for allowing him to shelter their horses in Father Julio's stable. He had fed the animals, but didn't remove their saddles, blankets and bridles in case they needed to leave quickly.

"You worked slowly," Sister said.

"Better not to rouse the horses or attract attention," he said.

"Of course, Yaquis are good with animals."

Cheve saw the rainfall pour at an angle, tapping against the rooftop and windowpanes, a tranquil rhythm apologizing for its earlier harsh treatment of the weary travelers. Even the distant thunder seemed to resonate their moans of relief. Resting his arms on the table, Cheve's head and shoulders sagged, eyes drooped and was about to doze when he heard Sister Carolina.

"Ángel sat in the back."

Cheve jolted upright as if he had just sat on a cactus. "Ángel, where?" He searched the dark room and saw with disappointment the silhouetted rows of empty desks.

"After learning Spanish," she said, "he became one of the top students. He recited long poems from memory with passion, and solved the hardest math problems before any other student. Sister Ana hoped he would go to the seminary to become the first Yaqui-born priest."

With all desire to sleep gone, Cheve stood and walked among the desks, careful to avoid the light. "Was this his seat?" He ran his fingers on the desktop, into the ink well, touched the cool liquid, pulled back his fingers, and smelled them. The pungent odor warned he should not taste it. He assumed it was for some type of paint for school drawings or holy oils students used to bless themselves.

"No, the last row. In the corner. Yes, there. Sister Ana placed him in the back away from the girls." The young nun giggled. "At first he was shy, quiet. Then he got the nerve to speak. We never heard a Yaqui voice, apart from servants and workers. Gentle, calm, respectful with that Yaqui accent. When he laughed, his eyes sparkled and deep dimples filled his cheeks. In his happy moments he glowed like an angel, just like his name. The girls called him 'mi Ángelito,' my little Ángel, and whispered if you kissed him you'd taste heaven. The bolder girls would pass notes inviting Ángel to share their lunches or to stay after school for a walk to the fishing boats."

Cheve touched his deformed lips and wondered if he would ever kiss anyone other than his mother, sister and maybe his horse. When the image of Jewel's twisted neck came to mind, he winced. If the schoolgirls saw him, they'd call him "*mi feito*," my little ugly one, and smooch their dogs before they kiss him.

"He was a strong athlete, outrunning and outthrowing any boy in the class," Sister Carolina continued. "But then, he is full-blooded Yaqui, is he not?" she said as if she were of the people.

Cheve chafed at the innocent reminder he was a half-breed.

"He pitched in our school's first baseball team, *Los Santos*."

"Baseball . . . what's baseball?" Cheve asked.

"A new ball game that some *Norteamericano* merchant sailors taught us to play. A man named Doubleday invented the game in *Nueva* York. The gringos said Ángel was a natural. That means he was good at throwing the ball so fast that no one could hit it. But when other pitchers threw the ball at him, he would make what they call home runs. He'd hoot as he ran around the bases. The sailors laughed and called him chief. When they offered to take him with them, to play on their team in *Los Estados Unidos*, I begged him not to leave. He laughed and said he wouldn't leave me for a bat and ball."

"I'm glad he didn't go either," Cheve said and wished he knew more about the Yankees' baseball. He'd asked Ángel to teach him.

"Several boys bullied him, mocking the deer dance and playing cruel pranks," she said. "Jealous. When Ángel had enough, he asked for a private meeting after school with the biggest bully, son of a sea merchant trader. The next day, the boy came in with two black eyes, a cut lip and a slight limp. Ángel had a slight cut over his left eye and bruised knuckles. When Sister Ana asked 'shadow eyes' for an explanation, he told her a bronco had thrown him. Ángel said he was also bucked from the same horse, but not as often nor as hard. When I giggled, Sister Ana smiled and shook her head. The boys quit their bullying."

Cheve slid into his brother's desk and tried to imagine Ángel sitting next to him sharing the secrets of books, numbers and the ink well. Since the departure of the Jesuits, the only way Yaquis solved the mysteries of the curls, circles, lines and dots was to go to Yori schools. In the darkness, he could almost see his brother's handsome face answering first difficult math problems, reciting with eloquence Spanish poetry, smiling at pretty brown, auburn, blonde-haired Yori girls who would glance or pass him notes. He visualized his brother's muscular body running on the playing fields like Maso outdistancing the Yori boys and winning prizes. Then he imagined the sweaty, bronzed Ángel clutching his medal in the crowd of admiring Yori youth. His chest swelled with pride at the scene of his big brother standing in a circle of boys with his fists cocked over the bloodied bully sprawled on the ground. Cheve wondered if Ángel had seen the Maso in the desert and perhaps gotten past the snake and entered the land of the Surem.

"How long has it been since you saw Ángel?" Sister Carolina asked. No one answered. "So long you can't remember?"

"Years, Sister," Luz lied.

Cheve shook his head, grateful for the darkness.

"At first he'd return to Pótam during holidays from school but then he stopped. We couldn't understand what had happened. My parents worried he may have died and the school hadn't told us. My father came to Guaymas to look for him. When he returned, he said Ángel was fine, but was busy with his studies and would come home when he finished. I think he shared more with my mother, who wept for several nights."

Sister Carolina sighed, stood and walked pass the first few desks and sat in one at a slight angle to Cheve. A shaft of light from the window cut through the darkness and revealed the bottom part of her torso. Against the black habit, the silver cross hanging from her neck and her white hands appeared to float in the air. Sister Carolina caressed the crucifix with her long white fingers.

"This was my desk when I went to school with Ángel," she said. "I, too, found him fascinating. Not just for his good looks but for his courage to come here alone among Yoris without family or friends. In his dark brown eyes, I saw the beauty and strength of your people. Even though I was too shy to write notes to him, he asked me to walk with him after school. We walked and sat at the boat docks learning each other's languages and customs while fishermen brought in their supper catch. I'm afraid he learned most of the foul language our shrimpers use when their catch is meager or their nets ripped." She laughed and her hand shook the cross as if the silver Jesus chuckled too.

"For three years, we learned together until the war with the Yaquis started again." She paused. "War is like a hungry lizard a person is forced to swallow. It slides down your throat and eats at your heart. All beauty and sympathy leave the world. Like Father Julio, one sees through the beady eyes of the reptile. His mother was killed in a raid on his family's hacienda. *El padre* took an arrow in the leg. He limps now, worse during bad weather. Not only did his gait change but also his voice, his look. He demanded the Order to stop teaching all Yaquis. Ángel grew sad when Sister Ana told him he could no longer come to school. He had fallen in love with learning, with Guaymas, with me."

She rose from the desk and blended into the darkness. Her footsteps knocked and the rustle of her flowing skirt swept on the floor until she placed her hand on Cheve's shoulder. He liked the feel of her hand, looked up at the nun and could barely see the features of her pretty face. His Spanish would improve rapidly with such an attractive instructor.

"I pleaded with him to stay," Sister Carolina said in a deeper voice. "I remember your father's visit and Ángel's struggle to say he couldn't come home. When the call for men came, he joined the local Indian auxiliary battalion." Her voice quivered at the last few words.

"He joined what?" Tomas snapped, stood and knocked over his chair. "He's a Torocoyori—a traitor. He may be handsome to you with his hair, dimples, and eyes, but he's hideous to all loyal Yaquis. His father will be shamed."

"In your eyes," sister said, "but he would be a traitor to his heart if he gave up what he cherished"

"What about his mother, father and people? Were they not dear to him? This will drive an arrow into Mateo's heart when he discovers his son rides under a Yori banner." Tomas struck his chest with a loud slap. He walked toward the back of the room knocking desks from his path. "Going to your school was a mistake. You've bewitched him. Taught him Yori ways to the neglect of his Yaqui duties, Yaqui law."

Luz rose and rushed to her protector at the back of the classroom. "Tomas, she didn't deceive Ángel. He was alone, far from home. She was kind to him. It's natural for a Yaqui to fall in love with a Yori like this." She touched his hand, but he pulled away.

"It's wicked for a Yaqui to become a traitor." He slapped his hand on top of a desk. "What value are Yori teachings if a man loses his place in his family, his people? This black-veiled woman says Ángel can recite Spanish rhymes and rattle numbers with ease. Who will that help? Yaquis or Yoris?"

"Both of us," Luz said.

Tomas raised clenched fists into the air. "When you can shoot poems from a rifle and cut a throat with a number, then I, too, will learn." He stormed toward the door breathing heavily. "This burro will sleep with the *caballos*." The Spanish word for horses pounded sarcastically. When he opened the door, a burst of cold air and smell of heavy rain rushed in.

"Tomas," Luz called, but he slammed the door behind him. She walked to the window. Through faint light, shadows of the rain trails on the windowpane crept down her tearless cheeks.

"Get away from the window, Luz," Cheve said. "Someone may see you."

"Yoris and Torocoyoris have treated him cruelly." Luz stepped back into the darkness. "He cannot forgive."

"Other Torocoyoris and men from other tribes join daily," Sister Carolina said. "Yaquis may fight alone."

"Cajemé is proud and many men like Tomas fill his army. They'll fight regardless of how many allies Yoris recruit. But Cajemé is also wise. I have a peace letter from him for the governor." Luz patted the pouch. She stepped toward the nun and Cheve at the front of the classroom. "Sister Carolina, your story's not finished."

Like the shy moon, half of Luz's face was now visible, the other half hidden in the darkness. "My brother stayed here for you. But your clothes..."

The veiled woman's hand pressed down harder and trembled on Cheve's shoulder. He peered through the darkness and saw her pretty face grimace as if she had just suffered a knife cut.

Sister Carolina's footsteps echoed on the wooden floor and stopped at the chalkboard. "These veils... these veils..." She lifted the black cloths that draped the sides of her head. "Were thrown on me to smother my feelings for your brother. My family refused to accept a Yaqui suitor. No Yaqui grandchildren for them. My father, Andrew Culpepper, III, is an *Americano* from Fort Worth, Texas. He owns many shrimp boats and trades with the Yaquis, gringos and other Indians on the river and coast. My mother, Manuela Montenegro de Ayala, is a descendent of Spanish viceroys and daughter of a local banker. My brother, Andrew Culpepper IV, was the bully."

Cheve stood and for a fleeting moment he wanted to shout his shame of his mestizo status to the sister. What would she think of him, then, he wondered? Would she still touch him? He went to Luz and clasped her hand. Sister's truth-telling chilled him.

The reluctant nun dropped the veils, lifted the cross to her lips, kissed it and let it fall to her chest. "I swore to them I would never marry another. My father decided then the convent would suit me. He offered me to the care of the Order of the Perpetual Virgins along with a promise of a steady flow of pesos to the Sunday collection plate. After a year here, I don't regret my love for Ángel Falcon," she said and sobbed.

"I'd gladly accept you as my sister," Luz said to the veiled woman. She and Cheve rushed to Sister Carolina.

"To be a Falcon. Cheve — my brother," she said, her voice trembling, and caressed his face.

He liked the idea and touched her hand. Suddenly, Cheve found himself hugging her and Luz in the empty, dark classroom battered by rain. All talk about Yaqui, Yori, religious, messenger or deformed boy vanished. In the darkness, he was simply a person sharing the ardor of human touch.

"Where's Ángel?" Cheve asked.

"Tonight he stands guard at the *Palacio Del Gobierno* as he has for the last year," Sister Carolina answered. "His post is close to the convent. I sometimes…"

The door burst open and a rush of cold air, rain and light startled Cheve. He clutched the nun and his sister tighter at the stomp of angry, Spanish voices and boots. Several men with kerosene lanterns stormed into the classroom, kicking desks and blinding him.

"Sergeant Bocagrande, we caught the rest of the horse thieves. Sister Carolina?" the black-cloaked Father Julio said, his mouth agape. "You, come here! What are you doing with these savages?"

The wind and rain had disheveled his hair and robes. The sway of the lanterns cast a shifting, mad light.

"They're not horse thieves," the sister said. "I gave them sanctuary."

"Sanctuary?" The fat priest bellowed and limped to the embracing trio, grabbed the novice by the arm and jerked her away from the Yaquis. "Are you insane?"

Cheve jumped on the priest's big back.

"Ahhh!" the cleric shouted. "Mongrel's got me."

A soldier jumped forward, pulled Cheve from the priest and threw him over the desks. The boy vomited in flight. The shifting lantern exposed angry Yoris staring at him. An invisible boot slammed into his face. He groaned and drew his arms over his head. He glimpsed another body emerge from the light. He winced and drew up his legs.

"Stop!" Luz screamed draping her body over her brother's. "We're envoys from Cajemé. I have a letter for the prefect."

"Where's this letter from *El Indio Caca*?" The priest scoffed.

Luz opened the pouch and hunted for the paper. "Fell out—it's somewhere here." She groped on her hands and knees on the schoolroom floor. "Where is it?"

"No letter? Your people can run, bark, howl and breed like dogs but certainly cannot write. Sergeant, get these *indios* out of my school and give them 'sanctuary' in your jail." The priest pounded his cane on the wooden floor.

"No, please Father Julio, allow them to stay," Sister Carolina pleaded. "They do have a letter from Cajemé—"

"*Silencio!*" the priest slammed his cane on a desk, the bang echoing in the room.

"I fell in the church!" Luz shouted in Cajita. "The letter is in the church."

Yori guards grabbed Cheve's and Luz's arms, jerked them up, and tied their hands behind their backs. They pushed the prisoners out of the school, into the rain and mud. Two soldiers wearing sombreros and bandoliers trained their rifles on Tomas, kneeling with his hands tied. Blood smeared the prisoner's forehead.

"It was a trap for burros," Tomas said.

"Did they hurt you?" Luz asked.

"*Quieto*, Yaqui whore," Sergeant Bocagrande shouted. "Move, *andale*, dog-tit-sucking savages."

Cheve moaned from a hard kick to his buttocks, toppling him into the mud. Forceful hands grabbed his arms and jerked him onto his feet.

"The mud is slippery, jackass." Yori soldiers laughed. "Watch your step."

"Did you cut his face?" Another guard looked at him. Several lanterns were brought up close to the boy's head.

"*Feo*—I saw a woman in the desert who looked like him. It's a *bruja's* curse," another sombreroed soldier said and made the sign of the cross. The others did the same, kissing their thumbs for extra, holy protection.

"*Muchachos*, do you want the rain to piss on you all night? Move the prisoners," the sergeant ordered.

Cheve trembled when he recognized the growling voice. Cajemé's wife's screams echoed. He searched the square for sight of the fat man grinding on top of her. "Ohhhh," he moaned. *It's him: the Yori rapist.*

Cheve walked behind Luz and Tomas, pass the church with the armed escort surrounding them. The outline of the *Palacio Del Gobierno* a short distance away loomed. His breathing grew more rapid as they approached the building. They were now on the square that fronted the Palacio.

Cheve nudged his sister. "Ángel's here," he whispered. Peering into the darkness the boy captive couldn't discern any figures except for guards who surrounded them.

Luz murmured, "Don't see him."

"He's here. I just know," Cheve insisted and saw they were going to pass the *Palacio*. "God help me." He bolted toward the building shouting in Cajita, "Ángel Falcon, brother."

"Cheve!" Luz screamed.

"Kill him," Sergeant Bocagrande bellowed. Shots and curses rang into the black rain.

CHAPTER TEN

✵

UNVEILING

"The nun is feisty."
"She thinks she's Yaqui."
"Oh no, another one who loves the poor Indians."
"Fat priest certainly hates Yaquis."
"He hates people who don't hate Yaquis."
"What a Christian."
"Vibrating Tree was correct about them."
"All Yaquis should have hidden from them."
"They will learn to defend or submit."

The sticky mud clung to Sister Carolina's shoes, weighed her feet down, making it difficult for the nun to keep up with Father Julio's urgent pace. Despite his limp and awkward gait, he plowed the cane like an oar in a sea of sludge. He propelled forward panting and grunting on each plodding step.

Pulling Sister Carolina along the mucky street, as wind whipped the rain and lightning scarred the sky, Father Julio growled, "You insist on disobeying me and your convent. When I report this to *Señor* Culpepper, he'll demand we punish you. And not with a mere scolding. Oh, no—a severe chastisement as the Inquisition has taught us."

The priest stopped to catch his breath like a winded mountain climber. Once recovered, he said, "What do you find so fascinating in these Yaquis? You forget your own people, your place. You shame your father's name."

The *padre* coughed and spit, some saliva spraying back onto the nun's face. She wiped it from her cheek with her free hand. "Is it this so-called Ángel? What a misuse of a Christian name! I'll have him flogged, banished from Guaymas. It's a sin for you to have any lustful desires for any man, especially an *indio*. You must learn discipline—much discipline, wayward nun."

Sister Carolina's arm ached from the priest's ever tightening grip. He could break it with a little more pressure. Feeling guilty for the Yaquis' capture, she'd underestimated the priest's hatred for them. She looked back and watched the Yori guards marching and cursing the Yaqui prisoners onto the square.

"Father Julio, you're right to be angry with me," she said. "I must confess my sins, do penance."

"Oh, Sister, you can be certain of that." The padre laughed sardonically. "You'll do penance—much penance. Allowing them to steal my horses, will you? If not for your father I would—" the priest's breathing and grunting grew deeper.

Her body shook from his body's tremors, channeling his seething anger. The priest plunged the staff harder into the mud and quickened the pace to a near run. His wobbly gait jerked her from side to side like a straw doll.

"My arm," she moaned from his vice grip.

He eased his hold but didn't release her.

"Your anger is justified. Please hear my confession, tonight, in the church." She pulled in the direction of the church. "If I die in my sleep, I may go to hell with sin weighing on my soul. Tonight, Father, before it's too late."

"No. I must think on your penance. It must be soul-cleansing, evoke true repentance." He raised his voice as if preaching to the Yori flock. "A penance that will keep you from the lowest level of hell where you'll surely go if you die tonight. You must repent before dawn to elude the other angel, Satan."

"But, Father, we're right here and I feel so much closer to the saints and God in the church."

"You'll defile the church," he said in a disgusted tone, "and it was just cleaned. In the convent—best place to hear your confession, in front of the other nuns. They must witness your cleansing. Novitiate, you must learn obedience."

As if on cue, thirty nuns from the convent rushed out. Several carried straps. "Give her to us, Father," a tall nun slapping a belt into her open hand said. "We know how to correct sinful nuns."

"See. This is what I've warned you about," Father Julio said. "Good Sisters. She's in love with a Yaqui. She needs cleansing."

"We'll wash her clean of all impurities, I assure you," the chief nun said. "Let me take her."

Sister Carolina gasped at the phalanx of black-robed women anxious to seize her. Even Sister Ana swung a rope in the air, meant to bind her.

"Father Julio, if you don't hear my confession in the church, I'll tell my father you treated me disrespectfully." She raised her voice to a high pitched, angry timbre. "I'll have him cut his donation."

The priest stopped before the church, dropped the cane and gripped the nun with both hands. Lightning rays illuminated the square, exposing a ghastly, twisted face that, in comparison to Cheve's, was more hideous. His mouth gaped open and his lips stretched tight, revealing teeth as if he were about to bite her. Alcohol stench reeked on his breath. She braced herself for a beating.

"Tell him! Tell him! And I'll tell your father you sought to deceive me again with your little ploy of wanting to confess your sins." His saliva spewed like a second baptism. "Your father doesn't frighten me. Tell him the truth—you wish to open your legs for a Yaqui!"

The nun averted her face from the unholy water.

"Is this what you look for?" The priest released her left arm and pulled a brown parchment from the pocket of his cassock.

By the dim street lamp, the paper appeared torn and crumpled.

"You found it," she said dismayed. She reached for it, but the priest pulled it away.

"Get on your knees here in the mud and confess your sins to me and the Order, Yaqui lover." The priest's hand pushed her down. "Get on your knees."

"Confess, confess, confess," the Order of the Perpetual Virgins chanted.

"Stop it!" She struggled to pull away. His grip anchored her. When shots cracked from the square, she twirled to the gunfire and heard angry, shouting voices and running feet. A lightning flash illuminated a fleeing boy with a group of men, pistols blazing, who gave chase.

"Cheve," she screamed into the rainy night.

"Shut-up, Yaqui lover, and kneel." The priest pushed her again.

Years of anger for love denied swelled within Carolina. Her breathing quickened, her body trembled and her back muscles tensed. She drew closer to his besotted face. "Yes, I am a Yaqui lover. I love Ángel Falcon."

With a hard swing of her arms, the nun knocked his hand from her and rammed her wiry body hard against him. Without his cane, the priest tottered.

"Ahh," he yelled, his hands reaching for anything to break his fall. He grabbed at the nun's veil and fell backwards. In an instant she found herself on top of the priest's fat body on the muddy road, her veil in his hand. When she saw the parchment floating, twisting in the wind, she scrambled to rise and give chase. Her long skirt tore. Looking down, she saw the fallen priest grasping the cloth and squirming like a beached dolphin.

"Satan whore," he yelled jerking harder. "Get her, Sisters."

The skirt ripped more as she fell backwards onto his head forcing his face into the mud. As he gagged, she jumped up and ran, tugging and tossing the wimple. Rush of cool wind and rain swept over her unleashed, rebellious spirit. She winced from the straps across her back, legs and shoulders.

"Sinner, confess, confess," the head nun screamed, flaying Carolina.

The liberated nun ran through a gantlet of swinging, howling sisters. Undeterred she plucked the letter from the air. The apostate hurled through the night, leading a flock of virgins.

"Ángel," she shouted to the lightning-charged skies. "I'm free."

CHAPTER 11

✦

YEEWE BICHOO

"What a joker."
"He should be a Pascola clown."
"We can tell him more jokes."
"Yaquis need to laugh more."
"They weep too much."
"Tell them saucy jokes in their dreams."
"I'll tell the joke about the eagle and the serpent."
"No, not again."

Cheve smashed hard into the nearest Yori guard, shoving him out of his way. The man moaned, drew up his gun and shot, nicking the boy's scalp. The boy yelped from the searing pain, stumbled, caught his balance, gritted his teeth and bolted.

"*Chingado*," the guard yelled.

"Cheve," Luz screamed.

"Ángel," Cheve shouted, churning his leather huaraches against the slippery wet plaza stones. The splash of frantic feet stirred. More shouts and high-pitched whistles shrieked. With his hands bound behind him, he strained to break the cords. Despite the bonds, fear lashed a ride and spurred him to an agile stride.

More rifle fire banged like a hammer slamming an anvil next to his ears. Sparks flew from the stone floor where the lead searched for him. He sucked air and cursed his legs' cries for rest. The boy wore sweat beads to this dance with death. The low flying clouds pummeled him in a gantlet of rain whips. The din of clanging rifles, belts, and buckles jarred close behind.

Cheve peered into the darkness ahead and saw a small light break the blackness. Two more flames flashed to life like a blazing trinity of salvation. Leaning forward and pumping his tired legs, he bellowed, "Run, deer dancer, like the Maso."

The illumination from the lanterns ahead grew, revealing shadow figures. Swift footfalls from behind closed in. The pursuer's heavy panting grew louder by the moment. Cheve darted from side to side, but the tracker appeared to anticipate his every dodge. A sharp pain, like a punch, ripped the boy's back.

The Yaqui runner flinched and craned his neck. The Yori slashed again with a long knife. Leaning forward, Cheve went airborne as he stepped off the square. Breathless, he flew as in his desert dream. Then, his body flipped forward and he landed hard against the muddy street. Wet slush filled his mouth. Spitting out the foul-tasting dirt, he sat and gulped for air. His chest and back ached. The square had rudely ended, dropping off several feet to the street below.

A nearby groan startled him. The Yori slasher, a body length away, curled in the road nursing his leg. The knife's shaft half embedded into the pursuer's hamstring.

Despite his own cut, bruises and fatigue, the boy climbed to his feet and limped toward the lights muttering, "Ángel."

A harsh voice demanded in broken Spanish, "Who's there? Speak or die."

Cheve answered, "Ángel Falcon." The Yaqui fugitive ran to the man with the lantern. A rifle barrel loomed from the darkness and poked him in the chest.

"You're not Ángel Falcon," the man said. "Don't move, *pendejo*."

When the man whistled a lilting pattern, Cheve recognized it as a variation of a Yaqui danger call. He said in Cajita, "I look for Ángel Falcon."

The man gazed at him. "I don't speak your Indian tongue," the guard said in Spanish, enunciating every syllable.

A clamor of heavy-breathing Spanish voices, rifles, boots and buckles swelled from the square as Yori guards jumped into the street. Some in their rush had forgotten about the drop off and hurled to a hard landing or were pushed over by the too impatient.

"Ángel Falcon," Cheve hollered.

The Torocoyori guard stepped back at the outburst. A Yaqui whistle flew back. The guard said in careful Spanish, "He comes."

Gleaming lanterns soon circled the boy, their glows revealing young men with Indian features. Cheve saw several point their rifles at him, others shook their heads. They mumbled in Spanish and several whispered in the tongues of the Seri, talking about the raindrop runner's deformed face.

He didn't recognize any of them as people from the Yaqui Valley. Cheve rotated at the sounds of the Yori guards close behind. He spun back to the circle of men and said in a desperate tone, "Ángel."

A man emerged from the darkness wearing a sombrero and a drenched poncho.

"Enough," he said, brandishing a pistol pointed to the troubled sky. The others fell silent and made room for him to pass. As if fearing the man's bullets, the rain abated until there were now scattered drops. The wind still whisked among the desperate. When he tipped back his sombrero to his shoulders with the barrel of his gun, lantern lights flickered over him. The boy sobbed as he saw Ángel's shadowy, handsome face.

"Brother," the boy shouted, stepped forward and leaned his head against the man's chest.

"Cheve?" Ángel said in a surprised tone and holstered the pistol beneath his poncho. He touched his younger brother's shoulders, wrapped his arms around and held him closer. "Your head—it's bleeding. Bring the lantern here," he directed the Torocoyori closest to him.

The boy flinched when his brother parted his hair to see the wound.

"The bullet grazed your scalp," Ángel said. "It will heal. Who did this?"

"A Yori soldier," Cheve said. "Luz brought a letter for the governor from Cajemé."

"Luz?"

"They have her captive."

"Where?"

"Out there." Cheve pointed to the plaza. He heard angry Spanish voices and saw the Yori guards emerge from the darkness, pushing their way through the gathered Torocoyoris.

The sergeant loomed with the gleaming stare of a ravenous mountain lion on the hunt. His mouth hung agape, his tongue protruding, and his sombrero cocked back on his shoulders. His large mustache dripped water. The flecks of light revealed long strands of hair on a balding pate. By his sagging face and pendulous belly, Cheve guessed the big man hadn't run much since his youth.

Brandishing rifles and pistols, the sergeant's men jostled their way through and forced the Torocoyori guards to stand in a semicircle around Cheve. He scurried behind his brother. Ángel and the panting sergeant stood face-to-face in the center of the circle of armed Yoris and their allies from the Sonoran wilds.

The sergeant pointed at Cheve and shouted, "That *hijo de la chingada* is mine. The ugly *cabron* escaped from me."

"What's he done?" Ángel asked.

"The *pendejo* and two other Yaquis were stealing horses from the crippled padre. We caught them at the school. But this one strayed from us. Cost me my best tracker, Paco, *El Conejo*. Knifed him in the leg. Come here, *cabroncito*," the sergeant ordered and reached out his big, beefy hand.

"Remarkable skill for a boy with hands tied."

"These *diablos* are clever. Used his feet." The sergeant raised and wiggled a foot. "Can't expose your back to them."

"You saw them stealing?" Ángel asked.

"No. I told you *Padre* caught them. Nun was helping them. Now give me the prisoner."

"A nun?"

"Some *puta* nun, good-looking woman." The sergeant grabbed his groin. "I ought to give her some copperhead for her penance." Several of his men chuckled. "Do you think she'd like my rattler, muchachos?"

His men responded with whistles and derisive hoots.

"Sister Carolina?" Ángel asked.

"Bravo. Sister Cute Vagina."

The Yori guards howled at the deliberate slip.

"Sweet Sister Vagina," the sergeant repeated, grinned and pumped his pelvis forward several times.

His men whistled and several imitated his gyration.

Bocagrande held out his open hand again and said in a sober tone, "I want *feo*."

His men's derisive laughter died away. They raised their guns. Cheve pressed his shoulder against Ángel's back.

The sergeant shouted, "Give him to me. Now!"

"Take him." Ángel whirled and pushed Cheve into the sergeant.

The boy's misshapen mouth dropped open. He shook his head in disbelief. Sergeant Bocagrande grunted, kicked Cheve's legs and cuffed him in the head. The boy yelped when the sergeant hit his open wound. Bocagrande's strong hands twisted him around until he faced Ángel. The Yori threw his arm around the captive's neck and choked him in a headlock. Cheve groaned at the feel of the man's facial bristles and the tequila stench.

"Looks like *El Conejo* got a piece of you before you knifed him. I'm going to cut more out of your Indian dog hide before morning. Rope!" the sergeant shouted.

A Yori guard came forward and handed it to him. Releasing his hold on Cheve, he dropped a rough noose over his head and tightened the knot around the boy's neck until it pinched his skin. Cheve gagged and wiggled his head up for more room to swallow.

His lips mouthed, "Ángel, save me."

His brother's expression showed no fear, anger or sympathy. He observed with an impassive gaze and revolved several times to talk to his men. The boy's heartache of abandonment hurt worse than the rope burn on his neck.

"Try to run again *cabron* and I'll break it." The sergeant jerked the cord hard and the captive's head snapped to the side. The rope cut deeper into his skin. Cheve gagged and his tongue hung out. "This chase and talk about Sister Vagina has made me limber. You got me hard, *feo*. If I can't have the nun, then the Yaqui girl is going to get a hot chile tonight. Don't worry, *muchachos*, I'm a Christian. I'll share like always. I just get first bite." He laughed and his men chuckled and nodded. "Your girlfriend will like me — won't she, *feo*? She'll like my rattlesnake." The sergeant jerked the rope. Cheve heard the bones in his neck creak.

"I'm coming with you," Ángel said.

"Don't need your help, *indio*."

Ángel stepped closer to the captor and whispered. "Some of the men here are Yaqui. I've heard them say they don't like the way you treat the prisoner. They plan to take the boy." Speaking in Cajita, he said to his men. "This fornicator of pigs, cows, and dogs will shoot the unarmed boy and rape his sister before they reach the jail. He'll report they tried to escape." Back to the sergeant, Ángel muttered in Spanish, "I told them you were the meanest *chingado* in Sonora and would not hesitate to cut off any Yaqui balls if they tried to interfere."

"*Bueno. Que macho.* How do you say *chingado* in the Yaqui tongue?"

"You say *yeewe bichoo* and move your fist up and down to show you mean it." Cheve saw several of the Torocoyoris avert their faces.

"Like this — *yeewe bichoo*." The sergeant formed a fist and bobbed his hand.

"Bravo. But say it with machismo and move your fist faster. Yaquis respect a macho."

"*Yeewe bichoo*," the sergeant growled and pumped his fist.

"*Olé.*" Ángel swirled to his men and said in Cajita, "Don't laugh. Jerk your fists as he's doing, nod and repeat *yeewe bichoo.*"

The Torocoyoris joined in the chant of "*yeewe bichoo.*"

Soon the Yoris guards were also shaking their fists in the air, repeating the Yaqui cheer.

"You see, sergeant, my men agree you are the meanest *chingon* in Sonora. In case this horse thief tries to run again," Ángel said, "I'll come along. I'm a good tracker, have a nose for their smells."

The sergeant said, "I don't—"

"*Yeewe bichoo! Yeewe bichoo! Yeewe bichoo! Yeewe bichoo!*" Ángel yelled and drowned out the sergeant's voice.

Laughing, the sergeant said, "Fine, come along. But no interference."

"*Yeewe bichoo.* These men respect you." Ángel spun to them and said in Cajita, "Men of the Yaqui River follow. The rest stay and continue the chant. Use no lanterns. Have your weapons ready. Wait for my command."

Cheve's head jerked forward at the guard's hard tug on the rope. He moaned and kept pace with the sergeant's steps lest the rope choke him. The chorus of Yori soldiers shouting, "I like to spank the donkey!" over and over surrounded them. Despite the pain, he smiled weakly at his brother's prank. With the throbbing scalp and back wounds, bruised arms and legs and now neck strain, he wondered if Ángel really had betrayed him or was he joking at his expense. He had expected an immediate fight to save him from the Yoris, a swift attack for the sergeant's lewd remarks about Luz and Sister Carolina. Perhaps, Tomas spoke true: in the ashes of his family's bones, he had read the dusky truth of the Yoris' savagery and the shame of his people's treachery.

Rising from his chest, a large sob swelled Cheve's throat but the tight noose refused to give. The boy choked like the snake swallowing the fat frog. He whipped his head back, opened his mouth and inhaled hard. A rush of air streamed into his nose and mouth and cleared his air passage. When he belched, a body-shuddering sense of relief filled his chest. He resolved not to give in to sadness since he didn't have the privilege to cry right now. *Be strong like Maso.*

Saliva, snot and blood mixed and crept from his forehead and nose and seeped into the crack of his face. He snorted and spit the copper-tasting fluid. The boy looked to the sides to see Ángel and his men, but the rope allowed little movement. His peripheral vision glimpsed only darkness. Up ahead he saw lantern lights belonging to guards who had remained behind to watch Tomas and Luz. They sat back-to-back in a small circle of four armed men who stared out to them. The chanting must have drawn their attention. His attempt to find help was futile — we'll die soon.

When they were within a quick dash of the umbrella of lights, a strong tug on the rope pulled on Cheve's neck.

The sergeant grunted and jerked to a stop. "*Chingao!*" the fat man exclaimed.

"Shhh. The *Indios* intend to take your prisoners," Ángel whispered. "I overheard them. Don't shout or show alarm."

"Where are they?"

"All around. They followed us with Mausers. There's about twenty."

"Let them try. My men will kill them and the prisoners."

"Yes, I know." Ángel slipped a dagger from beneath his poncho and as he seized the sergeant around the neck, he said, "Let go of the rope, *cabron*, or I'll slit your pig throat."

"My men — " the sergeant began, in a loud voice.

Ángel whirled around. "Quiet." He clutched the sergeant's genitals and pressed the knife to the fat man's prized possessions. "Would you like *huevos revueltos*, scrambled eggs?"

The man moaned and released the rope.

"Keep your hands up, away from that pistol." Ángel squeezed harder. "Good at this. Done it before."

"Ohhh," the Yori moaned, bent slightly as his knees quivered. His hands shook in the air as if he praised the gods for the rain's end. The Yoris' steady chanting of "*yeewe bichoo*" suffocated the sergeant's guttural protest.

"Your hands, Cheve," Ángel ordered.

The boy heard the knife snap the rope.

"Take his pistol," his brother ordered.

The sergeant's heavy gun trembled as he pointed it at the guard's head. With his free hand, he wiped the spittle, mucous and blood from his face. His breathing quickened and his legs tightened as if he were about to restart his run.

"Empty the bullets from the chamber," Ángel said.

The boy dropped them to the ground.

"Put the gun back in his holster."

Cheve hesitated.

"Do it."

The boy did.

When Cheve began to work the noose from his neck, his brother said, "No. Leave it."

As soon as Ángel released his grip, the sergeant exhaled, fell to his knees and cupped his balls.

"If you scream," he exchanged the knife with his pistol, "I will blow your piggy brains out, shoot off your worm and stick it in your mouth so you can chew it in hell. My men's weapons are sighted on you now."

The boy tried swerving his head to search for the armed Torocoyoris hidden in the darkness but a twisting pain stabbed his neck.

"Now pick up the rope, *cabron*, and lead your prisoner into the camp," Ángel said. "Careful, *hombre*. My pistol is on him but the bullets are for you." He crooked his neck to the darkness. "Fire on my command, but don't shoot the prisoners. *Yeewe bichoo, yeewe bichoo, yeewe bichoo.*"

Cheve's heartbeat quickened, but didn't panic.

CHAPTER 12

BOAT OF DREAMERS

"His Seataka is strong, this young one."
"Runs fast like Maso."
"Shall we let him see us?"
"No, not yet. Maso must test him."
"He has much love for his brother."
"True, but his brother loves the Yori girl."
"Much trouble will come of it."
"The brother had wondered away like so many."

Ángel walked in a near slow-motion fluidity. His arms' and legs' feline speed sprang in supple ease when he grabbed the sergeant's balls or wielded his knife and gun. Ángel's synchronicity and nuanced voice soothed Cheve's jittery nerves and probably eased the trigger fingers of his men.

The boy's senses heightened to every splash, shade of darkness, and musky smell on the rain-slicked plaza. Watching his sister's desperate gaze as they approached closer, he yearned to run to her. The rope grew tauter as Cheve quickened his pace.

The lead members of the chanting Yori soldiers entered the guards' umbrella of light. They continued to pump fists into the air and encouraged the waiting guards to join them in the grand gesture. Some of the men laughed, lowered their weapons and took up the chant.

Cheve giggled and in a weak voice echoed, "*yeewe bichoo, yeewe bichoo.*"

The illumination exposed Luz's and Tomas' bewildered stares as they met Cheve's bemused smile. He resisted the urge to cry out to her—to tell her Ángel was present.

"Quiet, Luz," Ángel growled in Cajita.

Reunited Falcons stood in the Yoris' light as the chanting continued.

A tall, slender Yori holding a rifle went to Luz, pulled her to her feet and wrapped an arm around her. "She feels stiff, my sergeant. Let me loosen her up for you."

The other Yoris hooted.

Ángel dashed, grabbed the Yori's rifle barrel, jerked the weapon from him and clubbed the man's leg.

He yelped, released Luz, falling to one knee. The other guards raised their weapons, pointing them at Ángel. Metallic malice whipping to attention echoed. All chanting died, replaced by the Yori guard's moaning and cursing.

"Prepare to die, Sergeant *Huevos*," Ángel said.

The fat face grimaced, his mouth and eyes widened and scanned the darkness.

Kill him, Ángel.

"My men will shoot you," the sergeant said.

"Spill our blood together." Ángel pressed his pistol to the fat man's crotch. "On my fire, shoot off the Yoris' *chiles*. I'll blast the sergeant's worm," Ángel shouted in Cajita and repeated in Spanish.

The Yori guards shifted on their feet and stared into the darkness around them. Some cupped a hand over their crotches. Ángel cocked his pistol. The metallic click of the hammer snapping into place broke the tense silence into a thousand jagged edges.

"Don't fire," the nervous sergeant shouted and held up his hand.

"Tell them to put their guns on the ground," Ángel ordered.

"*Bueno*, Ángel. You've tricked me this time. I see you want the woman, yourself. *India bonita*, go to Ángel. When you finish, let me know. I've got a Yaquita now, but she drinks too much and has grown fat like me." The sergeant laughed, revealing missing teeth.

Cheve slipped the noose from his head and followed Luz to Ángel.

After he cut her bonds, Luz embraced her younger brother and reached for Ángel, but he pushed her to the side.

"The guns," Ángel shouted louder, pressing his pistol barrel deeper.

"Do as he says. Put your weapons down." The sergeant motioned with his hands toward the ground. A furrowed scowl replaced the grin on his fat face.

"Who's this?" Ángel asked in Cajita, tilting his head to the Yaqui prisoner now standing.

"Tomas, my escort," Luz said. "He's protected us."

"Do you wish to join my men?" Ángel asked in the Yaqui tongue.

Caked blood smeared Tomas' forehead. "Traitor, I prefer to kill your men."

Ángel shrugged. "Spoken like a true Yaqui. You'll stay with the Yoris." He gestured his free hand to Tomas. "He's yours. You see, you don't leave empty-handed," Ángel said.

"I don't want him. I want you," the sergeant said. "You were too clever for me, tonight. But I will catch you one day, Ángel. Oh yes. I will cut you like Comanches gut gringos."

The sounds of rushing feet approached. A disheveled, tattered-dressed Sister Carolina ran into the circle of light.

"I have Cajemé's letter… I have the letter," she panted, her garbled words barely understandable. Standing next to Ángel, she waved the paper in the air as if the letter were a raven struggling to take flight.

"Ángel, my love." She tried hugging him, but he held his hand up.

Without a habit and a torn gown, the nun exposed golden hair and shapely, shimmering legs. The running had flushed her face, giving it a natural rouge tint. "They came to deliver this letter from Cajemé to the prefect. I allowed them to stay in the school. They stole no horses. Father Julio lied."

"You look *bonita* with so little clothes." The sergeant leered.

"They're innocent. Let them go." Sister Carolina took the letter to the sergeant.

The Yori's lecherous gaze wandered over the nun's body. The fat man brought the parchment close to his face. His bellowing laugh erupted. "It says, Sister Cunt needs to show me more leg."

"Don't dare talk to me like that," Sister Carolina ordered. "You can't read."

The sergeant held up his hands, blinking his eyes and wiggling his fingers. "I'm blind. Allow me to read your body."

The nun backed away.

"With your permission, grand trickster, we wish to leave. We've had a great misunderstanding. Sister Cun—I mean Carolina, thank you for solving this disagreement." He crumpled the letter, tossed it to Ángel, took off his sombrero, bowed and swept it across the ground. Holding his bent position to stare at the nun's exposed legs, he exhaled loudly and said, "*Ay, Dios mio!*"

Ángel caught the letter, straightened it and struggled to read silently in the feeble light.

"Tell your men not to shoot," the sergeant said rising. "Or we'll shoot back. *Muchachos*, pick up your guns and let's allow Sister's cute cunt to baptize Ángel's dong." The men laughed.

"The guns remain, Bocagrande. You leave with your peckers. *Que vaya con el Diablo.*" Ángel pointed his pistol at the fat man's chest.

"*Chingado, hombre.* You ask for too much. I can understand taking the women, but our guns are like our children. We can't leave our sons and daughters."

"Then I'll make them orphans."

"I'm going to kill you with these, Ángelito." Bocagrande held out his open, beefy hands. "I swear it on my whore mother's grave." Bocagrande made the sign of the cross and kissed the knuckle of his right thumb.

"Your bitch mother birthed a mad dog, *pendejo*. Go to hell."

"We'll see who goes to hell first. When we meet again, Ángelito." He swiped his closed fist across his throat.

"*Muchachos,* leave the guns for now. *Vamonos.*" He waved his men forward.

On hearing the Yoris' grumbling, Cheve's pride soared at the way Ángel had shunted them away. He kept looking at the Yoris' retreat and glancing back at his brother. As the lanterns faded, they were soon swallowed by the darkness.

"The letter?" Luz asked.

"Cajemé tricked you," Ángel said. "He had sent the official emissary the day before you left on your mission. He asks the prefect to grant you safe passage home."

"What? Why would he do this to us?" Luz asked.

"He had no choice when you volunteered before the assembly," Tomas said. "He assumed there were traitors still among us. Untie my hands, Torocoyori."

Ángel walked to the bound Yaqui and slipped his knife from under his poncho.

"Thank you for your care of my sister and brother." Ángel worked the blade on the rope. "And they'll need you to return to the Yaqui."

As soon as his hands broke free, Tomas rubbed his wrists and arms.

"You knew?" Luz asked her escort.

"Yes. The mission was too dangerous for you to go alone." Tomas stared into the darkness. "We hoped to draw out the traitors. Better if we leave now. How many men do you have?"

Ángel sheathed the knife underneath his mantle and chuckled. "None."

"We were bait?" Luz said, shaking her head.

"Good bait. We caught a traitor. Unfortunately, it's your brother."

Cheve and the others peered all around them and saw the bouncing lights of the Yori party about a hundred meters away. The quiet plaza revealed only shadowy outlines of distant buildings that surrounded the large square. The fresh, cool air, after the evening storm, soothed him. Moonlight glimmer shed its evening halos onto the party.

"You out-smarted them, Brother." Cheve put his arm around Ángel.

"Not so clever." Ángel shook his head. "Thought I had left my Yaqui allegiance behind. But when I saw Cheve and then you, Luz, bound — well, I went crazy-coyote. Bocagrande knows I can't stay in Guaymas. He'll report me to the *comandante* tonight who'll order me killed on sight. He assumes if Cajemé catches me, he'll hang me from the closest mesquite. I'm trapped."

"Not true, Ángel," Luz said. "Come back with us. Father and Cajemé will welcome you. You've been away too long. Our mother and father miss you. We need you now. Isn't it true, Tomas?"

"He'll answer to Yaqui Law," Tomas said in a stern tone.

"And what about God's Law?" Luz asked. "Do we not all answer to Him? Please come with us. Cajemé will understand and accept you among the people. You can tell them all you know about the Yoris."

"You shouldn't have come. I want to be with Carolina." Running to the novice nun, he took her into his arms. "It's been too long since I touched you, *mi amor*."

Carolina caressed his face. "Oh, Ángel, to see you this close." She kissed his lips and cheeks. "Please, understand." She and Ángel walked away a short distance.

Luz and Tomas also drew away together into the recesses of the darkness. Murmurs of animated voices ruffled the nocturnal silence. An occasional female voice of "No! . . . No!" crackled the shell of privacy from both corners.

The soothing, soft voices of the women would seal the cracks of the males' hostility. Soon a duet of calming cadence flowed in harmony from the pairs.

Cheve's head, back and neck ached even more in the darkness. He rubbed his neck, feeling the peeled portion of his skin. It stung to the touch. After all the raucous noise and beatings, pliant voices and after-shower tranquility settled over Cheve. The day's turmoil weighed on his body. Despite the wet plaza stones, he sat on the ground, brought up his knees, bowed and curled his hands around his head. He sobbed and rocked until he heard familiar singing above the couples' voices. It was a lively, stirring melody that dampened the memory of taunts and torture. Looking up, he wiped his eyes and nose and listened for the source. From the docks, the heart-warming tune wafted across the rain-slicked plaza. He stared hard but saw only the outline of the cathedral and the distant mountains.

"Maso calls us. Wants us to follow." Cheve jumped to his feet. "Must go now. Yoris come." When the couples didn't move, he shouted, "Run!"

"Cheve, what's wrong?" Luz rushed to him.

"Maso's out there." Cheve pointed into the darkness. "Wants us to leave before they come." Ángel, Carolina and Tomas surrounded the boy. "Brother, hear it?"

"He's right," Tomas said looking at the Palacio. "Your master must not be that stupid, Torocoyori. He brings more men and guns."

"Maso will save us," Cheve said.

"Yaqui superstition," Ángel said. "But men and bullets are real. We leave."

"Where?" Luz said, holding up her long skirt.

"Maso will take us home," Cheve said.

"Go," Ángel said drawing his pistol. "I'll delay the Yoris."

"Too many." Carolina pulled on his arm. "You tricked them. They'll kill you."

Shouts of angry men, dancing horse hooves reverberated.

"*Mi amor.* I want you alive. If you die, what happens to me?"

"Gun," Tomas held out his hand to Ángel. "Quick, Torocoyori. Time to collect Yori debts."

"Hurry," shouted Cheve. "Maso calls."

Ángel yanked off the lariat tethering the pistol, slipped bandoliers from around his shoulders and handed them to Tomas. "Moving target harder to hit."

"Yaqui heart harder." Tomas, shrouded in darkness, raced toward the approaching Yori mob.

Grasping hands, Carolina and Ángel chased after Cheve and Luz. Shortly, the boy heard a Yaqui battle cry and pops of gunfire. Like a wave splashing into a pier, Yori guns sprayed the plaza. Stray bullets pinged and sparked the stone floor close to the fleeing Yaquis. Occasional flashes of fire bursting from the opposite side drew the Yoris away. Horses neighed in panic. Men cursed the leaden night.

"Mother Mary, protect my Tomas," Luz uttered to the sky, running after Cheve and his Maso.

A faint outline of the magic deer's pointy crown antlers shimmered and bobbed as its sleek head swayed with the wilderness song. Propelled by elation at chasing the mystic deer of *Sea Ania*, the enchanted world, and desperate to flee gun-toting Yoris, Cheve bolted.

His sister's running speed, her step by step cadence, surprised him. Her body leaned forward, arms pumped to and fro in an easy, fluid flow. Beneath her long skirt that hid her taut legs, the rhythmic tapping of her feet echoed her strength and grace. She shot like a Falcon, feet splashing across the brick floor. Against the flashes of red and white gunfire bursting spasmodically, silhouettes of Ángel and Sister Carolina trailed.

At Cheve's howl, "Run faster," they grunted and quickened their tempo. He gasped at the clear sight of Maso prancing at the dock where anchored shrimp boats bobbed in Guaymas Bay. The deer lifted its head, mewing melodic lyrics that painted the beauty of flowers, desert animals, and the *Surem*. Cheve lifted his voice only to hear it fall flat as his running deflated air from words. The richness of the deer tune filled his heart with joy and legs with energy.

"My Maso." Cheve stretched his hands out and sniffed the air for the Maso musk. "Wait!" He ran onto the wooden dock, reached out within a few feet of the gigantic deer when its light vanished. The boy touched rain drops. "What . . . Where?" Cheve twirled in a circle. He flinched at his sister's touch.

Doubled over, she gulped for air.

"Maso... Maso," he wheezed with his hands outstretched like a blind, deaf boy stumbling for his bearings. No familiar antler or fur, no deer singing remained. Ángel and Carolina soon ran onto the dock, panting and trembling.

"Tomas cannot keep them away for long," Ángel said.

"Maso led us here," Cheve said in a faint voice. "Did you see him or hear his singing?"

"What are you talking about?" Ángel asked.

A sudden rapid pounding like nails hammering into the pier erupted. Splintered wood, some striking the fugitives, shot into the air.

"Quick. The boat. To the front." Ángel ran to a small moored craft. The single-mast boat, about twelve feet long and six feet wide, bobbed in the dark bay waters. The boat's sail clung to a fourteen-foot high mast at the back.

Ángel helped Luz and Carolina into the shifting vessel. "Cheve, come on."

"Maso led us here. Where did it go?"

"To hell," Ángel said, "and you'll join him if you don't get into this boat now." He ran to Cheve and pushed him toward the craft.

More bullets sang overhead some hitting the dock in staccato hisses. A large chip slapped Cheve's cheek.

Ángel grabbed his brother by the waist and threw him into the boat.

He moaned as he landed hard onto the deck covered with the shrimpers' netting. The boat reeked of the crustacean.

"Come here, Cheve," Luz whispered.

He crawled quickly to the sound of her voice and slid in next to her and Carolina, crouched at the prow, their heads bent low.

Ángel scrambled to untie the boat and push it from the dock. As it glided into the water, he ran alongside, leaped at the end of the dock and caught the side, his legs dangling into the bay. He grunted as he pulled himself up and landed on his back on the deck.

"Shhhh," he hushed.

Yoris' angry voices growled louder and closer. A glow of fleeting lights flickered past the canvas.

Cheve peeked around the mast. Many men, pistols drawn, fire light shifting over their gyrating bodies, looked like dancing, killer phantoms. He placed his hands over his ears to muffle their harsh, Spanish voices, calling, "*Chingados Yaquis. Hijos de putas.*"

More firing erupted from the cathedral square. Cursing men ran toward that direction, leaving the dock in darkness.

Ángel kicked Cheve's huaraches. "The sail. Help me."

Cheve rose, grabbed the rope Ángel held and pulled with him until the canvas unfurled.

A slight after-shower wind filled the sail, pushing the boat faster from the docks. Like two giant arms, the dark land reached out to the water, outlining Guaymas Bay. Between the arms, a couple of small islands rose like protruding heads. Beyond the isles lay the open sea that separated them from Baja California. Leaving the roiling land swarming with men hungry to kill, the calm waters offered refuge.

The boy sat in silence with the others, watching the receding lights. Occasional gunshots grew fainter. Water lapping the sides of the boat and the flutter of the sail relaxed him. After their stormy, violent visit to Guaymas, exhaustion stooped his shoulders.

"Rest. I'll steer the boat." Ángel sat next to the tiller at the back of the boat.

"How can you steer in the dark?" Cheve asked.

"I know this bay, Brother. I've sailed in the night before."

"Did you see Maso? Hear his singing?"

"I heard gunshots and guards. Smart of you to lead us to the boats. Sleep now."

Carolina rose and rocked her way to Ángel. While he held the tiller with one hand, he placed his other arm around her waist as naturally as a well-developed habit. She leaned into him, her head resting on his chest.

Ángel was the bravest man Cheve knew—even more so than his father, Mateo. With his big brother navigating the boat ever farther from the Yori shores, Cheve's fears receded. He lay next to his sister who sat staring at the shore.

"Did Tomas get away?" she asked.

Cheve couldn't see her face, but her sad voice projected a forlorn big sister.

"Can't catch him. Too fast and tough. A true Yaqui warrior — smart and swift. We'll see him again." He hoped he sounded convincing. A sudden yawn overwhelmed him and his eyes struggled to stay open on the easy-swaying craft. "Let's sleep while we can, Luz. Maso protects us."

"God watches over us," she said.

"Yes, God and Maso will protect us," he murmured, sailed to the sea of sleep and dreamed he danced and sang in the *Yo Ania* with the deer.

CHAPTER 13

TROUBLED WATERS

"Ángel's a traitor."
"Loves the Yori girl."
"He's confused on his loyalty."
"Should give her up."
"No, love makes you blind to your differences."
"He led the Yoris to Cajemé's wife."
"Allowed them to rape her."
"Deserves punishment."
"His confusion is his penalty."
"Must ask for forgiveness."

After the stars filled the night sky, Ángel quit looking and listening for any Yori pursuers. He instead listened to the soft snoring of Luz and Ángel. He had first regretted they had come to Guaymas, but then gratitude surged at the sight of Carolina. Would they have ever found the courage to escape from Guaymas?

Steering the sailboat from the bay toward the Sea of Cortez with the wind at their backs inflated pleasant memories. With Carolina's family away on business or personal visits, she insisted, despite dangers of going aground, to go sailing at night. One fleeting kiss convinced him prying eyes couldn't see through the dark or on the sea. As before, the breeze and cool mist from the lapping waves soothed and eased his worries. The fresh touch of their bodies and the renewed scents of their passions fanned his desire for her, especially after their forced separation.

Carolina tore off the dangling veil and tossed it into the sea. Her blonde hair that she refused to cut lay pinned in wet curls against her head. She slipped off the pins, lodged them in her nun's garb, and brushed out her hair its full length with her hands.

Ángel slid his free hand over her hair, up to her neck. "You are the best-looking nun the Romans ever allowed in a convent. It was sinful to force you into that sack cloth."

Bending, he meant to kiss her when she called out, "Rocks!" To the immediate right, the dark outline of a stone close to the shore of the last island leading into the sea jutted out. He veered to the left and scraped the shore. Carolina pulled away and sat up. "Better you watch the sea for now."

"Come closer. I want to hear and feel you breathe," Ángel said. "I promise to steer straight."

She leaned against him.

He grabbed her waist and brought her to his chest. Kissing her lips and cheeks, he pushed the silver cross away.

She pulled back and said, "Your brother and sister."

"They're asleep."

"No. Not the same as before. They came for you. We escaped capture. Where shall we go?"

Ángel looked at the Sea of Cortez, which they now entered. A slight southerly breeze pushed the craft along the small waves.

"To Arizona, California or Texas as we had planned. We'll marry and ranch."

Carolina placed her arms around his neck. "Together, finally. Away from all this fighting and hatred." She nodded toward the sleeping forms of Luz and Cheve. "First we'll take them back to the Yaqui. They've come a long way for you. Your parents—"

"What of them? I've told you I don't answer to them. I'm on my own." His voice took a hard edge. "And what of your parents? Your father will accuse me of kidnapping. He'll demand the governor send the army after us."

"Shhhh." She placed her hands on his cheeks and took him into her arms. "When I'm your wife, no one can ever separate us." She kissed him on the lips.

He released the tiller and wrapped both arms around her. The boat swayed in the easy waves, drifting in the bay as it had before.

After a while, Carolina pressed his chest away from her and whispered, "Enough—not here, not now—not before we're married."

Her "nots" aroused him. His breathing grew rapid and his hold desperate.

"Stop it!" she said.

Reluctantly, he released her.

She stood, walked gingerly to the side of the boat. "We must restrain our desires. Can you wait until we are free of Yoris, Yaquis, fighting and running?"

"When I couldn't see you, I had no choice. But with you so close—it's torture."

"Patience, my love."

"I've no patience for patience." Ángel moaned. He pointed to the shadowy land in the distance. "Going into the Yaqui will be risky. Cajemé will fight back. His men will seize all the boats."

"By land in the dark to the Yaqui. You know the way."

Her voice had a strange, cold tone. Despite the moonlight, it was hard to see her expressions. *She doesn't know about the raid, does she?*

"Still dangerous, Carolina."

"We live in perilous times."

"Sit next to me, Carolina the Courageous. I'll only place an arm around you—nothing more, like nights before when we recited the story of the Montagues and Capulets, my Juliet."

Carolina sat next to him.

He rested an arm on her slender shoulders.

"No church, parents or war will separate us again."

"Till death do we part."

Carolina tensed her body. "Why did you say that?"

"Our love will never die."

"Not the same. Say it, Ángel." Her voice cracked and body shivered. "Say we're not going to die for a very long time."

He glanced at his sleeping brother and sister and then at Carolina. "Of course. We'll die when we're asleep in our beds, our children and grandchildren sitting around."

"Say it, then." Carolina raised her voice and grabbed his shirt.

"We're not Romeo and Juliet. We're Ángel and Carolina who'll live for a long time together. Better?"

Behind them, flickering lights of Guaymas winked. Looming farther east, the shadowy outlines of the Becatete Mountains rose. The sea's cool breeze chilled their bodies clad in wet clothes.

Carolina shivered and snuggled closer. "Sleep," Carolina said. "I can steer to Yaqui land. I know the way."

Her hand drew his face down. Her pleasant fleshy mouth warmed the navigator's face. His senses reflected the outline of her mouth, the smoothness of her skin, the taste of her lips, the feel of her breath on his tongue. At the parting, he exhaled in a high, almost feminine tone and chuckled at the sound of his voice.

"It's been so long since we did this. I forgot how sweet you tasted," he said. "Sleep, Carolina."

"Wake me if you feel tired. I can steer as well as you," she said.

"Yes, my captain."

She slipped down to the deck, wrapped her arms around herself, and curled up her legs against her chest. In a drowsy voice, she said in Cajita, "Promise me you won't leave me, my Ángel."

"Never." He clamped his lips tight, but couldn't hold back the waves of passion suppressed by the long year of forced distance. Her cherished voice fed his hungry heart.

"Good man... strong Yaqui," Carolina murmured and soon snored softly.

In the moon rays, her closed eyes, her parted lips, her hair draped partly over one eye, she appeared like the drawing in their school book of Juliet after taking the sleeping potion. He found it hard to keep from staring at her.

Luz breathed rapidly and occasionally cried out. She still ran in her dreams from Yoris. His sister was naïve to think a sheet of paper would keep them from coming to the Yaqui Valley. Having lived among Yoris, he knew they considered natives of Sonora primitive, uneducated fanatics and inept landowners. The government in collusion with rich hacendados and miner owners was determined to work the lands for cash crops and ores. Like all other *Indios* of the Americas, Yaquis could not be permitted to block the road to México's growth.

From his history lessons, Ángel learned strong countries conquered weaker ones—it was the natural order: *Los Españoles* conquered the Americas and ruled until Simón Bolívar and Miguel Hidalgo united their people to overthrow the Spaniards. Several years later, Benito Juárez led his people against the French invaders who supported Maximilian, the so-called emperor of México. Now it was time México grow stronger or face conquest from another foreign power like the *Norteamericanos*. The gringos already had taken half of México's land. There was rumor the Yankee government would incite a war to seize Sonora.

Ángel and other Yaquis didn't find it difficult to side with the Yoris. They were paid pesos, wore nicer clothes, ate and drank as much as they wanted, slept in soft beds, and sometimes took a Yori woman. The Yoris treated the natives well when they shared their knowledge of the wild lands, tongues and customs in service to the Mexican government. He looked again at Carolina and guessed had he stayed on the Yaqui, he never would have kissed or held this blonde, brainy beauty. Her love washed away any maltreatment by some like Father Julio and her parents. If forced, he would admit to his brother and sister, he loved Carolina more than the Yaqui and his family.

To her side lay Cheve's motionless, curled form. Although he couldn't see his face, Ángel could tell by his deep, slow breathing, his brother slept in surprising tranquility. He had almost forgotten the reach of Cheve's ugliness. He found it hard to admit his brother had grown uglier—the gash in his face appeared to have widened, the pock marks deeper. As a child, Cheve's face was smaller and when he looked closely, he could see some patches of Falcon beauty. The dark eyes were even set with a slight shift upwards at the ends hinting of a distant Asian past. The eyebrows were thick and their curls accented his eyes' deep brown brilliance. But all traces of childhood beauty had transformed to adolescent distortion.

Ángel recalled seeing his brother lying in the dirt outside of Cajemé's house at the raid. Sprawled on the ground, blood streaming from his nose and mouth, moaning, Cheve appeared like one of the Yaqui mythical, bewitched, underground half-man, half-monster that crawls out to eat humans. A urgent desire to ride away from the pitiful sight of his hapless brother bit—but the rape of Cajemé's wife and the cruel beating of Cheve disgusted him. Falcon blood ties pushed him to fight for his brother again.

He, like other Torocoyoris, was angry Cajemé had eluded them. With his death, Yaqui resistance to Yori influence would end. He had volunteered to lead the assassination team through little known trails in the dark to Cócorit. But there was a more personal reason for killing Cajemé. A successful mission would impress Carolina's parents he was worthy of marrying her. Instead, the failed raid touched off a new cycle of revenge and war. He would probably never gain the respect he sought from Carolina's father.

Cheve's open mouth of shock deformed his appearance even more. His worst fear, that his family would recognize him had come true, and its horror was reflected in his brother's face. He hadn't planned on the rape of Cajemé's wife. But the men had ridden a long way and their blood lust had roused. Like a wounded bull in a corrido, Sergeant Bocagrande ravished the woman for sport and revenge.

Ángel caressed Carolina's hair and knew if Luz and Cheve hadn't come, they wouldn't have found the nerve to flee Guaymas. They would have had to settle for long-distance looks, furtive waves, secreted letters and lonely memories. Instead, he could savor again her honeydew kiss and caressing touch. He owed them safe passage for their gift of reuniting them. Still he risked capture and death by Yaqui warriors.

He recalled waking one night in his youth to his father's and his men's angry voices. Several warriors stood outside their hut, pointing toward the desert. He overheard sporadic words: "Torocoyoris... ropes... knives... mesquites." When several of the men cursed, he ordered them to stop and pointed to the hut. They bowed their heads, murmuring apologies.

Slipping out of their house, without his mother's notice, he ran after his father and men but lingered far enough behind to avoid notice. After a short distance into the desert, he lay on his belly close to where the men encircled four tied captives, sitting on the ground. The Yaquis held torches, their guns trained on the prisoners.

His father exploded in rage, cursing, kicking, spitting, slapping, and punching men who were probably Torocoyoris. Ángel bowed his head to the ground, his hands over his ears. The prisoners whimpered, moaned and cried from the assault.

"Stand them up," his father barked. He held out his hand. A Yaqui warrior placed a knife into his palm. His father ran around them in circles, slashing and plunging their chests, backs, faces, legs, wherever the blade could reach. Torocoyoris howled, their bodies spilling blood from their wounds. One tried to run away, but the warriors pushed him back.

Huffing and sweating, his father shouted, "Traitors, you'll not be buried. Your bodies will be thrown into the desert for the coyotes and buzzards. They'll shit you out for the flies. We'll tell your people you were killed by Yoris. Good lies to avoid their shame."

"Mateo, you drunken coward," the shortest Torocoyori screamed. "We know what you and your men did to the Yaqui woman and her Yori husband in the desert. You're the filth. Raising the ugly bastard will not atone for your sins. Cut your own throat."

"Hang them!" Mateo ordered.

The four men's bloody bodies soon swayed from the branches of a large mesquite. He ran back to his hut, reeling from the torture and hanging. He now wondered if his father would cut and hang him as he did those Torocoyoris the night he faked sleeping. "Drunken coward." He never could get those words out of his memory. The other was "bastard."

Peering at the shore, he saw faint lights, but couldn't hear any gunfire. Tomas had little chance of escaping the Yori guards. If they caught him, they'd torture him to get the truth of his mission. Should he survive the cuttings and beatings, they would send him to the *Islas Marias*, the prison islands down the coast or even farther south to a place called Yucatan. There, he'd work in the henequen fields alongside Mayan slaves. Tomas wouldn't see his Yaqui home for many years, if ever.

The Sea of Cortez and the night hid the troubles of Sonora. Death, war and hate stalked the sierra leaving a trail of Yaqui and Yori bones and crosses. As long as Mexicans sought and seized land and Yaquis refused to leave their ancestral homes, fighting would continue.

The Yaquis were a backwards people: if only they embraced civilized rule, Yori ways, they would discover a life of clean beds, medicine and education.

Shifting his weight to ease the stiffness in his neck and arm, Ángel gazed on his Yori beauty, leaned to one side. He sang softly, "On the other side, other side, land of the deer and flowers / on the other side, I will play the drum and flute for the dancers and the bees—"

He stopped singing, stared into the sea of darkness, and pointed at the shadowy land. He might die soon on the other side.

CHAPTER 14

DANCE OF THE DEVILS

"Tomas has fire in his soul."
"We must bring him to us."
"Misses his family."
"Teach him how to fight, run and love."
"He'll never love again."
"Lost his manhood to the fire."
"Luz can teach him."
"She's not strong enough."
"Never walked with a man."
"Lead her to him – make her courageous."

The plaza reeked of acrid gunpowder as rifle and pistol shots rang around Tomas. He lay on wet stones, listened for horses and men and elevated his aim. Glints and chimes of spurs spaced out on the square surged toward him like speeding, bobbing fireflies. He squeezed six, quick shots.

Horses screeched and danced chaotically. Hard thumps of animals falling echoed in the square.

"*Chingado*, Yaqui… *hijo de puta…*" Yoris shouted and fired back.

The whistling lead flew just above Tomas' head. After the burst, the Yaqui rose to one knee and reloaded as the clap of hooves approached. A speeding shadow of the animal charged from the left. He raised the gun higher and fired. A scream flew past and faded. Running, he chased the moans across the plaza.

His back and face still throbbed from the beating he had taken from the Yori guards. If captured, he would suffer worse before they actually killed him.

That would not happen – not again.

Tomas's burns and pain was partially relieved with the curer's mushrooms and herbs. Unable to tell day or night or how many days had passed, he wafted between dreams, visions, and agony. Never again would he float in purgatory — not on this side of the river.

The sounds of hooves reverberated through the ground. Frantic barking of dogs clamored. He tripped. His groans mixed with the grunts of a body he tumbled over. As he hit the stone floor, the gun sailed from his hands caught by the darkness. Tomas reached all around him for the weapon.

The wounded man gurgled, vomiting hot blood onto Tomas' arm.

He wiped the slop on the fallen man's chest and face. "Die, Yori," he whispered. In the wounded man's holster, he found another pistol, picked it up, slipped the bent sombrero from the Yori's head and put it on.

"My chest… can't breathe," the man said in Cajita. "Mary, Mother of God, save me."

Tomas startled to hear his tongue spoken.

"Torocoyori, I'll save you from your traitor life." He drew his knife and slit the gurgling man's throat.

With pistol and blade in hand, Tomas ran toward the cathedral. Yoris had expected him to look for the closest escape from the city. They massed their men along the streets surrounding the plaza. Shots from the dock rang.

Found them. Torocoyori couldn't save them. I'll avenge your deaths.

By the light of the lantern hung over the church entrance, Tomas spied Father Julio standing by the door. He appeared bedraggled in his soiled black cassock, tousled, wet hair and mud-streaked, fat face. The priest stared intently, shifting his gaze from side to side.

Draped in darkness, Tomas smiled at the man who refused them sanctuary, who lied about their horse thievery. *His desire to witness the capture of the Yaquis exceeded his fears of them. Time to confess your sins, padre, and do penance.*

At the crack of gunfire, the priest trembled and searched the darkness around him in quick, jerky movements.

Yoris' yells, their mares' neighs and dogs' barks drew closer behind the fugitive. Tomas stepped forward quickly with his head down, the sombrero's wide brim over his face.

The minister yelped in fright, jumped back, slipped and fumbled for the church door.

The Yaqui sprinted and grabbed Father Julio as he entered his sanctuary. Tomas' momentum pushed the two into the House of God. His weight knocked the man of the cloth to the clean floor. The fugitive slammed the door shut, pulled out his pistol and placed an index finger to his lips. When the cleric opened his mouth, Tomas pointed the gun barrel at his head.

"No," the priest cried, his eyes widened in a frightened gaze. He threw up his hands as if to swat a mosquito bullet.

He gestured for Father Julio to get up.

The *padre* groaned as he rose to one knee. His hand reached for the back of a pew.

Tomas scanned the crepuscular church. Red and white candles at the altar and along the sides in chapels gave shifting glimpses of ornate statues, paintings and columns. Shadows stood in the corners like sentries waiting for dawn. The grey, marble floors glimmered from the candlelight. Except for the cleric's panting, the church lay quiet, clean and peaceful, unlike the Yoris' curses and dogs' yelps just outside the church doors. Death waited patiently for Tomas to step into the mud.

Angry voices and lights flared louder and brighter as the church door creaked. Tomas pushed the priest into a dark corner, leaned against his captive and shoved the barrel into the cleric's mouth.

The door opened wider. The wind shifted the candle flames to a sinuous dance. For a moment the light splashed into the corner, revealing the distorted look of fear on the fat face.

Two Yori soldiers with pistols drawn walked in. One held a pit bull on a leash straining and whining to run. The dog's barks echoed obscenely in the near-empty church. After the door closed, the Yoris blessed themselves with their guns. They shifted their sombreros off their heads to their backs. They gazed around the church as they tracked slush and rainwater onto the polished floors.

When one of the Yoris looked in their direction, Tomas pressed the gun deeper into Father Julio's mouth. Despite the darkness, the whites of the priest's eyes glowed. The Yaqui whispered a sibilant "shhh" into the cleric's ear and watched for any signs of detection.

The Yoris walked down the center aisle, guns poised, sweeping from side to side. At the front of the church, they blessed themselves at the feet of the larger-than-life wooden statue of Jesus on the cross. They went up the altar steps, walked toward the side and disappeared into a recess Tomas took for a door.

The *padre* squealed.

Tomas pushed the man's head into the wall with a dull thud. He squeezed his neck. "Silence or death. Choose," he whispered, unsure if the cleric knew Cajita.

The bug-eyed cleric nodded as if he clearly understood.

"One sound," Tomas swept the gun barrel down one cheek and up the other, "and they'll call you the holey man." He slipped the gun back into the captive's mouth.

The pit bull barked.

Tomas discovered the Yoris in the center aisle.

One looked directly at him as if he could pierce the dark like a killer owl. Tomas guessed he could get off two shots before they returned fire. To kill in a sacred place troubled him. But then he remembered his discovery of a Yaqui church where Yori soldiers had trapped Indian families. The savages had set the roof afire and shot, hacked and clubbed worshipers as they tried to escape the flames. Tomas would never forget the smell of charred flesh, bashed heads and gaping wounds on the men, women and children. Their cries grated on his ears.

As the door opened, another surge of wind and rain burst in.

Pressing the *padre* to the wall, Tomas gazed calmly at the new intruders.

A Yori who stood outside shouted to the others. The dog growled and pulled the chain taut as it strained to run toward Tomas. The dog handler jerked the leash. The pit bull yelped as the Yori soldiers ran to the entrance.

After the church door banged shut, Tomas chuckled. He slipped the barrel out of his prisoner's mouth.

The cleric coughed and wrenched, his hands reaching for his throat.

The Yaqui dragged the pastor to the church door, pointed to the lock and made a twisting motion with his wrist.

With the gun pressed against his belly, Father Julio fumbled for the keys in his pocket. After a couple of tries, he inserted the key into the hole and locked the door.

"Get going, priest-hater-of-Yaquis." He shoved him toward the altar. "Let's have a Yaqui Mass."

His mind raced between whether to stay in the church with *padre* through the night, or to escape now. Angry voices outside bellowed the danger. The longer he stayed in church the greater the chance of capture. A day escape would fail. Eventually, they would come back with more dogs, guns and chains. By morning, Yoris, nuns and parishioners would seek Father Julio for confession, Mass and indulgences.

The priest would be his personal savior, or his personal executioner—whichever way, the cleric chose. Better to persuade him to choose wisely. Tomas pushed the *padre* up the red-rich, carpet-covered steps and onto the platform before the altar.

A large, gilded cross stood on the altar between gold and silver candelabra. A filigreed wall accented with niches of painted statues of angels and saints stood in ethereal gaze. Latin words in colorful, shimmering tiles close to the ceiling pronounced indecipherable sacred messages. A loin-clothed, lean-muscular Jesus loomed on a wooden cross.

In contrast to the dirt-floors, stucco-cracked walls, and leaky wooden ceilings of the Yaqui churches, the Yori God's Sanctuary was lavish. Yaquis endured long, sleepless nights of guard duty at festivals, ceremonial marches in a bull mask at the Lenten drama of Christ's rise from the dead, ritual cleansing and repairs to the church. Yet their holy house lacked gold and silver, sculpted saints and angels, marble floors. God gave the Yoris shiny metals and mansions and the Yaquis the mesquite, Bacatete Mountains, Yaqui River, deer and lion.

Tomas smiled: God favored Yaquis.

He pushed Father Julio toward the door at the back of the altar. After Tomas pointed at a lit altar candle, Father Julio picked up the candle to illuminate the shadowy room. As they entered, Tomas found a wood-paneled chamber. Silver chalices studded with red and blue stones of various sizes stood on a shelf. Crystal bowls that refracted orange and green light perched on a ledge next to wine goblets. Burners with their long chain handles hung from ceiling hooks. Incense and wine sweetened the air.

Tomas went to another door at the back. When he couldn't open it, he pointed toward the key hole. After the priest unlocked the door, the Yaqui opened it and peered out. The unguarded church barn stood across the empty street. He quickly closed the exit.

Tomas opened a tall closet cabinet, and discovered red and black cassocks and white, silk surplices. He grabbed a cassock, slipped it on and began to fasten the long column of buttons down the front.

"Stop." The servant of God waved his hands.

After Tomas pointed a finger to his lips, the cleric threw the candle at him. The Yaqui ducked and chased the *padre* into the church.

"Help!" Father Julio shouted as he ran into the central aisle.

Tomas jumped on him at the altar stairs and tumbled to the floor. Under the stony gaze of the saints and angels, he slapped the minister about the head with the pistol. Rosettes of blood surfaced.

While the wounded man yelped and cowered on the carpet, Tomas grabbed his arm and jerked the priest to his knees. As he pulled the cleric's hair, a tear ripped the air. The Yaqui looked at the toupee in his hand, then at the priest's bald pate. "Hairless Chihuahua!" Tomas threw the hairpiece to the carpet, grabbed the front of Father Julio's collar and pulled him up to his feet.

The priest curled his lips. "Bastard, Yaqui."

Tomas kneed him in the stomach. "No cursing in church."

In a heap, the cleric fell at the foot of the altar. With whimpers, he curled his legs up to a fetal crouch.

The Yaqui finished fastening the cassock over his wet clothes. The Yoris were smart to sew in place so many buttons to fight temptations of the flesh.

He went to the lit candles at the sides of the altar, picked up the candelabra and held it up. "For my family and all the Yaquis your people burned. May God have mercy on my soul." Tomas lowered the candles to the altar sheet.

The white mantle burst into yellow flames and rekindled the memory of his family's death, the smell of their burning flesh.

Father Julio howled. He grabbed the burning cloth from the altar.

Tomas hammered the man's arm with the butt of his gun.

The cleric released the cloth as he slumped to the floor.

Tomas ran to the sacristy, threw open the vestment doors and tossed candles onto the colorful surplices and albs inside. In a dash through the church, he lit hymnals, tossed them around the church, tumbled candles, and poured burning wax over the statues. He sprinted back to the sacristy where flames licked out and up from the vestment closet. The fire crackled and heated the smoke-filled room. Back in the church, he saw flames dance about the pews like teen devils at a satanic festival.

In the midst of the blaze, the priest stumbled down the center aisle toward the doors.

The growing heat invigorated Tomas as he bolted after him. With a firm grasp of the priest's collar, Tomas jerked him toward the altar.

"This way, priest. One more soul to save."

The cleric clutched a pew.

"You are Satan incarnate," the *padre* whimpered. "Go back to hell."

The shifting flames shot arrows of light all around. Faces of the saints transmuted to sneers and malevolent grins. Gold, silver light flashed across Jesus' skeletal body like the lashes of Pilate's men.

Tomas hauled the priest with him to the altar. The acrid smell and crackling wood inflamed memories of his children's screams for their father to save them. He towed the cleric into the smoke. The intense heat from the burning vestments seared him. Tomas dragged a coughing Father Julio to the back door. He peeked out, saw the street still empty and stepped out. With his mouth open wide, he inhaled the cool, fresh air. The barn door stood about thirty meters away. Not much time left — they would soon discover the holy smoke.

"Get into that barn, cow-priest." He pushed Father Julio into the stable, walked to the stall of his horse and whispered.

The animal whinnied.

Tomas pulled his and Luz's horses' reins to the middle of the stable — glad he had left the horses bridled and saddled. At the stable door, the Yaqui fugitive saw smoke billowing from the sacristy, but still no soldiers.

"On the horse," he shouted. "Get up" Tomas kicked the cleric, who lay on the ground strewed with straw and feces.

Father Julio yelped and rose.

"No... no more, *por favor*," the priest pleaded.

"Get on." Tomas pointed at Luz's horse.

"*Ay, Dios mío.*" The minister grunted as he slipped his foot into the stirrup. He groaned as he pulled himself up by the saddle horn.

As soon as Tomas pushed opened the stable door, the acrid smoke stung his nostrils and made him cough. Church mice shrouded in white clouds fled out of the back door. Yellow flames bobbed and danced to the beat of a satanic band.

Despite the chill, Tomas' body grew warm. He forced himself to tear his sights from the fire and jumped on Deer Chaser. He brandished his pistol.

The cleric's face contorted. "My beautiful church! You will go to hell, *Indio.*"

"Stay with me or get a bullet here in the stable and meet Satan tonight?" Tomas poked the barrel into the captive's chest. He then slipped the pistol into the front of the cassock with the butt barely exposed. For the sake of a passerby, they were two servants of God out to do His work.

He breathed easier at the feel of Deer Chaser's firm, strong muscles, beauty of its angular neck and switch of its tail. His horse's musky odor calmed him. Holding the reins to his fate, Tomas could die in the saddle on Yori land.

When his mare whinnied, backing up at the sight of the fire, Tomas rubbed its neck. "Calm, Deer Chaser, we go home now."

The horse edged forward.

Tomas peered along the street. No one appeared. He had trotted halfway down the empty road when he noticed he didn't hear the other horse's canter. Swirling, he found Father Julio staring at the smoke billowing out of the door. His hands were outstretched to the church.

"*Fuego... fuego!*" the cleric shouted.

Tomas trotted to him and slapped him with his reins. "Judas, shut up." Grabbing the reins, he pulled the *padre* after him. As he neared the end of the street that opened to the square, Tomas slowed.

"*Fuego... fuego!*" the cleric shouted the alarm.

Soldiers patrolling along the plaza streets stopped at the cries. They pointed, shouted "fire" and ran to the church.

Tomas peered at the darkened road from which they had entered Guaymas. If he bolted now, he might escape.

The church doors exploded in a fiery burst, a fireball swooshed out and flames licked the sky. Expanding and bursting wood popped and squealed. Stained glass windows shattered into colorful shards, showering the streets and people.

Deer Chaser jumped, prancing on its hooves.

Horsemen galloped from the darkened path Tomas had intended to make his escape. Bearing rifles and machetes, they were waiting for him.

"*Fuego... fuego!*" Tomas took up the alarm. He pulled the minister with him in a slow trot, and then stopped as the soldiers ran toward them. "Judas, this is for you." He slipped out the pistol, pointed it at the cleric and tucked it back into the cassock. "*Fuego... fuego.*" Tomas pointed at the church.

Gun-toting soldiers on foot surrounded them.

Father Julio looked nervously from Tomas to the soldiers as the imposter placed his hand over the gun butt. The *padre* pointed to the church. The soldiers nodded and raced toward flaming shrine.

The bogus priest heard one of the soldiers with rifle in hand talking at him. One quick move and he could shoot the Yori. But then he'd draw the other soldiers to him. He paused and then raised his hand in a sweep to bless the Yori. The soldier looked puzzled and made the sign of the cross.

"Yaquis... Yaquis!" Tomas shouted.

"Yaquis?"

"Yaquis!" Tomas pointed to the burning church.

The soldier ran toward the house of the burning bush shouting "Yaquis" to the others.

A large crowd of soldiers who had stood a safe distance from the church door ran to the back.

"Yaqui!" The priest pointed at Tomas. In the darkness, no one seemed to have noticed him expose the holy pretender.

"*Yaqui, sí, fuego, sí,*" Tomas chanted with a chuckle and a clap.

Fire alarm bells rang at the *Palacio*. More men rushed across the square. Shop owners, women holding children, prostitutes, bakers, and fishermen, some half-dressed, others with mismatched clothes ran to the conflagration.

Flames burst through the roof and danced about the turrets like Satan's children at a lost souls ball. The crowd shouted in anger, cursed the Yaqui and wept. Nuns bearing straps knelt in the mud praying. Several curled charred on the ground, caught in the path of the fireball.

Several bucket brigades formed. A mix of incense, smoke, curses and prayers filled the air.

From a far distance, possibly from the Yaqui, Tomas heard a woman and children crying in Cajita for help. The sight of his wife wrapped in flames and his son crawling on his hands and knees with his head on fire sprang before him on the dark path leading out of Guaymas. Tomas pulled the *padre's* horse down the darkened way past rushing firemen.

Father Julio shouted, "Yaqui... Yaqui... Yaqui!"

The fire starter yelled, "*fuego... fuego... fuego!*" laughing and weeping.

CHAPTER 15

✵

INTO THE MIST

"They're on Yaqui land."
"Danger awaits them."
"Ángel knows the way."
"That Ángel is arrogant."
"I wish he knew the way back to his Seataka, his Yaqui people."
"Cheve has strong Seataka."
"He brings them allies."
"The Yori girl speaks Cajita well."
"She's a witch."

Water lapping against the boat, Cheve snoring and
Carolina mumbling gibberish awakened Luz. She stared at
the early morning sky shrouded in white gauze fog. To her
side Cheve shivered, his arms wrapped around himself to
catch his body's warmth. By the tiller, Carolina curled up in
the tattered remains of her heavy, black habit, her golden hair
stretched across her face. The run-away-nun swatted the air
to block some phantom attack.

Luz yawned, stretched her arms, and winced as her back
ached from the hard, wooden, boat bottom that no longer
rocked. She stood upright and found the boat ashore,
wrapped in morning mist. *Ángel's gone.*

She whiffed smoke and meat. Her mouthed watered at
the delectable scent. A red glow emanated from the gray mist.

Climbing out of the craft, she walked toward the ruddy
cloud and saw a dark outline of a man. The closer she
approached, the clearer she saw her brother, kneeling beside
an open fire. The sight of him holding a skewered fish
roasting in the flames whetted her hunger.

"Brother, where are we?" she asked.

"In a bay."

Several fat, long fish lay at his feet. They looked brown, ready to devour.

"Hungry?" he asked.

Luz nodded.

"Wake Cheve and Carolina."

"Are we safe here?" Luz stared at the surrounding trees. In their specter glow, they appeared like tall, dark, ominous sentries guarding the passage to the Yaqui desert. Slow undulating gray sheets curtained the desert. Sea fog blanketed the banked boat and Sea of Cortez. The waves sounded like a dog lapping water. Neither sights nor sounds of Yoris or Yaquis by land or sea surfaced. She gazed up again to see if Yoris had grown wings.

Ángel had sailed into a harbor of tranquility, hidden and safe. They could stay at the shore, build a hut, fish and hunt for game, far from the fighting and killing. She and Cheve could rekindle the fire of their relationship with Ángel, and convince him to come back to them. Father and Mother would accept him and Carolina. He could marry the white girl, live with them, have children and show the Yaquis and Yoris how they could love instead of hate.

"We'll never be safe in Sonora after last night." Ángel shattered her daydream. "Yoris will send their best trackers. They're good at finding their man. I trained them to track Yaquis," he said with a proud smirk coupled with a mischievous gleam.

"Oh, blessed Mary, we need to leave." Luz looked again at the sentry trees. She feared the fog would lift soon and the morning sun would expose them. Their flight to the boats, burst of gunfire rattled her memory. She expected to see the sergeant loom in boats filled with armed Yoris.

"You're shaking, Luz. Come closer to the fire."

She didn't stir.

"You'll run faster with some food in you."

At the touch of Ángel's hand on her shoulder, she yelped, "Oh, Mother!"

"Luz, we have a good lead. They'll not catch us." Ángel smiled a big, warm grin she remembered from their childhood. His confident voice and handsome face calmed her a bit.

In their flight, she hadn't taken a careful look at her brother. His wide shoulders, muscular build, thick, black hair and good looks reminded Luz of their father, Mateo. He had grown taller than their father. His white teeth gleamed against his dark skin.

"You were brave to come to Guaymas. Thank you for bringing Carolina back to me."

She tried to smile, but instead tears flowed. Cajemé and her father had fooled her to think she could actually negotiate a peace treaty with Yoris. She could normally detect when people lied or masked true intentions. Her mother had taught her to watch people's eyes, faces, hands, heads and hands when they spoke. Truth would flow easily from honest ones as evident in their body's harmony. With practice and attention, she had learned to watch how skilled liars would betray their motives in twitch of their lips, droopy eye, hand to chest, flutter of fingers, foot tap, lop-sided smile, rate of breathing. Her desire to bring Ángel home had overwhelmed her truth-divining senses. But then the truth was she had hidden her true intentions from Cajemé and her father. Petra had told her truth was like an egg: its fragility calls for careful handling if it's to yield a good life.

Her flowing tears gave her some relief. She consoled herself with finding Ángel. Will the truth of his Torocoyori life endanger him and his family's lives? Could she tell the truth to her parents?

"You must be brave for the trip home. If Yoris spot us, we'll need to run and fight again. Can you do that, Luz?"

She nodded and wiped her eyes.

"Wake the others," Ángel said.

Luz revisited the boat and stirred Cheve and Carolina from their sleep.

Carolina ran to Ángel's embrace. Cheve and Luz trailed behind and smiled to one another. Ángel kissed his woman, told her to sit and handed them each a fish skewered on a stick, dripping in its own cooking nectar.

Luz savored the morsels of sea food. "Wonderful." The juices dripped from the corners of her mouth.

"Slow down, Brother," Ángel said. "It can't swim away,"

"Good!" Cheve slowed his chewing.

After eating, Luz sat close to the fire with the others to warm up from the morning chill, her clothes still damp from the rain.

"Did you sleep, my love?" Carolina asked.

"Enough." Ángel touched her cheek. "Fished in the night—like before."

"So clever, my dear."

"Use your wits, Brother, to get us home," Cheve said.

"Do you think Tomas got away?" Luz asked in a cracked voice, searching the sea.

"He looked tough and skilled at killing. He might have made it out—with luck," Ángel said. "But so many soldiers-"

Carolina nudged Ángel.

"Of course, he escaped. That Yaqui's strong and fearless." Ángel snapped his fingers and turned to Luz. "Did you walk with Tomas?"

Luz blushed and looked into the fire.

"What does walk mean?" Carolina asked. "The way you used the word."

Cheve chuckled.

"Walk has several meanings, *cariña,*" Ángel said. "One way is to walk as you and I did at the Guaymas docks. Another is to share sleep blankets. But I asked if Luz and Tomas were in love—do they walk together?" He fluttered the fingers in both hands, side-by-side.

"Oh, you mean like we walk together." She imitated his finger signs.

"Yes, like us."

Luz wondered about this too. She enjoyed the feel of Tomas' arms around her and his looks of concern. But he carried much anger like an anchor from the past he couldn't release. His resentment moored him.

"I hope he comes back," Luz said, averting her gaze to the fog-shrouded sea.

"I hope Maso comes to protect us," Cheve said.

"Maso is a myth, Brother," Ángel stated.

"The deer led us to the boats in Guaymas. I saw and heard it sing."

"What's he talking about?" Carolina asked. "What's a Maso?"

"Maso is a magical deer of the *Yo Ania*, the Yaqui world of enchantment," Cheve said. "If you learn deer language and show courage, Maso will share its power."

"Yaquis delight in talking animals and witches." Ángel laughed. "Superstition and ignorance. Hunger stirs foolish ideas."

"Ángel, you once believed in Maso," Luz said.

"That's before I went to Yori school. I've no need for Maso, *Yo Ania*, *pascolas* or *chapeyekas*. They're fun to imagine as a child but as an adult—" Ángel shook his head.

"You once were a deer singer. Father boasted you were the best among all the eight villages."

"I've learned new tunes—love songs." He held Carolina's hand.

"I like the way you sing." Carolina hugged him.

"Shouldn't we go?" Luz stared at the tree line. She grew annoyed at the constant attention Ángel paid to Carolina.

"Yes," Ángel wrested himself from Carolina.

"Sail away?" Cheve asked. "Can't track us on water."

"No, Yori boat patrols will trap us. And right now, Yaquis are holding several of our boats as ransom."

"Our boats?" Cheve asked. "You mean Yori boats."

Ángel smiled a mischievous gleam. "I once was a Yaqui and I once was a Torocoyori. Now I'm—" He shrugged his shoulders and raised his empty hands to the air.

"You're *mi amor*. Yori, Yaqui, it doesn't matter." Carolina took his big hands and kissed them. "And we owe thanks to Cheve, Luz and Tomas for bringing us together again."

"My love, as much as I enjoy seeing your golden hair and beautiful legs, you will need to wear your nun robes on this trek. If Yoris stop us, they must believe you're on a holy mission and we're your Yaqui escorts."

Carolina touched her hair and torn skirt. "Not that veil. I'm not a novitiate nun anymore. I'm your woman."

"You're a free woman. But to stay free, we must carry on the deception for a short time longer. Yoris are looking for a white woman with blonde hair and shapely legs. Let's disappoint them. Once we're free, I'll insist you never cover your head. I'll want you to wear your hair in the latest Paris fashion. But you must hide your legs or I'll be forced to carry a gun to protect you from lustful men." Ángel touched her hair and kissed her.

"You must be a nun until we're among the Yaquis. They might not accept your present clothes."

"Where shall I find such a habit?"

"There." Ángel pointed at the boat. "The sails."

"But they're red." Carolina placed her hands on her hips.

"You're of the order of the cardinal, my love."

"Never heard of such an order," Carolina said.

"You'll be the first and the last." Ángel laughed.

Luz, too, found it amusing, giggling with him on the shore of tranquility.

"The tailor shop is open, *mademoiselle*. Allow me to show you the latest Paris styles." Ángel rinsed his knife in the river and walked to the boat.

Within an hour, Carolina stood garbed in a red gown and veil with a golden cross lying on her chest. Pieces of the shrimpers' net served as a rope girdle.

"Hmmm, I like it, *monsieur* tailor. I will pass your name to mother superior. Ángel, is it not?"

"Ángel Falcon, *mon chéri*." He bowed and kissed her hand. "I reserve my skills to one customer."

The Red Nun curtsied.

"Leave now?" Luz asked.

Ángel nodded and threw dirt on the fire.

Cheve helped with the remaining embers and kicked them into the river.

Ángel scraped a tree limb over the fire pit, smoothing the dirt.

"Brother, help me with the boat," Ángel said.

The Falcon brothers pushed the boat from the shore.

Luz watched it drift into the bay." *If only we could be invisible.* As they made their way from the shore, into the trees, Luz worried Ángel didn't intend to stay home. His words about Tomas' fate sounded hollow. She searched the Sea of Cortez to catch sight of him. As the fog enveloped the boat, she heaved a heavy sigh. If they hadn't been separated, if they were back in Potam, she would have walked with him many nights along the banks of the Yaqui River. Despite his wounds, they would have found other ways to walk as husband and wife.

"Luz, stay with us." Cheve said.

"Come home to me, Tomas," she whispered to the sea. The Falcon woman followed her brothers and Red Nun past the trees, through the fog and into the desert.

CHAPTER 16

✳

HORSE RIDE

"She's getting closer."
"Cheve is the prize."
"He's vulnerable with his self-pity."
"Ángel is an unbeliever."
"He believes in Yori ways."
"He should leave. Go far away to gringolandia."
"Avoid Texas. They hang Yori lovers."

By mid-morning, the fog had receded to pockets exposing the Yaqui desert. The rising sun's heat dried Cheve's damp body. With his belly full, grateful for their escape, and surrounded by desert silence, he found it easy to keep up with Ángel's quick pace.

Although Carolina struggled, she and Luz stayed close to them. They had agreed they would try to reach Pótam by nightfall.

There was little talk. Instead, Cheve watched the visible desert flat lands for signs of Yoris or Yaquis. He knew in the wilderness with nowhere to hide, friend or foe would spot them easily.

Lizards and rabbits scattered from their paths in desperate flight. Desert aerial predators wafted high above, occasionally diving and soaring back up with their morning prey squirming in their talons. Bones of small animals littered patches of the desert. Except for dispersed prickly cactus and bushes, the brown landscape stretched in all directions with the similar flat vista. Toward the east rose the Bacatete Mountains, the site of many Yaqui battles, escapes and raids during their many years struggling to stay free.

A break in the fog exposed wild horses grazing on a small hill a few meters to the front. Pointing to them, Cheve whistled softly.

Ángel placed his arm around Cheve's shoulders. "You from the right, I from the left. Don't scare them."

Cheve nodded and ran hard, soon reaching the foot of the fog-covered hill. Under its cover he slowed to a walk, calmed his breathing and approached a sorrel at the top. He saw Ángel emerge from the land cloud talking to a horse near him and suppressed a laugh. His brother lacked wings, harp and halo to complete the heavenly tableau.

Cheve took slow steps, careful not to make any sudden moves as his father had instructed him when catching wild horses.

The sorrel raised its head from the brush, training its big brown eyes on him. The sight of the tawny face, white spot on its forehead, bore a strong resemblance to Jewel. As the familiar grief coursed through his chest, he averted his gaze too late. The image of Jewel lying on the muddy slope with its neck twisted flogged his feelings. He wiped tears from his eyes.

The rustle of horse beats pounded as Ángel chased the mares into the fog. The sorrel looked up once at his companions' flight and resumed its grazing.

Cheve held out his hand. "Gentle horse... let me ride you." He walked a few more steps, stopped, hiked his right leg in a deer pose.

Raising its head, the horse swayed toward Cheve. Large muzzle sniffed the air.

The boy bowed to the ground as if to eat from the same brush. Cheve peered with his peripheral vision. The horse's big, brown glassy eye reflected his face. He rose.

"Gentle horse, let me touch you," he whispered close to its pointy ear. Cheve placed his hand on the animal's neck and stroked. "I'm not going to hurt you. Just want to ride you." The horse gargled a resonant grunt.

He swept his hand over the horse's back. The mare munched on the sparse brush, flicking its tail against its rump. Cheve imagined throwing his leg over, sliding onto the sorrel, just like he did many times with Jewel.

"Good horse… let me mount." With an easy leap he had learned like other Yaqui boys, he landed on the animal's back.

The horse shook, neighed, bucked, kicked and jumped.

The boy leaned forward, grabbing the mount's mane. Its powerful muscles rippled beneath him as it bolted down the hill, into the fog. Riding again on a galloping mare enchanted him.

Cheve tucked his legs in closer, hunched lower along its long neck. He reveled in the wild rush of jerking, pulling gyrations, accelerating speed, touch and smell of horse flesh and hair.

At first, Cheve didn't care he lacked control of the sorrel until it ran farther away, deeper into the gossamer air. In his search for land, he found himself enveloped in whiteness and stillness. He propelled through the air without the balancing sight of passing desert life and colors.

"Slow down, Horse. Back, go back."

The animal ignored his remarks in a torrent of a full gallop.

He could jump; but, the clap of rapid hooves stirred fears of an injury he couldn't afford on this trek. Fleeting bits of the desert floor flew below. He worried the mare would fall as Jewel had fallen. This time the landing would hurt.

"Stop, Horse, stop, I'm lost."

The sorrel bolted faster through the fog.

He recalled the songs of the Maso and the *Sea Ania*, flower world, and leaned forward toward the animal's ear, raised his voice to the melody of the Other Side.

Cheve sang of the *Sea Ania* beauty, of the beasts and insects living there, of the Little People who joyfully played. The rider revised the words to emphasize the grandeur of horses, highlighting their powerful speed and grace. The mount slowed to a walk.

"Good horse, there now. Rest, horse," he said, breathing easier.

"Good horse, there now. Rest, horse," the animal repeated in perfect imitation.

Cheve startled, nearly falling, inhaled sharply, shivered and pulled his hand from the mane. His mouth dropped open in disbelief on what he had just heard.

How could this happen? Was he dreaming?

The mount cackled, bobbed its head and twisted its long neck toward the rider.

He gasped at the sight of a woman's disfigured face—the same one he had seen at the hut in his dream. Cheve leaped from the mare, tumbling away. The fog ebbed creating a halo around boy and beast.

"Don't you want to ride? I promise not to slip nor break my neck." The sorrel swayed its neck from side to side. "Get up, Jewel, get up, boo hoo."

"What are you?" Cheve's voice trembled.

"You know me from the hut, my son. You've come searching for your father, haven't you? I know where he is. I can take you to him. I know him well. Get back on, Cheve. We'll take a short ride to him."

"Witch." Cheve crossed himself.

"I can cure your face. Make you look pretty, like this." The animal's angular face transmuted to an image of Cheve without the familiar facial tears.

He gasped, drew closer to the phantasmagoric face and touched his own. The unblemished Cheve was symmetrical, strong and handsome. When the face beamed, it grew bright and happy. The boy gleefully imitated the toothy smile.

"Want to look like this? No ugliness. Handsomest man to run through the desert. Ever walk with a girl? Time you learned the touch of a woman? You'll grow tired of mounting horses. Jump on. Just a short ride to find your new face."

He watched transfixed at how his handsome self spoke without slur or nasal drone. From different angles, Cheve admired the symetrical mask that he yearned.

"Begin your ride to your father and beauty. Get on."

"Will you take me to Maso?" Cheve pointed in his desired direction. "To the mountain cave?"

"At my fastest speed." The sorrel pounded his front hooves, kicking dirt into the air and leaving prints in the ground.

A sweet-sounding song swelled from a distance. The boy spun to the music. "Come on now, Cheve." The horse insisted. "We must go."

"Someone's coming. Someone who knows the song." He peered into the surrounding fog at the words sung in deer language. "Do you know the deer melody? Maso sings. Maso's coming."

"Let's ride, Cheve," the equine shifter ordered in a low, raspy, woman's voice.

When Cheve twirled, he saw the visage alter to the witch's hard, scarred face. "Don't you want to find your real father? He cursed you with that freakish face. Make him pay." The nag walked around Cheve. Its hooves kicked up a cloud of brown dust, tail swaying high and from side to side. "Come away, son, to beauty, pride and manhood."

"But Maso, he's coming. He's closer." Cheve opened his arms wide in the direction of beating hooves rhythm.

"Damn you, hideous boy, and your bitch Maso!" the horse-witch screamed, galloping into the fog. A woman's wailing grew fainter as the deer's singing grew louder.

When the proud horns and head of the Maso emerged from the fog, Cheve shouted, "My Maso, I've missed you. Don't leave."

The deer's crown swept up and down like a mesquite tree swaying in the wind. Its large, beautiful face glistened: oval, dark eyes gleamed. Brown fur clung to the deer's torso like a woven, sculpted blanket. Maso's coat bunched up at the chest, tapering along a sinewy, sleek torso. Its muscly legs danced effortlessly as if jumping through rope circles.

The large deer stopped in front of Cheve stirring up brown dust, blurring vision. The boy coughed and waved the dirt from his face.

"Little Deer, why were you talking to the witch?" The Maso said in his lilting, deer tongue.

"She promised me a handsome face."

"Witch is full of hate and lies. She stalks your soul. Beware."

"It wasn't a dream." Cheve ran to the Maso and touched its plush hair. "Take me to the *Sea Ania,* to the mountain again. I want to dance and sing. Want to enter the snakemouth. Look." He crouched to all fours to begin the deer dance as he remembered it.

"You're not ready."

"When, then?" Cheve rose.

"Perform brave works for your people. Show you think of others and even risk your life for them. Attune to the stream of feelings flowing around you. Use your *Seataka* and wits to beat the enemy. Then you will find the *Yo Ania.* Take this as an ally." With the shake of its head, Maso broke off an antler into the air. The crooked branch flew, landing at Cheve's feet.

He picked it up and caressed its smooth, hard surface and pointy end. "In the *Sea Ania* will I have a smooth face? Will I lose this?" Cheve placed his hand over his deformity.

"You'll have the beauty you seek. Little People will welcome you into their homes. You'll learn how to sing and dance new songs. Animals of the claw, water, hoof and air will bring you peace."

Cheve's chest swelled with excitement. "How do I begin?"

"Find your people. Go, Little Deer. Help them. Follow your heart. It will lead you to them." The Maso ran a little way and stopped. "Beware of the witch's lies. Go now." The deer plunged into the fog and out of sight.

Cheve ran to the edge of the fog line, holding the antler high. "Thank you, my Maso, for the gift." He shouted and laughed louder than ever in his sixteen years in the Yaqui.

Alone and lost in the whiteness, staring all around, Cheve couldn't remember from which direction he came. As he followed the bewitched horse's tracks, he found the path, his landmarks and bearings through the desert of his youth. Maso was his ally who would lead him to beauty, *Yo Ania*, Little People. Cheve was unafraid of the witch with the protection of the deer. Even if she transformed into a winged-burro, he wouldn't fear her.

He ran faster along the horse tracks. His legs swelled with energized muscle and bone. His feet kicked the desert floor like a jackrabbit chased by a cougar. The familiar speed coursed through his body, feeling no fatigue as he raced past cactus, shrub and animal bones. As he breathed through nose and mouth, his stomach swelled with each inhale and his chest collapsed at exhale—a rhythmic, caterpillar wave. Sweat spilled from his hair onto his face, salty flow seeped into his mouth. Pores flew open to the desert's bright colors and joyful pain.

A small hill loomed. Cheve accelerated with a churn of his arms. At the start of the incline, he kicked harder, faster. He propelled like a hurling arrow, flew up the hill, his heart pounding. At the crest, he saw Ángel, Luz and Carolina standing in the distance where he had left them.

Cheve waved. He tried to shout, but couldn't gulp enough air. He ran down the hill, nearly tripping forward from the momentum of speed and slope. At the foot of the next hill, his velocity accelerated. He shot forward, giddy from the run, tumbling to a stop at the feet of his companions. Lying flat on his back, unable to speak, he panted and smiled.

"Cheve, thank God you're back." Luz said going to him. "Why did you ride away?"

He sat and rubbed his legs. "I didn't—" Cheve couldn't finish his answer.

"The sorrel was wild. Strange it didn't buck you off," Ángel said. "Did you jump off?"

Cheve shook his head. "Maso." He pointed at the distant hill and placed his hands on his head and spread his fingers in the formation of horns.

"The magic deer. You saw the magic deer?" Carolina asked.

Cheve nodded and stood. He yearned for water.

"Are you sure you didn't fall on your head?" Ángel asked.

"It was Maso... He was at the skeleton hut and in Guaymas... He's out there now... Maso's my ally... He gave me this." Cheve held up the antler. "The horse was a witch. She tried to trick me in going with her. Maso saved me."

"Fantastic! A witch and a magic deer," the Red Nun said. "I'd love to see them. What did they look like?"

"Carolina, stop. Not real." Ángel smiled with a shake of his head. "His imagination. Yaqui superstition. A deer shed the antler. Proves nothing."

"I believe in angels—your moniker." Carolina said. "I haven't seen one, but I still believe in them. What's the difference?"

"I don't believe." Ángel said. "There's no God."

They all grew silent.

Cheve had heard of unbelievers, but he never knew anyone so bold. He stared hard at his brother. The desert fog evaporated, exposing him in bright sunlight. A worm surfaced from his eyes, crawling away. Ángel loomed big, strong, handsome, intelligent and lonely. Without God, saints and *Yo Ania*, a Yaqui would lack protection, allies and strength. Like a lizard on a rock, he'd have to run and hide from predators. Even animals had the power of the *Yo Ania*. Ángel lacked armor, shell or scales depending instead on his wits, gun and knife.

"Brother, you can't believe that." Luz broke the silence.

"I believe in myself. If you need God and myths, then you delude yourselves. I won't."

"Do you believe this too?" Luz said to Carolina.

"No. I believe in God and the saints," Carolina said. She went to Ángel. "You promised you wouldn't talk about this." She gripped his arm and grimaced, her sweet face cast into a hard mask. "This is the only difference between us."

"I don't want my brother and sister fooled. You must learn to live by your natural intelligence." Ángel pointed at his head. "Learn to read and think. Another world will open. Don't be a slave to what you've heard and have been taught on the Yaqui."

"It's more important to live by your soul's calling," Luz said.

"Live as you like. But for me, I live by my senses and my woman." He placed his arm around Carolina's waist.

"You've been gone too long, Ángel," Luz said stressing his name.

"If it gives you satisfaction, call me fallen Ángel." He laughed. "I, too, have horns." He placed his hands on his head with his index fingers pointing up. "What do you think of renaming me Lucifer, my love? Does that suit me better?"

Carolina pulled away from him. "Don't joke like that. I believe in the devil, angels and God. I believe they are as real as we are. Your brother said he saw something out there that scared him."

"Then convert this heathen, sweet Sister Carolina of the Order of the Cardinal." Ángel bowed his head.

"Stop mocking us," Carolina said.

"How many believe in their bellies. I'm thirsty and I'd guess so are all of you. Let's keep walking and look for a well or pond." Ángel went to his brother. "You run like a Falcon soars. You can even outrun me. Enough about God, let's find H2O to baptize our throats."

"H2O?" Cheve asked.

"Chemical formula for water." Ángel said. "You can learn the periodic table in school."

Despite Ángel's disbelief and strange language, Cheve scanned the horizon for signs of Maso or witch. Certain of what he saw, heard and touched, he marveled Ángel had not ever witnessed Maso. His brother was strong and brave but he had lived among the Yoris too long, studied too hard and learned a new religion: scientific self-reliance. He was in danger of losing his *Tekia*, his connection to the *Yo Ania*, the enchanted world.

Recalling the magic deer's counsel to prove worthy for the *Yo Ania*, Cheve resolved to act bravely through sacrifice for the Yaqui. Let the Yoris and witches come: Maso was his ally now and gripped the antler.

* * *

Cheve kept glancing at Ángel as they scanned the ground for game. If his father discovered his involvement in the raid on Cajemé's hut, he'd disown him. His disbelief in God would place him in deeper scorn, brand him an outcast, mark him for death.

What mystified him was his insouciant attitude as if Yaqui ways were childlike. Ángel scoffed at their belief in the witch and Maso. His brother was proud of his accomplishments, giving no credit for his prowess to the Falcon family or God. Despite the red habit, Cheve decided Carolina a worthy match for his brother. She could persuade him to leave his godless world, coax him down the path of saints to the house of God. What more ideal mate for a fallen Ángel than a reluctant nun.

The hair on the back of his neck rose. He inhaled sharply. They weren't alone.

The horses' neighs and low male grunts broke his reverie. Five mounted, armed vaqueros formed a circle around them with rifles and pistols trained on them. They must have ridden so fast from behind, none of them had heard them on time to run.

A bandoleer-wearing vaquero with a long scar running along his left cheek to where his left ear should have been rode close to Carolina. He shouted, "Sister, what are you doing here?"

"I'm on my way to the Yaquis to build a mission school." Sister Carolina fixed her cross over her chest. "These good Catholics are escorting me."

The vaquero sniffed the air. "They've got the smell of Yaqui."

"We've been on the road and, yes, we do smell like pilgrims. But no worse than you."

"Sister, we're at war with Yaquis. They'll cut your throat while you sleep. As you can see they whittled on me and took an ear." He swayed his head for a better view of his quarter ear lobe. "I swapped it for the devil's eyes, nose, tongue, fingers and — well, he won't bring any more Yaqui rats into this world. I carry his parts in this pouch. Care to see?" He held up a lumpy bag attached to a string that hung on his chest. He laughed and his comrades pealed their enjoyment.

Carolina held up her cross. "My God and my faith will protect me."

"*Dios* sent us to protect you." He made the sign of the cross. "Come with us to the Hacienda Garcia, two kilometers away. Don Garcia will give you food, water and a place to rest. Savages are running wild over the lands and rivers. Two ship owners reported to *Don* Garcia *Indios* stole several merchant boats. Animals won't respect your veil and cross." The vaquero edged his horse closer to Ángel. "I don't like the looks of this big one. You kill many Yoris?" One-Ear ran his index finger across his throat.

"They don't speak Spanish. I speak Cajita," Carolina said.

"I speak a little Cajita," a flat-nosed, gap-toothed, diminutive vaquero close to Luz said. His voice had a high, tinny tone. "I'm big enough to satisfy you. Give you pesos, *bonita*." He held his hands a foot apart.

She drew back from his leering smile and shook her head.

"Don't talk filthy to her." Carolina said. "She's chaste and devoted to the Virgen Maria."

"Chato, shut up," One Ear said. "Muchachos, search them."

As the men dismounted, Luz's breathing grew more rapid. She grabbed Cheve's arm and pulled away from the vaqueros.

"What are you hiding, pretty one?" Chato said. "I like you playing hard to get. Let me search your clothes, *chica*." He touched her skirt.

Cheve stepped between the little man and his sister. She crossed her arms over her chest.

Chato took out his pistol and pointed it at Cheve's face. In the man's small, pudgy fingers, the gun looked too big.

"She your woman, Yaqui? Don't want to share? Want to fight for her?" The other vaqueros laughed. "*Comprendes?* I have a woman, too—*nalgas grandes*." The midget vaquero held out his hands to his sides and puffed his cheeks. "When I get on her and she starts bucking, I have to hold on with both hands or I'll fly off. She looks more my size. Let's swap *viejas*."

Cheve's arm muscles tightened, his body shook and his breathing quickened. "Don't provoke him, Cheve," Luz said in Cajita. "He'll shoot."

"He won't touch you."

"I like pretty Yaqui girls. You, boy, are ugly." Chato distorted his lips and cocked his head. "I'll kill you to get her."

"Chato *chango*." Cheve grimaced, contorted his twisted face even more and squatted to the man's eye level. He hopped around grunting simian shrieks.

The vaqueros laughed.

"I think you found your twin, *chango*." One-ear slapped his leg, unable to hold his guffaws.

"You want to die, Yaqui? You want to die?" Chato brandished the gun. The diminutive man jumped from side to side as if trying to get the best angle for a shot. He hopped like a manic marionette ready to tip over from the weight of the gun.

"This one's clean," a red-haired, bushy-bearded vaquero said standing next to Ángel.

"We're on a holy mission, I tell you, "Carolina said. "Haven't there been enough killing, raping and suffering to satisfy you?" Carolina asked. "Don't you men have any decency? Did your mothers not teach you to respect women?"

One Ear's expression shifted from a droll to somber cast. He opened his mouth to answer, his lips quivered, but words refused to jump out. The others sat tight-lipped, avoiding eye contact with Carolina.

"On your horses, *muchachos*. To the hacienda with them," One Ear said. "Chato, give Sister your pony."

"What? Not Flying Dragon!" The small vaquero rattled a stream of curses.

"Thank you, *señor*, but I prefer to walk. Allow Chato to ride his dragon." Carolina raised her eyebrow and rolled her eyes. "I promised *La Virgen* I would walk all the way to the Yaquis as a sign of my devotion to her."

"*Hay Chihuahua!* Walk then, Red Sister, with your Yaqui pets."

"Be brave, Luz, Carolina." Cheve whispered in Cajita. "Ángel and I will protect you. Right, my brother," Ángel nodded.

"Don't bray that donkey tongue. *Cristiano* only." One Ear pointed to the top of the hill. "Now walk."

Chato stuck out his tongue and wiggled it at Luz. He winked, blowing a kiss to her.

Cheve grabbed his crotch and held up his hand to the Flying Dragon rider. He opened his thumb and index finger about a half inch and increased the spread to about three inches. He strained to open his fingers farther, his hand trembling.

Despite their effort to suppress their amusement, Ángel and the vaqueros erupted in laughter. Chato howled and cursed, flailing his arms in the air as if priming to fly away. Luz and Carolina joined the chorus punctuated by Chato's high-pitched allusions to anatomical size, mothers, mice and dogs.

CHAPTER 17

KIKO ORGU

Stray cows scattered at the approach of the party. One Ear stopped, stood up in his saddle, hand to brow, eyes squinted.

Luz and the others strained to see what attracted the vaquero's attention. A faint, cloudy ribbon tinged in black curled from the ground. More cattle and horses wandered toward them. Her nose wrinkled at the piqued, smoky odor.

"Yaquis! The dogs raid the hacienda." One Ear pointed at the smoke.

"What about them?" Chato asked.

"Bring them in. Shoot them if any trouble. Ride, *muchachos*."

"As ordered." The small man pulled out his pistol and trotted Fire Dragon behind the travelers. "I shoot to kill. Give me trouble *Indios, por favor*."

"Don't provoke him. Caution," Ángel said in Cajita.

"No talking. Run," Chato screamed.

Luz saw him shaking in anger, his face skewed in rage.

"No one look at me. Anyone falling, I shoot. Run!"

"Dragon ass," Luz muttered, kicked dirt with the others and bolted forward.

Carolina lagged with her long skirt restricting her strides. Ángel ran alongside her, urging her on. Cheve led the pack in an easy lope.

Luz reached him and whispered, "Not so fast. Carolina." He nodded and slowed his pace.

More smoke spirals rose from multiple fires raging about the hacienda grounds. The acrid smells of burning wood and corn stalks filled Luz's nostrils. Horsemen chased one another across fields in haphazard directions, shooting and cursing. Puffs of smoke, delayed bangs from gunfire poured from the main hacienda building. Hapless horsemen slumped forward and fell. The only semblance of order was the men and boys who formed bucket brigades at the burning huts. Others beat flames with blankets or threw dirt on burning stalks.

Luz jumped at a nearby crack of gunfire. A vaquero shot a man who lay on his back. By the fallen man's feathers and clothes, Luz recognized him for a Yaqui. The Yori jumped from his horse, kicked the man, tied a rope to his feet and dragged him away. The body bounced with every jolt, leaving a bloody trail.

"Oh, Jusacamea. Angelina's younger brother," Luz whispered to Cheve as her eyes teared.

"Look away," he said. "Don't let them see you cry. Pretend you don't know him." She averted her gaze, but couldn't block out the sounds of rustling fire, rumbling curses and firing pistols. Her jaw clenched.

Cheve led the run to a large stucco-white, red tile-roofed hacienda where several armed men gathered. Luz stopped next to him panting, sweat pouring from her face, her body tingling with energy.

Bullet holes and arrows pock-marked the hacienda wall and door. Small huts and sheds stood on both sides of the house where men, women, children and barking dogs ran between the huts, chasing chickens and pigs the Yaquis failed to take. By the people's peasant whites, tall heights and dark complexions, Luz took them for Yaqui hacienda field workers.

A bald man, waving a riding whip, wearing brown, leather pants, stomped, cursed, and barked orders. One Ear stood behind him. Two younger men with rifles stood on either side of Baldy. When a woman and three young girls opened the door and crept out, he shouted, "Get inside. Now." At the crack of his whip, they startled.

The woman nodded and directed the children back into the house. Before they went in, one child carrying a wooden toy rifle aimed at Luz and Cheve, yelped, "Pow! Die, Yaqui dogs!"

The sound of approaching yells and hoof beats swelled. Ángel and Carolina ran to them with the small man close behind, waving his pistol in the air, bellowing curses. Chato entered like a slave master chasing runaways.

Carolina bent over, panted, flushed-faced, hands pressed against her ribs.

"Stop, right there." Chato shouted. "Move and I blow you to hell with the rest of the filthy, thieving Yaquis."

"What are you doing, you red-ass monkey?" One-Ear yelled. "Why did you make the Sister run? She's not Yaqui."

"She's a Yaqui lover," Chato said. "She's ready to give up her sacred muffin to the big one. Look at how she touches him."

"Go help the others." One Ear waved him away.

Chato sneered before swirling his horse into the fray.

One Ear approached the nun. "*Mi jefe*, allow me to introduce Sister Carolina of the Order of the Cardinal. Our patrol found her and these others in the desert. She says she's a missionary to the Yaquis."

"A missionary to the devils?" The *hacendado* burst into laughter. "Has the cardinal drunk too much wine?" He stepped forward. "I know you from somewhere." Baldy poked Ángel in the chest with the crop. "Strong. I'll recall where I saw you."

He stopped in front of Cheve and probed the boy's face with the whip, shifting it from side to side. "I've also seen you before—in my nightmares. Chato's got a brother." The vaqueros laughed. "What have we here?" The hacendado stood in front of Luz. "A desert flower. What do you think, boys? Want to pluck her petals?"

"The Sister said she's chaste," One Ear said.

"We can break her of that habit." The *hacendado* laughed. His men cheered, several raising and waving their hands, volunteering for the assignment.

"*Caballero!*" Carolina shouted.

"A mere joke, Sister." The *hacendado* winked at her. "We respect all women here, Miss Order of the Cardinal. You may stay in the hacienda with my family but the rest will go with the field hands to help with the cleanup."

"I promised this girl's mother her safety," Carolina said. "She can help in cleaning the house and preparing meals."

"Yes, Sister, a good idea." His eyes lit up. "She'll stay in the hacienda. Safer there."

Excited yelling rumbled closer. Yoris dragged a bleeding man before the *hacendado*.

"I wish I could give you a proper welcome. But you see, I have unexpected company I must attend to," Baldy said. "Stand him up."

Two vaqueros forced the Yaqui raider to his feet, holding him by his arms.

Luz winced at the sight of the gaping chest wound as dollops of blood fell to the ground.

The captive forced his head up, staring back at the *hacendado*. "Get off our land, Yori," he said in Cajita.

"What did he say?" the *hacendado* asked.

A Torocoyori standing nearby shouted the translation and added "bastard."

"Bastard?" the *hacendado* hollered. He lashed the prisoner's face. "I'll show you what this bastard can do. Get the rope." He waved at One Ear and struck the wound with the butt of his whip.

The Yaqui howled.

"Bring him." Leading the onlookers of Yoris and Torocoyoris, Baldy walked to the closest tree.

"They're going to hang him." Luz rushed to Ángel and held his hand as if he were the executioner. "He's going to die. Stop them, Brother. Don't let them kill him."

"I can't. If we try, we'll be killed. Don't look, Luz. Carolina." Ángel waved for her to come.

The Red Nun put her arm around Luz, diverting her from the wounded man. Cheve shaded her eyes with his hands, but she brushed them both away.

"No, I must witness. He can't die alone like this," Luz said. "Carolina, your cross."

The nun lifted the chain over her head and handed it to Luz. She raced after the lynch mob. The crowd blocked her vision of the Yaqui prisoner until they lifted him onto a horse. Pushing her away through the gathering, she stood next to the mare. At close range, a jagged bullet hole torn in his bloodstained shirt flared before her. Despite his grimace, he cocked his head at an angle in the all-too-familiar, Yaqui defiant pose.

Since childhood, Yaquis were taught to respect the mysterious beauty of their rivers, desert, mountains, animals and Maso. No man was permitted to defile the *Yo Ania* with claims of ownership. Their passion to shape their lives around their beliefs and customs heightened with Yori incursions. This was Yaqui land and only Yaqui Law mattered in the heart of the man on the horse.

"Your name?" Luz touched his leg. "Your village?"

His gaze transformed to a surprised expression. "Why do you want to know?

"To tell your wife and mother you died bravely, your last words."

His bold gaze transformed to a flash of fear. "Am I going to die now?"

She nodded. "Your soul never dies." Luz held her hand over her chest.

"Kiko Orgu from Tórim. Tell my wife and children . . . in the next life. I embrace them in my heart."

"Christ sits on the horse with you, Kiko Orgu. Ask His forgiveness for your sins." She stretched her arm up, the cross gleaming in the sun. Bending to kiss the silver-haired Jesus, he groaned and sat erect. "I kiss him for you." She brought the cross to her lips.

He smiled weakly, his breathing slowed. "You're pretty."

One Ear threw a rope over the branch hanging above the Yaqui and tied the other end to the tree trunk. He jumped onto the horse and pulled the noose down to fit around the prisoner's neck. After securing it, he jumped down behind the animal.

The *hacendado*, his armed guards and several mounted vaqueros pushed their way to Kiko.

The press of bodies forced Luz back into the crowd.

"Loosen the rope," the *hacendado* ordered.

A vaquero on horseback reached over and opened the noose.

"You Yaquis, I'm fair and treat you well. I pay you what I can and give you plenty to eat. You're like my children. I came here to raise cattle and corn and take care of my family. I didn't deserve this." Baldy swept his whip over the burning fields. "This Yaqui is a wild cougar. Cajemé wants war and sends his *locos* to steal and kill. But I'm merciful. I'll spare this man's life if he renounces Cajemé and asks for my forgiveness. Tell him." He pointed to a Torocoyori.

He repeated the *hacendado's* words in Cajita and added, "Kiko Orgu, this is your last chance to see to your wife and children."

The prisoner sat straight, winced and shouted in Cajita, "Cajemé... my Cajemé lives forever. This is Yaqui land. God gave it to us. Yoris, get off our land." Then in Spanish, he bellowed, "Baldy, kiss my Yaqui ass."

The gathered Yaqui hacienda workers gasped, some laughed. They mumbled, some wept and whispered their approval.

Luz said, "Say a quick prayer, Kiko, before you die."

"Damn Yaquis. Damn all of you to hell. Tighten the noose." As the *hacendado* rushed to the horse's rear, a mounted vaquero tightened the cord until Kiko's neck bent acutely to the side.

"To hell, Yaqui scum." The *hacendado* whipped the horse's rump.

The death horse neighed and bolted across the horizon, rider-less.

Luz tottered from the animal's lurch, but regained her balance. She stood transfixed at the sight of Kiko swinging and twitching.

He gagged, gurgled, his face contorted and his tongue squirmed like a headless snake. His body convulsed for a minute and then relaxed, his head falling forward. He swung like a busted piñata with all the candy disemboweled.

"Death to all Yaqui renegades. Bastard Cajemé is next." The *hacendado* struck the swinging Yaqui with his whip. "He hangs the rest of the day." Baldy and his men broke through the gathered Yaqui witnesses in his rush to the hacienda. Gunshots rang in the corn fields.

Luz stepped forward, looking up at Kiko's death mask. She touched his feet.

"You must leave him." Ángel pulled her away from the suspended corpse.

"His name was Kiko Orgu." Luz wept. "He had a wife, children."

"Live to carry his last words to his wife."

She stared at the swaying body. Chato, standing on the back of his horse, hung a sign in Spanish around the dead man's neck.

Luz read, "Good Yaqui."

CHAPTER 18

✦

CORN MONSTER

Ángel and Cheve joined Yaqui field hands in the fiery cornfields. They threw dirt over the flaming stalks or cut them to prevent the blaze's spread. Smoke wafted around them stinging noses and eyes. Mounted Yoris rode along the corn rows, hunting for wounded Yaqui raiders left behind.

"Kiko died like a true Yaqui." Cheve bowed his head. "Died for the *Yo Ania*. A good death."

"Superstition, Brother, is never a good reason to die." Ángel swept his hand in front of him. "Can you see through this smoke? Can you breathe clearly?"

"No."

"Superstition is all smoke. It clouds the thinking and traps you in the dark. Science, math and logic blow the smoke away and open your eyes and mind to clear-headed paths." Ángel touched Cheve's shoulder. "Come with us, brother, while you can. Leave this fighting and go north to Texas or California. We can bring Luz too. We'll start a new life. You can go to school."

"What about Mother and Father?"

"You think they'd leave the Yaqui?"

"Not sure I want to leave. I still believe in what you call superstition. Even if I did, I'd want to speak with our parents first. They'd think we were killed or rotting in a Yori jail."

"We can sneak out tonight through the corn fields." Ángel pointed toward the west. "By morning, we'll be close to the Yaqui and Pótam. After a quick visit with them, we head out to *gringolandia*. Carolina can teach us good English. We'll speak as well as any gringo *caballero*. We'll buy a farm, raise children and crops. Here—" Ángel shook his head.

"What about Luz and Carolina? They're in the hacienda."

"We'll get them out."

"How?"

"By our wits, by reason — not dancing like a deer fool and praying for a miracle. Use your brains more and your heart less." Ángel tapped Cheve's chest and head.

"Did your brains trick you into falling in love with a Yori? Did your brains fool you to pine for her after she entered the convent? Did your brains dupe you to save us from the soldiers? Brother, it's hard to listen to your brains when your heart aches."

Cheve smiled at Ángel's surprised look.

"Spoken like a Falcon. You've learned some wisdom for so young."

"From the *Yo Ania*, brother."

Ángel winced. "Enough!"

Cheve followed several cows along a row when he tripped and fell to the ground. He heard a moan and found a body lying face down.

"Ángel, wait." Cheve crawled over to the man and turned him over. A gray haired, wrinkled-faced raider with deep-brown skin and a puckered chest wound lay with eyes closed. A pistol lay next to him. Before Cheve could reach it, Ángel swooped down, grabbed the gun and tucked it into his shirt.

"He won't need it," Ángel whispered. "Let's go."

A gunshot exploded a short distance away. Cheve stood. A vaquero pointed his weapon at the ground. He jumped off the horse with a rope, tying the end to his saddle horn.

"Eeeehaahhh," the Yori shouted and galloped through the field with the dead Yaqui in tow.

"Run, my son."

"What?" Cheve said and stepped back from the man who now opened his eyes.

"If they find you, they'll kill you."

Cheve covered the old man with cornstalks.

"I'm dying," the old man rasped.

"Leave him," Ángel yelled.

"We'll be back for you." Cheve placed the last cornhusk over the man's head. Rising, he followed Ángel along the row. A low moan called. The old Yaqui rose to his hands and knees. He groaned as his body uncurled. Panting, he stretched out his arms. Like an unsteady corn monster with maize leaves stuck to his hair, clothes and chest, he stalked forward.

"Ángel, look."

"Walk away, Cheve," Ángel said. "Leave him."

"My son? Where's my son?" The corn blades fluttered as the man shook his hands in front of him.

"Here, Father. I'm here."

"Cheve, what are you doing? Get away from him."

"He's dying, Ángel."

"Let him die."

Instead, Cheve shuffled through the smoke to the tottering, wounded Yaqui. With the old man's mouth agape, amber saliva poured from the corners. The goo complemented his blood-shot, half-opened eyes.

"Is this hell, son?"

"Almost. You're hurt. Lie and rest."

"Can't. Cajemé needs me." The old man swayed. "Yoris coming. My gun... got to light up."

Cheve raced to his side and curled his arm around his waist. "You've been shot, old man. Lie before you fall."

"No, son... not afraid of bullets... never shot... plenty brave."

"Aow." Cheve winced at the hard cuff to the back of his head.

"The vaqueros will find him," Ángel said. "He's going to die. Drop him."

"He's searching for his son."

The old man sagged, his full weight resting on Cheve.

"His son's dead. Dragged his body through the fields. Leave him."

"My son?"

"Yes, Father," Cheve said.

"He's not your father." Ángel shoved Cheve.

The old man touched Cheve's face. Blood smeared the boy's nose and cleft cheek.

"Wounded... brave Yaqui." His knees buckled, dragging Cheve down with him. "Son!" He shouted from the ground.

"Here, Father." He knelt next to him and felt a sharp kick to his buttocks. Looking up, he saw Ángel gesture for him to rise.

"Crazy midget riding this way." Ángel said. "Get up before he spots you with the old fart."

The wounded touched Cheve's face. "Mother... love."

"I will love her."

"Brother... love."

"I love him." He glanced at Ángel.

"Sister... love."

"I love them all."

"Son... love."

"I..."

"Good son." He wheezed and his body quivered.

Cheve slipped the old man's hand off his cheek and placed it over his chest. "Rest, Father."

"Chato! Chato, over here! We found one." Ángel waved his arms. He whistled a high-shriek tune.

Churning through the smoke, the small vaquero on his horse cut a path toward them. Despite his firm grip on the saddle horn, he bounced and slipped in his seat. The empty stirrups flopped like leather pendants against the horse's belly.

"Why did you alert him?"

"To get you away from corn monster."

Cheve scanned the wounded Yaqui's craggy face. His deep-brown, leathery skin, crisscrossed with wrinkles around the eyes and forehead looked like other old Yaqui warriors, survivors of the fighting, disease and hunger of their youth. He wondered if he would still carry the Yaqui fire in his old age. The boy had intended to find "El Feo," the ugly one, the man who raped his mother and gave him the look of shame. But after encounters with Maso, his search steered from finding a disfigured man to seeking the *Sea Ania*: the land of the Surem. The path to the Yaqui mystic lands passed through the valleys of ordeal, over the mountains of compassion. Ángel followed the trail of Yori knowledge, reason and science. But the gringo promise land seemed joyless and lonely.

"Ángel, you've traveled far away from us for too long," Cheve said. "We're Yaquis. Come home."

His brother knitted his brows marring good looks.

"Clean the blood from your face," Ángel said.

Cheve wiped his hand over his cheek which only smeared it further. He cocked his head to his brother. "Yaqui war paint." He stared at Ángel.

His older brother grabbed the boy's shirt, but released at Chato's arrival.

The little man pulled up Flying Dragon, glaring at them. A rush of wind blew a thick cloud of smoke over Chato, causing him to erupt in a paroxysm of coughing. He shook like a hooked fish pulled out of the water. His head jerked forward while he jumped in his saddle as if the horse bucked.

When his pistol fell, Cheve picked it up, slipped it into his shirt and pulled Ángel along. "I have his gun," he whispered.

"What?"

"Run, before he notices." Cheve ducked behind the horse, waving to Ángel to follow. He surged forward as corn leaves slapped his face.

After he broke through to the clearing, he waited for his brother's arrival. A heavy stench stung his nose. A bonfire with Yaquis milling around it lay one hundred meters away. Cheve was drawn to the conflagration.

Several Yaqui men and women on their knees made the sign of the cross, their lips moving in silent prayers. Some kneaded rosary beads. Yori vaqueros, wielding rifles, huddled nearby, smoking or drinking from a bottle passed among them.

At a closer range, Cheve stopped at the sight of a hand reaching out from the tree limbs. As if to confirm his impressions, a Yori rode up dragging a body. He threw the rope to the men who picked up the Yaqui and tossed him onto the fire.

Cheve touched the pistol in his shirt. He could shoot at least two before they returned fire. He started at the firm palm on his shoulder.

"The gun?" Ángel said.

"Here." Cheve touched his waist.

"Keep it hidden."

A horse broke from the corn stalks behind them. Chato dragged the old man's body, trailing leaves, to the pyre. The idle vaqueros hooted and whistled at his arrival. Several bobbed, mimicking the small vaquero's ride.

He motioned to two kneeling Yaquis to pick up the body. The men rose, shook their heads and ran away. "Come back, dogs."

"Quick, this way." Ángel bumped Cheve and led him into the crowd of Yaqui field hands a short distance away.

The boy stared at his "father."

"Yaquis don't like you much, Chato," a vaquero shouted. "We don't like you that much either, but we'll help."

Lifting the limp figure, two Yoris with a strong, steady swing, heaved him on top of the pyre. Sparks and flames sprang up as he hit the wood.

His head and arms hung from the flames. Opened eyes appeared to stare as the rest of his body burned. He started convulsing, his head bobbing up and down, arms and legs kicking as if he swam in a sea of flames. "Aaaaahh!" he yelled.

Cheve peered hard at the pyre. Gooseflesh rose on the boy's neck at the sight of the burning man reaching out from the orange, dancing fire. "What? No!" Cheve ran back to the pyre and felt its heat on his face. "Father." He stretched up to touch the outstretched hand. He winced from the licking flames.

"Blessed Mary Virgin, he's still alive." A Yaqui field worker gestured to the human torch. Others stopped praying, stood and pointed at the top. Some grunted, shook their head and raced toward the human oven. Their grumbling grew as they neared the burning of the Yaqui dead and near-dead.

"Help me, son... I'm in hell," the old man cried.

"Get back." Chato trotted his horse closer to the fire.

Cheve groaned as the flames seared his fingertips. The foul stench of burnt flesh filled his nostrils.

"Get back, ugly boy, or I'll shoot." Chato reached for his empty holster.

"Looks like you lost your sling shot," a vaquero yelled. A gun flew from the Yori bunch, landing at Flying Dragon's front hooves.

"Pick up the gun. Hand it to me," Chato ordered Cheve. "Hurry, fish face."

The boy looked at the pistol and then at his "father" howling and gyrating in a bed of red and yellow flames. Was this why the Maso had led him here? Had he not told his mother he wanted to kill his father?

"Help me die, son. Aahhhha! Send me home." His burning head whipped from side to side as if to douse the fire that ate his flesh.

"Aaaahhhhaaa." The little man mocked the fiery man. "I'll send you home, you ancient goat, to your Yaqui hell."

"Father, forgive me." Cheve picked up the pistol, his eyes blurry from tears. He tossed the fire arm to Chato and shouted. "Go to the other side, my brave father."

From the midst of the flames and smoke, close to the burning face, a deer's visage emerged. It sang a melodic tune as if the fire burned musical notes about the beauty of the Other Side.

"Die, old goat." Chato fired.

The head and fire exploded, spouting blood, bone, brain, yellow and red sparks into the air. The warrior convulsed once then sank into the burning wood.

The vain vaquero held the smoking pistol up, smiling over the onlookers. "*Numero uno* Yaqui killer, muchachos!"

Yoris hooted their approval while Yaquis moaned. As vaqueros ran to the fire to admire the head shot, several grunting field hands ran toward the small man. He trained his pistol on them. Their cheering quelled by Yaqui growls, Yoris whipped out their guns.

The killer perched high on Flying Dragon rose instantly to ring leader of the Yori avengers. "Go back to your huts. Get away from the fire." Chato swept his clenched pistol from side to side. "Push them back, *hombres*. Aim for their *Indio* balls. They fear castration."

The Yaqui mob raised their fists, kicked the dirt and shouted Cajita curses.

The vaqueros erupted in grunts and groans as they exchanged Yori obscenities, their pistols and rifles drawn in a row like a wolf's bared teeth. The air filled with a barrage of bilingual curses. Occasional English profanities of "Sons of bitches" and "Fuck you" marked the presence of Chicanos in the Yori bunch.

"Cheve, the bastards have blood lust. Come away." Ángel dragged his brother back into the gathered Yaquis.

He stared at the shattered remains of the old man he called Father. "Forgive me," he shouted as Ángel escorted him away from the Yori phalanx.

"Let me go. I'll kill the devils." Cheve reached for his gun in his pant waist. "Shoot them in their mice balls. Kill them all." He strained against Ángel's firm embrace.

"Shut up. They'll massacre us." He picked him up off his feet and hauled him through the crowd toward the Yaqui huts.

"Let me go... he killed my father... release me." Cheve's anger surged through his body. "I'll shoot the runt—" He erupted in tears, his body convulsed in frustration. "He killed Father... they burned him." He lost all sense of time and location, tossing in his sea of rage. The tempest roiled his desire to kill the killers. The image of the old man's head exploding rebounded against his skull. The sight of the Maso's face, its singing filled him with an ardor to fight.

When his paroxysm of crying eased, his sobbing and whimpering slowed. He opened his eyes to find himself lying on a dirt floor inside a large, thatched hut filled with crepuscular rays streaming from cracks in the bamboo-slatted walls. Several seated men surrounded him. The rays illuminated their outlines as if they were silhouetted saints.

Cheve lay still on the ground, glad to rest from the running, killing and weeping.

"Calmer?" Ángel asked.

He sat up and reached for the gun at his waist.

"Took it before you had us all shot. You did right to give Chato the gun. Gave the old warrior a quicker end."

Cheve's eyes adjusted to the dim room, watching his brother's features form to his left. Ángel held a bowl and tortilla. A late sob racked the boy's chest. He wiped his eyes with his hands, his nose on his sleeve.

"You're a mountain lion, young one. But Chato would have killed you in a blink if attacked," a tall, lanky man said leaning back against the wall. "Your brother saved you. Some food?" He stepped forward and handed him a bowl.

The smell of the soup and corn tortillas stirred his hunger. Cheve took it, slurped down the corn gruel and ate the tortillas in two bites.

"More." He handed the bowl to the hospitable Yaqui.

He smiled. "Eats like a mountain lion, too."

Ángel nodded. "You own a strong fighting spirit, Brother. But you need to ride it like a bronco. As long as you stay on, you're in control. Fall off and the wild mustang will plant you with your small ass sticking up for anyone to kick. Learn to tame the beast—you become the kicker."

Gathered Yaquis, sitting and standing, grunted their approval of Ángel's advice.

Angry voices outside the hut approached. Several men entered, grumbling and cursing.

"Damn Yoris. Penning us in like chickens." A big, barrel-chested Yaqui stomped the ground with each step. "They herd us into huts."

"Why?" Cheve asked.

"They fear our numbers." Ángel tipped the bowl up to his mouth.

To Cheve, the men in the hut appeared strong and young. Working the fields, eating well off the land fortified their natural prowess.

"But we don't have guns?" The barrel-chested man held up his hand holding an imaginary pistol.

"Wait until dark when we escape. Their bullets will fly blind." Ángel swept his hand at the thatched ceiling.

"You're talking rebellion." Lanky went to the hut door and stuck his head out. He grabbed his ears. "Some doors can hear."

"Before, they thought you children. But with the raid and your show of anger out there, they'll kill some of you to control the survivors."

"How is it you know how they think?" the burly man asked.

"Lived with them in Guaymas."

"Doing what?"

"Eating, sleeping and screwing Yori women."

When Cheve and the others chuckled, he felt guilty laughing so soon after the murder of the old man.

"Now, can we talk as Yaqui warriors?" Ángel set his bowl down.

The men looked around to one another.

"Go on—what are you called?" A one-eyed Yaqui wearing a patch sat next to Cheve, asked.

"Ángel, Ángel Falcon from Pótam."

"I'm his brother, Cheve Falcon."

"Fighting Falcons—your plan?" the burly one asked.

"We'll escape by the ashes of our dead brothers. Listen well." Ángel swept the dirt in front of him with a stick. Yaquis in the shadowy room drew closer to catch lines in dirt exposed by sun rays.

Cheve's spirits soared as his brother explained in cool detachment and low voice his scheme to save them tonight from Yoris. The sight and sound of Maso filled him with hope. He clutched the deer antler.

CHAPTER 19

✵

GUN AND BIBLE

After Luz cleared the plates and utensils, she stood in the kitchen, eating the remains of the meal. Although the day's killing had dampened her appetite, Luz thought it wise to keep up her strength. Baldy lit a cigarette while his wife, son and Carolina sat with him at the dinner table. The *hacendado's* three young daughters played with dolls in front of the lit fireplace radiating a warm glow.

Luz had never seen dolls made of white plaster, the faces painted so colorfully, wearing beautiful dresses, blue eyes and golden hair. Yaqui children played with corn husk dolls stitched together with maguey leaves and straw.

Lanterns illuminated the room, forcing shadows into the corners. The smell of cooked beef, spicy beans and coffee hung in the air. A tri-colored Mexican flag, eagle and serpent coat of arms in the center, hung above the stone fireplace. Hardwood floors and smooth stonewalls were a pleasant change from the hard packed dirt floors and crooked wood-lined walls of Yaqui homes. Their bedrooms impressed Luz with their big, fluffy pillows and thick mattresses covered with embroidered, colored sheets. She could dream sweetly with such beds offering soft comfort. The appeal to Ángel for Yori life grew evident as she recalled Yaqui nights sleeping on ground mats, fighting bugs.

On a table in the corner sat a lit candle inside a cylinder glass with an image of the *Virgen de Guadalupe* drawn on the transparent surface. Along with crosses of various sizes, a scene of the Last Supper hung on the walls. Underneath a painting of a blue-eyed, auburn-haired Jesus surrounded by children, lay a table of rifles and holstered pistols near the door.

The image of Kiko hanging from the tree in the yard by his twisted neck haunted Luz. How the *hacendado* could act sanguine after hanging the young Yaqui astonished her. Hatred plucked out the eyes of his morality like ravens on a carcass.

Baldy raised his cup to Luz.

Careful to avoid spilling the wine, she eased the spout to the urn. Luz avoided his staring red-tinged eyes.

"Did you care for the animal I hanged?" the *hacendado* asked.

"*Si, señor.*" She retreated from him to the kitchen.

"Stop. Come back here."

Luz walked back to the table, her head down.

"Your name?"

"Luz." She looked at Carolina.

"Where did you learn *El Español?*"

"My mother taught me."

"And where did she learn it?"

"Jesuits taught her."

"Luz, are you the light of the Yaquis?" Baldy inflected 'light." "A shining star?"

"My mother said I brighten her life." She lifted her head. "Like a lamp in the darkness."

"You pitied the savage. What was his name, coo-coo, or *caca*? Do you side with Cajemé and his rebels?"

"His name was Kiko Orgu," Luz said with too much emphasis on his name. At the mention of the Yaqui, Luz felt sadness creep over her. She resented his talking of the hanged man. The Yaqui fought the tears swelling and her breath growing shallower.

"*Señor*, Luz is a good Catholic and an innocent girl," Carolina said. "She doesn't get involved in such things. She believes in the Gospels and is an example of the good Yaqui who's loyal to God and the Mexican state."

"Are you loyal to México?"

"I'm faithful to God, Mary and the saints."

His cigarette smoke curled into her face. She coughed and her eyes watered.

"Would you care for wine?" He offered the cup.

Luz shook her head. "I don't drink."

"I'm told the name Cajemé in his native tongue means 'the one who does not stop to drink water.' True?"

"*Sí, Señor.*"

"Do you know this Cajemé?"

"*Sí.* I know him."

"What kind of man is he?"

Luz raised her eyes to the *hacendado.* "Cajemé's passionate about his dream to rid the Yaqui of Yoris. He inspires young men like the man you hanged to fight and die for Yaqui land."

"Enough questions, husband. She's tired from walking all day and serving us. She's innocent and can do us no harm. Let her rest."

"After today, I don't trust any of them. Go, *señorita*-lantern-in-the-darkness." The *hacendado* waved her away with the back of his hand.

Luz returned to the kitchen, set the jug down and moved out of the *hacendado's* sight. She trembled and tried to slow her breathing.

"And what of the others that came with you, Sister? The big one looked like he could fight. The other one has some kind of facial leprosy." He contorted his face.

His three daughters laughed, distorting their faces as well.

"I'll kill him for you, daddy." one of the girls held up a wooden toy rifle. "Pow, pow." She pointed it at Luz.

"You are so brave. One day, I'll take you Yaqui hunting. Play now with your dolls, dear."

"My escorts are loyal Christians," Carolina said. "Tomorrow we plan to take leave of your hospitality and continue on our religious mission to the Yaqui."

The *hacendado* raised the cup, drank and set it down. "No, tomorrow you go with my wife and daughters back to Guaymas."

"What? *Señor*, I bring the word of God to the Yaquis."

"Very holy of you but you don't know the Yaquis as well as my son and I. You look very young. You haven't seen what they can do to a white woman when they catch her alone. I don't want to say more in front of the children." He took another drink.

"I'm willing to take that chance."

"They're beasts, Sister, and ungrateful for what they've been taught by the Jesuits. They kicked the good priests out of the Yaqui. Ignacio, tell her what you know of the *Indios*." The *hacendado* looked at the young man to his right, a curly-haired, male replica of him.

"My son is a Franciscan seminarian in Mexico City." Baldy's wife placed her hand over her son's arm. "Top of his class. He's visiting before he goes back to take his final orders."

"I don't wear the cassock because I want to live these last few days with my parents as their son before I take my Holy Orders. I'm sure you understand."

Carolina nodded.

The seminarian rose and walked to the candle of the Virgin Mary. "We Franciscans are missionaries as you know. I had intentions to go to the Yaqui to teach them the Gospels. But my superiors decided with all of the fighting, it would be wiser if I waited."

Luz regained interest in the discussion, walked from the kitchen and stood at the edge of the room. She thought Ignacio looked too young to be a priest. His smooth skin, fine locks and effeminate voice and mannerism tipped her to the difficulty the Yaquis would have accepting him. Her mother had told of the struggles the Yaquis had with the Jesuits. But she had the impression these priests were as tough as the Yori vaqueros. This altar boy didn't fit the rugged mold.

"In preparation, I had studied the Yaqui folk ways through talks with my father's field hands," he said. "I learned they honored the Virgin Mary. But they also said Mother of God had performed miracles, appeared to them

159

and said to rid or kill us if we didn't leave the Sonoran lands. Some of their leaders claimed to be prophets with a God-ordained mission to kill all Yoris. What a twisted view of God." His voice rose and his hands flicked through the air. "I pray the fighting stops soon. Then I can visit the Yaquis. Your mission is righteous, Sister, but trust my father when he advises you to go to Guaymas with my mother and sisters. The Yaqui are too dangerous for you now." He frowned and like a metronome swayed his index finger back and forth. "You've seen what they're capable of doing. After they're defeated and pacified, we can return." He smiled at Carolina and took his seat. "May I have some wine, please?" The seminarian held up his cup to Luz.

She picked up the pitcher, walked to the young man and filled his cup. Luz resisted the urge to explain to him they were better Catholics than Yoris. The Jesuits were kicked out because they profited off the Yaquis' free labor. They grew tired of the slavery cloaked in service to the Catholic Church and decided they could honor God without the priests' rigid control.

"Another for me." The *hacendado* held up his cup.

"You've had enough, tonight," his wife said.

"Pour it, Yaqui girl," Baldy barked.

Luz did as ordered and went back to the kitchen. "Sister, I've worked too hard to build this hacienda in the middle of this wilderness. I intend to give this place to my children when I die—one of the best gifts I can give them. God gave this land to me. The Yaquis had their chance to do something with it. Instead, they let it go to waste and now steal what they need from us. But we were ready for them. That wild boy I hanged was just an example of what I'll do to all of them if they steal from me."

"Please, Jorge, don't get excited," his wife begged. "You'll scare the children."

They had stopped playing with their dolls and stared with nervous gazes at their father. One held up the toy rifle.

Luz guessed the *hacendado* had scared them before by his drinking and shouting.

Carolina cleared her throat. "Ignacio, I respect your concern for my safety. But like the apostles, priests and nuns have braved dangers in foreign lands. Saint Peter and Saint Paul and many missionaries have lost their lives preaching the word of God. I accept the risks. I've also studied the Yaquis and know they're Christians and believe in Jesus, Mary and the saints. They love their land and resent people coming onto their soil without their approval."

Luz wanted to shout for joy at Carolina's defense of them.

The *hacendado's* laughter filled the room. He stood, waving for Luz to come to him. With his eyes squeezed tight from his peal, he touched his protruding belly. "Oh, it's beginning to hurt," he said between laughs.

"Control yourself, husband. You're treating Sister Carolina rudely. She's serious about her mission, but you make light."

"It's hilarious to think an Indian girl can civilize this wilderness. Look at her." Baldy grabbed Luz's arm and pulled her forward. "Do you think, Sister, this savage can transform the land from shrubs and cactus to a rose garden?" He released Luz who retreated, feeling hot shame on her face.

"Sister, you've heard the parable of the talents?" Ignacio asked.

Carolina nodded.

"The master was most pleased with servants who used their talents instead of burying them," he said. "I know Yaquis have skills. My father taught them how to farm and raise cattle. They learn well and work hard. The *indios* need our help to know the true meaning of God, to lift their lives from the desert dirt to a civilized life. First they must surrender their arms."

"Or we'll take them," the *hacendado* said.

"Did you consider God is pleased with the way they worship Him and their way of life?" Carolina asked. "You think our way of life is the singular one God desires. I don't mean to offend you, but God is not Mexican. Before we came to this land, the natives knew no diseases such as smallpox and measles. We killed millions when we exposed them to our plagues. Have you listened to their beautiful songs or seen their deer dances? Their melodies, words and movements honor the creatures of the desert, especially the deer. They lack envy because no one owns the Yaqui. God gave the land to all of them. Ignacio, I go there to serve and teach religion but also to learn how they've been blessed by God so I, too, may share in His blessing. If I'm killed in this effort, then I die in His glory."

Luz's tears welled. The Red Nun preached as well as her mother, swelling her with pride. Her precious love for Ángel spilled over to the most human of people. She'd selfishly sought to lure Ángel away from Carolina back to the Falcon family. Luz beheld the first budding thoughts surface to convince the Yaqui lover to live with them, to learn more of their beauty.

"You have grand illusions of acting the Joan of Arc to the heathens, but tomorrow you leave with my wife and daughters. I'll not suffer the ridicule of the cardinal because I allowed a zealot nun to consort with devil Yaquis."

"*Señor*, you have no authority over me. You cannot tell me what to do."

"No authority?" The *hacendado* rose, went to a table and picked up a book and a pistol. He held them up high as he walked to the dinner table and held the items over the nun. "Sister Carolina, I believe in the power of God and power of the gun. God gave me this gun to bring peace to this land. I'm as holy a warrior as Cortez was a fighter for the Catholic faith. I will not allow this land to become a heathen wasteland of animal worshipers. My mission is to teach the *indios* obedience to God and to México.

"There's a time for praying," the *hacendado* held up the Bible, "and a time for fighting." He held up the pistol and waved it in front of Luz. "Now is a time for the gun. My men will scout the region for more Yaquis. If we find them—"

The *hacendado's* wife hurried to his side and touched his shoulder. "Calm yourself, husband. You frighten the children." She pointed to the three girls.

Luz saw they had dropped their dolls and toy rifle, whimpering with frightened looks. One sucked a thumb. The other two placed small hands over ears. Their mother went to them, cuddled and consoled them.

"Papa, please lower your voice. You've made your point," Ignacio said. "I'm sure Sister Carolina now understands the seriousness of your intent to civilize the lands. *Por favor*, sit down."

Huffing and grunting, the *hacendado* stood trembling with anger over the nun. Carolina's initial look of dismay changed to defiance: face grew nearly as red as her habit, eyes narrowed to slits and lips pursed.

"Enough," the wife urged holding the three children. "Please sit down and leave Sister Carolina alone."

The *hacendado* lowered the pistol and Bible to the table and went back to his seat.

His bullying disgusted Luz. She feared he voiced the sentiments of most Yoris. At the back door of the hacienda, she gazed into the night. Overhearing the *hacendado* mention an outpost not too far away caught her attention.

"Please, husband. The story scares the children."

"Then take them into the bedroom. Sister needs to know what awaits her."

Luz watched Baldy's wife pick up one of her children.

"I'll help you with them," Sister Carolina said.

"No, stay and hear about my dead brother, Victoriano," the *hacendado* commanded.

"Papa, he found his glory many years ago," Ignacio said. "Sister Carolina will accompany Mother tomorrow to Guaymas. Let's leave it now and get some sleep. We've all had a difficult day."

"I'm not sleepy. This would-be-martyr deserves to know the truth of her beloved Yaquis. You do want to know all about your blessed *indios*, don't you?"

Luz saw Carolina's look of resignation to the inevitable tale. "*Sí.*"

"Papa, can you find forgiveness in your heart?"

"Sinners must first ask for forgiveness. And I've not heard any of these damned bug-eaters shedding tears for their past sins."

"You've drunk too much." Baldy's son rose and went to help his mother with the children.

Luz drew closer but kept close to the walls, behind the *hacendado*.

"You're good at farting and praying. Too bad you can't fight."

Ignacio stopped, swirled, his lips tightened, body tensed, and took a deep breath. "Your hatred for the Yaquis has made you cruel. Release the anger, Papa. It leads you to sin."

Baldy didn't look up at his son and waved his words away like swatting flies.

Instead, the *hacendado* turned his gaze across the table to Carolina.

The young priest shook his head, and went into the bedroom.

"Victoriano and I came to this wilderness many years ago to make our living. We were both young and full of fire and *chile. Sí*, we wanted to make money, but we also wanted to raise our families, to cultivate this land. He helped me build the hacienda but grew tired of the work. He decided to open a trading post among the savages. I warned him he risked his life out there by himself. He ignored me, set up the post ten kilometers to the south."

Luz realized he spoke about the abandoned hut where she found the two skeletons. An ominous feeling about the bones came over her. She recalled Cheve's strange attachment to them and stepped closer to the *hacendado*.

"He married an ugly Yaqui girl. Big open wound on her face. You could see inside her mouth. I had tried to convince him to marry a pretty Mexican woman. He said this girl was bewitching. Ha! He didn't know how true his words were.

Sister, do you know about *la brujería*, witchcraft?"

Carolina shifted in her seat with a puzzled look. "Witchcraft? I've heard talk about it, superstitious stories. Some believe in it."

"You don't?"

"I believe flesh-and-blood Satans walk the land."

Luz saw the lanterns and candle lights flicker. Shadows chased one another around the room. A chill wrapped her. A mischievous wind must have snuck down the chimney.

"I didn't believe in *la brujeria* until I met her — Floratina. Her voice was raspy but enchanting, her walk alluring revealing strong thighs, and except for her face, her slim waist and heavy breasts gave her a rough beauty hard to resist. Her Indian eyes were like owls, wide and penetrating. This may embarrass you but men are attracted to such female charms. My brother dressed her up, taught her Spanish and dancing. He'd play the guitar and the two would sing and dance into the night. She loved roses. So he planted a rose garden next to their house. Despite their differences, my brother was captivated by her."

The *hacendado* paused, rubbed the back of his neck and cleared his throat.

"Our work kept us apart, so it wasn't unusual for me not to see him for months. But when a year had passed I grew worried. The animals were raiding again the haciendas. I rode to the hut with several men. What remained of him lay on his bed. The trading post was in shambles.

"We found Floratina, bare-footed, hair disheveled, dress torn, squatting on the ground by a mesquite eating raw field rats. Through the clothes tatters, her bulging belly stuck out. When I asked her what had happened, she screamed and shouted '*Chingado* Yaquis.' I guessed Yaqui raiders had killed my brother. She pulled out clumps of her hair and ripped her clothes off, wailed and ran naked into the desert. We went after her but never found her.

"I brought back my brother's remains and buried him. Two months later I found his grave opened and his bones gone." The *hacendado* lit another cigarette, sucked on it and blew out a puff of swirling smoke. The tobacco haze wafted between the desert boss and Yaqui servant. She drew back as if in fear of its miasmic smell.

"My *indio* help tell me they hear Floratina some nights, crying for a lost child. They think she came back, dug up and stole my brother's bones."

Why do you think she's a witch?" Carolina asked.

"Because I saw her again one morning a year ago. I was riding alone on horseback from Guaymas through a fog when my horse reared. I caught a glimpse of her through the mist and saw that horrible scar. She growled and ran as fast as a mountain lion. I swear I saw her running on all fours. My men found the remains of a deer, gutted and torn to pieces."

"Still doesn't make her a witch." Carolina said. "She sounds mad."

"Sister, my men buried Floratina's bones three years ago. They found her body at the abandoned trading post, lying in her rose garden and buried her there. Floratina preys on deer and travelers and seeks vengeance for Victoriano's death. She's cursed the Yaquis and any who stand by them. I pray for her success." The *hacendado* laughed. "*La bruja* is my ally. Long live her haunting."

Luz's thoughts swam in a whirlpool of images. She recalled her mother's insistence they not go, the skeletons at the abandoned post and Cheve's desire to keep the bones. A knot called Floratina tied them together. An urgency to run to the Yaqui, to escape the grip of the angry *hacendado* and the vengeful witch seized her. Cigarette smoke and fireplace fumes made her gag. The children wept. The *hacendado's* droning voice about the evils of the Yaquis sparked a headache. She walked to the back door.

Stepping out into the open air, she recoiled at the stench. She walked a little way and saw a bonfire in the short distance with silhouettes of men moving around the blaze. Faint voices and laughter drifted to her.

A strong hand clamped over her mouth, startling her.

"Shhh, Luz. Quiet," the familiar voice said. The hand released its grip from her mouth.

She spun around. "Ángel, what are you doing?"

"Escaping. Where's Carolina?"

"Inside. The *hacendado* wants to send her back to Guaymas tomorrow."

"Never."

Luz heard his footsteps go to the hacienda's backdoor. "Where are you going?"

"I need to see her—make sure she's safe."

"He'll see you." She heard the door creak open and saw a flash of light slice the darkness.

His breathing quickened as if stoking tears.

She put her hand on his shoulder and felt his muscles quiver, defying his ever-confident façade.

He closed the door, drew back away and whimpered. "I won't lose her again. I'll kill him if he hurts her."

Luz held his clenched, rough hands. "Use your wits, Brother. Save your fists and get us out alive."

"When you see the fire on the hill." He pointed to the distant direction. "Get Carolina and wait here for me. I'll come for you. Remember the escape signal is two dead mesquite trees burning on that hill. You can't see them now but you will when the fire starts. Get ready."

Luz covered her nose and mouth and stared at the distant flames. "That stench. What are they burning?"

"Yaquis. They may start burning more of us by tomorrow or even tonight. They're drinking and angry. Yoris get mean with tequila. Their thinking dulls, movement slows. Easier for us to kill and escape. They treat us like frightened children. Tonight, we'll see who's the snot-nosed."

Cold metal pressed into Luz's hand. She drew it back. "What's this?"

"Chato's gun. It's loaded with six shots. Use it, Luz. If they discover our escape, they'll kill you and Carolina. Yoris hate Yaquis outsmarting them. Take it."

She opened her fist and grabbed the handle with one hand and the barrel with the other. The pistol weighed heavier than expected.

"Never shot a man."

"Pull the hammer back, aim and squeeze the trigger. Aim for the chest. Simple. When the fighting starts, Yoris will kill anyone they catch—women and children."

She saw his shadow spin, his footsteps treading across the ground.

"Ángel, in all this running from danger, we've not…"

She heard his steps stop.

"We've not what?"

She opened her arms wide.

His strong arms encircled her, holding her close. A peace settled, caught in the warmth of fraternal love, nestled in childhood memories and sealed with the strength of the Falcon blood bond.

"Be brave, Sister. Remember, when the trees burn, be here waiting with Carolina." He broke from her.

"Cheve?" She heard his footsteps running away.

"He'll be with me," he said in a harsh whisper. "Use the gun." His voice trailed off. Tense silence swallowed his rapid plodding into the night.

A shiver replaced the warmth, skeletal firelight appeared ominous, and her confidence quaked. A full moon silhouetted the dancers before the pyre, gyrating like devil's disciples. Without mercy of clouds, Yaquis would make easy targets for Yori marksmen. She hoped they were as drunk as Ángel assumed. A prayer sprang to her lips but fell limp at a wail close by. Pressing back to the wall of the hacienda, she stared into the darkness.

"Who's there?" she asked in Spanish.

Distant laughs, songs and the *hacendado's* bawdy voice nearly drowned the moans. Yaqui huts showed no lights. She listened closer for a signal from them. When none came, she went to the back door, but stopped with her hand on the knob at a faint cry.

"Are you hurt?" she said in Cajita. Gooseflesh erupted on her arms, rising to her neck in several rows. The cold metal of the knob reminded her of the pistol and brought it up. In astonishment, she realized she was about to enter the hacienda with a loaded gun.

In his present foul mood, the *hacendado* was capable of shooting her on the spot and explaining to his wife, son and Carolina the lesson of never allowing Yaquis in the house bearing a weapon. She slipped the six-shooter under her blouse. It slid down to her waist and to the side.

Although her keen hearing brought her luck, she still wondered who or what cried: perhaps a stray tom in search of a mate or on the scent of a field rat. Full moon nights seemed to make the yearnings of God's creatures more desperate.

She turned the doorknob, stepping into the warmth of the room.

The *hacendado* droned about his desire to bring modern ranching to the Yaqui desert. His face looked skewed.

Luz stepped to the side of the room.

By her sagging eyes and droopy lips, Carolina appeared to wither at the *hacendado's* slurred speech. The guns appeared untouched on the table except for the pistol the *hacendado* had waved in front of her.

Grabbing a broom leaning against the wall, Luz swept toward the couple. Sweet smell of spilled wine filled her nose. A few sweeps closer and she spied the red-bound Bible with the gold Gothic letters lying next to the *hacendado's* right hand. A big, silver pistol with a pearl handle lay on top of God's holy words.

"Would you like more wine, *señor*?" Luz asked.

"What?" the *hacendado* said, twisting to her.

Carolina shook her head.

"You spilled the wine." Luz pointed.

"What about you, Sister? Do they allow you to have some? Mother Superior Holiness isn't here and I won't tell." He laughed, slapping the table.

Luz brought a jug of wine and poured it into Baldy's cup.

"Pour a glass for her," the *hacendado* ordered.

"No, *señor*, thank you, but I don't drink," Carolina said.

"Just one, a small one. My wife and son don't drink. I don't indulge in front of the men or Yaquis. But I like your spunk. Come now. Show your appreciation for our hospitality. Take a sip." He switched to Luz. "Yaqui girl, didn't I tell you to pour it?"

Luz retrieved a glass, set it before Carolina and filled it half way.

The Red Nun glared.

"Leave us, girl." The *hacendado* waved Luz away.

She retreated to the back of the hacienda, leaned against the wall into the shadow.

The *hacendado* swigged the glass, pushed the Bible and pistol aside. He leaned forward, smiling.

"Do you ever get lonely in the convent?" he said in a soft voice.

"No, *señor*. I live with fifty nuns."

"I mean do you ever miss what your mother and father had — intimacy?"

"Please don't trouble yourself with my feelings of loneliness. But, I am exhausted from the day's travel from Guaymas." Carolina rose. "If you could please show Luz and me where we'll be sleeping, we'll make our evening prayers and take rest."

"Not until you drink the wine." Baldy lifted the glass from the table, offering it to Carolina. "It's inhospitable to not drink with the host."

Luz placed her hands to her face. She regretted putting Carolina to the test. The drink needed to dull his senses even more.

The reluctant nun reached for the glass.

He grabbed her wrist before she touched the wine. "You're very pretty for a nun. I can see your blonde hair." He pulled her to him. "Show me how much you appreciate your host."

"*Señor*, let go of me. Your wife and children. Your son the priest. They're in the next room. Please release me."

Luz touched her belly for the outline of the pistol. She reached into her blouse and drew the gun out. It shook in her hands, hot and heavy, as she pointed it at the man raging with lust.

He embraced Carolina, kissed her cheeks and groped her body. The more she pushed and shook, the stronger he clutched, drawing her closer to him.

As the gun trembled in her hands, Luz feared she would shoot Carolina accidently. Her breathing quickened, perspiration showered her face. The salty sweat stung her eyes. She wiped her hand over them.

"*Señor* Garcia, please leave me alone," Carolina cried.

Luz cocked the hammer. Her finger slipped over the trigger. She jerked the gun from side to side tracking the couple's struggle. A clear shot at Baldy seemed elusive. She feared the bullet passing through him, into Carolina. Grabbing the pistol by the barrel, she thought she would hit him on the head instead.

A hard knocking beat at the door.

"*Jefe... Jefe*," the voice shouted.

The bedroom doors opened. The *hacendado's* wife and son rushed out.

"Husband, what are you doing?"

"Papa, she's a nun. Let her go."

"*Señor*. The Yaquis... the Yaquis."

Luz hid the pistol behind her skirt, relieved by the wife's and son's sudden appearances. Her body quivered.

"She's a woman, I'm a man. More than I can say for the two of you." Baldy pushed Carolina away. "Shut up, Chato. I'm coming." When he opened the door, bright light from distant flames showered the room.

"They're escaping, *señor*. Yaquis running away. Just like you said they would." Chato pointed back to the fire. He jumped and shook as if the flames where searing his buttocks.

"*Chingado* Yaquis," the *hacendado* roared. "I treat them well and this is how they repay me."

Luz followed the Mother and seminarian to the door. Two mesquite trees at the top of a nearby hill burned. She backed away, grabbing Carolina's hand.

"Come," Luz whispered in Cajita. "We've must go now."

Carolina's habit was awry, exposing blonde hair, left sleeve torn, shoulder flesh. The Red Nun looked stunned.

"Chato, stay here with them. I need your horse. *Chingado* Yaquis planned to leave me without saying *adiós*. I'll give them a warm send-off to the devil... every damn one of them." Baldy grabbed his silver pistol from the Bible, lifted a cartridge belt from the table and slung it over his shoulder.

"Let me go with you, *jefe*. I don't want to miss the fun of chasing them." Chato hopped up and down like an excited child waiting for his chance to bust the *piñata*.

"No, *cabrón*." The *hacendado* grabbed the little man's leather vest, lifted him from the ground and shook him. "Stay here and protect my family from crazy Yaquis. If any of them are hurt, I'll throw you into the fire."

"*Si, señor*," Chato said. "As you ordered. I'll stay. Good hunting. Please, take my horse."

"And my men?" The *hacendado* set Chato down.

"Most are in position. Some are at the pyre. Others are on their horses chasing the Yaquis down like fleeing rats. Looks like they're running to the burning mesquites. Must lead to their escape route. There's some more bad news. I'm sorry to say this... Please don't get angry with me."

"Say it."

"Many of the men are drunk. Some can't stand. But I didn't drink. You can smell my breath." Chato blew into the air. "Not a whiff of tequila. I see you've drunk. But you're different, *señor*. You can hold your liquor better than any man I know. Alcohol is like milk to you--"

"Shut up, *pendejo*. Get out of my way." The *hacendado* pushed him aside and staggered to the waiting horse.

The little man wobbled but quickly regained his stand.

Luz shuddered. *The escape has started. Ángel was correct about the Yoris' drinking.* Her courage grew stronger, energizing her desire to flee. She led Carolina to the rear door, stole a quick glance. All attention riveted on the fiery escape.

When they reached the back of the house, Carolina followed Luz outside and closed the door.

"Ángel's coming," Luz whispered and pulled Carolina to the edge of the house.

"How do you know?" Carolina asked.

"I talked with him here. Chato's right: Yaquis are escaping. We must wait here for Ángel and Cheve."

"The *hacendado* was about to attack me in his home." Carolina sobbed. "Man has no shame. He reeked of wine."

Luz hugged her.

"He wouldn't have hurt you."

"Yes, he would have. I saw it in his face. He's the kind of man who lusts for power. If he doesn't get it, he strikes out."

"He wouldn't have hurt you." Luz took out the pistol and touched Carolina's hand with it.

"A gun."

"Ángel gave it to me. To save your honor, I would have killed him." The familiar fear snaked over her body. She couldn't hold back the tears.

"But you didn't." Carolina placed her hand on Luz's shoulder. The two women embraced.

"I'm glad Chato came when he did. He saved me from taking the *hacendado's* life and life-long guilt. Sinful to take a life."

"Hard to accept, but I think God in His infinite mercy would have forgiven you for killing a man who was about to rape or kill."

"You sound like a nun." Luz pulled away. "I'm throwing this away. I don't want to face that choice again." She tossed the gun into the darkness.

"Why did you do that?" Carolina asked. "We might need it. Where's Ángel?"

Small black figures ran and galloped in and out of the light of the undulating flames. From the cacophony of screams, moans, jeers, cows mooing, dogs barking and horses neighing, surrounded in floating embers and smoke, Luz thought they were at the gateway to hell. Satan walked the night in wicked abandon, eating barbecued souls.

"Our Ángel will come soon. Have faith," Luz said. She heard weeping. "Don't cry anymore, Carolina. They might hear you."

The Red Nun muffled her sobs with her hands.

In the near distance, Luz watched wild men chase the desperate Yaquis to the blazing, arboreal freedom gates. She thought of the Jews' exodus from Egypt, the pillar of fire holding back Pharaoh's chariots. But now they had no Moses to dip his staff in a sea long enough for them to escape. Instead, the Yaquis used the desert as their passage to their promised land. Their love for freedom, belief in God would lead them to their homeland of ant milk and bee honey.

She heard a wail. "Carolina, quiet. No crying."

"I'm not."

Luz heard the wail again, closer.

"My husband... they killed my Victoriano," a woman howled in Cajita.

"Who's there?" Luz asked.

"I want my son—they took my son," the raspy voice said.

Luz edged closer to Carolina and grabbed her hand. "Who are you?" She feared she knew the answer.

"We've met."

"Where?"

"At my home in the Yaqui. You and my son, Cheve, visited me and my husband and disturbed our sleep. But you took Cheve away. Give my baby back."

"He's not yours." Luz clenched her fist.

"Do you not see him?" The woman's body illuminated in a red glow, her face jutting forward. When she pulled her long hair to the side, Carolina and Luz gasped and drew back. The familiar gash erupted traveling up from the corner of her left lip, cut across what should have been a left nostril to her cheekbone. The rupture glared green, exposing the red skull underneath. The smell of roses hung heavy about her.

"Go away. God is with me." Luz made the sign of the cross. She heard and smelled the weeping woman approach closer.

"God left the Yaqui long ago," she screeched. "Satan walks among us tonight. His stench is in the air. He's everywhere."

"Floratina — you're the *bruja* Floratina," Luz said.

"My husband called me, '*mi florita*'. He'd play his guitar and I'd dance with his songs floating in the breeze. We'd make love till the morning." She danced, twisting with grace, swaying her skirt. Floratina smiled, closed her eyes, wrapped her arms around herself and hummed to the tune of the imaginary Mexican guitar. She kissed the air and moaned.

Floratina stopped, bowing her head. "But then they killed him." The witch's howl sounded like a goat's bleating. "I want my baby... I want my Cheve." Her face contorted like a red candle dripping green wax.

Fear slapped Luz into alarm. The witch could trap Cheve when he arrived. She pulled Carolina by the hand. "We must go," she whispered.

"But I thought Ángel —" Carolina protested.

"No, the witch will kill them. Come." Luz led her in a quick step from the back of the hacienda.

"How will they find us?"

"They'll track us or die trying." Luz waved to Floratina. "We'll lead you to him. We'll help you find Cheve. He's over here. Come with us." Luz tugged Carolina by the hand, leading her into the checkered-lit, blistering night of fire, flight and freedom.

"Floratina, let's find your baby... your baby."

The witch howled, "My baby... my Cheve."

Tres desesperadas ran into the melee of flames, fears and fury.

CHAPTER 20

✦

BURNING TREE

From his perch on the top rung of the corral, Cheve saw two trees explode to fiery life. Their limbs shimmered in incandescent brilliance from a wind fanning the flames. The blaze combed through the branches as if the mesquites had been roused from their slumber and opened their eyes for the night's fateful work.

The leafy umbrella offered refuge from the darkness to the fleeing Yaquis who raced past the burning limbs, baptized as free men and women of the *Yo Ania*. Some fell in forlorn poses, shot by angry vaqueros, their hands stretching out to the desert. The lucky and swift fled through the searing light, into the darkness beyond. Their life-candles flickered but still aflame.

Ángel whispered from inside the corral. "Cheve, mount, but don't ride away."

The smell of horse manure lay heavy about them.

The Yaqui boy dropped down to the ground and saw the horses' silhouettes. The mares stirred. Cheve thought about mimicking the deer again, but recalled the ride of the mystic sorrel. Instead, he listened for sounds of the Maso, stretched out his arms and stalked a horse's shadow. When one brushed him, he crept to its side and jumped on. The animal startled for a moment. Cheve calmed the animal with gentle hand sweeps along its neck.

"Ángel, I'm on," Cheve whispered. "Let's go."

"*Chingado*, Yaquis!"

Cheve tensed at the angry voice behind him.

In the moon's glow, two men embraced in a death dance against the fence. As their bodies slammed against the corral, they moaned and grunted, their feet churned the ground.

Horses whinnied, shuffling and bumping against one another.

An arm shot up, metal refracted distant fire. The man slashed over and over into his opponent. With each shimmering thrust, the stabbed man whimpered. He crumpled, fell to his knees and dropped face down to the manure-littered dirt.

"*Chingado*, Yori," Ángel said, breathing hard.

Cheve sighed.

"Here, you now have a gun and bullets," Ángel said. "Grab this!"

The young Yaqui took the gun and draped the cartridge belt over his shoulder. "Is he dead?"

Ángel didn't answer but rode to his side. "Have you fired a *pistola*?"

Cheve smelled his brother's blood-stained sweat. "Rabbits and rats."

"These rodents don't move as fast, but they're bigger and shoot back."

Cheve recalled Maso's words to defend his people. He touched the gun handle. The distant flashes and crack of gunfire by Yoris demanded a fierce Yaqui response. Eager to join the fray with Ángel at his side, he'd give the Yoris a send-off to hell.

"We'll first ride by the hacienda and find Carolina and Luz. Then, we head east."

"East? I thought you told the others we'd reunite in the south at the trading post."

"Just to draw off the Yoris from us. If we can't find them, then we go to the trading post."

"Brother, you used them as decoys."

"To increase our chances of making it out."

"What about the people? They trusted us to lead them to the Yaqui. We were going to fight our way out together."

"Keep your voice down." Ángel looked from side to side. "We're outgunned. Do you want to die like that Yori rat? If you're so eager to fight, charge into the flying bullets like a hero and get your face blown off. Half those Yaquis will die tonight. For me, it's simple. Ride to the hacienda, find the women and leave. I take care of my blood first."

Ángel's response stunned Cheve. He followed him to the corral gate. While Ángel opened it, Cheve beheld in the moonlit night a brother who had lost his *Yo Ania*, his love of the Yaquis. Confused by Ángel's deception and motives, he thought of Maso.

He remembered the deer's singing, dancing and magical beauty. With the Maso, he uncovered natural strength and courage to leap forward as a protector of his people. Until Ángel mentioned it, he had forgotten his face. He put his hand to it, feeling the familiar deep skin folds, exposing his teeth and cheek muscles. To his surprise, the shameful feelings had fled. The heaviness around his head and shoulders had lifted, replaced with a vitality he found dancing with the Maso. What if his face were shot off? In the defense of his people, he accepted the loss. If only Ángel could meet the deer, he would accept the beauty of the *Yo Ania* and duty to fight for the Yaqui.

Cheve trotted after Ángel toward the hacienda. To the south, past rows of corn, the desperate howled. Their maddened pursuers bellowed. Gunshots echoed, men yelped, women screamed and dogs barked in a dissonant clamor to freedom's birth.

Up ahead, Cheve saw the dark outline of the hacienda. A shower of light washed the night through the open front door.

"They wait behind the hacienda," Ángel said.

Slowing to a walk, Cheve followed his brother's horse, peering ahead. "Carolina... Luz," he called. No response. "They're not here, Ángel."

"I told Luz to wait with Carolina. Must still be inside. I'll kill the bastard if he's hurt Carolina. Tie your horse to that tree and take out your gun. Do it now."

After tying the reins to the tree, he followed Ángel to the back door.

"Stay close. Shoot when I tell you." Kicking hard, Ángel broke the door open and charged in with *pistola* drawn.

Cheve came up close behind and looked all around at the lamp-lit room. He saw neither Luz nor Carolina. Instead, he found Chato, standing at the open front door, mouth agape.

Ángel pointed his *pistola* at the man's head. "Touch that gun and you die."

Chato stood still with a simpering smile. "Don't shoot. I'm calm, see?" The small man held his hands up and revealed missing and rotting teeth.

Ángel slammed shut the front door.

Cheve remembered the little man's mocking smile, his bullying in the desert. But most of all he recalled how the man had dragged the old Yaqui through the cornfield, shot him in the head on a pile of burning wood. Deer Dancer pressed the muzzle to the man's head.

Chato yelped and cowered.

"Like killing people, don't you?" Cheve said.

"It's a sin to kill," the seminarian yelled from a doorway.

Cheve gazed at him.

Ángel aimed his *pistola*.

"The nun and Yaqui woman?" Ángel asked.

"Gone. I don't know where," Baldy's son said. "They were here with Father a short time ago."

Cheve cuffed Chato's head. "Stop your whimpering."

He slapped his hands over his mouth.

"Cheve, go look."

As ordered, he went to the room where the priest stood. After peering inside and finding no one, he exited and shook his head.

Ángel pointed at another room.

The boy went to the door, opened it and saw the *hacendado's* wife with weeping, frightened children huddled behind her.

"Get back, filthy Yaqui. get back!" The mother's crazed look told she was ready to fight for her children.

Cheve retreated.

179

"Not in there. Chato's right," Cheve said in Cajita. "They snuck out the back, escaped."

"My father will return soon with his men," Ignacio said.

"Damn it. I told her to wait," Ángel growled in Cajita, punching his left fist into the air. "We need to find them. Let's go and bring him."

"Him?" Cheve pointed at the seminarian.

"He'll act the hostage. But first, get Chato's gun."

Cheve slipped his *pistola* into his waist and slipped the little man's gun from the small Yori's holster.

"No, give me the extra gun." Ángel held out his hand.

Cheve realized his mistake too late as the little man made a swift grab for the grip and pulled the weapon out. As soon as the boy pushed Chato's hand away, the gun exploded.

A second gunshot rang from behind, leaving a ringing in Cheve's ears.

A stream of warm blood sprayed across his cheeks. Some splashed into his mouth and the folds of his face, tasting sour and thick. He tripped and fell onto his back. Looking up he saw Ángel run forward.

He shot Chato again and reached down to pick up the gun.

"My God, I'm bleeding," Ignacio said. He slid to the floor cradling his stomach.

"My son. Oh, blessed Mary, not my boy." The woman ran from the room and knelt next to him.

Her other children, their little arms and hands outstretched, ran crying after their mother. Their huge eyes stared in fright at Cheve and Ángel. They clutched their mother's back, grabbed her hair and pressed their faces into her dress.

"Come on," Ángel shouted.

Cheve jumped to his feet. Chato lay on his back with two, jagged holes in his face. He wiped the blood splatter from his own with the back of his hand.

"Let's go." Ángel stepped backward toward the door, his *pistola* aimed at the wounded man and his mother and children.

"Dirty Yaquis. You shot my son."

"She thinks we shot the man—we didn't do it. The little man shot him." He pointed at the body.

The woman howled, "You, it was you."

"No, I didn't do it. It was him." Cheve pantomimed the man shooting the priest.

"Mama, mama, save us from the ugly Yaqui," a girl cried.

Cheve went to the fallen young man and knelt.

"*Hijos de la Chingada.*" The woman spat on his face and slapped him.

He drew back, wiping the saliva from his cheek.

Ignacio cradled a gaping stomach wound. He grimaced and moaned.

"Get out, leave. Your Yaqui whores left the back way. I hope they get shot. I hope my husband finds you and cuts out your hearts."

"You better pray he doesn't hurt those women." Ángel brandished both *pistolas*. "You won't have to worry about birthing more children."

"My husband will hunt you down."

Ángel squatted an arm's length away from her.

"No, Ángel. Let's go."

His brother held up his gun-clenching hand for silence.

"Shooting your son not enough? You hate your husband so much that you want me to kill him for you? When he comes back, do it yourself and blame it on us. Put your children in the room, wait by the door and blast him in the head when he enters. You'll be rid of him as you secretly desire." Ángel laid the gun before her and stared.

The woman's eyes widened and her mouth gaped open. By her silence, she affirmed Ángel's penetration to the subtle truth that caught her unawares.

"You, *madre mía*, are the whore," Ángel stated.

Many men had gazed into his brother's hot, penetrating stare before the darkness sealed. He was death's doorman — no tips required.

The woman burst into tears. Her children wailed louder.

"Carolina," Cheve said from behind. "We need to find her and Luz. They're out there, in the fighting." He worried the woman would take the gun, start shooting at them. "Luz, Carolina?" he shouted.

Ángel gazed at Cheve as if just recognizing him. "Yes. Need to find her." He rose, ran to the door.

Cheve followed, stealing a backward glance. The woman stared at the gun while her daughters wailed and her son moaned. He ran to his horse, untied it and jumped on.

"Why did they leave?" Ángel said, slapping his leg, astride the horse.

The young Yaqui stared at the chaos and maze of the night's riotous escape. "What if Yoris see us?"

"We're on horses. They think only Yoris ride. Their blood lust and tequila will blind them to us. Be ready to shoot when I tell you. You'll have no choice, Brother. They'll not hesitate to kill you." He wiped his brow with the back of his hand. "Draw your *pistola*. Hold it out, ready to shoot. Stay close. Watch for Luz and Carolina." With a dig into his horse's flanks, Ángel trotted into the battle fury.

Cheve did as ordered, comforted by his brother's brutality. He guessed Ángel had killed many men in gunfights. He seemed at ease with the *pistola* as if it had become a natural extension of his hand, an extra thumb and knuckle.

It felt heavy, unwieldy for him. He tried to steady his grip but the gun shook. With a watchful eye on Ángel, he imitated his posture and angle of his arm. He leaned forward, like him, resting his left arm on the horse's neck.

A powerful stench swept over them, forcing Cheve to avert his face as they passed the lynched Kiko Orgu, dangling from the tree limb. In the moonlight, Cheve saw the outline of his young face. He remembered Luz's final words and touched the leg, causing the body to sway.

"Look for the women!" Ángel sounded angry Cheve had bumped the body.

Gazing up at the tree, he recalled Chato's sardonic smile, his grotesque facial wound. Death rushed to the disrespectful and desperate.

This night many Yaqui candles would extinguish in their flight to get past the sentinel trees, into the desert. They would die with outstretched hands in its fiery shade, knowing their last race on this side was for the Yaqui as free men and women. Agonizing screams and wails of the fallen in the darkness just beyond the apron of light resounded their frustration to cross over to the *Yo Ania*.

Cheve passed the bonfire where the old Yaqui raider had died burned alive. Some skeletal, scorched remains of the captured hung from the top as if crawling from their bed of flames. Yoris stoked the fire with the near and newly dead. Sickening metallic stench of roasting flesh filled the air. Vaqueros raced their horses about the hacienda lands, several passing within an arm's length. The smell of tequila and gun smoke left a pungent odor in their wake.

"Don't see them, Ángel. But the killing must stop."

"Can't stop it. Keep searching for Luz and Carolina."

Cheve troubled over Ángel's reluctance to help the other Yaquis escape until he saw two women racing for the burning mesquites.

"Look. Is that them?" Cheve pointed.

"Perhaps."

They were near the top, inside the flames' light, when a Yori rode up from behind. He shot them in the backs.

The delayed pops of the gun floated to him, chased by the woman's distant cries. Cheve watched as they fell writhing, reaching out for one another. The shooter jumped from his horse, drawing a knife. The blade shimmered from the flames.

Cheve knew what was to happen, but at the same time didn't want to believe it. He screamed, "Noooooo!"

His delusion vanished when the blade man grabbed them in quick sequence, one at a time, pulled their heads back and slashed their throats.

"He killed them. He butchered them." Cheve growled like a dog. He lifted the *pistola* with ease, shaking it at the distant vaquero.

"Come on, but don't shoot," Ángel said. He slapped his horse's rump.

Cheve galloped a short distance, then slowed at the sight of the Maso at the top of the hill. The large antler crown swayed, their tips shimmered red in flames. Maso trotted from one tree to another, seemingly untroubled by the heat and fire. Thick brown fur transfigured to a golden hue from the fiery glow. Tilting its large head back, the deer sang, "My people die at the hands of the cruel. Free the Yaquis! Return to your river home. Fight, Yaquis!"

"I will fight, my Maso," Cheve shouted. A hot surge of blood lust pumped through his body. He charged up the hill to the vaquero now stooped over the bodies. He couldn't slow his horse in time, galloped past him to the top of the slope. The Maso was gone. Intense heat from the burning trees sizzled. He dodged the stings of fiery motes, floating underneath the limbs like immolating fire flies. His unfortunate horse whinnied in pain.

The night had transformed to brightness keener than the day. At the outskirts of the umbrella of firelight, he saw men, women and children churning upwards. Their frightened faces expressed the night's drama of flight from mayhem.

"Yaquis, Maso will protect you," he yelled.

They howled when they spotted him.

"Wait, I'm Yaqui," he shouted in Cajita.

But they ran instead, cresting the mount into the desert darkness where gunfire greeted them. Some fell. Survivors ran or limped back down, howling from wounds.

From this vantage point, Cheve saw the lights from the hacienda, the burning Yaqui huts, the bonfire, gun sparks, and quick shadows chasing slow shadows. In a wide perimeter around the hacienda, fire flashes of *pistolas* spewed their guts of lead.

A trap, the Yoris had set a trap. The lucky and the swift would survive the night. Someone had tipped the Yoris to their plans.

Stewed anger, seasoned with years of shame for his face, boiled. *Ángel's wrong. Maso's right, we must fight.* He glared at his older brother training the gun on the vaquero as they talked.

"What?" Cheve's mind reeled from the profane scene. "Kill them all." He aimed his *pistola* at the vaquero. Stooped over the horse's neck, he charged, squeezed a shot that missed the Yori.

"No, Cheve!" Ángel raised his hands.

He rode his horse to the Yori who reached for his gun. Cheve fired. The vaquero grabbed his chest, swayed and fell to his knees. He tried holding himself up by pressing down on the face of the younger, dead woman.

Cheve jumped from his horse and landed next to the Yori who wheezed, spitting up gouts of blood.

"What's possessed you?" Ángel said. "He told me he saw Luz and Carolina race up to the trees earlier. He was going to point out where."

Cheve placed the gun next to the vaquero's head. "Get your filthy hand off her." He fired again.

As his head blew apart, the vaquero fell back.

The young executioner wiped the brain and bone shards from his own face. He panted, his heart raced. The *pistola* warmed his hand. For the first man he killed, no guilt, no sorrow, no sin lashed, but instead satisfaction swelled at the man's frightened look, the sight of skull and tissue flying. The power the gun gave him, to change events to his preference, thrilled him. The future of his people rested on bullets and bravery not on civility and compromise.

Cheve steered his horse to the women's bodies. Their similarity suggested mother and daughter, but not Luz and Carolina. "Did you say they went up the hill?"

"Yes, damn it. You shouldn't have killed him." Ángel mounted his horse.

"Yoris are waiting up there." Cheve jumped off his horse and mounted the dead vaquero's horse. "They've set a trap, have us surrounded. We must fight—not talk our way out of here." Alongside the saddle he found a holstered rifle. He slipped his gun into the pouch around his chest and pulled out the Mauser. Similar to the ones the Yaqui warriors carried, the rifle hefted more lethal than the *pistola*. Then he drew out the Maso antler. He truly was ready for war.

Ángel drew his horse next to Cheve. He grabbed him by the shirt and pulled him close. "You're a killer now, are you? Fighter for the people?"

Cheve drew back. "You can bargain with the devil in words. I barter in bullets." He brandished the rifle. "He sliced those women's throats because they wanted freedom. How do you know he didn't kill Luz and Carolina somewhere else? He would have led you to their bodies. Brother, he deserved to die."

"Eeeeeeiah!" Ángel howled. "You're a Falcon, a Yaqui killer." He released his hold, drew back, smiling and shaking his head. "Tonight, the devil hunts for souls. Let's give him plenty of Yori eggs to fill his basket. You don't need the rifle. *La pistola* is the best weapon for close fighting. Let's see how good a killer you are."

Cheve followed his brother up the hill. At the top, the young warrior pointed to the line of flashes in the near distance.

"They still could have made it past them and are out there," Ángel said. "Or they're still down the hill waiting for the firing to ease."

"Let's surprise the Yoris," Cheve said. "We'll ride along behind them and shoot them in the backs."

"I will. You need to lead the Yaquis up the hill, into the desert."

"I can protect your flank and back. You'll be alone and outnumbered."

"Brother, I was the best assassin in the Yori army. I kill better alone and in the dark. I'll trap the trappers, like the cougar catching the coyote that caught the rabbits. With four or five quick kills, I'll open a big enough hole for the Yaquis to escape. The rest will scatter. Learned this trick fighting the Apaches. Many braves never saw Arizona again."

"How will we know you've done your job?"

"If not finished in ten minutes then it won't matter. Charge up the hill. If you make it to the top, then I've done my job. If not—you'll know I'm dead. You may die as well and we'll discover together if there's a heaven or hell. Clear, Brother?"

"Yes, Ángel."

"Draw your *pistola* and reload."

Cheve did as instructed, elated to prepare for battle under his brother's guidance. Their father would beam with pride if he knew they were defending their sister and family from rapacious Yoris. With time, he thought, Ángel could accept the Maso, bathe in the Yaqui and take his place among the warriors, deer singers, and Falcons.

"Ready, Brother?" Cheve said.

"If one of us gets shot, the other must go on. If we survive, I'll meet you two kilometers north beyond the trees." Ángel pointed at the fiery leaves.

"But I don't know if I can do this, Brother."

"You must. Carolina and Luz are out there. If they're alive and we miss them, they'll go to the hut with the rest. Understand?"

"Yes."

"Brother, shoot at the Yori flashes. Move before they shoot back."

"I will."

"Your hand, Brother."

Cheve edged his horse closer and took Ángel's outstretched hand.

"I regret the raid on Cajemé's house and the rape of his wife. Loreto Molina told me we were going after Cajemé.

When we didn't catch him, the men lost their senses and acted like desert rats. They shamed me. Do our parents know?"

"No, but Luz does. She saw you. We went to Guaymas to work a peace with Yoris and you. I don't understand, Brother. Aren't you Yaqui?"

"Tonight, I am, eh?"

CHAPTER 21

CHARGE THE HILL

Ángel's smile shimmered next to the shiny metallic *pistola* barrel pressed to his cheek.

His eyes gleamed, his nostrils flared, his hair fluttered. By the screams, gunshots, fire, smoke, running, bleeding, he reveled on the night of mayhem. Bangs exploded, men, women and children howled, their horses stirred. Another wave of Yaquis was repulsed from the hill.

He grunted. "Time to free our people. Come, Brother. Tonight the Falcons unsheathe their talons for Yori guts. Let's kill with grace." The Yaqui assassin released Cheve's hand. He charged into the darkness behind the Yori lines, his *pistola* drawn, a killer Ángel swooping in on Egyptian sons.

Cheve rode his horse down the hill at a trot. He slowed to a walk as he approached the base.

"Ten minutes," he whispered to hidden Yaquis. "Ten minutes we charge up the hill." He peered into the shadows. Away from the burning trees, darkness shrouded the people. The closer he approached the plain before the hill, the louder their breathing and whispers sounded.

"I'm Cheve, a Yaqui!" His shouts startled some. Moans and cries from the wounded greeted him in eerie welcome. He pointed to the hill. "Up there is the way out. We're surrounded. They'll close the noose, kill you and your family. We can break through the lines if we rush it together. I'll lead you with this gun and rifle."

The cracks of gunfire exploded from the hilltop followed by cries of alarm and panic, neighs of panicked horses, and the frantic shuffling of feet.

"My brother, Ángel, attacks them now. He opens a path for us. Everyone must come. Carry the wounded and old. Maso is with us."

The gathered people jostled and whispered to one another. "He's right. No other way out," a strong, male voice rang out. "We must rush the hill together."

"Another trap. Only Yoris and Torocoyoris have horses," a frightened voice warned. "Is he a traitor?"

"I'm Cheve Falcon, son of Mateo Falcon. Many of you saw me today. I'm the one with… the scarred face."

"Yes, the ugly one," another invisible voice blurted from the dark.

Cheve winced from the remark.

"But look how brave he acts. He's no traitor," a woman's voice rang. "We have no choice — we must follow him or die."

"I can't leave my wife's and son's bodies here," a man shouted. "They need burial in Yaqui soil."

"Their spirits are free," Cheve said. "They wait for you in the desert to escort you home. Stay here and your body will lie next to theirs. Honor them: live and kill Yoris in their memory. The dead are free."

The night clouds parted and shed moonlight on the hacienda plain. In a specter glow, Cheve saw the grounds crowded with Yaquis, huddled together. Torch-bearing Yoris on horses poured from the hills at the sight. Their yelps, whoops and gunfire lashed over the Yaquis, foretelling their death. Little time remained.

"They're coming for us!" a boy shouted.

Cheve looked up at the long, steep slope before them. He thought ten minutes hadn't yet passed. Ángel needed more time.

"Have any of you seen my sister, Luz Falcon, or the Red Nun, Sister Carolina?" He trotted a little way, asking, "Has anyone seen a nun?"

A woman's raspy voice said, "I saw them killed. Shot in the heads."

Cheve halted his horse. The night grew colder. He shivered at the vaguely familiar voice.

"No — what?" he said.

"They were calling for you: 'Cheve... Cheve.' But you didn't come. After the Yoris had their pleasure, they shot them."

"No!" Cheve shouted, bowed, placing his hands overhead. "No! Luz, dead. My sister, gone." Ángel would never believe him until he saw their bodies. He'd insist on continuing to search for them. But why would the woman lie?

"This way," the woman said. "I know where their bodies lie."

"No, we must wait."

"You would leave your sister's body for the Yoris to defile and burn? What would your mother think of you?"

"Cheve, where are you?" a breathless voice shouted behind him. He recognized the urgent tone.

"Luz, you're alive. This woman said you were killed."

"Get away from her. She's a witch."

"A witch —" He heard a shriek and winced at the sharp pain to his face. He pulled away from the *bruja's* reach.

"Flee, Cheve," Sister Carolina shouted.

He peered at the voices. Luz and Carolina stood waving behind the witch.

The crazed woman howled. "You're my son, Cheve. Come to me, baby... my baby."

Gooseflesh rose on his arms and nape when she stepped into the light, revealing her tortured face. He had seen the face before on the mystical horse in the desert, at the trading post, in his reflection at the Yaqui River.

"You're not my mother," Cheve said pulling his horse back away from her.

"I am," the woman said and screamed a nerve-piercing howl. She sprang for him, hands outstretched.

"Run away, Cheve," Luz said.

"Come to me, my dear son."

"Run. Don't stop," the nun shouted.

The urgency of their voice and the sight of the woman charging stirred him to swirl his horse to the hill.

"I'm not your dear son. To hell with the ten minutes. We'll not die soon." Cheve charged up the hill howling, "We'll not die soon" and looked back at the witch as she ran after him with outstretched arms.

The people roused like awakening bats, flapping their wings and seeing in the dark with their night eyes and sonar senses.

"It's time," a woman yelled. "The boy is leading the charge."

"Follow him," a man shouted. "He's yelling 'we'll not die soon.' Run up the hill." Yaqui mothers scooped up their children. Fathers and young men ran before them as shields. All grunted and encouraged one another to leave the dead behind and to climb.

As soon as Cheve broke over the top of the hill, the dark lands ahead of him stirred. The witch's shrieks of, "my dear son… my dear son," sounded closer. Bullets whistled past and struck the first line of Yaquis cresting the summit. The fallen made little noise as the survivors streamed past them shouting, "We'll not die soon… we'll not die soon."

In his mad charge, Cheve rode past the first line of Yori shooters as they fired or swung their rifles at him. Several groaned and fell, reaching for a star to hold them up.

The fleeing Yaqui glanced at Ángel on his horse, his gun barrel smoking in his hand.

"Cheve, shoot them," his brother shouted.

He shook his head. "No… I can't… I forgot how," he screamed.

He rode on and saw Baldy shouting at his men.

"Kill the rats. Don't let them escape." The *hacendado* fired his gun into the streaming Yaquis.

Cheve heard a distinct howl, looked back and saw the crazed woman leap onto *Don* Garcia. She grabbed his head and plucked it from his shoulders like a cork from a wine bottle. The body tottered as the stump gushed blood and fell in a heap.

La bruja held up the head in the moonlight. "Bad man will not harm you, my son. No one will hurt you. You'll not die soon." She tossed the head into the swarm of Yoris attacking her, shrieked and plowed into them. The vaqueros fired, screamed and scattered as she tore limbs and testicles from any within her reach. With feline speed, she jumped up with a Yori, bit into his leg, gripped the wound and clubbed his comrades. The gutsy died quickly in pieces, the cowardly scattered intact.

Cheve crouched forward on his horse, kicked its flanks and heard the witch's high-shriek lisp battle call, "My dear son… my dear son," as she slaughtered drunk men with guns on a hill.

The desert darkness swallowed him whole.

CHAPTER 22

✵

DEER SLAYERS

Tomas rode out of Guaymas until his horse collapsed in the dark desert from two bullet wounds, one in the rump and another in its left hip. He decided not to shoot his horse in fear of attracting predators or Yoris. Instead, he covered its eyes with cut strips of the horse blanket, and sliced its throat with a swift, deep slash. Sitting a little distance away, he stared at the wilderness while the animal gurgled, gagged and dropped its head to the ground. Careful not to step into the blood, Tomas covered the horse's carcass with rocks and brush, in hopes the ground litter would hide the animal from the night hunters. He knew he deluded himself to think the stench would not attract the clawed scavengers, the *Huya Ania's* desert cleaners.

The Yoris had soon discovered his ruse after escaping from Guaymas with Father Julio. In their pursuit, they fired into the dark, hitting the priest and his horse. The cleric and mare yelped in unison as flying lead ripped through them and zipped past Tomas. He released the reins of the *padre's* horse as hostage and animal tumbled to the ground. The killers couldn't stop hunting him now lest they take blame for the priest's death.

Tomas ran through the dark until growing fatigue forced him to stop. He climbed a tall mesquite, tearing more pieces of the blanket and rigged a make-shift sling between the forks of two branches. Yaquis had learned over the years better to sleep high in tree hammocks to avoid beastly and human night traffic.

He slept fitfully. The stirring sounds of horses woke him, but he couldn't see where or who rode. Afterwards, he heard the growls of a prowling cougar. He feared the cat would hear or smell him and climb to his perch. When no danger pounced, his eyes closed again.

He dreamt of the times he took his son hunting. Fleeting images of them stalking deer, chasing game into the mountains pleased him. Late in the evening, they would carry the prize back to his wife and younger son, wary of hungry lions and coyotes. His first-born proved a good hunter, learning quickly the art of stealth and patience, for the precise time to kill.

His dreams shifted to his training as a *Chapeyeka*, a religious clown, like his father. Images of the Lenten season rose when he would act the role of Christ's enemy. His sons would laugh at his wild pantomime mocking Jesus. His older son would imitate his dog-like postures as he searched for the scent of the Messiah actor.

The visions flitted to the time he and his boy searched in the wilds for wood to carve a new clown mask. He couldn't decide whether to shape it into a caricature of a horse, dog, monkey or human image such as a Yori or gringo.

His son, too young to wear a disguise or to dance in their company, would practice the comical acts with him. He'd follow his arms' and hands' movements in synchronized elegance. After a while, they were twins in style, fluidity and speed—like two eagles soaring and veering with the same strong wind. Clowning came easy to his son. He developed a skilled style as good as his and any other in Pótam. Tomas felt confident that in time his eldest would earn the rank of *Chapeyeka* captain.

His two-year-old son, frightened by masks, enjoyed playing with his ball and cornhusk dolls. The boy resembled more his mother with his whimsical smile and bright eyes. The jingle of ankle bells, Tomas had made for him, chimed through their hut when the boy ran with peals of laughter.

When dream images swam to his wife, tears seeped from under his pressed eyelids. Her laughter, head tilt, walk and scent conjured why he sought her as a mate. When he married, he hadn't realized how much his love would blossom. She wasn't beautiful but her bright smile, jokes and kisses enraptured him. Like other Yaqui women, she was physically and emotionally strong and outran all of them. Their love-making spent him—a remarkable feat for a man who took pride in his stamina. He longed for her sensuous screaming, "Tomas... Tomas" with lusty inflection on the nights when she desired tenderness and more. The next day, her simple nod and smile, in the presence of others, would cause him to blush, grin and look away. She prepared deer and other smaller animals for meals so tasty he had to work harder to lose the weight he had added after their first year of marriage.

Then sweet images crinkled to nightmare reenactments of flames licking his body. His wife's and children's screams rankled as he recalled seeing them rise engulfed in fire from their sleeping mats. He had heard such guttural shrieks in the midst of hand-to-hand fighting with Yoris. To hear his own family's howls terrified him.

The blaze attacked his legs and climbed to his genitals. Scorching liquid pain had seeped into his pores, searing muscle, bone and nerve. "Ahhhhhh!" he howled.

With a start, his arms stretched against the sling, his legs kicked the bark. The echoes of his cries fled into the darkness. Fearing he had signaled his presence to two- and four-legged hunters, he froze. Tomas listened and peered down, careful to make no sound. When nothing rustled, growled, sniffed or slithered, he relaxed.

He accepted Yaqui life was hard and painful, but his heart still ached for his wife and sons. Their loving absence filled him with a yearning to kill Yoris and Torocoyoris. The lethal desire percolated with each passing year without them. The feel of his rough, scaly skin on his stomach, legs and genitals whetted his desire for vengeance. Tomas grappled self-pity as a mortal enemy and refused to drink from the well of depression. Like many Yaqui warriors, he found the heft of guns, knives and arrows some solace to his woes.

When Luz had stood before the assembly, he suspected a woman's love could ease his loneliness. Her courage resembled his wife's self-assured mannerisms, graceful movements, and winning smile. But many Yaqui women walked in that fashion. *Why was he especially attracted to Luz?* She was of the age when she would start looking for a mate. Her long looks, touch, and hugs on their mission exposed her longing for him.

Cheve, and especially Ángel, troubled him. Yaqui Law required he report Ángel's treason to Cajemé. Such news would infuriate her father. Mateo would never forget who reported the deceit. Luz would never forgive him for exposing his brother's love for the golden-haired Yori girl or his treasonous alliance with the Yoris. When forced to choose between Yori girl and Yaqui loyalty, Ángel sided with love for the pretty nun. Stretched out on the branch, he realized he now faced a similar dilemma: win Luz's love or expose her brother.

Damn, Ángel, for forcing him to choose. He struck the closest tree branch and felt the make-shift hammock wobble. He lay still to stop the shaking.

Tomas consoled himself that he had escaped from the Yori capital, snake nest. "Well done, Tomas. Well done," he whispered. He gazed up to the starry sky. His wife and children probably smiled on his cleverness.

He shivered as a cool breeze swept over him. Air-stirred leaves whispered to him, "Sleep, Tomas. We'll stand guard." Above the branches, the immaculate, sparkling sky shimmered and danced. In the desert, the soft sounds of nocturnal animals seeking their prey, a full moon hanging low, a whiff of mesquite wood cooking food allowed his senses to whisk up to the stars. He no longer feared the dangers of the night. Sleep snuck into his hammock and embraced him.

The next morning he woke refreshed. Untying and storing the strips of cloth in his shirt, he climbed down. He gazed at the desert awash with colors from the rising sun. He set out in the brisk air Pótam-bound and estimated a day of walking and running would take him home. With luck, a horse would cross his path.

Since the night predators had retreated to their holes, rabbits, roadrunners, rats and quail scurried from their desert lairs in search of morning meals. They still feared the shadows of the winged slayers that now soared. Like Tomas, they tuned their ears, nose and eyes for rampant raiders.

Tomas trekked for several hours until he saw a well-armed Yori patrol. He flattened to the ground. After the vaqueros passed, he rose, ran about three hours until he found the abandoned trading post where they had stopped two days before on their way to Guaymas. Tired, dirty and hungry, he went to the well, drew water, drank and poured the liquid over his head. The post hut appeared unchanged from their prior visit. Drawing his pistol, he walked into the darkness. Darting shadows scattered. Tomas knelt on one knee and listened to the scurrying. Leaping to his right, he hammered the gun handle down and heard a squeal.

He repeated his hunt until satisfied he had killed ten rats. Lifting them by the tails, he took the black, furry catch outside. Having never developed a taste for rodents as other Yaquis, he sought bigger game. He pierced the neck with a knife and laid a trail of blood starting about thirty meters away to the hut. He planted the rats about forty paces apart. The last one he sat upright onto the bed, its narrow visage staring at the open door.

Climbing to the roof, he tore off parts of the thatched mesquite branches and a large piece of timber used to support the limbs. After descending, he went to the corner of the bedroom, sat and covered himself with branches and its scent. After two hours, the sounds of bones crunching neared. Between the branches he saw his prey's snout poke into the room. It bent low, sniffed, kicked up dust and hesitated. The animal twisted its head from side to side, beady eyes searching the room. Finally, the red raider stole in, following the trail of blood.

Tomas smiled at the full, adult size fox.

Jumping onto the bed, the pointy-eared scavenger bit into the bait and sat.

He erupted from the branches, striking a glancing blow with a club to the fox's head. The stunned scavenger howled, dropped the rat, stumbled from the bed, and tottered.

Tomas pounced again, bashing its head.

The animal fell to the side, legs flailing, jaws biting. Bits of rat meat fell out of its mouth. The fox stopped kicking.

He poked it with the club until satisfied it could no longer bite. Dragging it outside by its bushy tail, he startled a bird of prey feasting on a vermin's remains. It soared into the air with the rat dangling from its talons.

Tomas had to eat the fox soon. Smell of blood would attract bigger animals, possibly a cougar. With his knife, he cut along its underbelly up to the neck. He forced his fingers along the edges of the tear, ripped open the skin and gutted his dinner. Without fire, he ate the heart, liver and leg and back muscles raw. He drew more water from the well and poured it over his body to wash away the scent of the fox. Covering the blood trail with dirt, he threw out the fox's and rats' remains several hundred meters away from the hut and rested in the shade against the wall.

A warm wind swept across the desert carrying a scent of smoke. He stood, studied the western horizon, but saw nothing. *A distant Yori camp had started their day's meal with the grace of a fire.*

Sitting again, he hoped Luz and the others had reached Pótam by now. If they had stayed the course, they would have sailed the Yaqui River to home. They're probably eating with Cajemé now, telling him of their escape. He wondered if they would tell the truth about Ángel and his Yori woman. He had known of Yoris taking Yaqui women as wives or mistresses, but never had he witnessed a Yaqui man walking with a Yori woman. It seemed outrageous. Then, again, Yaqui men were handsomer and braver than Yoris. *Perhaps, he would take a Yori woman.*

"No, never," he said aloud, feeling guilty for betraying his wife and sons with such thoughts. Luz's soft voice echoed in his ear. He smiled recalling her concerns for him. If she would walk with him, he could better endure the hardships of war. He might have more sons and daughters, teach them the ways of the *Chapeyeka,* laugh again. Drawing down his pants, he stared at the scars of blistered skin. His breeding days were petered out. He laughed sardonically and allowed a solitary tear to escape. Perhaps they could adopt a boy and a girl from the many war orphans.

The scent of fire grew stronger, inciting his anxiety. He rose, walked farther into the desert, swirled in all directions and scented the smoke strongest from the west. *Higher, he must get higher to see.* Up the tree, standing guard next to the house, he climbed. A plume of gray smoke about ten kilometers away snaked up. *More fighting.*

Cajemé didn't wait for their return to retaliate for his wife's rape. The desert war would boil as hot as the Sonoran sun. If a Yaqui were caught, the Yoris would torture him to extract information about Cajemé's army's location and strength. Yaquis would do the same with Yori captives: such was the way of desert war. Fox eats rat as man eats fox.

Tomas weighed the risks of making a night or day run with predators lurking throughout his race. Spanish words wafted with the smoke to his sensitive nose and ears. The rapid beat of hooves kicked up a baby tornado hurling toward him. The riders' flying raised the hair on his nape and his scalp tingled. *Deer shit.*

Twenty riders emerged from the dust. Their high-brimmed sombreros, silver buckles, lariats and rifles shook and rattled like castanets striking a discordant tune. They rode around the hut. One of the horses carried a large weapon with a barrel almost as big as a cannon strapped to its back. Many Yaquis had lost limbs and lives rushing into the mouth of big barrels.

Tomas climbed higher until he was near the top, hugging the dark trunk to blend as much as possible with the wood.

The men dismounted, drinking the well water and feeding it to their horses. Several went into the hut, flopping into its shade.

He had to restrain a grunt at the sight of several Torocoyoris squatting among the Yoris. The traitors must have led them here. *I could die here and take some with me.*

His question about leaving during the day or night was decided. Through the hole in the roof, he saw the Yoris smoking and eating. By some of their punctuated words, he figured they jabbered about Cajemé and Yaquis. Otherwise, he didn't understand their Spanish. Harsh tones, stiff hand swipes into the air translated into curses for his people.

They carried repeating Winchester rifles, accurate at long distances. The guns fired quicker than the older carbines the Yaquis carried. They also holstered pistols called Colt, probably bought from Texas gunrunners. Tomas' pistol, taken from a dead Yori several years ago, jammed often and bullets were hard to find.

After about an hour, a short, mustachioed, muscular Yori stood, spit on the ground and barked orders. Jumping up, the men grabbed their weapons, took last gulps from their canteens and followed their *jefe* outside.

The Yori leader kicked several men sleeping with their sombreros drooped over their heads. He pointed to the horse carrying the large gun barrel. A vaquero unpacked the weapon while another unloaded a metal bar and several boxes of ammunition. Others mounted horses.

El jefe led the two dismounted men a short distance from the tree to a small rise overlooking the post. The mound lacked cover except for the scanty shade of a nearby mesquite. Bossy swept his hand in a 180-degree arc in front of them. The two men nodded. After the Yori chief tightened his sombrero's chin strap, mounted his horse, he led the rest into the desert.

Tomas relieved his aching feet with a shift of his footing. If he shot from the tree, he knew he had slim chance of hitting both men before one shot back. Caught in the branches, he'd make an easy target. He had no intentions of becoming a trapped fox. Glaring at the descending sun, he welcomed the darkness. Tomas watched the men convert the metal bar into a three-legged stand on which they mounted the barrel. A vaquero fed a bullet belt into the machine while his *compañero* sat behind the weapon swerving it from side to side.

A deer with a fawn trailing drew the Yoris' attention. The doe stopped, stuck its nose into the air, searching for danger. The fawn halted, looked at its mother and searched around, as well.

Tomas heard a metallic click, click.

The gun burst to angry life. Bullets kicked up dirt, flying to the fawn. The furry animal cried as it hurled back and up into the air, its guts spewing into a purple and red necklace. Mother deer bellowed at the sight, running to the fawn. But another burst from the mad gun sent more bullets screaming, stitching holes across her flank. The deer fell, blood pouring from the wounds, legs kicking.

The Yori gunners howled at their lethal shooting. They ran toward the deer, leaving the gun unattended.

Tomas climbed down and raced to capture the rapid-killing machine. He winced as he forced his numb feet to kick across the desert floor. He lay next to the weapon, touching its warm barrel. Spent, hot shells lay all around him. Kneeling behind the gun, he grabbed the protruding handles and swiveled the barrel from side to side on the tripod.

Two shots startled him. He looked up to see both men with *pistolas* drawn standing over the bodies. Their laughter danced across the plain in mischievous delight. The Yoris grabbed the two deer by their hind legs, dragging the dead animals behind them, and leaving a trail of innards, fur and blood.

Tomas hunched lower and squeezed the trigger spitting shells and bullets quicker than he ever shot before. An electric joy charged his body at the feel of this wicked, gringo gun.

As the first burst of bullets flew over the Yoris' heads, the men dropped the deer and hugged the ground.

Tomas shot again, lowering the angle of the barrel. The bullets peppered the dirt right between the two prostrate men.

They raised their pistol-packing hands, shot back and cursed him in their *El Español*. Bullets sang a hostile tune over Tomas' head.

In their large sombreros, the Yoris made easy targets as he swept his fire over them. Their screams filled him with joy. Lifting the barrel with the bullet belt dangling, he ran forward. Shots had ripped through the dead men's sombreros, blood poured over their faces. He put the big gun down, stripped the pistols from the Yori bodies, strapped on their holsters and took off their bandoleers.

"Pedro, José, I didn't give you permission to kill deer for sport in the Yaqui," Tomas told the lifeless men. He dragged the bodies back to their gun placement and propped them up into sitting positions leaning against one another. He placed their sombreros over their heads to cover their faces. He mounted the gun on the tripod.

Cajemé had taught his army that to defeat the Yori, they had to learn their fighting ways. As a young man, the Yaqui's captain-general had fought alongside Yoris, distinguishing himself in their battles against Mayos and Apaches.

He taught Yaquis the Yori cavalry maneuvers, how to build military fortresses and the lethal power of cannons. But Cajemé had never talked about the rapid firing gun Tomas now held.

He planned a reception for the other Yoris when they arrived. Like Cajemé, he would seek vengeance for the assault on his family. But unlike Cajemé, his wife and children were dead. He had even more reason to kill Yoris than their Yaqui leader. Again he smelled the smoke, this time stronger. The fighting, burning and killing stalked him.

He checked the dead Yoris' Winchesters and pistols to see they were loaded, ran to the well with canteens and filled them. He took the rifle, gun, box of bullets and canteens into the hut.

Untying the horses, he led them one hundred meters, tied them to another mesquite tree. He ran back to the machine gun emplacement and lay next to the dead Yoris. When he noticed the dead men leaning to one side, he straightened their positions.

"Sit up, *amigos*. Poor posture will hurt your spine."

The sky streaked red. Night hunters would soon stir. Sitting in sight of the setting sun, watching the desert vista of scattered trees, rocks and shrubs, sleep ambushed him. He soon dreamed he heard flutes, drums and harps. Rising from the ground, he followed a dancing goat through the desert to a large hole sloping into the ground. The goat danced in a circle, shook its tail and trotted into the hollow. Lured by music and bright lights that flowed from the burrow, Tomas went in. He found himself walking a well-worn, dirt path into the village of the Little People.

They danced with him, took him by the hand, giving him food and drink. The Little People told him he could see his family again if he had a good heart. They knew how they had died, of his desire to avenge their deaths and his burns. To help him, they taught him to run faster and longer, shoot straighter with bows and guns, fight and endure pain tirelessly. They gave him herbs to eat and to stave off hunger and thirst.

The music grew louder. The goat danced even more frenetically. Without a good-bye, the Little People released his hand, retreating deeper into the village. He stood transfixed, watching them leave until a jolt to his buttocks knocked him to the ground. The goat hopped away into bright light as his eyes opened.

In the receding rays of the setting sun, the outline of the trading post loomed. The music faded, replaced by approaching hoof beats, syncopated with Spanish voices.

CHAPTER 23

✶

WARM WELCOME

Tomas reached for the machine gun when the horsemen were about five hundred meters out. From their gallop, they appeared oblivious to his presence. Within two hundred meters, he hunched down behind the gun, peering over the barrel. The gun sights framed two columns of fifteen men.

He smiled at the thought that many of them would die in a few moments.

"*Amigos*, your *hermanos* are coming to join you." Tomas told the dead Yoris on either side of him. "Don't look sad, I'll give them a warm *bienvenido*,"

The men were now within one hundred meters when they began to slow their pace as if to give him a better chance to pick his targets. At thirty meters, the enemy's horses trotted. The machine gun fire drowned his chuckles.

The rat-tat-tat muffled the men's screams as their arms flew into the air and the rest of their bodies catapulted from their saddles. Their sad, scared expressions thrilled Tomas. The shooting lasted about a minute when the gun quit its mechanical cursing. He pulled the trigger, but only heard a click, click, click. With pistol in hand, the ambusher stood and fired at every moving target.

More men fell, others scattered, shouting, "Yaquis!"

When he stopped firing, five men lay still in front of him. Three others squirmed and moaned from their wounds. Their bleeding horses lay scattered around them, some neighing in agony. He picked up the rapid firing gun and pulled the trigger — still didn't shoot.

Throwing it to the ground, he danced as the machine barked bullets. One whistled and clipped his right ear. Calling on his *Chapayeka* moves, he leaped as more bullets struck the ground around him, spitting up dirt.

Yoris called out the names Pánfilo and Enrique. Tomas shifted to the sitting bodies. "Which one of you is Pánfilo?" He sat behind them, picked up the arm of one of the dead men, and waved his hand, shouting, *"Viva Yaqui... viva Yaqui."*

The Yoris shot back. Tomas ducked as the bullets whistled into the dead men. Blood and gore showered over him until little remained of the overly dead vaqueros.

Tomas yelled, *"Olé... olé."*

By the sound of their weapons, he estimated they were fifty meters diagonally to his right. He rose, lifting the gun, its tripod legs hanging like those of a fat infant. His weapon wailed deafening machine gun fire. Another stream of gunfire replied to his bullet barrage, forcing him to drop to the dirt. When the firing eased, he stood with the big gun, his muscles bulging from the strain, and ran to the mesquite tree by the hut. Bullet holes peppered the clay walls.

He looked from behind the tree, lurched and immediately pulled back. Fresh firing slammed into the wall and tree. Running sideways, he blasted the Yoris' position, ran into the hut and sat in a corner. Breathing heavily, sweat pouring over his body, he scanned his body for any wounds. Finding none, he aimed his new friend toward the hut entrance and waited for foe and night to come. He grinned. Tonight he could die showered in Yori blood.

The enemy shouted to one another until one barked orders over the other voices. Uneasy silence settled.

Darkness rolled in like a stumbling drunk. A waning moon shed amber light. A few men moaned and pleaded for help — but no one stirred. After listening for an hour to the lamentations, Tomas stood, went to the hut door and peered out. He relished the power of the rapid firing machines in his hands. Yaquis could kill as many Yoris as their governor dared to send into their lands. His people must trade with the *Norteamericanos* like Yoris to get more of these guns. Their fastest warrior and mighty fighting spirit couldn't dodge the speed of the hummingbird bullets.

Forced to make their gunpowder because of the Yori's arms blockade, some Yaquis resorted to fighting with bows and arrows like their ancestors. Tomas replaced the notion of dying too soon for the urgency to live long enough to show Cajemé the weapon.

The fighting strengthened Tomas, loosening his muscles, quickening his reactions. His earlier sadness had fled with the sight of Yori soldiers falling, screaming. Vengeance, opium to his emotional malaise, left a sweet euphoric glow.

A whistle pierced the air. "We wish to pick up our wounded and dead. Then we'll leave. Don't shoot."

Tomas went back into the hut. The barrel pointed out the door like the head of a snake. The sounds of horses approached and Yoris whispered. He aimed the gun at the source of the moaning. *Would they be so kind if they had the gun? Would they spare the Yaqui wounded?*

"Hell no!" he shouted and ran out the door spraying death. Sparks from his machine gun fire illuminated faces of terrified men reeling and falling.

Lead rained from above. He looked up to find a gun sparking. He swerved and swept the barrel up. A quick burst ripped the sniper. The man fell through the roof, landing hard inside the hut.

"Mercy time, *amigos*." Tomas walked to each wounded Yori lying in front of the hut. He hushed them to eternal silence with bullets destroying their dream gears. He took a water canteen from one and drank, listening to the fading gallop of horses. Shivers from the thrill of killing Yoris tingled his sweaty body.

"For you, my wife and sons." Tomas held up the canteen to the witness stars and drank.

The shadow desert resumed its predatory drama of hunter and hunted. Back at the hut, he dragged out the dead Yori to keep his breathless mates company. Tomas took to the shelter, sat in the corner and cradled the machine gun like a prodigal son. He closed his eyes hoping to revisit the *Sea Ania* and dreams of the Little People. Instead, he saw fearful, shocked faces of the two Yoris he had caught in the open field. Their moans and groans echoing in the night reverberated in his ears. *The way of war: today he killed Yoris and someday Yoris will catch and kill Yaquis on the plains. We're no better than desert stalkers that prey on one another. The beasts of the night: smell of blood will lure them.*

Whispering, feet-shuffling men loomed closer. He gripped the machine gun, praying he hadn't snored. *Yoris desire more bullet soup. Come, Yoris, come and slurp up.*

He rose, went to the bullet box and wove another cartridge strand into the machine gun. He walked out for more deadly work, peered and wondered if he was dreaming. Had the Little People guided his wife and children to him? The closer the crest of the human wave approached, the more distinctly he heard women comforting their young.

"Yaquis," he shouted. Several women screamed. "I'm Yaqui. No live Yoris here. Welcome, my people."

A disheveled, dust-covered man walked forward, stopping within a few feet. "Your village, Yaqui?" the man asked.

"Pótam," Tomas responded. "Where are you coming from?"

"Hacienda *Garcia*. Cajemé and his men attacked today. Two Yaquis who drifted in with a nun stirred a rebellion. We escaped before the *hacendado* and his men killed us all. Many of our people died back there." The man pointed to the desert. "They still hunt us."

"Several ended their prowling here. Skin them for drums. Eat their horses." Tomas gestured with his machine gun to the bodies. "Drink from the well and rest. Just beyond that tree. My people, the well is this way. Rest, brave Yaquis."

As if waiting for the invitation, more men, women and children swarmed around the hut and well. Several moaned or yelped when they found the Yori bodies.

"Cajemé and his warriors caught them," the dust-covered man said. "We can beat them."

Tomas chuckled, deciding not to reveal the desert destroyer. He didn't think they'd believe he was the Yaqui Sansom, wielding a metallic jawbone.

Some men stripped the bodies of their boots, guns and bullets. What food they found in their pockets, they ate or shared with their women and children. Other dragged the bodies into the bushes, away from the women and children, to mutilate their remains in the names of their dead kin. A man took out a long knife, cut into the dead horses' hunches and passed around hunks of meat.

Tomas' loneliness vanished in the presence of his Yaqui brothers and sisters. More trudged in until it appeared over a hundred survivors gathered. Walking among them in search for Carolina and Luz, he heard the nun's Spanish-accented voice talking to Luz. Her veil gone, disheveled hair sprouted in curls, knots and shoots. Her tattered skirt exposed glimpses of pale skin. Luz carried an infant in her arms. As equally unkempt, she appeared like a desert Madonna cradling a dark Baby Jesus. The child cried weakly as its small arms and legs trembled.

Tomas walked to the women. "Yoris can't kill a Yaqui ghost."

Luz looked up in surprise and smiled through tears. "Tomas, you escaped. Thank God. I prayed you would get out alive. Carolina, Tomas is here. Look." Luz drew closer and touched his arm. "Your ear. It's shredded, bleeding."

"Not serious. I can hear your voice. Must have the charm of the *Yo Ania*."

She handed the baby to Carolina and strode into Tomas' open arms. They embraced for a long moment. Their bodies warmed at each other's touch.

"Baby isn't breathing," Carolina said.

Luz broke the embrace, took the infant back into her arms. She rocked the child, calling, "Wake up, dear. Don't sleep now." Placing her ear to the baby's mouth, she touched the child's chest and caressed its cheeks. The limp infant appeared deep in slumber.

"Baby's gone," Carolina cried. "Yoris are barbarians. God help us!" she screamed, her hands stretching up to the night sky.

Luz drew the child close to her chest and rocked. "Oh, baby, sweet baby. You die too soon." As she wept, Tomas placed his arm around her shoulders. "I saw the child's mother shot and fall in the cornfields. Went to her and found the infant lying next to her. Bullets struck the mother's head and the child's small shoulder. Carolina and I took turns carrying the baby. We hoped we could make it in time to Pótam, to a healer."

"Your kindness eased the baby's death—Where's Cheve and Ángel?" he asked.

"Out there. We were separated. A *bruja* stalks Cheve," Luz said. "We couldn't wait for them in that terrible place."

Tomas gazed at the Yaquis feasting on the horses. "Better to bury the baby now—farther out."

CHAPTER 24

DESERT MAGIC

"Cheve, slow down," Ángel shouted. "Yoris gone. Fighting over."

The boy looked back several times and slowed his horse.

"Stop, Cheve. We need to water the horses, eat and sleep." Ángel rode up to his side. His younger brother shivered.

"*Bruja.* Where's the witch?" Cheve gazed into the desert in all directions.

"Witch?"

"I saw her back there. Said I was her son."

"Were you shot? Any wounds?"

"No, I don't think so. Where are we?"

"The desert. We're safe here. Need to find shelter."

"A post out here. Tomas found it." Cheve swept his hand over the right. "In the dark it's hard to find. I first saw the hag and Maso in a dream there—Luz and Carolina. I saw them back there."

"Were they safe?"

"Safe? No one was safe back there. They were alive and told me to flee the *bruja.*" His voice trembled. "Rode up the hill. Witch chased me. Didn't you see her? She was ugly. Tore Baldy's head off."

"You should have brought them out. Brother, how could you leave them?"

"Told you I was chased by a witch who looked like me. Called me her baby. I'm frightened, Brother." He stared into the dark, jerking his head around and about. The desert night grew colder with a slight wind. After the cacophony of guns and screams, Cheve's ears still rang with the clamor of war. The dark chill and echo of terror exacerbated his tremors. The witch's screams, "My baby... my baby," clamored.

211

"Cheve, calm down. There are no witches. A crazy, strong woman mistook you for her son. *Brujas*, saints, devils and even angels come from imaginative minds intent to control yours."

"How do you know this, Brother? What proof? I saw her. She was ugly, vicious."

"Science, Brother, shows us the truth — not faith. There's no God, no *Yo Ania*, no Little People, Maso and all that Yaqui rubbish. Don't make the sign of the cross — break the cross Jesuits strapped on the back of our people to make themselves fat and rich. You're scared like a pup from lightning because of a screaming, wild woman. Many more men and women will go mad with this war."

"Science?"

"Science is a way of knowing the world. It uses facts, reason and logic to see truth. Learn to read and you'll meet the greatest minds of history. In Guaymas, the library was my second home. Carolina opened my heart and books opened my eyes. I was content as a Torocoyori when the prizes were love and truth. And then you came and brought out the Yaqui in me I thought I had given up." Ángel sighed. "I'm disappointed in myself, Brother. I've lost Carolina and my books. I'm the one *embrujado*."

"Ángel, what happens to the men we killed tonight? Do they go to heaven or hell?"

"No such places, Brother. We make our own heaven or hell here on Earth. Have you wondered why you were born with that face?"

Cheve inhaled a quick breath at the suddenness of his brother's question. "Mother said a man called 'El Feo' fathered me."

"Mother would like you to believe fairy tales."

"Fairy tales?"

"Children's stories. But you're not a child any longer, are you? If you wish to know the truth of your face, study science — even if it hurts. If Mother doesn't tell you the truth, I'll do it someday — Lights, see them?" Ángel pointed.

Smells of meat cooking and the hums of distant voices wafted to them.

"We're close to the post," Cheve said. "I'm hungry."

"Reload your pistol. We'll eat or die trying. Watch for Yori patrols. They're hungry, too, but for Yaqui meat. We'll wait here to make sure they don't intend to trap us with our own bellies."

* * *

Cheve flinched when his chin hit his chest, nearly falling from his horse.

"Wake up, Brother," Ángel ordered.

"I'm sleepy. Let's go to the hut or somewhere to rest."

"Wait a little longer."

Cheve straightened up and tilted his head. "Do you hear, Brother?" he whispered.

"I hear people's voices."

"Someone's singing. It's getting stronger, coming from that direction." He pointed toward the left.

The galloping came upon them too quickly to escape the collision. Ángel's horse screamed, falling to the side, shoving against Cheve and his horse. The boy's mare danced trying to catch its balance. He grasped the reins, bent down and shifted his weight against the fall.

Ángel moaned as his mount rose from the ground.

In the moonlight Cheve watched a large deer gore Ángel's horse, lift with its antlers and toss man and mare up. The hapless pair crashed in a heap.

The deer spun to Cheve. The boy's horse whinnied and shimmied. The antlered beast raised its regal head, sang a high tune and danced, swinging its antlers.

"Maso, you've come to save us," Cheve said.

The deer jumped over Ángel and the horse lying atop him. The deer sang a traditional Yaqui poem about the *Huya Ania*. He remembered his mother often chanted the song at night when she was content.

213

"To the other side… to other side," the lyrics repeated. The song's sweetness, the deer's melodic voice exhilarated him with a soothing calmness. He started singing and followed the deer until he heard Ángel's stern voice.

"Help me." He struggled to squirm from underneath his wounded mount.

Cheve leaped from his mare and grabbed the other horse's reins. "Up, up now."

Ángel rose, moaned and rubbed his legs. "Sore, but unbroken. Why were you singing? A crazy deer just rammed my horse and you sing?"

"Maso, Brother. Maso."

"Probably ate some mushrooms and went berserk."

"Didn't you hear the Maso singing 'To Other Side'? It sounded like Mother singing to us."

"Heard nothing. My horse is done. Won't make it." Ángel unbridled the mare, took off the saddle and slapped its rump. "Can't shoot it. Gun blast will draw attention. Bad luck. Coyotes or cougars will take him. We'll ride together the rest of the way to the post before another crazed animal attacks or what… sings?" Ángel strained to mount Cheve's horse. Once in the saddle, he held out his arm to his younger brother and pulled him up.

Gazing into the dark wilderness softened by a starry sea and lunar isle, Cheve searched and listened for any sign of Maso. His slender body warmed to his ally's encounter, deflecting the sting of the cold wind.

Better not to reveal Maso had attacked him because of his denial of the *Yo Ania*. He couldn't hear the singing because of his disbelief. Ángel had adopted a new faith—the religion of science, blinding him to desert magic. *He's a falling Ángel. I can't catch him.*

Cheve sighed.

CHAPTER 25

✸

BASTARD CHILD

Petra's hands grew blacker by the hour from the gunpowder she scooped into the bags intended for their men's guns. Like other Yaqui women, she worked long hours during war to keep husbands, sons and fathers armed, fed and clothed. The cloth veils they wore to avoid inhaling the powder muffled talk. But she was comfortable with the silence. While other women sought relief sharing fears, she found solace praying, working and gardening.

She and Mateo grew alarmed by the escort survivors' report they had engaged Yoris, resulting in several Yaqui deaths. Thinking about Luz and Cheve in hostile lands brought her to quiet tears. Most of the Yaqui women filling powder bags had lost a family member to the never-ending fight. Witnessing their pain at news of death's reach prompted her to pray mourners would never come to her home.

Led by Cajemé, Mateo had joined three hundred men armed with rifles and bows to scout their lands for Yoris, to seize more weapons and to recruit more allies. Their captain-general wasn't yet ready to challenge their enemy in a pitched battle. Anastáscio Cuca, Cajemé's second-in-command, was left in charge of the rest of the warriors to guard the women, children, livestock, cornfields and food supplies from Yori raiders. They were better prepared for surprise attacks since the rape of Cajemé's wife.

Petra distrusted the captain-general's intentions. At first opportunity, he would order raids of the closest haciendas to quench his anger over the assault. His rage would goad him to risk the lives of his men for a few cows, chickens and horses. Cajemé was reckless and a war lover. For now, he offered vision and courage to the Yaquis they could keep their lands as long as they were willing to fight and die. He roused their pride and whetted their hunger for the days when Yaquis ruled the land without Yori incursions. They had fought with neighboring natives, but no tribe ever eradicated an entire enemy people. Since Cajemé's arrival to Pótam and his aggressive, daring attacks on the Yoris, Petra wondered if their enemy would permit any of them to live.

After a day of powder making, the work crews went to the Yaqui River. She wrapped a rebozo closer to her body to ward off the dusk's chill. A few stars hung shyly close to the night's stage before the stellar performance. Like others, she dipped buckets into the waters and poured it over her hands, arms and faces. Despite the cold air, the river's cool water soothed Petra.

The workers dispersed to their homes to eat and rest for the next day's work.

At her hut, Petra prepared a fire in the stone oven lying outside the door, cooking corn, tortillas and cactus. Since her children had grown older and Mateo away attending Cajemé, she found herself often eating alone. She didn't like solitary meals.

Lantern lights squeezed through the interstices of the cane-slatted houses. Like her, the families would eat and fret about the fates of their kin in the desert. They'd talk about the coming war with the Yoris. No, she thought, that was just part of what they discussed. They'd speak about hunting in the mountains for deer or cougars, fishing in the river or the gulf, feeding the horses, tending their gardens. Mothers praised their children on how well-behaved they acted in the presence of their elders, how the girls learned to cook tasty meals and the boys to hunt with bow and rifle. Fathers reminded them about brothers, sisters, grandfathers and grandmothers who would never eat with them again in this world.

At the table, she took a few bites of the corn and tortillas and thought about Cheve and their last talk in the church. She had waited too long to tell him the truth or half-truth. He had grown too quickly, sought too many answers about the past.

Petra sighed. If only they could forget yesterday and live each day as if they had just been born, life's woes would vanish. The Yaqui past was too painful—the future hopeful. But memories followed her like a hungry goat, crying for the milk of atonement and wouldn't stop wailing until the kid received its full measure of penance.

She lost her appetite, went to bed, closed her eyes and reluctantly remembered the rebozo-wrapped woman standing at the door, soaked from the pouring rain. A lightning strike illuminated the woman and a dark boy holding two horses by the reins.

"Where's Mateo?" the woman asked with a lisp.

"Not here," Luz said. "What do you want with him?" He had taken Luz and Ángel on a fishing trip.

"I bring his son." The woman carried a bundle close to her chest. "Visited several Yaqui towns. Told I would find him here. Boy needs his father's care."

Wind-blown rain came down hard, whipping into the carrizo cane hut. Even though the woman and package were getting soaked, Petra didn't want her to enter.

"I carry truth that stings. Yaquis led by Mateo killed my husband, Victoriano. Mateo raped me." She opened her *rebozo*, exposing an infant sucking on her breast. When she pulled the baby from her, the baby yelped, mouth dripping milk. With outstretched arms, she offered the boy to Petra.

She stepped back from the wailing child, but the wet woman entered the hut's light.

"The baby needs a warm, dry place to grow, a father." Lanterns exposed gaps in the infant's face. Looking up, Petra saw similar deformities in the woman's mouth.

The stranger placed the baby on the ground. "He's called Cheve, desert lover." She raced to her horse.

"No, wait. My husband wouldn't rape anyone." Petra rushed to the door, but the woman cackled.

"You're a fool." The ugly visitor and dark boy rode away through the rain.

Petra ran after them. "Come back! He's not mine!"

The woman galloped away into the wet night, kicking mud from rain puddles.

Petra trudged back to the hut soaked from the shower, and stared down at the infant. The baby cried, distorting his face even more. *Would have been better if Cheve had found his glory at birth.* A pang of guilt swept through her. Stooping, she picked up the boy.

"You bring us sorrow." She slapped the baby's face. His arms and legs wiggled rapidly in the air. Blood trickled from his distorted nose as he bellowed a loud cry. Petra shuddered at the fact she had struck the child, and stared at Cheve through wet eyes.

"Is it true? Is Mateo your father?" She pressed a cloth to the infant's face, dabbing the blood away. She went to a corner, sat in a chair and rocked him to sleep. Placing the baby to the ground, she lay next to him, fighting the temptation to roll over him, and end the struggles to come.

Her family wasn't expected for another week. Meanwhile, Petra fed the infant goat milk, cleaned and clothed him. Rain visited for several days, giving her good reason to stay in the hut. But when the showers stopped, Petra strapped the baby to her back and went to the Yaqui River to draw water.

She avoided the womens' stares of amazement. "Have you never seen anyone draw water?" she stormed. "Why do you gawk?"

The women looked away.

On the day Mateo, Ángel and Luz returned, they stared at the child in her arms.

"Where did this baby come from?" Ángel asked.

"Luz, Ángel, go to church. Now." She gestured with her head. "They need help cleaning."

"Whose kid is this?" Mateo asked, after the children left.

"Yours, I'm told."

Her husband frowned, and stepped back. "Mine?" Thoughts raced across his face, twisted, swerved and then stopped at the realization his past sins had caught him.

Disgusted with her unfaithful husband, she shoved the infant at him. Tears welled and her hand went to her mouth.

"I'm so--," he said, head bowed.

"Listen. His name is Cheve. His mother says you raped her. Were you drunk again?"

Mateo walked toward the door. "Yes," he said. When the infant began crying, he rocked the child.

"What's the woman's name?" Petra demanded.

"I don't know." He ran his fingers through his hair.

"Did you not ask before you raped her? How can you not know? Let me help you. She has the same type of disfigurement as the child." Petra took several steps closer to him until an arm's length separated them.

"I never raped a woman."

"Don't lie to me." She slapped his face. The infant howled. "How many other women have you had?"

"Petra. Enough. They meant nothing."

"They? How many? Where?" She pulled his hair.

"I don't want to talk about it." Mateo took several steps back.

"I do," she screamed, thrusting her hands into the air.

The baby flailed his arms and legs, and howled, making an even uglier face.

"Keep your voice down. Don't shout at me."

"If you're man enough to unleash your dong to breed, then be man enough to wag your tongue to tell the truth."

"I will... I meant to for some time." Mateo went to a corner, staring down at Cheve. "Several of us rode to Guaymas for food, tools and guns. After the long ride, we went to cantinas where Yori women would drink with the men. We had them."

"You still drink?" Petra shook her head.

"Yes, but not here, not in front of our children."

"How many did you have?" she demanded.

"How many drinks?"

"No, you drunk." She pantomimed drinking with her right hand. "How many women did you screw?" She thrust her hips.

"What difference does it make?"

"It's important to me to know," she shrieked, upending the table. The bastard howled.

"Many—more than I can remember," Mateo shouted over the crying.

Petra moaned as fresh tears spilled.

"Do you recall raping a woman with a disfigurement like his?" She pointed at Cheve.

"Many of the women had scars or missing teeth, but none had such a face."

"This child's mother said she was married to a man named Victoriano. Do you recall the name?"

Mateo shrugged his shoulders and shook his head.

"Could it be you were so drunk you don't remember what she looked like?"

"Possibly." Mateo lifted his head, walking closer to Petra. "I'm sorry. I can take him into the desert. He'll not bother us ever."

Petra stared at the baby. Cheve would find much cruelty and ridicule because of his face, and his bastard birth. Disgust and concern for this defenseless child tore at her. Then again, if Mateo took the child to the desert, the problem of explaining the infant to Luz and Ángel would disappear.

"Get rid of your son." She motioned with a sweeping hand. "I don't want to raise another woman's bastard child. Get him out of my sight."

"Poor boy is cursed." Mateo left the hut with the pitiful bundle.

Petra fell to the ground weeping at the ugly truth. She had heard wives in hushed tones talk about temptations their men faced. Yaqui women went to mining camps and Yori cities looking for work only to prostitute to survive. Young Yaqui men faced many hardships or risked death. Some sought respite between the legs of other women, Yori or Yaqui.

She struggled to accept her husband's repeated deceit with several whores. *How many children had he fathered throughout Sonora?* The anger swelled in her. She could never trust him again. *Leave for another village, and damn the talk of others.* But she knew the shame would follow her wherever she went. Better to confront the humiliation on familiar grounds. Why disrupt the lives of her own children for a bastard and his selfish father?

The gentle voices of Luz and Ángel crept nearer.

She wiped her eyes with the back of her hand and found her children and Mateo with the infant in his arms at the doorway. Before she could get up, Luz and Ángel ran to her and grabbed her hands.

"Mother, look at our new baby," Luz said.

She rose, allowing them to pull her to Mateo and the infant.

"Father said a woman gave us the baby to keep," Luz said. "But there's something wrong with his face. Father said God breathed too hard into the baby's lungs when He delivered him to his mother. And now she doesn't want him. She thinks he's too ugly. I don't."

Cheve sucked his thumb with his eyes wide open. For a moment the baby took it out and smiled broadly at Petra, expanding his facial gap.

"I can't get rid of the child if he's mine." Mateo said in a broken voice. "Despite what you may now think of me, I'm not heartless. I must atone for my sins to my family."

"Why are you crying, Father?" Ángel asked.

Petra strode to Mateo, lifted her head as if to kiss him and whispered into his ear, "You selfish pig. You don't deserve us." Lifting the child into her arms, she went to the reed mat on the floor, sat and rocked the infant.

"Ángel, Luz, go get the goat. The baby needs milk. Cheve is now your brother," Petra said.

The children ran to the yard.

"I don't like his name," Mateo said. "I wish to change it."

"No. I don't care what you like. I want you to remember how he got the name, dear, desert lover."

Mateo sat next to her. "I'm sorry," he said weeping.

Over the years, Petra's children grew and treated one another as loving siblings. Luz and Ángel defended Cheve from taunts, the older brother fighting Yaqui boys of all sizes. He grew to become one of the toughest brawlers in the Yaqui.

Petra never again questioned Mateo about the disfigured, raped woman. Through talks with other Yaqui women whose husbands had been unfaithful, she learned that some Yaqui men had a weakness of the flesh and mescal they could never overcome. Petra's love and respect for her husband waned. She transmuted uxorial to maternal love for her children.

When an itinerant nun or priest came through, they might stop by the hut to leave a toy, shirt or even pesos. They said an anonymous friend sent the gifts for Cheve. Petra refused them, telling the Sonoran magi to stop bringing presents. But the offerings continued to come throughout the years, left at the Falcon's hut door.

The Yaquis of Pótam accepted the deformed child in respect and fear of Mateo, lest they stir controversy about his personal faults or sins. Or worst yet, their wives' suspicions might stir unwelcomed inquires. Besides, continuous stockpiling of arms, food, and fighting Yoris took most of their time and energy.

Petra opened her eyes to the hut's darkness, drove away the painful reverie, rose from the mat, went to the door and saw fewer lanterns shined than earlier. With some of the men away again, she prayed there were no raids, drunkenness, or feuding. She feared since the killings would begin anew, Yoris would escalate their brutality. From taking prisoners and raping women to torturing and killing, they would terrorize the survivors.

After going inside the hut, she lifted from the corner a rifle Mateo had given her. She insisted he teach her how to shoot. Although she had never fired at another person, she would shoot to kill any Yori or Torocoyori who attacked their village or tried to violate another woman.

Cradling the rifle, she walked to the rape site of Cajemé's wife. If she had had this rifle, she would have opened fire regardless of the danger. Sordid images and sounds swam to the surface of her mind forcing her to grimace and moan. For Yaquis to ravage and kidnap other Yaquis filled her with disgust, a yearning to kill. Yoris were barbaric, money-craving, lazy Catholics. But they had the excuses of stupidity and pride. How sinful for Torocoyoris to kill or terrorize their Yaqui brothers and sisters and inflect Yori cruelty. Such sins deserved the eternal fires of hell.

A knot in her stomach swelled, as she remembered Cheve's angry words in the church. Ángel was a Torocoyori… her eldest had ridden with the raiders when they raped Cajemé's wife before her children. Could she condemn her own son to hell? She screamed, pointed the rifle into the air and fired several rounds.

"Ángel, why?"

Dogs barked, lanterns blazed, doors burst open and people rushed out.

"Yoris!" voices shouted. Yaquis brandishing guns and knives ran toward Petra.

"No Yoris," Petra shouted and brought the rifle down.

But they didn't stop their charge.

The fastest man reached Petra first. "Where are they?" he asked, wielding a machete. Others half dressed, breathing hard, aimed their rifles, pistols, and bows into the darkness at the phantom foes, and gathered around her.

"No Yoris," she said again in a quieter tone.

As soon as Anastácio Cuca arrived, the crowd of men allowed him to pass. The lanterns illuminated the area around her like daylight. She winced at the brilliance, looking down embarrassed at the disturbance her shooting had elicited.

Anastácio escorted her a little distance from the others.

"No Yoris," she said.

"Shots. I heard shots," Anastácio said.

"I accidentally fired."

"Why do you have the rifle?"

"Safety."

He drew closer. "Have you heard from Luz or Cheve?"

She shook her head.

He sighed, facing the gathered people. "I'm proud of the way you came so fast. It shows you're ready to fight should the Yoris raid again." Anastácio raised his gun. "Petra and I had planned this test to see how long it would take you to respond to the firing. Well done, my people. You have proven ready for an assault. Now go back to your families and rest. Stay on guard."

Despite Anastácio's protective words, Petra heard some men grumble, and curse for disturbing their rest, time with their wives, dinner and games. One joked the running helped loosen his bowels. He could now complete his nocturnal relief. Another laughed he needed to run even faster back to make sure his rotund wife didn't eat his portion of their meal. An older man stumbled around, and asked if anyone had mescal to quench his thirst from the scramble. The banter soon faded, leaving shifty shadows in their wake.

"I know you're alone, Petra. Your family's away on missions on behalf of the Yaqui." Anastácio said. "I admire the Falcons. Allow me to escort you back to your hut."

His kind words comforted her. She had attended his sister's wedding, and had been at her side when she died giving birth to a second child. Petra had sung, and given the eulogy at her funeral Mass. She mourned with the family the customary nine days.

Anastácio had ensured all the mourners had enough to eat and drink during their dancing, singing, and praying. His popularity among the Yaquis had captured Cajemé's attention. By appointing him second-in-command, the captain-general secured steadfast support from the man's friends, and followers.

When they arrived at the hut, he asked, "Are you worried for your children and husband?"

Her chest swelled with the sadness, said nothing in fear of crying, and nodded.

"I, too, worry for them. But if we surrendered our lands to the Yoris, we would become like all the other *Indios* without homes, without hunting, without our language, customs, and beliefs. Our children would forget the deer dance, *pascolas*, *matachines*. They would no longer believe in the Little People and the *Yo Ania*. Instead, they'd work for railroad men, *hacendados* and miners. Our valley would dissolve into a wasteland and lose its sacredness. Our Yaqui River would clog with Yori merchants eager to sell us tequila and whiskey to weaken our spirits and minds. The Yori would deport us to Yucatan as slaves for their haciendas."

"I love the Yaqui Valley as much as anyone." Petra said. "But I love my children more."

Anastáscio picked up some dirt at Petra's feet. He poured the soil into her empty hand. "We are the land. Many Yaqui sons and daughters spilled their blood for this dirt. I've heard you preach the saints walked the Yaqui to define our borders. They anointed the Yaqui as sacred."

"I'm a loyal Yaqui. I know too well our history of struggle, and sacrifice for the land." Petra opened her hand and spilled the dirt to the ground. She rubbed her palms. "But not a grain of this or any land is worth a drop of my family's blood."

Anastácio nodded. "You're a good mother. I'm sorry I upset you. My wife will stay with you tonight."

"No, thank you. I wish to be alone."

Anastácio stepped back away and smiled. "Rest, Petra. We have much work."

After he left, she lay on the reed mat, the rifle next to her.

They could flee from the Yaqui Valley, even from México to the north. Many Yaquis now lived in the *norteamericano* state called Arizona. She had heard of a city in Texas called Fort Worth that welcomed hard-working people. If Mateo chose not to go with her and the children, he could easily find another woman. Let him continue to prove his machismo to Cajemé.

She hummed a lullaby she used to sing to Luz, Ángel and Cheve when putting them to bed. The song told of a land where children chased one another in fields of flowers, swam rivers, and danced with deer. The lyrics told of the games they'd play with the Little People and how much their parents loved them. The melody carried her away to sleep amidst echoes of her children's soft snoring.

CHAPTER 26

✦

BLANCO AND NEGRO

The pounding of horses' hooves stirred Petra from her bed. "Mateo," she called but quickly remembered he was gone. She aimed the rifle at the door. The horses' heavy breathing lumbered closer to her hut.

"Petra, come out," a woman's familiar lisp called.

"Oh, no," Petra moaned. "Go away."

"As a mother, you have duties to perform. For the sake of your husband and children's lives and souls, come out."

Petra's heartbeats quickened. Her breathing grew shallow as she stepped outside into the cool night. She gasped at the sight of two large horses, one black, the other white, their red eyes glowing. Manes stuck up on their long necks in a bristle a meter high. A woman, with the familiar facial deformity and lisp whom she had seen sixteen years ago on a rainy, night sat on top of the white horse.

"Cheve is my son. You cannot have him." She pointed the rifle at the woman who wore the same *rebozo* from the first time they met.

"I regret leaving my son with you. But I'm not here to take him back. I come to bring him home. A witch stalks your children in the *Huya Ania*. A strong mother can break *la bruja's* curse."

Petra paced and gripped and un-gripped the rifle. "My children—a witch?"

The woman nodded to the black horse. "Get on *Negro* and leave your gun. Bullets will not help you. Your *Seataka* is your weapon."

"Why should I believe you?" Petra kept the gun pointed at the woman. "Perhaps you're a witch."

"What do you know of *brujas*?" The woman laughed. "I'm a witch killer who knows their sly tricks and disguises. I track them by their foul smell and the terror they leave. Only a deer or brave mother can kill them. I don't see your fur, antlers, hooves or tail. The witch enslaving your children is strong. It'll take two mothers to trap this evil. Your children cry for release. I come because I need your help to free Cheve. If you're too afraid, then I'll save him alone. But know this: I'll keep him, my reward for risking my life and the lives of my precious horses. *La bruja* can enslave pretty Luz. They especially like virgins."

"Ahhhh!" Petra dropped the rifle and felt for the knife hidden in her blouse. She raised her clinched fists to the air. "I'd never allow *brujas* to harm my children. Take me to her."

The large, black horse bowed its head, allowing Petra to grab its mane. She thrust her right leg over the horse's back but couldn't mount. The deformed woman edged her horse closer to Petra. She bent down. "Grab my hand."

The Yaqui reached and clutched her cold, firm grip. She was surprised at the woman's strength as she pulled her up to the back of the black horse. Mother Falcon winced at the smell of roses. She had never sat so high on a mare. If thrown, she surely would break bones or die, she feared.

When the deformed woman yelled, "*Blanco, Negro,*" her steeds snorted and bobbed their heads. She slapped *Blanco's* rump, gave a high shriek and galloped forward. *Negro* followed close behind, charging through the sleeping Yaqui village, past the church graveyard filled with crooked crosses and into the wilderness.

Riding above the large mount, Petra's thighs vibrated to the strong muscles undulating underneath as the horse's powerful legs pounded the ground and kicked up dirt. She clutched *Negro's* mane with both hands, riding at a speed faster than ever before. Trees, shrubs, and cactus flew past in a blur. Fleeting glows of rabbit and owl eyes winked and faded. The wind pressed her face and blew her hair back in long tresses. She rode up to the Yaqui River.

Instead of slowing, the horses quickened their pace. They leaped at the bank. Petra held tighter, bent closer to *Negro's* neck and looked down at the river, appearing like a rippling ribbon. The horses suspended in air longer than she had ever seen. Not even Pocho, the best horseman of the village, could jump as high or far. She inhaled as her butt lifted from the horse's back, her legs dangling behind. On descent, she felt her stomach slide forward and opened her mouth to catch her breath. *Negro* landed absorbing the shock of the fall and resumed its rhythmic gallop into the wilderness. Petra rose to her normal riding posture, pressing her thighs tight on the horse's flanks. Like a child riding for the first time, she took delight in the memories of riding with her father. But they never rode at night because of the danger of their mounts stepping into a hole or crashing into a tree. If *Negro* fell, she hoped she would soar far away from the animal, lest it crush her.

To her side rode the strange woman astride *Blanco*. She swept the *rebozo* from her head and bared her crooked smile as if the two were sisters sharing a deep secret. Moonlight exposed her in a shadowy glow, distorting her oral gap even more.

Despite the huge horses and the woman's disfigurement, Petra didn't fear her. She tried to think about how they were to rescue her children from the witch. The Yaqui mother felt comfort in the knife she sheathed in a leather pouch cinched tight around her chest. A few inches beneath the dirk lay her true strength: the heart of a mother who'd fight any human, semi-human or super human that threatened her children.

Galloping over the silent desert, she recalled Mateo telling her about Ángel's infatuation for a Yori girl. He had seen the two together on one of his trips to Guaymas. When he told his son the folly of the relationship, Ángel shouted at his father and begged him to go back to Pótam with his old Yaqui ways and superstitions. He found Yori life more satisfying than the Yaqui world. At first chance, they planned to leave México and go to Fort Worth, *Tejas* where Carolina's family could help them settle and find work.

The Yori girl had bewitched her son. This deformed woman might know how to break the spell and redirect his love to his Yaqui home. The Yori flirt lured Ángel away: she must be the *bruja* to kill. Petra rubbed her knife.

They had ridden an hour when Petra saw in amazement they were near Red Mountain. *Negro's* speed shortened what normally took half a day's trek through the desert. Was she dreaming, she wondered? At the foothills, they rode through thick brush. Leaves and branches slapped against her legs as if to pull her down. The stalwart horses strode, and panted in their ascent.

The scarred-face woman screamed, and cursed bilingually: Cajita and *El Español*. She blurted, "Damn you, Maso. I'll kill and cook you one day. I'll carve your bones into flutes, combs and bowls. *Te mato, animal salvaje*." She lashed a whip at deer that burst from the brushes in front and sides, darting in all directions.

Petra found herself and *Negro* in the midst of a jostling deer herd. For a short distance, the deer darted close to them, and kicked, and gored the horses. She pulled her legs up. Their antlers brushed close, and left streaks of blood along the horses' flanks. Riding higher up the steep slope, the woman stopped her cursing and whipping as the deer dispersed.

The hostile deer behavior had astonished Petra. The witch killer's fury assured her the woman could combat *brujas*. The whip rider cackled. "*Blanco, Negro*, we beat the filthy deer again. Up, up, my beautiful horses." Black and White bobbed their heads in agreement, their muscular legs pounding the mountainside, their sweat glistening their surging bodies. As the lunar glow dimmed, the air scented sweeter as the fir fragrance enveloped them.

With an outstretched hand to the lowest branches, she touched the bristled leaves and tottered. "Ah!" She grasped *Negro's* mane.

"If you fall, deer will gore you," the woman warned. "They hate strangers."

The searching moonlight seeped through the branches, casting a shifting shadow and light show of the horses. They blew misty plumes through their large snouts into the cool night air. *They must have keen eyes to avoid running into trees. Or else, they know this mountain path well.*

Screaming, shouting, and pleas for mercy swelled over the galloping claps. Anguished, human cries reverberated around her. Men raced in all directions, chased by growling mountain lions in close pursuit. Skeletons hung by their necks from tree limbs. A bony foot scraped the top of Petra's head. Boulders bounced and rolled down the hill.

Is this where Yaquis driven mad by war fled, and died either by their own hand or beasts' claws?

Negro broke through the line of fir trees and continued to climb up even rockier terrain. Petra shivered from the cold air. The jostling grew rougher and higher, but she didn't tire. By their steady, steep ascent, they could climb to the pearl moon. Stars glittered like a bejeweled crown on Red Mountain's rocky head.

The desire to save her children injected the energy of a Yaqui girl. The auras of danger, grace and power exhilarated her. The rushing, chilly air against her skin ironically roused in her an ardor to fight anyone or anything that would harm her children.

Petra galloped to the crest, and stopped before a fortress-like rock structure, blocking most of the wind. Rocks encircled ashes and bones of previous fires. A large desiccated head of a deer stood impaled on a stake in the center of the ring.

The ugly woman jumped off *Blanco* with ease, rubbed its head, whispered in the animal's ear, laughed and slipped a treat into its mouth.

Petra slid off *Negro* and flopped on her buttocks. When she tried to pat its head, the horse pulled away, and went to the other woman who stroked the horse's long neck.

After she kissed the black beast, she snuck a morsel into its wide-open mouth. The horsewoman said to Petra. "Do you still want to save your family?"

"Yes, of course."

"Are you willing to see the truth, no matter the pain?"

Petra nodded.

"Is your *Seataka* strong?"

"As strong as any."

"We shall see how strong. Come with me." The woman led her a little way to a dark cave.

Petra followed the sounds of the woman's scraping feet. A flash of light grew to small flames and then burst into a bright fire.

The witch hunter stoked the fire until the flames shut up and illuminated the entire cavern entrance. The floor was littered with bones. Whether animal or human, Petra couldn't discern. The woman stood before the fire staring into it for a moment. Her neck bent to the side as she moaned, "I miss my son Cheve. I regret my mistake in giving him to you." She ripped off the *rebozo* from her body and tore open her blouse. Exposing and cupping her pendulous breasts with large, brown areolas, she said, "Cheve should have sucked these nipples, not yours."

Petra stood dumbfounded, staring at the bare-chested wailer. "You gave me the child — don't you remember? I had no choice but to raise him like his mother. I loved him as much as my other children."

The woman cackled. "Love? I'll show you the ways of your loving family." She lit a cigarette with the fire. She whispered to it and released it into the air. The cigarette floated, glowed and circled above them a few times before shooting like a flaming arrow out of the cave.

Petra recognized the *Choni*. The magical cigarette could spy and sometimes kill with a touch of its burning tip. Her grandmother had command of the *Choni* and had used it to find the body of her husband, killed in battle. It took much *Seataka* to wield such a magical tool.

The woman waved Petra to her. "I have important news that can save your family."

The Yaqui walked closer, but stopped a few meters away.

"Victoriano fell in love with me the instant he saw me at the bordello *Cielito Lindo* in Guaymas. He was one of my frequent customers. Said he could never tire loving me. You wonder how a man could fall in love with an ugly whore. But I tell you my body was the most attractive in all of Sonora. I brought him a little heaven when we were together in bed. Only a man with the heart of a lion could see my beauty. And your filthy husband took him away from me," she wailed.

The woman clapped. "My *Choni*... my *Choni!*" The burning cigarette hovered in front of the woman. Admiring the roll-up as if it were the finest tobacco ever grown, she nestled it between her fingers. "Let's see what your noble husband is into tonight." She brought it slowly to her lips inhaling. Closing her eyes, she opened her mouth, allowing smoke to ooze out of her half smile. The vapors swept up to her nose and covered half her face in a small fog. With opened eyes, she offered the *Choni* to Petra.

She laughed. "What did your husband say he was doing?"

Petra stepped back. As soon as the woman released the *Choni*, it floated to Petra.

"Kiss the *Choni*. With a puff, you will know his heart." The cigarette flew closer to Petra. "If your *Seataka* is strong, you should have no fears. Inhale the *Choni* and blow out the truth."

Petra slipped the thick, sweet-scented cigarette between her fingers. She hesitated to lift her hand to her lips, nervous of what she would see. Did she really want to know?

"For your children, for your self-respect, smoke," the whip woman shouted.

God give me the power to forgive. Petra brought the leaf to her lips, inhaled, smoke wafting in her mouth. A pleasant rush tickled her throat. She closed her eyes and held her breath. Soothing warmth radiated through her entire body.

On exhaling, colorful, bright images loomed before her suspended in air. Although the scene was at night, she could see a man's back as he sat on the ground with a woman. In the corner, two children slept. The couple spoke in hushed tones, making it difficult to hear. Tears welled to Petra's eyes when the view shifted to reveal the man's face. Mateo leaned forward to caress the woman's cheek as he had done often with her in the first years of their marriage. They were soon on the ground in each other's arms. She swiped at the smoky images, sobbed and wept into her hands.

The deformed woman covered her eyes with her hands, mimicking her sobbing. "Mateo mounts another woman tonight. Lustful, he is." She danced around the room with her hands formed into a phallic symbol pumping it from her groin. "He's a bull. One cow is not enough. Those children in your *Choni* vision are also his. Mateo, the great inseminator of Sonora." The woman laughed and pranced around the fire.

Petra wiped her eyes. "Why did you bring me here? To mock me? To torment me for loving Cheve? Do you seek revenge?"

"To test you, Petra. To learn if your *Seataka* was stronger than the witch's. It isn't. You're too weak."

Petra pointed at her. "*Bruja*." She snatched a burning stick from the fire and waved it at her. "Go to hell with your master Satan."

"I curse you and your Falcon family. Suffer, like I've suffered, bitch." The witch reached out.

Petra threw the fire stick at her, but the *bruja* caught it, tossed it up and swirled it like a blistering pin wheel. Shadows raced around the cave wall at her direction. The witch spoke in a strange, guttural tongue, and ran about the chamber pointing and cursing Petra.

The Yaqui mother crouched, regretted not bringing her rifle. She reached for the knife. She pulled it from its leather sheath, held the dagger in front, poised to slash.

"I'll burn your pretty face and scar it." The witch sliced the air with the fire stick. "You'll know why Cheve cries like a calf. He's ugly in a family of pretty faces and nothing will change unless you become hideous. If you love Cheve, slash your pretty face. Prove your love for him. Slice yourself now." The witch tossed the torch into the air, caught the handle and ran screaming toward Petra.

The Yaqui ran for the cave entrance but stopped when she heard horses galloping into the cave. She jumped to the side to avoid trampling by *Negro* and *Blanco*. They neighed in a high-pitch as if crying for their mother. Their tails arched high, almost perpendicular to rumps. They shat piles of dung as if to mark their trail. The horses raced to the witch, their flanks streaked with bleeding, gash wounds. The *bruja* howled. She swung her fists and threw the fire stick to the cave entrance.

The ground vibrated and the beating sounds of many hooves echoed in the cave chamber like drums. As the tom-toms grew stronger, Petra pressed her back against the cave wall. She clutched the knife before her.

A large deer with a crown of blood-tipped antlers trotted forward. Bending its head, the antlers stopped a few inches from *Madre* Falcon's face.

She heard the beast make deep, garbled grunts, its musky smell filling her nose. To her surprise, she understood the animal's instructions. She raced to escape the cave.

"Come back," the witch shouted. *La bruja* mounted *Negro* in a swift leap. She trotted forward, but stopped when the deer blocked her. The witch charged. "I'll kill you Petra and this filthy beast."

Antlers bent down, the deer swept up just as *Negro* was upon it. Deer sliced the black horse's throat, then plunged its horns into its right flank. The gored horse neighed as it swung from side to side like an impaled fish out of water. The witch catapulted into the air, landing hard onto the horses' dung.

She rose, bolted to *Blanco* and leapt onto its back. As the deer charged the white steed, the ugly rider swept up several burning sticks into its face. With its strong legs springing up, the horse hurdled over the antlers to land in feline ease.

"Petra," *La bruja* screamed, her hands reaching out to her as Blanco charged. The Yaqui darted to the side, pressed her back against the cave wall, knife raised high. The deer howled a low, deep bellow. Wincing at a burning streak along the side of her face, the Mother Falcon yelped in pain.

The shrieking *bruja* on *Blanco's* back galloped out of the cave, wielding fire sticks. Petra ran after to discover the mountain top covered with a sea of antlers, the moon looming large behind them.

Witch and white mare ran a gantlet of slashing antlers and hooves. Deer pressed around the speedy horse, but it weaved, jumped and charged too fast for the phalanx of antlers to trap or kill it. *La bruja* swung her fire sticks from side to side, searing and burning hide from her tormentors. The mighty horse toppled deer like toy dolls, leaped high and vanished into the darkness of the mountain side.

Petra heard a commanding voice behind her. The deer stood majestically with crimson antlers, massive chest and legs. Flecks of blood streaked its furry flank. *The deer should take out the remains of Negro to stop the desecration of Red Mountain.*

As if reading her mind, several deer dashed into the cave, the black horse perched on their antlers. Others scooped up dung with their horns. More deer lowered their horns, grunted, forming a semicircle around Petra. Blood dripping from its leaf-shaped antlers, deer chief ordered them back.

"Maso," she whispered.

The deer's bellow was answered by a chorus of deer army thunder.

Petra shook from the mountain chorus.

"Witch scarred your face," the deer said.

Petra placed her hand to her cheek, tracing the cut. She reflected her wound on the knife blade.

"The witch's cut will never vanish. She intends to cut out your heart and kill all you love. Your *Seataka* must threaten the *brjua*."

"Then I'll kill her first."

"Many have tried. This *bruja* is strong, stronger than all the *brujas* I've slaughtered. She has slain many priests, nuns and deer who have sought to destroy her."

"I look for my Falcon children. Lead me to them."

"Too dangerous now with the fighting. Rest here for the night. When there is light, begin your journey home. Deer will protect you on Red Mountain."

Petra nodded. Perhaps, her *Seataka* was strong enough to withstand the witch's rage. With Maso as an ally in her search, *la bruja*, unfaithful husband, traitors, and savage Yoris couldn't stop her.

She would sleep on Red Mountain, close to the fire and regain her strength. In the morning she'd not go home, but instead start her search. How could she return to Pótam and allow the witch to hunt her children? Tearing a strip of cloth from her skirt, she pressed it to her cheek to staunch the bleeding. Back into the cave, she lay close to the flames, and wrapped her arms around herself to guard the truth withheld from Maso: the witch had not scarred her.

CHAPTER 27

FLIGHT OF THE FALCONS

Pablo Estampe, leader of the escapees from the Hacienda *García*, stood in front of the gathered Yaquis outside the hut. With arms outstretched, he asked, "Where do we go from here, my people? Yoris and Torocoyoris wait for us, hungry for our blood." He pointed to the wilderness.

"We fight or die." Cheve stood. "We barely escaped from Guaymas."

Ángel tugged on his hand, shaking his head.

Cheve pulled away. "I must talk. By the grace of the *Virgen* and Maso, we escaped from that Yori city as you have from the hacienda."

"Brave. But what do we do now?" Pablo asked. "Wait here until Cajemé's warriors find us? Send a messenger to bring men? Or leave together to our homes?"

Cheve stepped forward. "I know my way to Pótam. Can ride fast and reach it in one day."

Luz shook her head. "Cheve's too young, inexperienced."

"I've no wife, sweetheart or children," the boy shouted. "I'm blessed with *Seataka* as a swift runner, rider. Maso gave me this." Cheve held up the antler. "I've seen, heard Maso sing four times."

"What's Maso look like?" a man asked.

"He's larger than our biggest horse and wears a crown of antlers." Cheve stretched out his arms above his head. "The Maso danced like this." He swayed front and to the sides in fluid motions. His feet shuffled in strong steps. Arching his shoulders, he thrust his head up. A deer song flowed from his mouth that told about the Other Side and the Little People.

The assembly clapped and shouted their joy at the sweet words and dancing.

238

"He's a deer dancer not a fighter," Luz said. "Sit down, Cheve."

Tomas rose, closed his eyes and remained silent. When his lids opened, he faced the assembly. "The boy is undisciplined, has self-pity because of his face."

Cheve shook his head, stared at Tomas and sat.

"But when we were caught in Guaymas, he showed much courage and a willingness to fight. If not for this deer dancer, Yoris would have hanged us in Guaymas. He's young, foolhardy, but a loyal Yaqui. I prefer loyalty, courage to age and good looks. The boy doesn't fear death, has a strong heart and speed. Enough to reach Pótam." Tomas sat next to Cheve.

He smiled at Tomas, touching his shoulder.

Luz groaned. "No, please don't send him into the desert."

Carolina leaned closer to Ángel, whispered into his ear, and touched his hand.

The nun lover inhaled, exhaled slowly. He stood. "Cheve has a chance to reach Pótam. In the wilderness, the boy saved me from a wild deer. Said it was Maso, but I think he had deer fever. I'll go with my brother. If one of us is killed or wounded, the other will still have a chance to reach the Yaqui River before the sun sets. He'll bring back help in less time. We'll go on foot, leave horses for you. Falcons are strong runners. If not back by tomorrow, assume we're dead."

"Well spoken." Pablo walked forward, arms in the air. "You've heard their offer. Do we accept?"

The crowd's discussion swelled in a chaotic Cajita, then gradually subsided. A man, his arm in a sling, rose and pointed with his good hand at Cheve and Ángel. "Let them go."

"If not back by tomorrow, we take our chances in the desert night," Pablo said. "God protect you." As he touched Cheve's and Ángel's heads, many in the assembly nodded. A low hum of praise rippled through the Yaqui fugitives.

Luz rushed and held Cheve's right arm. "Don't go. This isn't bravery—it's deer madness."

"I'm a Yaqui man." Cheve pulled away from her.

"You're a boy."

"Let him be a man," Ángel said and stepped between them.

She exhaled in exasperation. "Cheve, run like Maso. Don't stop, Brother."

"My swiftest." Cheve posed in a running stance. He stood upright at the sight of Ángel embracing Carolina.

White and brown faces touched cheeks; hands pressed, clutched and enveloped one another like overlapping feathers. The buzz of talk, wind, and time completely stopped. All froze in place at the rare sight of Yori/Yaqui transparent love. She caressed Ángel's face for a moment, then her fingers climbed to run through his hair. His black strands protruded like stalks of grass through her white knuckles. The Red Nun kissed brown Ángel on the lips as if the two breathed as one. When her cheek pressed against his and slid to his left ear, Cheve and others leaned forward to catch the whispered words reserved for paramours risking lives and likes.

Amazed at the wondrous sight, they had never seen nor heard a nun kissing a Yaqui man. Despite obvious differences, their love mined the barriers and found the secret passage to the other's heart. The Yori/Yaqui couple was reckless, rebellious and defiant of their peoples' traditions. Such love exploded myths of master and slave, civilized and savage, beauty and brute. Wayward passion cracked stony stares.

Cheve sensed Ángel studied science to salve the wound of his loneliness. *Better they had never come and instead escaped to Texas, Arizona or California. They sacrifice too much.*

He stepped close to the entangled pair, "Go north now before it's too late. You've done enough for us."

Ángel released his hold and smiled. "And what would happen to you, my brother?"

"Tomas can go. He knows this land better than you. With him, there would be no question about loyalty. There's danger here for both of you."

"Before I leave the Yaqui, I must speak with our parents."

240

"Carolina, leave with him now."

"I want to flee this fighting and hatred. But Ángel would always regret he didn't see his parents again. Despite what he says, he's still Yaqui in here." She placed her hand on his chest.

"Yes, you are Yaqui, aren't you, Brother?" Cheve said smiling.

"By birth—hopefully not by death," Ángel said.

"Time to fly, Brother."

The older Falcon tossed his sombrero to the ground, wrapping a bandana around his head. He tore a sleeve from his shirt and tied it around Cheve's head. He slung the cartridge belt over a shoulder.

"A firecracker," Ángel shouted.

Tomas came forward, handing him a gun.

The two men exchanged cold gazes as Ángel took the weapon and tied the pistol with another strip of his shirt to his chest. In their make-shift garb, they transformed to desert assassins.

"Don't flinch from killing Yoris. If they catch us, they'll torture us with pleasure before they execute us." Ángel placed his hand on Cheve's shoulders, drawing him closer. "I was never a traitor to my heart."

Cheve hugged him and buried his head in his brother's chest. "I missed you."

Ángel hugged him tight. "You'll certainly miss me if you don't keep up."

Cheve laughed. "I have deer speed."

"You have deer smell." Ángel held his nose.

When word traveled that the Falcon brothers were ready to leave, the crowd parted and opened a path. A woman sang "Other Side." Soon others joined in until most of the assembly intoned the beauty of the Little People's world.

Cheve smiled wider than ever in front of his melodic people.

A light-skinned girl about his age with long, brown hair held out a willow cross attached to a string. He bent down for the girl to drape it over his shoulders. "Your name?"

"America," she said.

A dark-skinned girl with two pig tails brought clay cups of water for the runners.

"And what are you called?" Cheve asked again.

"México," she said.

When he chuckled at the curious names, the surrounding crowd joined in the laughter.

Luz embraced him, "Run fast, brother."

As soon as his sister released her hold, Carolina hugged him. His face flushed.

"Come, Brother," Ángel said. "Enough hugging and kissing." When he puckered his lips, Cheve drew back.

The Falcon brothers walked side-by-side through the crowd. Deer Dancer felt pats on the shoulders and head. He waved, baring his face bolder than ever in his entire life. The old shame had flown away from his shoulders.

Over the Yaquis' singing, Cheve cried, "I love you, my people."

Ángel picked up the pace to a slow trot and once outside the crowd, he raced.

Cheve loped effortlessly abreast of him. No witches, demons or Yoris could restrain him from saving the most human of people. With every beat, the willow cross struck his chest.

The sound of the Yaqui crowd quickly faded replaced by the soft sounds of their rapid footsteps and easy breathing. The brown, Yaqui desert vista spread out before them, inviting them to run their race of salvation. A soft wind pushed them forward, cooling their moist torsos.

Cheve felt his body's supple muscles respond well to the race. To his side, Ángel ran in a natural rhythm of synchronized arms and legs rotation, his head balanced on broad, dancing shoulders. His face shimmered from sweat.

"Falcons!" Ángel grinned wide.

"Falcons!" A giggling Cheve echoed with his crooked smile.

The two runners clutched hands for a short distance, then hit their full strides. They flew across the desert grounds.

CHAPTER 28

✦

MERCHANT FAMILY

At dawn, Petra awoke to the first sunrays that painted light on the Yaqui world.

Outside the cave, leaves of the tall firs rustled, whispering a good morning. The ground's frost oozed a stirring chill awakening her to an even greater desire to begin her rescue. A bird of prey soared soundlessly above. *Do you see my children?*

She recalled *la bruja* and her horses, *Negro* and *Blanco,* and searched for signs of them. *A bad dream? Had she run in her sleep to Red Mountain? Where were Maso and its deer legion?*

She touched crusted blood on her cheek. Last night was no hallucination — more *Blanco* and *Negro* nightmares.

A faint child-like cry echoed from the cave, drawing her to its entrance. When the howl echoed again, she plodded farther into the cave, calling, "Who's there?"

The yelp sounded more plaintive now.

"Come out." She waited. "Show yourself."

From the shadows, she heard rapid clopping swell. A white goat jumped forward. Petra fell back onto her buttocks. The short-horned critter danced around her, shook its tail, kicked its legs high and pranced away as if to lead her from the cave.

She followed the goat, walking to the edge of the mountain summit. The rising sun had chased back most of the darkness, illuminating beautiful colors of the fauna. Shades of brown and orange spread out before her like a checkered desert quilt of soil and rock. The greens of the mesquite and cactus dotted the landscape. Red nopal flowers stretched like an arrow flying toward its bright, solar target. Large stones appeared like silver coins scattered over the land. Other than wide-winged birds soaring, she saw no evidence of animal or human—a deceptive desert ruse.

The wilderness teemed with life as reflected by the scouring, hungry predators. A panoply of insects, birds, small and large animals, plants, cactus, trees and precious water breathed crystal air. This was *Huya Ania,* the "Other Side," the source of beauty, the home of the deer and *Surem,* the Little People. The bones of her ancestors lying in the soil anchored the living with their memories.

When the goat rubbed her leg, Petra petted its head. "You wish to join me on this journey?"

She knelt, closed her eyes and prayed for the *Virgen's* help to bring her children home. On her descent with the goat leading the way, she thought the deer must have sent the goat to accompany her on her quest, to amuse on this trek. Stepping over rocks, gravel and bushes, her feet ached. She hadn't brought her huaraches in her ride to Red Mountain. Even though her soles were tough, she didn't think she could walk long across the desert without some foot covering. By the time she reached the mountain base, her feet seeped blood from scrapes and cuts.

The goat ran ahead, bleated as she followed it to the first clump of cactus. Petra walked gingerly to the spiny foliage, patting the goat on the head. She carefully scraped off the needles, broke off several nopales, and cut strips of plant skin. Petra sliced several large pieces and wrapped them around her soles. Next, the Yaqui mother stripped thin slices and threaded together the ribbons of nopal around her ankles and forefeet. Rising from the ground, the searcher tested her *planty* shoes. The desert skins provided cool protection on her soles and toes.

Cutting more nopal skin, Petra bent it into a crude cup.

"Come, goat. I'll not hurt you." She milked the goat for several cups. "Thank you, my friend." The grateful woman stroked its head. "I promise not to eat you."

The furry companion bleated as if to say, "You're welcome. Remember your promise."

The facial wound ached. Stripping more nopal skin, the Yaqui placed it against her left cheek to ward off infection. She intended to show Cheve that despite her marred, pretty face, she could live with physical and spiritual scars. Despite the witch's malevolence, the cruel woman had taught her how to help Cheve with his facial shame. Perhaps another slice would help him live like a courageous Yaqui. As the traveler lifted the blade to her cheek, a hard shove on her backside knocked her to the ground.

The goat cried and jumped away.

"As you wish, goat. One scar is enough." Petra sheathed the knife.

Yaqui lore told of magic goats with powers to make the trekker's journey lighter. The critters were the favorite animal of the Pascola dancers who were reputed to dream of them often. They taught Pascolas funny stories to share with their Yaqui audience. The dancers learned intricate, complicated steps that impressed onlookers at religious festivals. Pascolas welcomed the magic goat to urinate on their legs and feet in the belief they would dance stronger, longer.

Petra called to the goat, "Pee now. Come back and wet my legs." She extended them. The goat trotted away and urinated in a distant bush.

"Modest, are you? I guess I would be, too." She studied her surroundings, smelling the air, listening for any strange or hostile presence. In other desert trips to the seven Yaqui villages, she journeyed a few kilometers, but always in the company of her family, people of Pótam or armed men. The war years had compelled them to stay wary of attacks even in times of transitory truce.

The blue, smoky images of Mateo with the other woman and children slinked to the open field of her memory. A deep sadness swelled. After he had admitted he was Cheve's father, she had forgiven him, with time and effort, for his infidelity. But she couldn't forget. Suspicions of his continuing unfaithfulness never left her. Before, she hadn't questioned his frequent absences and explanations that

Cajemé needed him in their constant vigilance and preparations against the Yoris. She reasoned her husband's high office required the Falcons to sacrifice for their people's survival. Petra prayed to the *Virgen* to bury her mistrusts. Still, they rose from their tombs, haunting and howling at her when he was gone. Mother Falcon stood unconvinced Father Falcon had learned to temper his lust. Perhaps, *choni* visions were lies conjured by the witch to ruin her marriage. *La bruja* was a trickster like Satan, intent on ruining lives and devouring souls.

Looking back, she saw Red Mountain shimmered different shades of burgundy in the sunlight. The fir trees' foliage canopy couldn't hide the reddish soil that radiated a glow she found soothing. Rising from the ground, Petra headed west.

She had heard of Maso, but never saw the deer until last night. In a vain attempt to see the mystic animal, she looked back again at the mountain. The Yaqui stories about the deer were true, but then so were the tales of witches. The traveler recalled the other harsh truth: Yoris and their traitor cousins, *Torocoyoris*, roamed the land searching for her children. Petra had to muster her courage to survive in the intersections of mystical and murderous desert. Her scout's bleats, cactus crimson flowers, and sharpened wits guided her along the Yaqui path.

After several kilometers, she found her nopal shoes held up well on the desert floor. Her throat felt parched as the day grew warmer. She rested by a large, shady mesquite, near a clump of cactus. She closed her eyes to shade them from the sun's rays that pierced the tree umbrella. Unaware of how long she had rested, she snapped open her eyelids at the harsh snort of horses. Petra remained still.

Gazing to the front and from side to side, she saw no evidence of strangers. The goat standing a little way from the tree stared north toward the open desert. With feline stealth, she eased up to her feet and peered around the tree. A man, woman and two children rode four horses with a fifth horse trailing behind. By the clanging sounds of cooking utensils and bundles, she guessed they were traveling traders. Sometimes, the itinerant merchant would bring his family with him to help with bartering and safeguard the goods. He must not have known of the recent outbreak of war to risk roaming with his precious cargo so openly.

Petra was about to call out to them when she heard gunfire. Three men on galloping horses raced after them. The distance made it difficult to tell if Yaqui or Yori riders.

The trader shouted to his family. The woman and children whipped their horses, their mounts kicking up desert dirt. Gun muzzles flashed and banged as the swirling dirt kicked up around the fleeing family.

If Yaqui riders, why would they pursue the trader unless they were Torocoyoris? From the aftermaths of the traitors' assaults, Yaquis found Torocoyoris more brutal than Yoris. Torocoyoris had to prove their loyalty to Yori allies by their savagery to their own. *Judas Yaquis had sold their souls to their masters for pieces of gold that shriveled their hearts.*

The goat bleated.

Petra cupped her hand to her mouth. "Shhhh, goat, come here."

Instead, it ran away.

She waited a few seconds, then circled around the cactus brush and tree. With no concealing foliage, she pressed to the ground and lifted slightly her head.

Several mounted men trained their guns on their captured Yaqui quarry. They tied the trader's hands behind his back. His wife and children trailed him on their horses. When the hunting party headed for her position, she crawled away about fifty meters from the brush. Her hands burned from the heat of the ground, her knees chafed from crawling over rocks and dirt. Petra raised her head to see the pursuers had thrown a rope over a limb at the mesquite where she had just rested. They looped the noose over the trader's head until it slipped around his neck.

Maso, come now. Save them.

The merchant's wife screamed, pulled a gun from her blouse and shot the hangman and the man sitting on his horse next to her. Both men fell, yelling in pain. The third man fired several shots into her. The howling woman fired again. The Yaqui hunter's horse crumpled, falling to the side, pinning the rider. The children screamed for their mother.

Petra jumped up, racing toward them. When she neared, she saw the woman's chest pump blood from bullet holes, soaking her dress red. The wounded wife swayed in her saddle while her screaming children reached out to her.

The bound husband called, "Marisol, don't die."

First the gun fell from her hand, then she dropped hard from the horse. Her children leapt from their mounts to reach their mother, touching her face.

Petra darted to the closest tracker. A bullet rosette marked a wound between his eyes. She raced to the trader, pulled out her knife and cut his leather bounds. Petra saw fear in his eyes.

"I'm Yaqui. I won't hurt you."

Once his hands broke free, he jumped off the horse, stumbled and low-crawled to his wife and children. The wounded woman reached out to her children. As her lips quivered, red bubbles oozed from her mouth. She gasped for each breath. Her eyes glazed over.

Petra glared at the fallen men. Between-the-eyes lay dead. The other two still breathed, for now: one writhed on the ground holding in his bulging intestines. The grunting shooter squirmed to free himself from under his wounded horse. He succeeded in slipping out most of his upper torso. With a mighty strain, he pulled his legs free.

Petra took the dead man's gun from the holster. She pounced on *Señor* Gut Shot. Although the Yaqui traveler had never killed anyone, she cocked the pistol and aimed it at the Toroyori's head with cool ease. "Stop squirming. I'll make a mess. Children, look away."

"No, wait. I have a wife and children," Belly Wound pleaded in Cajita, one hand up poised to swat bullets.

"Like the family you stopped? *Chingado, Torocoyori.*" After their father covered the children's eyes, Petra's gun exploded. As the gun din and vibration abated, she felt no remorse, just disgust for the traitor.

Horse Tumbler had climbed to his feet, limping as he fled. Petra took chase, ran past and stopped before him. "Go back or die here. Your choice." The gun pointed at his chest.

"I'm from Tórim," he said in Cajita. "Mistook you for Yoris."

"Bad mistake, you lying cockroach," she said.

He shuffled back to the killing place.

The husband grunted, jumped to his feet, knocking the Torocoyori to the ground with a strong punch to the jaw. With the hangman's rope, he tied a strong knot around the traitor's waist. He looped the rope around the neck of the horse meant to buck him from this life and leaped onto its back. Gripping the rope firmly, his eyes widened, opened his mouth as if to swallow and keened, "Marisol!"

Petra sprang back as the man slapped the horse's rump. He raced through the desert howling and cursing Torocoyoris. In short time, the captive's body bobbed from the ground at times sitting up, flipping to his face, then his back. First arms, then legs, ears, finally head tore loose. He rode back without rope or Torocoyori, leaving desert scavengers to clean the mess.

"You must leave now before more of them come," Petra said. "Others may have heard the firing."

"Can't leave her here."

"Think of your son and daughter. If *Yoris* or *Torocoyoris* see this, they will not spare any of them. Protect them. Marisol would have wanted it that way."

"Who are you?"

"Petra Falcon of Pótam, searching for my sons and daughter. Come with me. Together we'll shelter our family from these devils."

Marisol gasped, her body stiffened and then settled back into the desert floor. The boy and girl wept. Their hands fluttered like doves in the air.

"She has found peace," Petra said, crossing herself.

The man jumped from his horse, bent down, wiped the blood from her mouth and kissed her. He picked up her body and placed it over the saddle of his horse.

"I'll take her home. To your horses, children. Thank you for your help. Now leave us."

"I'll come with you to care for them. They need a woman's comfort. I'll meet my own a little way ahead. Please follow the cactus flowers and you'll find shelter and water."

"Marisol," he howled, raced to his pack horse, took out a machete and ran to the dead Torocoyoris.

"Good Father, stop!" Petra shouted. "Your children!"

The wild-eyed trader, the long blade shaking in the air over the body, halted his swing. Dropping the machete, he wept.

Petra went to the crying youth. "Don't look at the dead men. Look at me. You are loved. You are good. Honor your mother with prayers." She touched their faces and rubbed their arms and backs.

After the trader mounted his horse, the survivors pushed on.

A cool desert morning breeze soothed the riders while the children wept for their mother. Petra sang songs she thought they'd know to distract them from their mother's body. She intoned about rabbits, owls, and foxes of the desert. When she'd see one, she'd point at the desert denizen. As if she had called their pet name, the critters would stop and stare. After enough refrains, the boy and girl were able to sing along. They chanted for about an hour until Petra heard the man sobbing.

He cradled his wife's bloody body. His children drew their horses around their parents to join in the weeping, searching for their father's face for comfort.

Petra's tears welled at the sight. Averting her gaze, she scoured the horizon for any signs of riders, deer or witches. The goat trailing after comforted her. Perhaps, Maso had sent the furry escort as a protector. The animal's fur was wet.

"Where's the water, goat? Take me to the water."

Her short-horned ally headed west. She looked back and saw the family still mourned, bent over the woman's body. Following the goat to a clump of mesquite, Petra tried slowing her horse, but it trotted faster. As soon as it stopped at the edge of a pond, she jumped off and bent to drink.

"Poison. Don't drink, Mother."

Petra pulled her long hair away from her face to see Ángel and Cheve standing by a mesquite on the other side of the pond.

"My sons." She held out her hands as she ran forward.

Cheve raced to meet her, stumbled, but Ángel held him from falling into the water. Once righted, the boy fell into her open arms.

She hugged and kissed him, repeating, "My sons, thank God you're fine. The goat led me to you."

"Don't let the horse drink," Ángel said.

Cheve broke his hug, grabbed the reins and pulled the mare away.

"Come here, my son. Please, Ángel, let me touch you." When he was within arms' reach, she embraced him. "It's been so long, my Ángelito, too long." She gazed at his muscular body, rugged look. Although he still bore the Falcon good looks, he had lost much of the boyish cheeks and eyes.

"I longed to hold you, my son." She kissed his cheeks, her tears wetting them.

"That scar?" Cheve brought his hand to her face. "What happened?"

Petra covered the cut with her hand. "A witch... Maso."

"The witch attacked me, too. I told you Ángel, Maso is here to protect us. Mother, he doesn't believe."

Petra gazed at Ángel, but had no desire to question him about his doubts after years of separation.

She hugged him again. "Cheve, why did you leave? We heard Yoris nearly caught you. Terrible fighting. Men died protecting you."

"To help Luz and find Angel," Cheve said.

"Luz is a little distance away." Ángel pointed to the north.

"We must save her." Petra grimaced. "Wait. The trader and his children." She ran beyond the pond, Ángel and Cheve following, past the dead animals surrounding the watering hole she hadn't noticed before. The Yaqui mother went to a small rise to stare at riders in the near distance. A large company of horsemen followed the goat to the trader family.

Father, boy and girl clutched one another as the men rode upon them. When they opened fire, their bodies danced like marionettes. They fell in a heap as if the puppeteer cut the strings.

"No," Petra cried.

"Bocagrande," Ángel hissed.

"Witch's goat," she said. "*La bruja* tricked me."

Horses scattered, one bolting in their direction.

"Come, Brother." Ángel ran and jumped on Petra's horse first. Cheve landed behind him on the horse's rump. They closed on the mare. As the riders came abreast of the horse, young Falcon leaped, reached for the horse's mane and righted himself on its back. They raced back to their mother.

"Mother, get on." Ángel pointed to Cheve.

She ran and mounted.

"Go back to the camp," Ángel said. "Warn them."

"I want to stay with you," Cheve said.

"No, you risk Mother's life. Go now." He slapped the rump of his brother's rescue horse.

"Save yourself, Ángel. Come home," Petra shouted as she rode away with Cheve. Her older son drew his pistol. He fired at the goat that jumped into the air straight for him. In mid-flight, the animal howled a deep, guttural roar, too loud for its size, fell, jumped to its hooves and stood on its two hind legs. Teats dripped blood on the white, curly fur.

Devil-goat stretched open its maw twice its normal size, two front legs shaking in the air and bellowed, "Give me, my baby, baaa!"

"He's mine. Go to hell, witch!" Petra screamed. "Baaa!"

Ángel rode in the opposite direction from his mother's flight, shooting at the goat and distant horsemen.

"Maso, Maria, protect my Ángel from desert *diablos*," his mother prayed. "This boy is mine." She hugged Cheve tight.

CHAPTER 29

✦

WALKS WITH ÁNGEL

Tomas formed a militia, directing the men to construct clubs and spears for the fighters and litters and bandages for the wounded. He assigned the younger men to guard the perimeters.

With their captured arms, the Yaquis could stand off Yoris for a time. The enemy that Tomas killed were buried in a shallow, mass grave, covered with detritus. Better to keep the dead concealed lest their comrades seek vengeance. Or his people's hunger lure them to the taste of human flesh. Besides, the smells and sights of bloating bodies grew unbearable.

Luz and Carolina joined other women to search for edible mushrooms, plants and nopal. They walked a little distance beyond the perimeter, within shouting distance of the guards.

"Carolina, I admire your love for my brother," Luz said.

"Mother and Father watched me closely." The nun stopped in her search. "They warned me to ward off probing touches and inviting smiles. Despite their cautions, I grew bold with Ángel. My desire was too strong to pull away. If Mother had her way, I would still be a nun," Carolina said pointing at her torn robe. "But Father preferred I become educated and cultured. He wished to send me to finishing school in Paris to learn French, to paint. I can draw, you know. I inked several sketches of Ángel. Kept them hidden in my books. When Mother discovered drawings of us kissing, she grew furious. Said I drew dirty pictures and showed them to Father. He threatened to castrate Ángel. Interrogated me, asking if the *indio* had touched me or as you say walked with me.

"It's good you came to Guaymas." Carolina took Luz's hand. "We were planning to elope. He wanted to do so right away, but I was hesitant. I regret we didn't. Watching you stand up to Father Julio in the church gave me courage to run away. You were so brave and strong."

"When you're hungry, wet and dirty or in love, you find courage," Luz said. "All Yaquis know this."

"Have you found the passion to walk with Tomas?"

Luz bowed her head. "Like your parents, mine sheltered me from men. Most Yaquis were afraid of my father. My mother stayed close at my side."

"Your parents aren't here." Carolina swept her hand around them. "They have good intentions, but sometimes they make poor decisions. This fighting will take many men. While you and Tomas breathe the desert air, show your love. When a man walks with a woman, it gives him courage to live longer, not to run from the enemy. His way of protecting you."

"Tomas shows no real interest in me."

"I've seen him look at you. Try to be alone with him."

"Here?" Luz chuckled and spread her arms out. "With this crowd? Now?"

"Yes, it's difficult. Still try to walk close by him. Let him yearn."

Luz laughed. And just as quickly took a somber tone. "I worry about Tomas' anger and what he'll do when we get back to Pótam. He might tell my parents all he knows about Ángel and Yoris. I hoped my brother could reconcile with our parents. I doubt it'll happen now. He'll be happier with you, away from all this." Luz took both Carolina's hands into hers. "Remind him we still love him."

"Can you read Spanish or English?"

"No."

"Can you get someone to translate?"

"Yes, we have a boy in Pótam who writes and reads both tongues. I know his parents. I'll have him teach me to write and read."

"I'll write often."

Running, shouting men interrupted their talk.

"Trouble has found us." Luz ran back with Carolina to the camp. When they arrived, Luz was shocked to see her mother. She hugged a dirt-covered Petra.

"How did you get here?" Luz asked. Before Petra could answer, gunshots erupted. Women screamed, snatched their children and searched for escape. Some hurried into the hut, hid behind trees or fell to the ground lying over their young.

A man shouted, "Yoris!" Rifle-bearing Yaquis shot back. Two mustachioed horsemen galloped into their camp shooting at anyone in their range. They trampled Yaquis too slow or too tired to run.

Luz and her mother dropped to the dirt. Bullets flew over their heads in a sinister buzz. An old man grabbed his chest where a red wound sprouted. He crumpled to the ground with a shout. Dragging himself along the ground, a boy trailed blood from an arm.

When they stopped shooting, the raiders drew long knives, circled back and stabbed at anyone within reach. They galloped out of the camp leaving a trail of dead Yaquis, mostly women and children. Cries of the wounded reverberated in the wake of flying lead and blades.

Luz helped her mother rise and escorted her into the hut filled with cowering, crying women and children. Pulling her mother closer to the entrance, she sat her on the ground. After an hour of sporadic firing, Luz ventured out.

Tomas directed men to different points along their defensive lines. He had the wounded lifted and brought to the hut where women tended to injuries or comforted the near dead.

She searched for Ángel, but couldn't find him. Instead, she found Carolina leaning against the wall, her eyes wide at the sudden killing spree. Taking her by the arm, she directed the Red Nun inside the house. Luz sat between Carolina and her mother.

"Mother, how did you get here?" Luz asked.

"A witch tricked me to follow her into the wilderness. Maso saved me from her. Pointed me into the desert where I found my boys. They rescued me from the Yoris."

"Ángel?" Carolina asked.

"You know my son? What are you doing here?"

"I walk with him, *Señora* Falcon."

"Walk with Ángel?" Petra's initial disbelieving gaze soon converted to sad understanding. "Mateo spoke the truth about the two of you. He's risked much for you... sinned against his people... Ángel stayed behind to draw Yoris away. Those two Yoris devils chased Cheve and me. We brought death here."

"Mother, where's Cheve?" Luz asked.

CHAPTER 30

SNOTTY ANTLERS

Cheve shouted to his mother to keep her head down as he rode to elude the bullets spraying all around. He stopped long enough to drop her off at the hut before he resumed his evasive ride. With two Yori vaqueros close on his tail, he dodged their bullets and curses.

"I'm Yaqui," he cried to the defenders. "Don't shoot me." Once out of the camp, he galloped farther into the desert, soon spying about thirty men sitting on the ground, eating and drinking. Well-armed men raised rifles, waved and shouted for him to stop.

"Shoot the *hijo de puta*," an alert Yori shouted. Several shots winged past striking the ground, tossing up dirt sprays at the bullets' point of impact. Vaqueros scrambled to their horses.

My candle's still afire.

After about ten kilometers, his pursuers fell off so far that he couldn't see or hear them. He returned to the poisoned water hole and the dead Yaqui merchant family. Coyotes and buzzards feasted on the remains. When desert dogs snarled, Cheve's horse whinnied, backing up. Gentle pats on the horse's trembling neck settled the mare.

"Nothing to fear, my friend," he said in a soft voice. "We rule here."

A coyote burrowed his snout into the smallest girl, tearing and chewing her stomach. At the sound of Cheve approaching, the predator started to drag her away. The Yaqui warrior shot the coyote in its belly, spewing its guts on the ground.

"Chew on that," Cheve shouted.

The buzzards took flight in a flurry of feathers and angry caws, sounding to the world their banquet had been interrupted by a rude intruder.

The bodies revealed the animals had mutilated their remains, left the trader family in a tangled mess of exposed bones, dried blood and red flesh. Cheve had seen Yaquis wracked from fire, disease, gunshot and knife cuts, but never eaten. Bites and tears disfigured the faces of the man, woman and children. Their torn torsos exposed shredded organs, ribs and muscles. He crossed himself, nudged his horse to a trot in search of Ángel's horse hoof prints. At wings flapping, he looked back. Buzzards alighted anew, strutting impatiently for him to leave. Their meal grew cold.

On tracking several horses' hoof prints for several kilometers, Cheve found a bloody trail on the desert floor that led to a dead mustang riddled with several bullet holes. As soon as he recognized Ángel's mount, he winced and scanned the area for the likely scenario. He imagined Yoris shot the horse from under him as he tried to elude them. His brother would have shot back. *If they killed or wounded Ángel, they wouldn't leave his body in the desert. They'd take it back to Guaymas as a prize. Or perhaps, that fat sergeant has him back in the Yori encampment.*

"Ángel, where did you go?" Cheve shouted. Human footprints, spaced in a runner's span, led away from the horse. Cheve followed the tracks in a westerly direction for about fifty meters and stopped at the scattered bullet shells. *Ángel made his stand here. More hoof prints but no more foot tracks. Unless Ángel sprouted wings, he had to ride out. But on whose horse?*

Hoof and human steps threw Cheve into a quandary: find Ángel or ride to Pótam?

He started after the horse trail, but stopped when he heard the familiar song, "Other Side." Gooseflesh rippled on his arms at the melodic words, routing all doubts. Maso galloped toward him until it stopped several meters away.

Cheve's horse neighed and backed away. "Easy," he muttered, stroking the mare's neck. "It's Maso."

The deer bobbed its antler-crowned head up and down, sinuous antlers tipped in red. Stirring up dust, its long legs shuffled. Deer Dancer's heart swelled at the singing presence of his magical ally. A yearning to dance with Maso swept over him, but before he could leap to the ground, the deer galloped away.

Cheve followed, riding in a quick pace, pressing his horse to keep up. He joined the grand deer in the singing of the Little People, recalling the desert beauty and the Other Side. He chased the stag up the slope of Red Mountain into thick tree covering where he lost sight of it. Maso's melodies acted as a beacon for Cheve's pursuit, hurrying as the song faded and slowing as it grew louder. From his hut dream, that seemed so long ago, he knew the journey's end. *Am I dreaming? My Seataka must be strong.*

As Cheve and his horse broke onto the summit, his deer guide danced from side to side in smooth, powerful leaps, keeping time with the lyrics.

His mare shied away from the mighty deer swirls, edging back, head bobbing. Cheve pulled on the reins, but the frightened animal neighed, reared and bucked him off. Free of rider, horse shot down the slope.

Stupid horse. He lay on the ground, his back aching from the fall. "My mount declined your invitation to dance."

Maso stood over him, making high, bleating sounds Cheve understood.

"You don't need a horse," Maso said. "They're witless and rude."

Cheve had never thought about horses in these terms.

"Do you dream?"

"Too well," Cheve said.

Maso shook its antlers. "Little Deer, you run, hunt and fight smarter if you exercise your speed, strength and courage in your night stories. Your visions give you faith in your talents. Your dreams will lead you to the *Yo Ania.*"

"Will dreaming give me a new face?" Cheve placed a hand over his disfigurement. "I remember once imagining I woke with a new one. Instead, this." He took away his hand.

"Do your night visions frighten you?" Maso asked.

"I recall a nightmare as a child when my mother left me on the ground in our hut. Beady, red eyes stared at me. Rats squealed, attacked and gnawed my cheeks. I twisted, swatted them, but they held tight, biting, tearing. I awoke tearful, shaken," Cheve's hands trembled. "at the bank of the Yaqui. I don't remember walking there."

"Phantom searches for your beauty. You were close to finding it," Maso said. "All men are ugly and you're not any uglier than others," Maso said. "Oversized heads, bushy eyebrows, puffy lips, crooked noses and yellow, brown, or no teeth. Wrinkles on top of wrinkles. Skin sagging like drooping candles. Men seldom bathe and smell foul. Without fur and antlers, you look like walking snakes. I ignore your looks and gaze into your hearts to find you." Maso bent its head until it touched Cheve's. "You possess the beauty and strength of a desert mesquite, strong and tough. To thrive in the *Huya Ania*, all life must learn to live with less. The hardiest will survive. Value little your appearance. Instead, dream well, nurture a good heart."

Maso strode to the center of the summit and swayed its head from side to side in a slow, steady swing. Shoulders and hind legs rocked in unison rippling the haunches' and back muscles with each leap.

Cheve clapped in joy to watch the magic deer perform for him a dance Yaquis practiced for years to perfect. He imitated the deer's sway, shift, dip and bob in *animan* synchronicity.

Maso quickened its pace, alternating springs from the front to the back and then from side to side. It rose to its hind legs and swirled in a circle around Little Deer like a furry tornado that swallowed a tree, all the while singing a lilting melody.

With sights on his hairy guide, Cheve pranced until his legs hurt. He panted, grew dizzy and doubled over. The world spun, his legs wobbled, stumbled to the side, tripped on a stone and crashed to the ground. Closing his eyes, he still whirled, but soon breathing resumed to an easy flow. When he opened his eyes, he beheld Maso's muzzle inches away. Black snout glistened sweat beads.

"You're not ready to dance. Rise," Maso said. "A witch hunts you."

Cheve rose. "Is she here?" He looked around.

"I smell roses." The deer lifted its muzzle up. "She's on the mountain, waiting for you."

"What does she want?"

"Your good heart and *Seataka*, to never dream or dance, to obey her, a slave son."

"Son?"

"She's your mother."

"No!" Cheve clinched his fist and drew them up. "My mother is Petra Falcon."

"She raised you. *La bruja* spit you out. Ate her last slave boy and desires another. She seeks vengeance."

Cheve backed away from Maso and shook his head. "I left my true mother in a camp. She's waiting for my help, to save her."

"To rescue one mother, you must kill the other. You must dream about slaughtering *la bruja*. She's devious. Will try to steal your wits." Deer shook its head, its crown of antlers rattling like swords against shields. A velvet bone broke loose and hit Cheve on the shoulder. "I give you a deer crown. You can dance through the night, run long distances without tiring, drive phantom dreams away."

Cheve picked up the light, short antler with pointy end from the ground. "I still have the other." He took it from his shirt and held up the pair.

"Come closer."

As he strode to the deer, Maso towered over him. The musky odor of its plush coat filled his nose. *Hadn't Ángel told him he smelled like a deer? An honor.* His hands hovered over Maso's fur. *Dare I touch him?* Youthful temptation ordered him to place both antlers into one hand. His free fingers ran deep through the deer's coat, exposing only the tips of his knuckles. He drew his face closer and rubbed his normal side on the Maso's hair. The piquant scent was strong and bittersweet. He brushed his deformity deep into the deer's furry robe. Eyes grew warm, wet as tears welled up. His weeping surprised him.

"I give you deep *Seataka*." Maso stepped closer to Cheve. "Makes you strong to fight." Don't be frightened of the *Yo Ania*—your strength flows from it."

Maso licked Cheve's deformed mouth and nose leaving it cool, wet and tingly. "Wash your face in the Yaqui River tonight. Your *Seataka* will bring you closer to the *Yo Ania*. Now place the antlers in each hand. Show me your palms."

As soon as Cheve exposed them, the deer snorted snot into them. "Paste the antlers to your head."

The boy planted his palms to his temples, pressed hard, released and found his hands empty.

"You possess the beauty and strength of a deer. Cry no more." Maso danced and sang about the Surem, dead Yaquis, their struggles, courage and strength.

Cheve joined in, swaying his new antlers with pride. He looked up to see them, but they were beyond his vision. His legs grew stronger in tempo with the Maso's. Little Deer's melodic voice rang forceful.

The deer stopped dancing, bellowed a lusty howl and bolted down the mountain. Deer Dancer ran to the mountain edge, but saw no sign of his ally. He stretched his arms out into the clear, blue sky. "I am Cheve, Yaqui warrior, son of Mateo and Petra Falcon, ally of Maso, deer dancer, defender of the most human people." His words echoed throughout the caves, crevices and cones of Red Mountain. He trotted down the slope. Without horse, he estimated he could reach Pótam by sunset.

Legs and arms in steady rhythmic cycle, heart beat accelerating, lungs expanding and deflating, body sweating, muscles engorged from his blood, Cheve loped. He sprinted faster than ever with grace and lightness, his feet skipping on the ground. His steps leaped like a deer with his mid-feet bounding and launching in steady descent. Reaching tall trees, he found woods enclosed him in brown bark, green shade and pine scent. Snapping cones echoed under his rapid footfalls.

When a roar reverberated through the trees, he peered at the forest gloom. His shoulder muscles tensed to the warning: he wasn't alone. The growl boomed closer. He surveyed the pines ahead, stopped and surveyed all around. Through the foliage, he saw a crouching jaguar at the foot of a fir staring back at him. To its side lay a horse, the mare he rode to the mountain, partly eaten.

When the beast growled, Cheve ran faster, cleared the tree lines and found the ground leveling, closer to the desert floor. He increased his speed, churning his legs in jack rabbit strides. The big cat chased him, jaws agape, closing within ten body lengths.

Cheve stood his ground, lowered his deer antlers, poised to charge. He howled like Maso, brandishing his knife to tear into the predator. Spittle dripped from his lips as he contorted his face.

After the beast took a few more tentative steps, it stopped, sniffed the air and gazed at him. Prowling from side to side, the animal appeared confused by the boy.

To help it decide, Cheve shouted, "Charge, jaguar. You'll taste your guts."

The cat held a paw in the air as if it forgot where to step next.

"Maso is my ally," Cheve shouted, beat his chest and howled.

Before the mission to Guaymas, he had never been alone in the wilderness. His parents told him it wasn't safe with wild animals. Savage Yoris or Torocoyoris shot Yaquis on sight.

With knife in hand, antlers on crown, he looked around at the desert scenery. Wild shrubs, mesquites, cactus and brown desert floor, framed by shapely mountains and blue skies, evoked a natural beauty defying fences. To take their land was to steal the Yaqui River, the desert flowers, Maso, birthplace of ancestors, their dreams.

Jaguar snorted, opened his mouth as if to snarl but stood frozen. It trembled, spun and ran back to his interrupted horse feast.

Cheve resumed his kicking, feeling deep respect for fauna, flora and his people for fighting to keep their holy land no Yaqui owned. The land belonged to God and *Surem*, the Little People, who lived hidden in the wildest and remotest regions. Deer songs revealed the Other Side, mirror world of this one. He recited lyrics in his mind to preserve the beauty of this creation for the beauty of the other realm.

The pull-push of his sinewy limbs, the effortless synchronization of arms to legs, the sweat beads shimmering his body and the rapid rush of air into lungs imbued him with a euphoric, mesmerizing awe of desert colors. Losing all sense of shame, he absorbed the *Yo Ania* spirit in pulsating pores.

He ran for several hours without fatigue or thirst. Stories of another people beyond the eastern mountains, who ran hundreds of kilometers kicking a ball without stopping, arose from memory. At the time, he thought them foolish to run so far when they could ride a horse. The intimacy of feet touching desert dirt with every step felt like kissing wilderness soles. Soil covering his body left him dusty with confidence he could cover long distances on holy grounds. Yaqui magic fortified lungs, legs and heart.

As the sun slid over the Becatete Mountains, he basked in dusky rays relishing the last day's warmth. When the faint melody and lyrics of "Other Side" wafted closer, he joined in. He strained to see Maso, but the darkness draped a blanket over the land.

Fireplaces burning from the distant huts of Pótam guided him. The deer's singing faded and left Cheve chanting at the Yaqui banks about earthly sacrifices and rebirth after death.

On other nights, chill would force him to curl with a blanket. His euphoria imbued him with an ardor for life. Alert and fearless, he found the trek to Pótam invigorating.

He ran to the wooden bridge spanning the river and jogged across, his feet echoing his arrival in huaraches' booms. Along the edge, he descended a path, knelt at the riverbank, scooped up water and washed his face as instructed by Maso. Cheve probed for changes and sunk into the all too familiar skin folds. After scooping more water and splashing his face, he again found nothing new. Stepping into the river, Cheve dunked his head and swept it side to side.

He rose and stared, by star light and moon glow, at a wavy reflection. As the surface calmed, goose bumps erupted on his arms. Bending to the river, he observed his face unfold on the surface: a smooth, handsome boy reflected in the river. His mouth gaped as he stared at Cheve Falcon the whole and smooth. The river face looked as attractive as any member of his family—just as good-looking as Ángel's. In the watery image, his eyes bulged.

He swayed his head from side to side. Cheeks were symmetrical, free of all holes. Small nostril flares accented. Nose shaft sloped in a smooth angle from between his eyes to the gentle, curved tip. Lips curved evenly like a ribbon bow. When he smiled, it was as if he were opening a pearly gift. An eagle's look, he thought, not a falcon's. His aqua visage appeared strong, lean and chiseled.

Cheve yelled in joy, danced and sang a deer song at the river's edge. He laughed until he patted his face and felt the familiar holes. A jolt swept his body that paralyzed his hands to his cheeks. He explored more of his visage and probed the familiar, asymmetrical expression. He bent again to the river, gazing into the watery mirror.

A passing cloud shielded the moon and veiled his image. Cheve groaned until the sky shadow drifted past the blemished lunar surface, freeing the light to shine on the river. From the Other Side, Cheve's proud visage stared back at the homely Yaqui on the bank. At the touch of his cheek, he saw the hand in the river caress the smooth skin while the ugly twin probed a jagged shell on this side.

Laughing at Maso's cleverness, he admired his shadowy smile as he stuck out his tongue. He changed his expressions to a scowl, fear and sadness. His wide grin transformed him to a youthful, attractive, deer dancer.

I will smile more to chase the ugly away.

He laughed again and then wept. *It doesn't matter: ugly or handsome, full-blood or half-breed, I am a child of the Yaqui — a beautiful boy. That's Maso's gift.*

His face dripping water, wearing a crown of deer antlers, he rose from the river and ran up the bank, shouting, "Cheve Falcon, deer dancer, desert runner, Maso ally is home."

CHAPTER 31

BOCAGRANDE DEALS

Twilight crept onto the defenders stirring Tomas to prepare Yaquis for the cold, desert night. He ordered them to light no fires, to remain quiet. Men posted in pairs all around the camp perimeter listened for any unusual sounds. As instructed, they knew to report as soon as they heard Yoris attacking. Most carried rocks, bows and tree limbs. In the dark, they would clash in the fashion of their forefathers: hand to hand. Despite the order to remain quiet, the wounded moaned and sobbed.

Able-bodied women without children joined the fighters. Should the men fall, they would pick up their weapons and avenge their deaths or die trying. Carolina and Luz guarded the southern end of the camp. They sat on the ground gazing at faint outlines of mesquites, brush, rocks, terrain. The hut lay about fifty meters to the rear. Shivering from the night's coolness, with no blanket, the woman warriors leaned against one another.

Rapid footsteps from behind approached. "Food. Eat." Tomas sat beside Luz, handing them tortillas and honey.

She devoured her cold meal in a few bites. *More, I wish there were more.*

"Yoris will attack on foot," he said. "Too dangerous to ride a horse. Mares fart and snort. Make much noise. We would target them by their smell and snot." The women muffled their giggles. He handed them each a pistol. "They're loaded. Use them if they come too close. Shoot for the chest and you'll not miss."

Luz held the weapon, recalling her last experience at the Hacienda *García.* What a child she had been when faced with the possibility of shooting the *hacendado* to save Carolina's honor. She gripped the gun, her hand holding the weapon steady. She had witnessed the terrible wounds that bullets left in flesh. With her mother in the camp, along with innocent women and children, facing merciless Yoris and Torocoyoris, she had two options: fight or die. Her breathing quickened knowing she must pray for the courage to kill.

At first the chant was faint, but more Yori and Torocoyori voices joined in the chant until the night resounded with *"Yeewe bichoo, yeewe bichoo, yeewe bichoo…"*

A light flared in front of them. Then another, and soon a third torch flamed.

Luz stared at the fire. *Oh, Mother Mary, let my bullets strike the enemy dead. Let them die quickly.*

"They come now," Tomas shouted. "Fight like Yaqui warriors. Fight for your families." His calm words sounded eerily soothing.

The chanting gradually stopped. "Don't shoot," A voice shouted in Spanish. "I want to parley."

Carolina interpreted to Tomas. "Tell him not to come any closer," he said.

She did so.

He shifted the machine gun barrel toward the darkness in front of him.

The Yori negotiator spoke in a deep voice that sounded familiar. The face of the fat Yori sergeant sprang from Luz's memory. She shivered when the corpulent profile in the light of the torch came into view.

"He's tracked us," Luz groaned.

"Who?" Tomas asked.

"Bocagrande," she said.

"No. It can't be," Carolina voice trembled.

"Look at the light. See his fat face. Listen to his voice. It's him."

"*Porcina!*" Carolina jumped up and fired several rapid shots at the big target she called swine.

The torchlight fell to the ground. Yoris shot back.

"Get down," Tomas shouted, pulling Carolina down.

Luz lay low. The din of gunfire and yells blasted around her. The desert quiet shifted to a night of exploding powder, flying bullets, screaming curses.

Tomas' rapid firing gun barked. He struggled to hold steady the machine squirms like a spoiled child. Rounds pummeled the enemy position with a rat-a-tat-tat. Rising to his feet, he ran forward. "Kill Yoris," he roared.

Luz winced from the surrounding frantic feet, yells, screams, thuds, sparks, flames and smoke. She jumped up, but didn't fire in fear she would shoot Tomas. At first, Luz didn't hear Carolina screaming at her.

"What?" Luz said.

"The firing's stopped," the Red Nun said close to her ear.

When she took her hands away, howls of freshly wounded men haunted the night.

"They've come for me," Carolina said.

As if he heard her, Bocagrande shouted, "Yaqui *putos*. I want to trade—not fight. You savages killed one of my men and wounded several. I know you have women and children. I don't want to kill them. But if you start shooting again, I'll tell my men to leave no one alive. Take your ass-wiping fingers off your triggers and from your ears. Listen to my offer first."

A strained voice interpreted the Sergeant's words into Cajita.

"Don't shoot," Tomas shouted. "We'll hold fire. Any tricks, you won't see your wives or children again." A Torocoyori interpreted Tomas' words.

"My men will not shoot as long as you are willing to bargain," the sergeant said. "Give me the white woman, Carolina, the pretty nun. She's crazy and will take you to hell. The nun bewitched Ángel Falcon. Enslaved him with empty promises of sex, money and status. Told him stories about running away with him. Would you trade the lives of your women and children for one crazy, white woman? Give her to us and we'll go away. That's all we want. You can then return to your dog rabies plagued villages."

Carolina picked up the pistol, pulled the trigger, but it didn't fire. The Red Nun stood and shouted in Cajita, "The Yori is a liar except for one thing. I'm crazy in love with Ángel and want to be his wife. That's why they want to take me back. They can't accept a white woman marrying a Yaqui, a real man." She sat and wept.

Luz placed her arm around her. "Tomas will find us a way out of this."

"Sister—or whatever you are now—Carolina, your parents want you home," Sergeant Bocagrande shouted. "If you care for these people, you'll come with us to stop this fighting and spare their lives."

"The white woman you seek isn't here," Tomas said. "All who fight are Yaquis. She's used her *brujería* to cleanse herself of Yori filth and is now Yaqui. Tell her parents, their daughter found no suitable man among Yoris and gringos. For every Yaqui woman or child you kill, we will slay twice that number of Yori women and children. I'll personally look for your wife and brats, you fat burro shit, and slice their throats."

After the interpretation, the sergeant laughed. "Find my wife and brats? You must be *loco*, too? You'll need to search and travel across México and Arizona. Every bordello in Sonora is home to at least one of my bastards. Let's reason and not play hero, Yaqui rat face. Señor Culpepper is rich and will pay a good ransom for her. I've brought five thousand pesos. Take it and buy another machine gun and bullets."

"You should leave the money as a good will peace offering, dog fornicator," Tomas said.

"You want a peace offering. I give you one, *hijo de puta*."

Torchlight burst and revealed three men. Two supported a limp man who stood between them. His head hung low. Pants and shirt were shredded, soiled. "If you shoot now, your sweet Ángelito will die first." The sergeant placed the gun barrel to the prisoner's temple.

Carolina screamed. "Ángel, my Ángel."

Luz held her from running to him.

A woman from behind shouted, "My son." Petra approached. "They've captured my son."

Luz went to her. "Mother, you shouldn't be here."

"My offer still stands," Bocagrande shouted. "You can have lover boy and the money in exchange for Carolina. We had to persuade him to tell us his girlfriend's whereabouts. He's not so pretty anymore. When I polished his pearls, I rubbed a bit too hard. How sad."

"Bring him closer," Tomas said. "I can't see his face from this distance."

"Send someone who knows him well. We'll not harm the man you send."

"I need to identify him," Luz told her mother. "I know what he wore, his weight, height, length of his hair."

"He bears a half-moon birthmark on his chest, beneath his left nipple," Petra said.

"Yes, I remember it," Luz said. "Tomas, I'm going out. Don't shoot."

Tomas grabbed her arms. "It's too dangerous," he said. "They'll take you captive, rape or kill you for our resistance."

"If you and Carolina go, they'll shoot you, take her captive and kill Ángel for spite. Then they'll kill all of us. Innocence has no place here."

Tomas sighed. "Brave, smart woman—don't shoot, Yaquis. A warrior goes to identify the prisoner."

Luz walked with the gun at her side. The closer she approached, the more anxious she grew. The hapless man's clothes and size matched Ángel's.

As if he read her mind, a Yori lifted the prisoner's head by his hair.

Luz gasped at the sight of a distorted face caked with bloody smears. Puffed eyes closed like the dark orbs of a fly. Bloody, snotty nose, swollen and crooked, bent far to the left. Cut lips covered with crimson patches smeared like misplaced paint. Dirty, matted hair wadded into blood balls. Right ear seeped a red trail. Jaw sat askew. His grotesquerie repulsed her, but she continued to stare unsure of who stood before her.

"Ángel," she said. The head teetered from side to side. "Who is your sister?"

"Luz," the man said in a broken voice.

She drew nearer, opened his shirt, saw the half-moon and wrapped her arms around him.

He moaned.

"Ugly, no?" Bocagrande said. "You had debts to pay, didn't you Ángel? I warned you we would meet again. What was that trick, *yeewe bichoo, yeewe bichoo.*" Torchlight exposed the sergeant's beefy face as he pumped his hand into the air. His piggish eyes squinted in delight. His men laughed, their hands mimicking their *jefe's.*

"Let me take him. He's no good to you like this."

"I'll consider it if we come to terms. If not, I cut off bits of him all night and feed it to the coyotes. His screams will not allow you to sleep. A pity, no?" He brandished a large knife and drew it close to Ángel's crotch. "The longer you wait, the less boom-boom ever after, ahhhhh." He pumped his hips forward. "We'll change his name to Ángelita, *qué lástima.*"

Luz clutched the gun harder, tempted to shoot Ángel and end his pain. She groaned. "My dear brother. I regret going to Guaymas. Mother was right." She released him and raced back to the Yaqui camp.

Carolina ran to embrace her. "Ángel?"

Despite Luz's opened mouth, crippled words lay on her tongue. By the time her mother and Tomas reached her, bitter tears flowed. "It's him. Tortured and beaten. But he lives."

Sergeant Bocagrande shouted, "I grow impatient. Give me Carolina or I'll cut Ángel's snake and toss it to you. I'll throw in tequila and my favorite Yaqui whores to the man who gives me crazy nun."

A Torocoyori interpreted and added "sons of bitches."

The torch-lit scene of Ángel held up between two Yoris loomed brightly against the desert darkness.

274

"Kill Yoris," Ángel shouted in Cajita. His strained voice cracking.

The sergeant slammed his pistol into Ángel's beaten face, whipping his head to the side, slinging blood onto one of the men who held him up.

Petra cried, "My Ángel. Leave him alone!"

Carolina screamed, "I'll go with you. Stop beating him."

"Carolina, don't go," Luz said.

Tomas ran to the Red Nun and held up his hand. "Wait. We'll kill them all."

"They'll murder Ángel before you can stop them. Can't let them kill my man. Besides, I'm not Yaqui. I'm *rubia*." She tore final remnants of her veil and threw them to the ground as she raced forward. She soon stood before her Yaqui lover.

Luz watched as she talked to him, touched his face and bloodied her hands.

The sergeant gestured for the men to take her. When the Yoris released Ángel, he crumpled to the ground. She screamed at Bocagrande, bent down to wipe Ángel's forehead with her skirt.

The Yori commander grabbed Carolina's arm. She resisted. He jerked hard, pulling her closer as if to dance a desert tango of death. Torchlight extinguished, draping the Yori drama in darkness. The Red Nun screamed, the sergeant laughed raucously, vaqueros hooted. Jingling spurs, creaking saddles, rapid hoof beats reverberated through the darkness.

Luz joined Tomas and other Yaquis racing to catch the fallen Ángel.

"Bring a litter," Tomas shouted.

"Brother, we're here. We'll care for you now," Luz said. "Mother is with us."

"My love… my life," Ángel cried as tears mixed with snot and blood smeared his once handsome face.

CHAPTER 32

✦

YAQUI MAP

Cheve howled, "I'm home, my people," as he ran past Yaquis gossiping in front of homes, children playing in fields, and dogs barking in dirt paths. A girl pointed and exclaimed to her mother she had seen a deer in the village. Smells of meat and tortilla whetted his appetite as he came upon armed men camped around fires. When he reached the graveyard of crooked crosses, he shouted, "Come to the church. Yoris trapped our people in the desert."

His raucous entrance sent men scurrying for their guns.

"I've come from the *Huya Ania*. News of our people. First, prayer." Cheve noticed fresh graves, sunflowers and purple mats strewn over them. A pang of guilt rankled, recalling how he had led the Yoris to Luz's escorts. He crossed himself before entering the church.

Women knelt and prayed before statues of the *Virgen* and saints. Crying infants swaddled in blankets lay on the ground next to their mothers. In contrast to the Yori church in Guaymas, the Yaqui church appeared poor in materials, but rich in spirit. Yori cathedral, constructed of marble floors, stained glass windows, tiled ceilings and wooden pews, rose majestic as an anteroom to heaven. Here, Yaqui worshippers knelt on dirt, surrounded by peeling plaster, rotting beams and few candles. A cracked statue of Jesus stood on a wooden altar. Despite their humble sanctuary, Yaquis devoutly served the Christ, without pretense. *La iglesia de los indios* seemed to sprout from the soil like a tree.

Cheve knelt at the altar. Blessing himself, he closed his eyes in a thanksgiving prayer for surviving the trek. Despite his efforts to calm his breathing, he found it hard to focus on the devotion, his river face kept leaping to his mind's eye. The harder he tried to suppress his handsome images, the more they sprang. Whether with closed or opened eyes, he saw his visage from the Other Side swimming up to his mind's surface, smiling back at him. He sighed, crossed himself again, stood and found a guard waiting. Outside the church, he was greeted by a large crowd.

"Blessings." Cheve held up his hand as his mother had taught him.

"Blessings," they shouted and peppered him with questions about Yoris, their response to the peace offering, their strength.

"Say nothing until you speak with Cajemé," the guard ordered.

Instead of looking away, Cheve held his head up, antlers visible to all. His legs trembled in an urge to dance.

"Clear a path," the warrior commanded.

Deer Dancer wound his way through the scattered homes, followed by the Yaqui throng, to the largest hut in Pótam. Surrounded by a high, mesquite wooden fence, Cajemé's headquarters was guarded by about one hundred armed men. Cheve's escort spoke to another warrior at the compound entrance and pointed to the boy. The guard opened a gate for the pair to enter. The hut's entrance stood about ten meters from the fence.

A tall cross loomed in the center of the yard with burning candles around its base. A Yaqui flag hung listlessly from a wooden pole planted in the ground to the side of the hut's door. A warrior, cradling a rifle along the path, gestured with the barrel the correct path.

The desire to dance vanished at the thought he would soon face Cajemé.

Several armed Yaquis who stood or sat on the ground, smoking or eating, gazed at him. Their curious expressions didn't annoy, but instead coaxed a nod and a smile from him. The closer he approached the hut door, the louder the hum of voices rose from inside. The antlered boy waited a moment before another sentry opened the door.

The lantern-lit hut revealed several men sitting on the floor around maps. Others stood or sat in another ring. A warrior pointed to the outer circle where Cheve should sit. Across from him, his stern-faced father sat cross-legged, next to the captain-general. The boy rose to speak to him, but stopped when Mateo placed an index finger over his lips and waved to the ground.

Still imbued with the joy of the *Yo Ania*, deer dancer smiled his lop-sided grin at the gathering.

"Your prodigal son returns." Cajemé said. "Or do you have two prodigal sons?" The boy squirmed at the captain-general's pause and stare. "You disobeyed my orders. I'm told you led the Yoris to my men. Several died. Explain."

Cheve stood and bowed. He glanced at his father who returned his gaze. He took a deep breath. "Captain-general, I grieve for their deaths. I wanted to protect my sister, Luz, from the Yoris, to find my brother, Ángel, in Guaymas. I meant no disrespect to you or my father. I'm a Yaqui warrior. I've killed a Yori."

"Killed a Yori, have you? Tell us, Yaqui fighter, of your battles."

Worried of the danger and shame he would place on his family, he gave a sketchy account of their escape and recapture. Cheve withheld any information about Ángel's role in the rape of Cajemé's wife, his joining the Torocoyoris and his love for Carolina.

His voice grew more animated when he told of his Maso meeting at Red Mountain, the deer's gift of the antlers. Lest they laugh and scoff, he withheld tales of his river face, or of his encounters with the witch.

"What an adventure," Cajemé said. "Maso, captures, escapes, fighting, killing, antlers," Cajemé said. "Despite your disobedience, you're a remarkable boy. Maso is your ally, you say. Right now I need magic cannons that shoot real bombs. Can you ask your antler friend to give me one or two? Will Maso deploy his deer army to fight alongside Yaquis? Can the deer whistle," Cajemé blew a high toot, "to the birds to shit on the Yoris and piss on the Torocoyoris? Were you shown the cave with the Yori candles? Tell me where it is and I'll send my best bean eaters to fart out their candle flames."

As the men chuckled, Cheve's body tensed. The familiar serpentine shame and humiliation slithered its way into his chest. He smiled and the shame retreated.

"A jest, Deer Boy. Laugh to drive away the fears. I need more men and arms than deer and antlers." Cajemé leaned toward Mateo. "You raised a brave fighter. I recall his courage in trying to stop the rape of my wife. And he disobeyed my orders, he says, to protect his sister. For your punishment, Cheve," the captain-general returned his gaze onto the boy, "you will guide some men back to our trapped people. Come closer. Look at this map."

He knelt before the drawings astonished by how someone could have drawn mountains, rivers, and towns. *The artist must know how to fly or stood at the peak of Red Mountain to capture the details.* Like a hawk, the boy soared over the Yaqui searching for his mother, brother, sister and Maso. By the proximity of the dots and lines, he realized they lived in close contact with the Yoris. They surrounded the Yaquis' land.

Cajemé traced the Yaqui River with his knife as it wound from the mountains and snaked through the Yaqui Valley to the Gulf of Cortez. Seven dots along the river represented their villages. The captain-general's knifepoint lay first on Pótam. Next, it glided and hovered over Guaymas. He handed the blade to Cheve. "Show me where our people stand."

The boy took the dagger from the gentle-faced, captain-general with the missing index fingertip. Cajemé's thin stature, short hair and wisp of a mustache gave him a teacher's look rather than the visage of a battle-hardened Yaqui commander. The knife point slid from Guaymas, traced along the coast, and then stopped. "We walked inland for a few hours. Came to a hacienda."

"Its name?"

"Hacienda Garza — no, it was Gar —"

"García," Mateo said.

"That's it, Father. Hacienda García."

Cajemé took the blade and placed the tip on a location north of Pótam. He dragged the end to a mountain formation. "Red Mountain is here. When you left the Yaquis at the camp in the afternoon, was the sun on your face or back as you traveled to reach the mountain?"

He remembered the sun's heat and sweat on his shoulders. "On my back."

Cajemé placed a finger on the map. "Mateo, there is a deserted trading post near the hacienda. You recall the location?" Mateo nodded. "Take ten men, your best shooters. Bring back our people."

"As you order," Cheve's father bowed his head.

"I can send Anastácio," Cajemé said.

"I'll bring them back. My wife and daughter are there."

"Go tonight." Cajemé stood and raised his arms. "Time to give the Yoris another lesson on Yaqui land ownership." The men whooped, shook their rifles, bows, and knives in the air. "Yoris want to enslave us for their haciendas and mines. The cowardly Mayos surrendered and now kiss their Yori masters' cheeks—face and ass. Some of our people have broken Yaqui law sharing our secrets, trails and tactics. We'll hunt the snakes and kill them."

Cheve gazed at his father who stared at the map. He hoped he wouldn't ask about Ángel.

"This land is like our mother. But Yoris want to rape her. As good sons, we'll fight to spare her from their lust. Are you brave enough to die defending her?"

All the men stood, shook their weapons and roared. *Mother was right: Cajemé was a preacher of war.*

When Mateo rose, Cheve went to his side. "I'm sorry, Father."

"Follow me." Outside the hut, Mateo picked up a lit lantern and shouted out ten names. "You men will rescue Yaquis trapped by the Yoris. Get your fastest horses, food, water and weapons. We leave in an hour."

The select grunted their understanding and ran to the corral.

Mateo led Cheve away. "Tell me more about your mother, sister. How are they?"

"When I left, they were uninjured, but they're scared. Yoris mean to kill them." His father's eyes stared hard as if searching for his wife and daughter in the folds of his tortured face.

"And Ángel?" Mateo asked. "Is he Torocoyori?"

Cheve winced at the question. He stepped back. His throat constricted, mouth dried and his breathing quickened. *Lie: Ángel is still loyal to Yaquis.* But he wasn't a good liar – not to his father. Despite the darkness, he averted his face. "Ángel walks with a Yori woman named Carolina. They wish to marry. Joined the Yori guard to be close to her." Cheve lacked the nerve to tell him he abandoned all Yaqui ways and God.

Mateo shook his head. "If I hadn't been so weak, you wouldn't have this." His hand caressed Cheve's face. "Ángel would ride as a Yaqui warrior now. Instead – "

Cheve couldn't hold back tears. "Maso gave me a gift. Come to the river, Father."

"We must be going – your mother, sister."

"Please wait and see this wondrous sight."

Cheve led Mateo to the edge of Pótam, past cornfields and down an easy slope to the Yaqui River bank. "Now watch the water, Father. Bring the lantern closer." Cheve knelt. On seeing his reflection, he dunked his head into the aqua image and brought it up. As the waves settled, he pointed and said, "Look at me." He soon saw his handsome face waver into view. Cheve giggled. "My true face is on the Other Side, in the *Yo Ania*."

Mateo gasped.

"Did you see me, Father – on the Other Side?"

"Don't know. It's too dark." He drew back from the waters.

"My face is smooth in the *Yo Ania*. Maso has shown it to me." He splashed water over his head and ran his palm over the river surface. "I'm like you, Mother, Luz and Ángel: a good-looking Falcon."

Mateo put his hand on his son's shoulder. "Doesn't matter to me what you look like—you're my son. This gift, Cheve, should be kept a secret. Others without *Tekia* might get jealous, try to harm you. What else did the Maso tell you?"

"The deer speaks in riddles. Said in order to save my mother, I need to kill my mother. I would never hurt her. What does it mean?"

Mateo clinched his fist. "She's back."

"Who?"

His sobbing father edged closer to the river. He hugged his son in a strong embrace. "You're a brave, clever boy."

"I'm a warrior, Father." Cheve formed a half-moon smile over here and a full-moon beam on the Other Side.

CHAPTER 33

✦

CONFESSION

Ten Yaqui warriors, Mateo and Cheve rode through the desert night. Deer Dancer jockeyed next to his father, who painted his horse's rump and legs white to assure his men galloped close behind. Their horses grunted and pounded the desert floor. Their hoof beats syncopated their mission like drummers sounding their fervent approach.

Predators' shadows crisscrossed their paths or snarled at the disruption of the meal. Yellow eyes glowed in menacing stares. Cool, night breeze wafted the scent of burnt mesquite and horse sweat.

After many night raids, Mateo developed owl's eyes, adjusting to the shifting shadows and shapes. He soon saw the outline of the Bacatete Mountains. The distant peaks summoned the ghosts of the foray he had led from the mounts sixteen years ago.

Yoris and their Torocoyori trackers hunted Yaquis for several months in the Bacatete. Angry over hacienda attacks by Cajemé's men, the Sonoran governor sent Yaqui prisoners to Yori haciendas to work as slaves, servants and field hands. The captured went to silver and copper mines to replace the men the Yaquis liberated. Resistance meant death, beatings and deportation to Yucatan or the National Valley in central México. After Yoris poisoned their watering holes, Cajemé ordered roundups of suspected Torocoyoris who may have led their enemy to their wells. So it went: a never-ending cycle of raids, rapes and rage.

Now he rode with his youngest who still thought him as a father worthy of respect and love. Would he continue to honor him if he discovered the truth of what happened sixteen years ago at the trading hut?

On his galloping horse, Mateo heard Floratina's wails all over again. In the lunar glow, he saw her standing naked, embracing Victoriano's body and cursing him. Peering at Cheve, he feared Floratina's bewitching reach to his family.

His blood son? Perhaps. But certainly, he was the son of blood. He regretted daily Cheve's suffering for his sins. Since his return, the boy seemed more content and at peace. The journey, despite the dangers, lifted his confidence. Mateo still couldn't fathom his son's image in the Yaqui River. What witchery conjured such a handsome, watery face? Cheve insisted Maso bestowed this vision of the Other Side. Or could Floratina still haunt his family with tricks, lies and magic to wreak her vengeance?

A strong wind redolent of roses slapped him across the face.

"Mateo," a voice whispered.

"What," he said to Cheve riding at his side. His son shook his head. Mateo sat more erect in the saddle, searching all around into the night. Shadows of his men's heads bobbed like an undulating tail.

The wind called again, "Mateo... Mateo... Mateo." A woman's distinct lisp chilled him.

"Slow your pace, men," he shouted, holding up an arm. The men's and horses' labored breathing pleaded for respite. "We'll stop here." He pulled on his reins, his horse nodding as if in gratitude.

The rescue party took out their water bags, stretched their legs and rubbed their backs. Others unwrapped food bundles.

Mateo approached his son, who shared water with his horse. He placed his hand on his shoulder. "You were brave for following your sister on her mission. I disapproved. Can't lose you both. I know it was hard to accept your—If I could trade mine for yours, I would do it."

"I disappointed you. When you looked at me, I saw disgust. I was outside—not a true Falcon. But since I met Maso, I found my *Seataka*. Maso's tongue on my face opened my eyes to the truth of who I am. Maso taught me to fight for my people."

"The truth... the truth is ugly." Mateo took his son into his arms. "Cheve, Cheve, Cheve," he said. "Not your face. I felt disgust for myself, sins I committed. You suffered for them. You possess something more important than a handsome face: a strong heart. It's as tough as any other Yaqui. Mightier than mine. Your perfect face lies on the Other Side. But your deer heart is with us." Mateo pressed his chest against his son's.

Cheve's body shivered and his breathing quickened. "I longed for your acceptance, Father."

"You have it, Cheve, my deer son."

"What sins?"

Mateo took a deep breath and audibly exhaled. "Come with me." He took Cheve several meters away from the warriors into the desert, their horses shielding them from ears and eyes. The stillness of the night belied his turbulent memories. "I want you to see with your ears. Listen to a story of how you were conceived. I'm now going to explain the riddle that Maso told you about killing your mother. No questions, just listen."

Sixteen years ago, Mateo had led four men under darkness upon the hut. They woke a man and woman, demanding food. Contrary to Cajemé's order not to drink when hunting the enemy, they forced the captives to give them Tequila. After many weeks in the mountains, living off snakes and rabbits, sleeping in the open, cold air, Mateo surrendered to the irresistible taste of the worm.

Despite his futile efforts to forget, their names surfaced: Yori storekeeper Victoriano and Yaqui wife Floratina. The couple traded tools, liquor and jewelry for pearls, reed mats and wood. Cajemé suspected them of relaying reports to the Yoris and Torocoyoris about their movements. Their mission was to discover the truth of their trade in the desert.

After the first swallow and tingle, Mateo the Man couldn't stop the release of Mateo the Mad. He tried to recollect the warrior's name who called for a rope. Then remembered: Mateo Falcon.

They took Victoriano outside, bound his hands and put him on a horse. One of his men reminded him that Cajemé had ordered them to interrogate not execute Yoris. The drunk ordered the advisor to tie a noose around the prisoner's neck.

Floratina pleaded for her husband's life on her knees. "He did nothing wrong. He was a simple merchant of goods and wares, not a spy."

"He's Yori," the Yaqui leader shouted. "His people poisoned my Yori mercy well. If you're a true Yaqui, why do you defend him?"

"He's my husband—Yori, Yaqui, it doesn't matter," she cried. "He's my heart. Please, spare him."

Floratina rose, ran to the well at the side of the hut. She drew a bucket of water, brought it back and offered it to Mateo. "Our water is clean. We poison no one." She drank a sip. "Please soothe your anger with our sweet well. I beg you, don't harm him." Floratina fell to her knees and held up the bucket gift as if propitiating an angry god.

Mateo kicked it from her hands.

"I give myself to you." She drew up her skirt to expose her white frills. "I was a whore in *Cielito Lindo* in Guaymas. I know how to please a man. You can all have me, but don't touch my husband."

"Get up, woman," Victoriano shouted. "Lose no honor for me. Yaqui drunks aren't worthy of you, *mi florita. Te amo,* Flora—."

Mateo slapped the horse's rump. Victoriano hung gagging, thrashing, swinging, kicking before his body fell limp.

"He can now share his *dulce* armor with Satan," Mateo said.

Floratina screamed, ran to the body and clutched her husband's limp legs. She pulled hard toppling the body down on herself. Clutching and rocking her husband, she kissed his face.

"Victoriano, *mi cariño,* wake my love."

Mateo mimicked her lisp and skewed his lips.

She grimaced, exposing teeth. Her nose curled to a twisted heap of skin and cartilage. "Damn you to hell," she screamed at the men. "Damn your families."

Mateo clutched her hair and jerked her away from Victoriano's body. He pushed her back into the trading post. "I'll now honor your offer, whore." He lifted her onto the bar, raping her while his men watched and hooted. When he finished, he told his men, "She's yours."

All the raiders took turns, tearing her clothes off, slapping and laughing at Floratina. They poured Tequila on her, bragged about who was the better rapist. She howled, scratched and pulled their hair. The waiting men struggled to hold her down. Several punched and slapped her.

Through the ordeal, she groaned, calling, "Victoriano… Victoriano, my love. Forgive me."

Mateo lisped, "Victoriano… Victoriano, help me. These men are so much bigger than you." His men laughed.

After the last Yaqui rose from her, Mateo pointed to the horses. "We've planted enough seeds tonight. She may have quintuplet bastards. Thank you, *señora,* or whatever you are, for the hospitality. You see, Yaqui men satisfy better than Yoris." Mateo yelped and jumped onto his horse. A naked Floratina walked to her dead husband.

Looking down on her, the lead rapist shook his head. "If only you weren't so ugly. Your body is magnificent, but that face — well, God gets bored sometimes."

She spit at him, splattering his feet. "I curse you, your family and all Yaquis. The venom in your blood will poison you. In this life or the next, I will see you suffer. You will scream for death, but it will not come until your loved ones suffer first. I promise you this. Your name, Yaqui filth?"

Mateo drew his pistol, but decided better to allow her to live with bitter memories. Besides, who would believe a Yaqui whore? "My name, slut, is Mateo Falcon, Yori killer." He blew her a kiss, waving his hand for his men to follow.

They howled and whistled. Over their hoots, he heard her screaming for all Yaquis to die.

Her lisping screams echoed in the desert. "Falcons, I curse you!"

After they reached their mountain camp, Mateo reported all their activities, except for the rape of Floratina. Cajemé grew angry about the drinking. He warned Mateo if he tasted another Tequila drop on patrol, he would personally flog him in the center of Pótam for all to witness. But he knew Floratina had never forgiven him for his drinking, killing and raping.

Ángel and Luz had learned from whispers, embarrassed looks, unanswered questions, their father's awkward handling of baby Cheve that some great sin accompanied their little brother's arrival. After enough probing and gossip, his eldest discovered the secrets like unwrapping leaves of corn to expose kernels of truth. His son grew estranged and moved away to become a Torocoyori.

Mateo placed his hand on Cheve's shoulder. "I'm so sorry. I was drunk… I don't know which one of us fathered you. But, son, know that I am your true father."

"Father?" Cheve took a few steps back. "You sinned greatly. You might not be my real father. I may carry the blood of any one or all of the rapists."

"I am your Father. I raised you. I cared for you." Mateo rushed to Cheve and tried hugging him. The boy pulled away.

"No, wait." He held out an arm to mark the desired distance. "I must think more about this terrible story." Cheve walked a little way, his hand touching his temple. "I see you better now. Mother, Luz, Ángel, Floratina, those other men and you knew and never told me."

"To protect you. You suffered so much as it is with your…"

"Face. My ugly, shitty face." Cheve slapped hard his distorted visage. "My mother's face."

"You've seen her, haven't you?" Mateo asked. "In your dreams."

"Yes. In my dreams and out there." He swept his hand toward the desert. "She's frightening, strong. She waits for me. Wants me back."

"She won't have you. I'll kill her."

"No, I must kill her. Maso said so. There's no other way."

"She may kill you."

"I'm Yaqui. We die every day for our families, our people, our land. I may be ugly but I know now I'm full-blooded Yaqui." Cheve slapped his chest. "Thank you for that."

Rustling bushes stirred, like an animal stalking. "Quiet." Mateo pointed his pistol to the darkness.

"Maso," Cheve said.

Mateo handed the horse's reins to his son. "I go alone." He walked into the bush, smelling the air for animal. Instead, he detected wild mesquite and desert flowers lurking in the shadows. Crushing sounds of paws or feet several meters ahead emerged. He aimed his gun. The stalker approached in a rapid pace. Mateo steadied his grip.

A voice called, "I'm Yaqui, don't shoot."

"You don't sound Yaqui."

The man yelped and ran back.

Mateo leaped forward and followed heavy breathing and running feet several meters. The shadow of the fugitive in front raced faster until he was within arm reach. He tripped him up with his feet, hurling the man forward.

"Get up," he said. "Others?"

"Yes. Several."

"Tell them to come out. We're Yaqui."

"We're not Torocoyori." The man whistled a high trill. "It's safe. Come out. Yaqui warriors found us."

Mateo soon heard more frightened voices. "Follow me but keep quiet." When they reached his men, the warriors gathered around the fugitives. "Give them water," he ordered. "What were you doing in the desert?"

"We escaped from the hacienda."

"It's him, Father. The brave one," a boy pointed at Cheve. "I remember his face."

The boy's father approached Cheve. "You saved us. I'll never forget you and your brother. Some families were caught by Yoris and Torocoyoris out there." The man pointed behind him. "They still hunt us. More of our people stayed at the trading post. Yoris surround them. Took our chances in the desert."

"Where's the trading post?" Mateo asked.

"About five kilometers away. Follow the twin stars." The Yaqui pointed to the northern skies.

"I can spare no guns. You can wait for us here or risk it."

"I want to go home," the boy said.

"Better to trek in the dark, far away from the Yoris," another Yaqui said. "They're crazy angry, carrying pistols, rifles, swords and knives. They'll slaughter us like chickens if they can."

"Horses, men." Mateo jumped on his mount and handed a pistol to Cheve. "You know how to use a fire cracker, don't you?"

"Yes, Father. Ángel taught me."

"You've learned too much. Stay close to me."

Cheve nodded.

"Travel in that direction." Mateo told the fugitives pointing to the south. With luck, you'll drink from the Yaqui River before dawn." To his men, he said, "We're almost there. Stay alert, save our people and send Yoris to hell."

His men grunted and raised their pistols, rifles and swords into the air. The fleeing Yaquis cheered.

Mateo galloped into the night, his hands trembling on the reins, returning to the hut where five drunks conceived Cheve on a Tequila bar. Kicking his horse, he feared Floratina awaited their arrival to send him to hell, to suckle Cheve on her cold tits.

CHAPTER 34

DESPERATE ENGAGEMENTS

Wispy clouds veiled and unveiled the witch's full moon in patches of amber light. The quiet desert night hid the desperados and predators in fleeting shadows of a macabre hide-and-seek.

The Torocoyori pushed the Yaqui guard's body to the side, wiped his knife on the dead man's leg, then whistled a soft alert. Several armed *Torocoyoris* rose from the desert floor with drawn guns and knives.

"Fan out. Quiet," the assassin whispered.

For the next hour, they crept to the guard posts, duped the Yaquis into thinking they had come in relief and clubbed or stabbed them to death. One of the assassins ran back to the Yori camp, reporting to Sergeant Bocagrande the perimeter was secure.

"*Los pinches* outnumber us, but have few firearms," the sergeant said. "Circle the post. When you hear my pistol bark, attack from all sides."

"Women and children?" a Torocoyori asked.

"Kill them all," the sergeant said. "If you capture Tomas, hold the *chingado* for me. I wish to shake his hands before I cut them off. I want Ángel's body. A promotion to the man who brings me his head. You won't mind, will you?" The sergeant told Carolina who sat on the ground. "You should pray for me now. I have work to do." He laughed raucously.

"No, leave the Yaquis in peace," she begged. "You agreed to spare them if I went back with you."

"Listen, Yaqui lover. I lie like Judas' mother explaining her son's death. *Señor* Culpepper will reward me *mucho dinero* when I bring you back. And a bonus for Ángel's head. Boyfriend not so pretty now, eh?"

"Leave him alone," Carolina screamed and lunged at him, scratching his face and pulling his hair.

"Whore," the sergeant yelled and threw her to the ground. He pointed to a soldier. "Watch her."

"*Con gusto, mi sargento.* I'll watch her good." He nodded, eyes opened wide.

* * *

Tomas' rancor for Ángel abated slightly at the sight of his beaten body. The Torocoyori was the most unfortunate man he had ever known—a man without family or home, willing to sacrifice his people's beliefs for a Yori woman. Yet he admired the risks Ángel took for his love. *Would I do the same? Yes, I would.*

Gazing out to the guard posts, he saw moonlight silhouette his men. *I should check their alertness, for signs of enemy activity.*

"Tomas... Tomas." A woman neared.

He recognized Luz's voice.

She stopped close to him, taking his hand. "We have little time. Thank you for your protection. If not for you, we wouldn't have lived this long. Your patience with Ángel and Cheve reveals your good heart."

He peered through the darkness to capture her eyes. "A good heart, you say. Since my family's death, a cactus replaced it. You transformed it into a jaguar heart." He drew closer to her. "When we reach the Yaqui, I'll ask your father if he will allow us to marry. Will you walk with me, Luz?"

She nodded. "Yes, my love. I'll walk, run and dance with you." She hugged and kissed him. "Carolina was right."

"About what?"

"About you... about us." She touched his face.

He took a step back still holding her hands. "The burns prevent me–"

A gun shot broke the night's quiet. Releasing her hands, Tomas reached for his pistol, his eyes searched the night.

Howls rang around their encampment like a rampant pack of dogs. Shadows raced past him. "Stop, come back," Tomas ordered. All around him, Yaquis fled from the perimeters. "Luz, go to the hut." He picked up his machine gun and cartridge belt. "My people, Yoris attack. Fight or die." He shot a volley at the perimeter to punctuate his words.

In response, firing and flashes erupted from all sides as Torocoyoris opened fire on the confused defenders.

Tomas recognized the ruse. "Yaquis, retreat to the hut," he shouted.

He ran to the thatched-roof shelter, his back against the wall. Hearing cries and moans of the women and children inside, he hoped Luz was with them. As his men arrived, he ordered, "Form a firing line." Twenty men dropped to the dirt in a semicircle.

Torocoyoris, unable to control their lust for killing, began shooting, exposing their location by their muzzle flashes.

"Shoot back, Yaquis," Tomas ordered. "Fight or die." Bullets buzzed around him and slammed into the wooden post. Chips burst into the air. "Send them back to hell." He ran to the hut entrance.

Attacking Torocoyoris bludgeoned or shot to death wounded Yaquis crawling to reach the trading post. Tomas sprayed the first line of attackers, stitching bullet holes across their torsos. The Yaqui warrior laughed at their mixed expressions of surprise, sorrow, confusion and pain as they toppled in loud thuds, moans, and cries. A flush of blood and guts spewing like an anatomical geyser showered the killing grounds. Yori and Torocoyori attackers slipped on their comrades' livers, guts and hearts.

Tomas fired another deafening machine gun burst, spewing bullets in a methodical sweep to the Yori guns. "Yaquis, death to the Yoris," he bellowed. He opened his lips to exhort, to enrage when a bullet splintered his skull. He dropped the gun, tottered and fell with a bright image of Luz walking at his side along the banks of the Yaqui River. His lips formed "Luz" as he leaped to the Other Side.

* * *

Ángel sat up and looked around through narrow-slit, puffy eyes. His head hurt from Bocagrande's pummeling that left a ringing in his left ear. Screams, wails and gun shots echoed like an interminable church's death knell.

"Mother," he shouted as he searched the dark room. "Mother."

"I'm here, my son," Petra said, placing her arm around him.

Ángel pulled her to him and whispered. "Everyone out. Run into the desert. Do it now."

The thatched hut's roof burst into flames. More screams erupted as women and children rushed to exit. Yellow flames ate the roof's dry mesquite leaves. Wood crackled and glowing embers dropped flaming confetti.

More shooting erupted. The first to escape the hut fell in heaps. Mothers, their children in tow, jumped or ran over the fallen into darkness. On the run, women snatched offspring at their dead or wounded mothers' sides. They stooped, dodged bullets in a desperate race to the desert. The air reeked of gunpowder punctuated with curses, grunts and whistles of the attacking Yoris and Torocoyoris.

Luz and Petra helped Ángel to his feet.

"Leave me. Go now," he said.

Luz pulled him to the hut entrance strewn with bodies. Smoke, straining their breathing, clouded their sights.

Just as they reached the hut doorway, they heard a child cry from the far end of the room. "Come here, little one," Petra called.

"I'm afraid of the fire, noise and guns," the youth said. "Where's my mother?"

Fire crackled, illuminating the room in a burst. The Falcons flinched at the sight of Floratina glaring at them with a smirk. The witch, a bulging bag in hand, ran and leaped onto the trading post counter. Fiery tears rained on her. The bag's contents clanged and knocked against one another.

"Mateo and his men raped me here as if I were their whore." She pointed to the bar. "I was the *Señora* García, wife of *Don* Victoriano García." The witch howled a deafening scream, jumped high, landing next to Ángel, and grabbed his arm. "I'll take this ugly one in trade. Petra, you took my son. This one's mine."

Luz and her mother pulled on Ángel who moaned from the tug of war.

"You can't have him, witch," Petra shouted as she struck Floratina about the face. Bouncing firelight exposed her twisted face's striking resemblance to Cheve's. The burning trade post grew hotter as the flaming tongues licked the furniture.

Petra and Luz dug their nails into Ángel's flesh.

"Ahhhhhh," he groaned.

"Mother, stop," a voice shouted from the door. Cheve and Mateo stood with guns in their hands.

"Son," the witch and Petra called in a discordant duet.

"Follow me, Mother," Cheve said. "Come away." He opened his arms. "Together we'll live in the desert, never to part again. Hurry, catch me, Mother."

CHAPTER 35

LAST OFFERINGS

Running into the darkness, Cheve heard one mother's pleas to come back while another screamed to flee.

He dodged bullets, eluded grasps, leaped over wounded and dead. Cheve dashed past warriors entangled in a dance with death. Muzzles flashed, lead hissed, arrows whistled, enemy hands sought their foe's throats. Deer Dancer sprinted faster than ever, feet skimming soil.

He broke free from the killing fields, away into the open desert. The wilderness hummed of wind, insects, rabbits and coyotes scattering from his path. Floratina floated above the desert floor close behind, her arms extended, her long hair trailing.

"Cheve, my baby," she wailed. "Come to me."

Fighters screamed and scrambled at the sight of the deformed boy stalked by *la bruja*.

His ride with his father exposed the foolishness of this quest for the man called *El Feo*—he should have sought *Los Feos*. The cumulative load of fatigue, lack of sleep, long runs weighed on him. Groaning, he forced his legs to churn. Instead, they rebelled, stumbled, fell, rose, raced again. His legs felt heavy, hard to lift. Pumping his arms, he strained to bolt, then collapsed to the desert floor.

The gliding witch hovered over him, her eyes glowing green, her hands extended. Her slow breathing contrasted to his panting. Cheve cringed, his back pressed to the desert floor, engulfed by the flowery smell.

"Not hurt you, my son. Give you gifts. Make you strong." She held up a jug. "Cool water to quench thirst."

His mouth ached for a taste of the liquid.

She poured the fluid over his face, some seeping into his mouth. At the first drops, his tongue stuck out, lapping up the sweet-tasting water.

"Up, my son," she said.

Cheve rose. When she reached for him, he flinched.

"Won't hurt you." She placed her fingers on the openings of his face.

Cheve drew back.

"No shame. Same blood—same markings. Know how you feel about your ugliness. Felt same shame until I met Victoriano, my sweet husband." She wept in loud screams, pulling on her strands of hair with both hands. The bag jangled. "Drunk with love. Content with our lives until Yaquis came. Your fathers hanged him. Five buzzards raped me—all your papas. Wish to meet them? I present the fathers you seek."

From the open bag, the witch pulled out four skulls suspended by chain.

"Behold, *Los Feos*." Floratina laughed, shaking the chain of skulls over him. "Tracked and killed all except Mateo, their leader. Saved him for last. Guided the Yoris here. Petra will feel many men between her legs tonight." As she cackled, her matted tresses shook like undulating snakes. "Mateo can witness her rape as he watched mine. Horrid men like him call me ugly when they are true sons of Satan.

"Follow me into desert. Teach you herbs' secrets, speak to plants, fly like raven, hunt like jaguar, swim like shark. Become stronger than any man. Never tire. Change your looks." She swept her hand over her face in a smooth flow.

By moonlight, he saw her transform to beauty. Her smile shimmered like the wings of doves, eyes scintillated like jewels. "Follow me, Son. Will change you to most handsome Yaqui man. Kiss me, son, all gifts yours." She opened her arms. Her puckered lips glowed red, as inviting and natural as a rose to a bee.

Cheve stood, kicking the skulls. He pulled the antlers from his head.

"Maso is my father. Behold my beauty, *bruja*." The antler tips swept to his feet and traced up his legs. In an instant, they transmuted to deer hooves, muscular, furry haunches. Floratina howled as he rubbed his back, arms, neck and head with Maso branches. The transformation came quickly as his body grew stronger, bigger, hairier. Bending forward, he stood on four deer legs and hooves. Cheve arched his neck up and down. Antlers sprouted on his head, shimmering a multipoint crown. Finally, his face grew a snout that sniffed the rosy aroma.

His head held high, the boy transformed bellowed in his deer tongue, "I am deer, Mother witch."

In an instant, Floratina's comely face contorted like a rotted pumpkin to the familiar lop-sided cheeks, flared nose, sunken eyes and twisted mouth. "Die, deer." She screamed, jumped on Cheve's furry back, embedding her claws deep into his ribs. As clumps of fur tore from his hide, the deer jumped and bucked off *la bruja*. Deer-boy charged, impaling her deep with his crown. Lifting the witch into the air, he swung his antlers from side to side.

"Cheve, my son, don't kill me. I love you, my dear son," she screamed.

"Oh, Mother, your torment and mine must end. You must die. Forgive me, dear. Sleep now." Tears rolled down his furry face.

Masoito ran into the desert with a crucified Floratina, twisting and howling how much she loved her baby, how much she needed her son to ease her sorrow, her shame, how she wished he was never born, how much she loved Victoriano. Despite his strongest bellows, Cheve couldn't drown her pleas in the desert.

Four skulls dangled, and clattered from an antler in time with the rapid hoof beats of Deer Dancer, leaving a scent of roses and wrongs.

* * *

The burning hut's fire lit up the night sky, exposing Yaqui defenders to the Yoris. Wounded men howled, struggled to their feet and fired guns or bows. The enemy's fusillade cut them down.

Luz, Petra and Ángel emerged to the smell of gunpowder, the clamor of shooting and dying. Behind them, the heat and roar of the flaming hut toasted backs. She assisted her mother in laying Ángel to the ground. Mateo moaned and grabbed his left leg.

"Father." She went to him.

"Take your mother from here. Hide in the desert," Mateo said. "Go now."

Petra went to her husband's side. Several of his men gathered around him, their guns firing at the attackers.

"There's too many," a Yaqui warrior said. "They're well-armed. We're surrounded.

"Fight or die." Mateo shouted. "Go back to your post. Fight your last fight, my brave men."

They backed away.

Weeping women and children crouched on the ground. When bullets struck, they jerked, cried and died in one another's arms.

Mateo struggled to his feet. "My gun."

Luz scanned the grounds. She spotted Tomas lying still and ran to him. The bullet hole in his head sliced her heart.

"Aiiiiiii!" she screamed. "Tomas, my love." Her chest swelled. Tears stung her eyes. She caressed his face, hair, then pulled him closer. His head flopped to the side exposing the wound on the back of his skull. Blood and brains oozed. Her arms clutched in a rocking motion. "We were to marry." After kissing him on the lips, she laid him down. His shirt opened to reveal burn-wrinkled skin. "Your suffering is over, my love," Luz whispered. "Go to your wife and children."

After a final kiss, she wiped her face free of tears and snot. Touching his blood, she smeared the Yaqui war paint across her face.

"*Chingados,*" she screamed, spit and picked up the machine gun. The weapon trembled in her hands at the sight of stunned Yaquis milling like frighten goats waiting for Yori butchers to slice their throats. "Fight or die, Yaquis," she howled. "Fight or die." Overcoming the weight of the weapon, she cradled the firearm.

More Yaquis retreated to Mateo's side. Women and children steadily died as the Yoris picked them off with ease.

She shouted, "All Yaqui women and men, pick up a gun, knife or club." When they didn't move, Luz fired a burst into the Yori darkness, "Now."

A disfigured, battered head flew into the crowd of Yaquis and tumbled to Luz's feet. She shuddered. "Mother, it's a baby's head."

"Yori bastards." Petra picked up a gun. She howled, "Die fighting on your feet, my people. Fight for your children."

"Men, follow my wife and daughter," Mateo ordered. "Obey them. Kill the Yoris and traitors."

Women and men grunted, picked up rocks, guns, sticks and knives. Crying children were left on the ground, tended by older youth or their fates.

A large booming Spanish voice shouted, "*Alto,* muchachos."

The shooting ceased, but the echoes of firing rang in their ears.

"Too many of you have died already," Sergeant Bocagrande roared. "Surrender your weapons. We'll let you go. If not, I'll butcher all of you, including your children."

Yaquis screamed as the shower of human arms, legs and ears flew into the camp.

"I'll wear your balls as earrings tonight," Petra shouted. Yaquis roared.

By the hut fire, Luz saw her people's looks of defiance. Her natural meekness transformed to a disheveled, dirty, rawboned fury. Pink gave way to red rage. She smeared Tomas' blood across her face and tongue. She was about to give the order to wade into the darkness when Ángel, mounted on a horse, trotted forward.

"You came for Carolina and me," Ángel shouted. "You have her and soon me. Take my head. You've won the battle. Spare your men and these people."

"Get down, Ángel," Petra ordered.

"My head means money. Better this way." He slipped a gun from beneath his shirt. "After I kill Bocagrande, the others will retreat to Guaymas. It's the way of cowards."

"No, Ángel," Petra said, pulling on the reins. "By killing you, their blood lust will swell. Get down."

Mateo, held up by two men, went to Petra's side. He placed his hand over hers. "Let him go. He wishes to atone."

"Not for Yaquis. For Carolina. My love." Ángel urged his horse forward.

"A Yori girl," Mateo said.

"Yes, rapist, a Yori girl—my woman."

"Kill the pig, my son, or I will," Petra said.

"I'll order my men to open fire soon unless I see Ángelito at my side in a few seconds," Sergeant Bocagrande bellowed.

"Coming, Bocagrande, coming," Ángel said.

"I'm so happy," the sergeant said in a falsetto voice. "We love you so much, Ángel. Pretty Carolina is waiting with open arms and legs."

Other Yoris laughed.

"Ángel, forgive me, my son," Mateo shouted.

The hut fire had died, draping the Yaqui camp in a shroud of darkness, leaving the crackling of embers and the smell of smoke. Luz went to her mother's side. Then clouds parted. Moonbeams shimmered over the desert desperados exposing the bold, Yori attackers. The pregnant silence felt ready to miscarry.

A group of cursing, Yori horsemen surrounded Ángel. Fire sparked from the rider's hand. Men growled, guns exploded, spitting darts of flames at the Yori lover.

"Carolina!" Ángel shouted, his body bucked, his hands shot up into the air, and for a moment it looked as if he would actually soar. Instead, he tumbled hard from the horse.

Yoris cursed as they shot into Ángel's body. Bocagrande ordered, "Cut off the *chingado's* head and balls."

Petra screamed, "Ángel. They murdered my Ángel."

Mateo howled, "Bastards."

"Yaquis, fight or die," Petra shouted. "Kill the Yori sons of bitches. Send them back to hell."

She and Luz led the Yaqui survivors in a charge guided by the bright light of the witch's moon. The killer shadows ran on a nocturnal hunt for human flesh. They screamed and screeched their desire to trim the skin from the bones of Yoris, allies, and their horses.

Yaqui women's long-flowing hair and high-pitched shrieks captured the fury of a *brujas'* coven attack. Brandishing knives, stones and guns, they plowed into the Yoris and cut, slashed, bit, punched, gouged and spat at the foe. Enraged by the death of their children, Yaqui women showed no mercy for the wounded Yoris.

Yaquitas fought in packs of twos and threes. When one fell, another lunged into place. Embolden by the women's ferocity, the Yaqui men plunged into the night ready to kill whoever escaped the females' clutches. Their killing rhythm accelerated on every bang and bawl.

Guns burst from both sides like low-flying, shooting stars. The smell of gunpowder wafted over desert fighters. Spanish and Cajita curses clashed with the moans and gasps of the dying. The screams of eviscerated Yoris skewered the night.

Petra charged toward the site of Ángel's fall at the head of a wave of black-tressed slashers. Yoris retreated at the onslaught shooting their remaining bullets over their shoulders at their predators. When a few tripped to the ground, blood-hungry, Yaqui lionesses swarmed them in fury of plunges.

Luz shot back and brought down a man two body-lengths in front. She ran to the man squirming on the ground with a chest wound. Petra ran to her side, swooped down with a fluid sweep of her knife. His gaped mouth now matched his slit throat.

"Yaqui necktie," Petra hissed. "Looks good on you."

Mother and daughter ran forward side-by-side, shooting, hacking, clubbing—death in skirts. Their sweat mixed with the blood of the men they slew.

Several Yoris fought back, tearing their killers' blouses, exposing their breasts. "Suckle on this," Petra howled as she drove the knife into their necks and chests. "Bitter milk, eh?"

They found Ángel on the ground, a weeping Carolina at his side. A few feet away lay a gut shot Sergeant Bocagrande.

"Serve me more tamales, *Madre*... I'm a big boy... more *frijoles, por favor... Padre*, stop whipping me. I promise to be good," he muttered.

The Falcon women touched Ángel's face and chest. He lay soaked in his blood. Bullet wounds lacerated his face and body.

"Ángel, my dear Ángel," Carolina said holding his body, her tattered nun's habit soaked in his blood. "Damn my father."

"Big mouth, I'll serve you *frijoles*." Petra rushed to the wounded sergeant, thrusting her knife into the man's belly. She ran the blade down to his genitals. As his intestines spewed, the sergeant howled. Petra cut open his pants, grabbed his testicles and lopped them off. "I'm tired of hearing you talk shit." She crammed them into his mouth and slit his throat.

Yaquis routed the enemy to complete the butchery the Yoris had begun. Yaqui women tracked the wounded foes, lopping limbs and balls in the names of their dead children and husbands.

Under the *bruja's* moonlight spray, the Yaquitas had transformed into blood-gorged, killer witches. Their victorious screams wrenched the night in piercing glee.

CHAPTER 36

DANCE OF THE LITTLE PEOPLE

"Time to leave."
"Maso comes."
"Yaquis were victorious."
"Cheve turned into a deer."
"He's a true deer dancer."
"Let's celebrate in the desert."
"Bring the horns and drums."
"Hurry, catch Maso."

By dawn, Cheve stirred from his sleep, sat up in the cool morning air. His legs felt strong, his head clear. As he rose, he winced at the deep slashes along his ribs. Recalling the fight with the witch, he looked at vultures a few feet away staring back at him with beady eyes. When he took a few steps, the scavengers took flight, cawing, "Cheve Falcon, witch killer… Cheve Falcon, witch killer."

The desert around him lay littered with bodies. Birds of prey flocked on the distant grounds tearing into the remains with avid determination. Several bodies hung from trees with their entrails dangling purple festoons. Dead horses lay on their sides, their long, spindly legs stiff as tree limbs. Packs of coyotes worked their red-stained snouts into unguarded Yori bodies.

Deer hoof prints surrounded him. Vivid images of transforming into a deer swelled his mind. Staring at his hands and feet, he found no remnants of fur or hooves. He touched his buttocks for a lingering tail and his face for a snout. His hands reached futilely for a crown of horns. Was it a dream? Four skulls on the ground lay at his feet. Picking up the chain of domes, he jangled them. "*Los Feos*, my fathers. I found you."

In his search for the skeletons' house, he passed Yaquis carrying their dead, laying them in a row. Battered mothers sitting on the ground cradled and wept over their dead children. Yoris with slit throats and slashed bodies, stiff in death poses, carpeted the land. Bullet hole-ridden Yaquis lay alongside the Yoris a short distance away. The sight of many women's corpses strewed alongside the male fighters or wrapped in death embraces with their killers surprised him. In their lifeless hands, they clutched knives, stones and guns. Their death masks skewed to angry sneers.

Mother, Luz, please not be here. Did you get away?

Cheve noticed a young girl who looked familiar walking in the field of dead. She had placed the cross around his neck. "America," he called.

At first, she grimaced, but then relaxed.

"Cheve, isn't it?" she asked. "Hurt? You're bleeding." Despite her disheveled appearance, her smile, lyrical voice and direct gaze stirred embers of joy.

"Some scratches. Where's México?"

"Lost. Good you survived the fighting. We walked in Hell last night."

"The fighting looks vicious. Were the Yaquis victorious?"

America shrugged her shoulders. "I think so. Why do you carry those skulls? Should we bury them?"

Cheve smiled. "Yes, later. But I must find my family first."

"Do you think this fighting will ever end? Why do we hate each other so much?"

Deer Dancer gazed at the field of silent dead and moaning wounded. Yaqui warriors walked among the bodies, quieting the injured Yoris with knife thrusts. "We can't see ourselves on the Other Side. We refuse to change, to cross the Yaqui River."

"I must find México. I hope she's alive and not wounded or dead." She walked away into the desert of death. "México, where are you?" America yelled.

Cheve resumed his search, scanning the distorted faces until he spotted his mother, father, Luz, and Carolina kneeling beside corpses. He ran to them, but slowed to a walk when he saw the bodies of Ángel and Tomas, lying side-by-side. His family wept and prayed over them, as did all other Yaqui survivors with their dead relatives. Cheve winced at the sight of his brother's bullet hole-ridden face. Handsome or ugly mattered little to the dead.

He wept. "Ángel, my love-sick brother."

Mateo and his men were *Los Feos*. The terrible truth drove Ángel to seek comfort in the arms of a beautiful, Yori woman, and what he called science. He sought to outrun futilely the sordid past. Luz had searched for solace by following her mother's devotion to the church. If Tomas had lived, she would have reveled in their passion. Shouldering the machine gun, Luz had steered her religious zeal to sending Yoris to their graves.

"Mother, I found my fathers."

"Cheve, you're alive," Petra said. "Thank God."

He dropped the skulls at Mateo's feet. "Old friends."

Cheve walked a few steps away from the mourners, stooped, lifted his hands, swayed his head, and danced to a silent drum and flute honoring the dead in their journey to the Other Side. Deer Dancer grinned, jumped among the unburied bodies, which would soon receive crooked crosses, and sang about the Little People.

Cheve hopped to a stop, crouched low, one leg stretched behind, an arm reached to a fleeting, dusty whirlwind topped with red-tipped antlers.

"Maso, my Maso, wait," he wheezed. The wound to his ribs soaked his shirt crimson.

Legs lifted high, feet dancing across the ground, arms swinging to and fro, mouth seeping blood-stained spittle, he sprinted toward the Other Side. Cheve Falcon chuckled at the

Little People's dance, cheer, music and laughter in his quest for serenity.

Petra, Mateo and Luz pleaded for their beautiful boy to come back.

"I must dance with Maso," Cheve cried. The scent of mesquite caressed his nose. The desert browns, reds, greens and yellows scintillated in his misty eyes. The curvy antlers grew the closer he approached Maso.

Within reach, he nestled his head into the deer's fur. "My Maso, show me the magic steps." Deer Dancer sighed. "See, I'm learning." His shuffling feet felt too heavy now, head sagged.

The Little People circled the pair, danced, clapped and chanted, "*Cheve found his papa... Cheve found his papa.*"

The grand deer raised its head, bellowing for all with desert *Seataka* to hear, "Cheve Falcon, witch slayer, people defender, desert runner, dream weaver, deer dancer is my beloved son."

Cheve slid to the bloody soil with a twisted beauty on his joyous face.

CPSIA information can be obtained
at www.ICGtesting.com
Printed in the USA
LVHW051435070219
606760LV00016B/491/P